## What Reviewers Say

"…well-plotted…lovely romance…I couldn't tu[illegible] fast enough!"—**Ann Bannon**, author of *The Beebo Brinker Chronicles*

"The author's brisk mix of political intrigue, fast-paced action, and frequent interludes of lesbian sex and love…in *Honor Reclaimed…* sure does make for great escapist reading."—**Richard Labonte**, Q Syndicate

"If you're looking for a well-written police procedural make sure you get a copy of *Shield of Justice*. Most assuredly worth it."—**Lynne Jamneck**, author of *Down the Rabbit Hole* and reviewer for The L Life

"Radclyffe has once again pulled together all the ingredients of a genuine page-turner, this time adding some new spices into the mix. Whatever one's personal take on the subject matter, *shadowland* is sure to please—in part because Radclyffe never loses sight of the fact that she is telling a love story, and a compelling one at that."—**Cameron Abbott**, author of *To The Edge* and *An Inexpressible State of Grace*

"*Stolen Moments…*edited by Radclyffe & Stacia Seaman…is a collection of steamy stories about women who just couldn't wait. It's sex when desire overrides reason, and it's incredibly hot!"—**Suzanne Corson**, *On Our Backs*

"With ample angst, realistic and exciting medical emergencies, winsome secondary characters, and a sprinkling of humor, *Fated Love* turns out to be a terrific romance. It's one of the best I have read in the last three years. Run—do not walk—right out and get this one. You'll be hooked by yet another of Radclyffe's wonderful stories. Highly recommended."—Author **Lori L. Lake**, *Midwest Book Review*

"Radclyffe, through her moving text…in *Innocent Hearts…*illustrates that our struggles for acceptance of women loving women is as old as time - only the setting changes. The romance is sweet, sensual, and touching."—**Kathi Isserman**, reviewer for *Just About Write*

**Visit us at www.boldstrokesbooks.com**

# Promising Hearts

*by*

RADCLY*f*FE

2006

**PROMISING HEARTS**

**© 2006 By Radclyffe. All Rights Reserved.**

**ISBN 1-933110-44-9**

This Trade Paperback Original Is Published By
Bold Strokes Books, Inc.,
New York, USA

First Printing May 2006

THIS IS A WORK OF FICTION. NAMES, CHARACTERS, PLACES, AND INCIDENTS ARE THE PRODUCT OF THE AUTHOR'S IMAGINATION OR ARE USED FICTITIOUSLY. ANY RESEMBLANCE TO ACTUAL PERSONS, LIVING OR DEAD, BUSINESS ESTABLISHMENTS, EVENTS, OR LOCALES IS ENTIRELY COINCIDENTAL.

THIS BOOK, OR PARTS THEREOF, MAY NOT BE REPRODUCED IN ANY FORM WITHOUT PERMISSION.

---

**Credits**
Editors: Ruth Sternglantz and Stacia Seaman
Production Design: Stacia Seaman
Cover Design By Sheri (GRAPHICARTIST2020@HOTMAIL.COM)

## By the Author

**<u>Romances</u>**

Safe Harbor
Beyond the Breakwater
Innocent Hearts
Love's Melody Lost
Love's Tender Warriors
Tomorrow's Promise
Passion's Bright Fury
Love's Masquerade
shadowland
Fated Love
Distant Shores, Silent Thunder
Turn Back Time

**<u>Honor Series</u>**

Above All, Honor
Honor Bound
Love & Honor
Honor Guards
Honor Reclaimed

**<u>Justice Series</u>**

A Matter of Trust (prequel)
Shield of Justice
In Pursuit of Justice
Justice in the Shadows
Justice Served

Change Of Pace: *Erotic Interludes*
*(A Short Story Collection)*
Stolen Moments: *Erotic Interludes 2*
*Stacia Seaman and Radclyffe, eds.*
Lessons in Love: *Erotic Interludes 3*
*Stacia Seaman and Radclyffe, eds.*

# Acknowledgments

*Innocent Hearts* was among the very first "full-length" works I wrote, and I had no aspirations to publish my stories at the time. The characters and I were all "innocent"—I because I had no real concept of what it really took to write a book, and the characters because they lived in a time when there were no words for who they were and how they loved.

Over the years I have come to understand that the story is the heart of any work, but the craft that brings that story to true life is plain old hard work. It can be exhilarating and frustrating from one second to the next. It is always rewarding. I was fortunate to be able to publish a second edition of *Innocent Hearts* (2005) in preparation for the continuation of the story of these brave, passionate women of New Hope. It was a real pleasure to revisit that work and add the subtle nuances I had missed the first time around.

While *Promising Hearts* happens to be set in a particular time in American history, romance and love are universal and eternal. It was a joy for me to write this book, and I believe the love and passion between these women will transcend place and time. I admit, however, to being a lifelong fan of the "Western," so this one was doubly fun to do.

Thanks to my tireless beta readers—Connie, Diane, Eva, Jane, Paula, RB, and Tomboy, my editors Ruth and Stacia, and Sheri, artist extraordinaire. And to Lee, for all the promises of the heart. *Amo te.*

Radclyffe 2006

# Dedication

For Lee
From the Heart

# Chapter One

*Appomattox Court House, Virginia*
*April 9, 1865*

The morning of the battle dawned gray and cold. Dr. Vance Phelps surveyed the low rise extending southwest from Appomattox Court House where Lt. General Ulysses S. Grant had deployed the Army of the Potomac after forcing General Robert E. Lee and the Army of Northern Virginia to abandon Richmond. Only a few hundred yards away, 30,000 rebel troops, all that remained of Lee's war-weary forces, prepared to mount their assault. Nearby, the assistant surgeons milled in a restless knot, awaiting orders as to where to establish the regimental field hospital. Vance was the senior surgeon by virtue of having served for nearly three years in the Pennsylvania 155th Volunteers—longer than any of the other medical personnel—and by being the only formally trained surgeon in the division. Many of the others had a few weeks of apprenticeship or no medical training at all. They'd learned the rudiments of their trade under fire.

"There." Vance pointed to a dense copse of trees on a knoll directly behind the close rows of muzzle-loading howitzers manned by Ord's 24th Corps. From long experience in skirmishes and battles too numerous to count, Vance knew that before long the air would roil with the clouds of lung-singeing black smoke spewed out from artillery and small arms fire. The walking wounded and stretcher bearers would have a hard time finding the aid station unless it was close to the battle line and clearly visible. "Set up the tents in front of that hedgerow."

"Gonna make a mighty fine target up there, Doc," noted Milton

Cox, the sergeant who served as her chief hospital steward. In his mismatched uniform of regulation Union blue trousers and a frayed, faded yellow shirt of homespun cotton that he'd most likely stolen off the clothesline of some unsuspecting Southern housewife, he looked more like a vagabond than a seasoned veteran.

"Might be," Vance agreed, her black eyes holding just a glint of humor, "if Lee's men are so unmannerly as to fire upon the hospital. But I figure we'll have the strongest section of the Union line in front of us, and just maybe the ambulance corps will be able to find us once the shooting starts."

The sergeant grinned, showing an uneven row of tobacco-stained teeth. "Well, you've been right more times than not."

*Just lucky,* Vance thought, swiping the sleeve of her loose blue officer's coat across the icy sweat on her forehead. Sometime during the night, when she'd lain awake on a thin blanket in the back of one of the medical supply wagons contemplating the upcoming battle, the congestion in her chest had relented enough for her to breathe without the stabbing pain that had been present for the last week. The cough and chills persisted, a remnant of the pneumonia she had been fighting since February. Now, her once long and slender form verged on gaunt, though her skin was tanned and roughened by sun and wind, her muscles sinewy from constant labor. As Grant's forces had cut deep into the South, the warm April days and the humid air of Virginia had helped ease the constriction in her lungs. She counted herself lucky not to have succumbed to consumption or dysentery or some of the other diseases that had taken so many on both sides of the war.

Not for the first time, she was bone-grateful for the good health and regular food she'd enjoyed before disguising her sex and enlisting in the newly formed U.S. Army Medical Corps in 1862. After so many losses at the Battle of Bull Run, when thousands died from lack of access to medical treatment and the general dearth of physicians among the regiments, recruiters accepted anyone with the vaguest sort of medical training. No one looked carefully at the credentials, or the gender, of the inductees.

"We're low on chloroform," Milton said.

Vance nodded, considering herself fortunate that they had any of the fairly new substance at all. Rumor had it that the Southern surgeons had been making do with ether for months, a far less reliable anesthetic. "We've plenty of morphine and laudanum if we run out of the anesthesia."

"Well, if I need any cuttin' done, I want you to be the one doin' it." Milton turned his head and spat a stream of dark brown tobacco juice. "Ain't none of the others as quick and clean as you."

"Thank you, Milton," Vance said, having long since lost count of the hundreds of limbs she had removed. "Make sure you keep the basin of carbolic full and close by today."

"Yep. Don't suppose we'll be runnin' out of that real soon, seein' how you're the only one usin' it."

Vance knew that Milton, along with her fellow surgeons, thought the practice of dipping her hands into the caustic liquid between surgeries was not only time consuming, but foolish superstition. Nevertheless, Dr. Lister's theories about sanitation made sense to her. She thought of how many soldiers she had lost, not to injury, but to gangrene. Far more than she had saved. Her face, thinned down to bone from subsisting on little more than hardtack and salt-pork for months, grew grimmer still. "There's little enough we can do for them. I don't see that it will hurt."

"Right enough." As if recognizing Vance's dark mood, Milton said quietly, "This war can't last much longer. Not with Lee's forces split and us between 'em."

"I hope you're right. There's been far too much death." With a sigh, Vance straightened her shoulders and turned to check the progress of the soldiers assigned to the ambulance corps who were erecting the hospital tent and bringing up the supply wagons. Her operating table consisted of a wooden door removed from a grand plantation house balanced across two empty ammunition barrels. Her instruments were her own, brought from Philadelphia when she'd left her post at the hospital to take her skills where they were most needed. Those she cleaned and cared for herself, carrying them in an engraved wooden case that had been presented to her by her father the day she graduated from the Women's Medical College of Pennsylvania. That day in 1861, she'd imagined a life very different than this. But since then, everything had changed.

The sound of small arms fire drew her from a past that had seemed so certain into the present, to a life that might now be measured only in fleeting moments. An eerie sound drifted on the pristine whiffs of white smoke that rose into the air beyond the Union lines like so many puffs of breath. A keening, undulating cry of defiance and, oddly, joy. The Rebel Yell.

"Here they come," Milton whispered with near reverence.

"Yes," Vance said, striding quickly toward the hospital staging area. She removed her coat and rolled back the cuffs of her white cotton shirt as she walked. Once there, she retrieved her surgical kit from the wagon and spread her instruments out on a rough pine bench next to the makeshift operating table. She doubted she would need more than the probes, the amputation knife, and the saw for the first round. Minnie balls and cannon canisters left her little choice but to amputate. She dipped her hands into the carbolic acid and shook off the excess, scanning the nearby rise for the first sign of wounded.

❖

"Look smart, men," General Philip Sheridan exhorted as he galloped up and down the forward line of the first of his three cavalry divisions, saber rattling against his thigh in its gold-braided scabbard. "Lee's infantry will be upon us before the sun burns the dew from the grass."

Sheridan's line of mounted cavalry, poised for the signal to strike, shifted in the sunlight like a huge black snake, the horse soldiers and animals alike agitated by the sound of weapon fire and men screaming. The light artillery, mounted on wooden platforms, bucked and belched fire as they disgorged their deadly hail of grapeshot. The ground trembled with the force of thousands of feet pounding the hard-packed red earth, and the air shimmered with the ominous thunder of war.

Vance heard the bugler signal the charge, and Sheridan's cavalry stormed toward the advancing rebel lines. Then from out of the smoke and shifting shadows she saw the first stretcher bearers emerge, running as fast as they could with their burdens of damaged humanity in tow. When the first man was laid upon her table, the battle receded from her consciousness. There were only the wounded now.

"Change the saw blade," Vance said as she turned from the table and immersed her hands in the blood-tinged antiseptic in the basin balanced on a tree stump by her right side.

"Ain't got but two left," Milton said as he sluiced the blood and gore off the wooden tabletop with a bucket of water.

Vance looked at the line of waiting wounded. Those who could walk were sitting under the shelter of the trees, bandaging themselves or their friends. She might get to some of them before the day was over, but those who weren't seriously injured would wander back to their regiments before she ever had a chance to tend them. They knew as well as she that there was little she could do beyond what they had already done for themselves. Those who needed her services were the soldiers with major injuries to body or limb, and these waited on the bare ground in a dense semicircle that stretched as far she could see.

"We'll make do with the one we're using for now," she said. It had taken her a little over fifteen minutes to amputate the last leg because the saw blade was so dull she'd had to wrench it through the bone by sheer force for the last half inch. She'd always been active, eschewing the carriage to walk whenever she could and working in the gardens that surrounded her family home in the spare moments between her studies. She was strong enough in body to do what needed to be done, but her heart suffered. "Next."

The boy looked no older than fourteen and might not have been, because as the war had dragged on, anyone who could carry a rifle and declared they were sixteen was welcome in the ranks. The cannonball had struck him just below the knee, destroying most of his lower leg bone and leaving only a mangled mass of muscle connected to his foot. She looked into the boy's eyes.

"I'm going to remove your leg, son, and you're going to live."

Vance nodded to Milton, who stood to her left with a cloth and a can of chloroform in his hand, and as he pressed the anesthetic to the boy's face, she tightened the leather strap around his lower thigh with one firm yank. Once again, she picked up the amputation knife bare-handed and swiftly cut down to bone, four inches below his knee. With a circular rotation of her wrist, she completed the incision around the stump and dropped the knife on the table in exchange for the saw. It should have taken her less than two minutes to transect the bone, but it required twice that long to worry the blunt teeth through the young healthy leg. When the destroyed portion fell onto the door that served as her table with a thump, Milton picked it up and tossed it onto a nearby pile of amputated limbs.

"Damn flies," Vance muttered, waving at the ever-present insects that buzzed around her head and the boy's motionless body, obscuring her vision. Milton passed her a straight needle threaded with black silk, and she rapidly located and sewed closed the major vessels in the stump. Then she covered the end of the exposed bone with a flap of skin and muscle and swiftly sutured it in place to complete the amputation. Somewhere behind her she could hear men shouting, even above the cannon barrage and general cacophony of battle.

"Move him to the evacuation wagon. Next."

When another body did not immediately appear before her, she looked up questioningly. Sweat and blood spatter ran into her eyes and she blinked, then automatically wiped her face on her sleeve. Seeing Milton gesticulating wildly as a lieutenant on horseback leaned down and shouted something at him, Vance called out, "What is it?"

"Lee has broken Sheridan's line," Milton called on the run. "We're to fall back."

Vance looked at the wounded covering nearly every inch of ground around her and shook her head. "We can't move all these soldiers."

"Then we'll leave them for Lee's surgeons," Milton said, hurriedly gathering drugs and instruments.

"No. Lee's surgeons will take care of their own first, and these men need attention now. You go. I'll stay."

Milton stopped what he was doing and stared at Vance. "If you stay, they'll make you a prisoner."

"That may be. But I'm a surgeon and I'll be valuable to them. Go on, Sergeant. Leave me enough medicine for these men and go."

"I don't think I can do that, Doc." Milton moved up beside her. "We fought together side by side these three years. Wouldn't be right. Besides, my mama didn't raise me to leave a woman to stand alone when times got hard."

Vance stared into his placid brown eyes. "You know?" He nodded. "Does everyone?"

"Can't say. You wouldn't be the first, and most choose not to remark on it, even if they know." He shrugged. "Seen some pretty damn good fighters, myself. And never a better surgeon than you."

"Thank you, Milton. Let's get the next one up here on the table."

Vance worked on, the sounds of battle growing closer. As the war closed in around them, the air grew thick with smoke and misery. The pain in Vance's chest returned, skewering her with each breath. She coughed and shook her head, flinging sweat from her thick dark hair in an arc around her. Incongruously, the sun broke through for an instant, and crystal droplets danced on the sunbeams before falling into the blood that pooled around her scuffed black boots.

"That's the last one, Doc," Milton said. "Now we gotta skedaddle."

"I believe you're right, Sergeant," Vance said, tossing the saw into her kit and rinsing her hands one more time. Reaching for her coat, she glimpsed the look of horror on Milton's face at the same time as she felt the earth shake. Then the world revolved crazily, and the next moment, she was lying on her back staring at the sky. A few small patches of brilliant blue still peeked through the dense battle fog. She couldn't hear through the ringing in her ears. She turned her head. Milton lay ten feet away, his neck bent at an unnatural angle, his eyes blank.

The pain came next, unspeakable waves of agony. Reaching out blindly, Vance felt the iron rim of the barrel that supported the operating table and, gripping the top, pulled herself to her feet. The left side of her body was soaked in blood. Her left arm hung uselessly by her side. Dizzy, she sagged against the table and hoped it wouldn't topple, struggling to sort out her injury. Bright red blood spurted into the air from somewhere near her elbow, the pulsations keeping time with her heartbeat. Of one thing she was certain—she'd bleed to death in another few minutes. Biting down against the pain and the screams that threatened, she found the leather strap she used as a tourniquet and cinched it down around her upper arm. The bleeding slowed.

A minnie ball struck the table and kicked splinters into the air. Not much time. She slid down to the ground, her back against the barrel, her damaged arm cradled in her lap. Then she closed her eyes to wait.

## CHAPTER TWO

*Montana Territory*
*May 1866*

The pain jerked Vance from her restless sleep, the shadowy images of danger and misery lingering on the edges of her consciousness even as she opened her eyes and blinked in the half-light of the stagecoach's interior. She met the curious stare of a young brunette seated across from her in the coach and fervently hoped she hadn't been talking in her sleep or, worse, moaning. She shifted on the hard wooden seat and realized that her legs spanned the short space between them and brushed against the young woman's traveling dress. Hastily, she sat upright and pulled back her booted feet.

"Sorry, miss," Vance murmured quietly, aware that the young woman's traveling companion, probably her mother, was eyeing her with scornful reproach. She imagined she looked unsavory, in the clothes she been traveling in for weeks. The dark gray woolen trousers, matching coat, and double-breasted shirt she had taken from her brother's trunk had been new, or nearly so, at the start of her journey. Her favorite ankle-high black boots no longer held a shine, but the fine workmanship was obvious. Still, even were she a man, her appearance would draw attention. Being female and so unconventionally presented always evoked scandalized expressions, even this far from Eastern society where it was slightly more common to see women out on the range or even in town dressed in masculine attire. She knew, however, that it was more than just her manner of dress that drew stares.

"Are you quite all right?" the young woman asked, knowing no polite way to express her concern that the mysterious woman's face was dead white and the dark eyes beneath a darker slash of brows appeared fevered. She'd taken her fellow traveler for a man at first glance, when she'd climbed into the coach just before their departure from Denver. But her face, though slightly square-jawed and perhaps too strong to be considered ladylike, had a refinement in the arched cheekbones and a fullness about the mouth that was most decidedly female.

"Yes, thank you." Vance was surprised that the young lady, perhaps eighteen years old, would go so far as to speak to her, a stranger and someone of whom her mother clearly disapproved. The brunette's silk dress, bonnet, and parasol were new and fashionably styled, and spoke of wealth and privilege. Such young high-society women, Vance well knew, were often exceedingly haughty and rarely ventured into circles considered beneath them. Nevertheless, the eyes that studied Vance were direct, part concerned and part inquisitive. "Pardon me for disturbing you."

"You didn't disturb me," the young woman said, extending a gloved hand. "I'm Rose Mason. And this is my mother, Mrs. Charles Mason."

Vance took Rose's fingers gently in hers and bowed her head politely. "Ladies. I'm Vance Phelps."

"Are you a...gambler?" Rose asked with barely suppressed excitement. She had heard of such women, but never thought to meet one.

"Rose," her mother said sharply, "your questions are unseemly and your manners even more so." She turned her steely gaze to Vance. "Please forgive my daughter's impertinence."

"Not at all," Vance replied smoothly, understanding Rose's confusion. Some more adventurous women did make their living by frequenting the gambling halls, often donning dapper male garb to enhance their reputations and garner invitations to the high-stakes games. "I'm afraid I have never been good enough at cards to make it a profession." She hesitated, then added, "I'm a physician."

"Oh, my," Rose breathed. "How exciting." Her gaze dropped briefly from Vance's face, skimming down her body and then returning. Once more, to her frustration, she could find no way within the bounds of propriety to ask what she truly wanted to know. "I imagine that's very…demanding work."

"Sometimes." Weary and hard pressed to keep up polite appearances or conversation, Vance wished she could surreptitiously slide the flask from the inside pocket of her traveling coat. The warmth of the whiskey, no matter how fleeting, would be welcome. Instead, she slipped the watch from her pocket and checked the time. "We should be arriving soon."

"New Hope must seem like a very dull place to visit after the excitement of the city," Rose went on, ignoring the sharp *tsk* of disapproval from her mother. Her visit to Denver as a birthday gift from her parents had shown her a whole new world that she had never realized existed, one far more thrilling than the plain frontier society in which she had been raised. She was determined not to sit quietly by ever again while life happened all around her. And here was just such an opportunity, for surely this woman had seen much of the world. Rose had never seen a woman dressed this way before or traveling alone. Nor had she ever seen anyone, man or woman, who looked so haunted. "Do you have family there?"

"No." Vance's tone was sharper than she intended, and when she saw Rose's dark eyes widen in surprise, she smiled to soften the edge of her reply. "No, not family. I'm going there to work."

"With Dr. Melbourne?" Rose couldn't disguise her pleasure. Now, she would have even more of an occasion to associate with this intriguing newcomer and learn more of what went on in the world beyond the boundaries of her tedious existence.

"Yes." Vance didn't care to elaborate. In fact, the coach brought a sense of relief. It seemed that she had lost the skill for courteous social interaction during the last few years. All she wanted was to be alone. Wondering why she had even made this journey when what awaited her held no appeal, she forced herself to say, "I'll be assisting Dr. Melbourne."

"Really? Oh. Well." Rose smiled brightly. "I shall surely avail myself of your services, then."

Vance smiled thinly. "I certainly hope you won't need them, Miss Mason."

❖

Jessie Forbes tossed a feed sack onto the pile in the back of her wagon just as the stagecoach clattered to a stop across the street in front of the hotel. She waved to the bearded, dusty man at the reins. “Afternoon, Ezra.”

“Howdy, Jessie,” the driver called back as he jumped down and secured the team. While the hotel proprietor hurried outside to welcome the new arrivals, Ezra clambered back up to the top of the coach and began handing down luggage to a third man. Jessie paid little attention to the familiar scene, noting absently that the Masons had returned as Charles Mason, the president of New Hope’s only bank, pulled his buggy behind her wagon. “Jessie,” he said as he hurried by on his way to greet his wife and daughter.

“Charles,” Jessie acknowledged, watching him idly as he crossed the street. Her gaze sharpened as another passenger climbed awkwardly down from the coach. Without considering her reasons or her possible reception, Jessie followed in the banker’s wake toward the stranger for whom she felt a swift and uncanny sense of recognition. Up close, she understood why. The newcomer was the first woman Jessie had ever seen dressed in men’s clothes in public, other than herself. Women out on the range might wear pants when it suited the work or the weather, but never in town. Jessie did because it was all she had ever worn, and it was what she was comfortable in. She had grown up in New Hope. The townspeople knew her and thought nothing of it when she rode astride looking exactly like one of her trail hands in typical cowboy garb—denim pants, cotton shirt, leather vest, boots, and western hat. Nor did anyone think it unusual that she wore a Colt .45 holstered against her thigh and carried a rifle on her saddle. She’d never given much thought to her difference until she realized she wasn’t alone. She stopped in front of the dark-haired woman who was almost exactly her height, if a good deal thinner, and held out her hand. “I’m Jessie Forbes.”

Vance took in the rangy blond, noting the tan on her face and neck that extended into the opening of her collarless cotton shirt, the wide black leather belt, the holster slung low on her lean hips, the scuffed boots. One quick survey told her this was a woman who worked on the land, but it was the intelligence in her blue eyes and the flicker of curiosity that held Vance’s attention. There was something else in her gaze as well, a look of understanding that was wholly without pity. It was that more than anything else that had her extending her own hand in return. "Vance Phelps."

"Staying at the hotel?" Jessie asked.

"Might be," Vance replied. "But I've got to see about a job first. Maybe you can tell me where I'd find Dr. Melbourne's office?"

Jessie half turned and pointed down the main street. The street itself was a double wagon-width wide, with permanent ruts carved into it from the passage of countless wheels and horses' hooves. The buildings were two-story wood structures with the exception of the bank, which was of a more recent vintage than most of the others and built of brick. Wide board sidewalks bridged the space between doorways and the street and allowed the ladies to keep their shoes and dresses dry when out walking or socializing during inclement weather. "About three doors down on this side of the street."

"Appreciate it."

"You're a doctor?"

"Yes."

"Well, welcome to New Hope." Jessie eyed the heavy valise that Ezra dropped onto the ground next to Vance, then regarded the neatly pinned up, and empty, left sleeve. "I'm going that way, if you've got more luggage."

"Just the one." Vance hefted it in her right hand, keeping her expression carefully neutral as the muscles in her left side burned. Ten cramped hours in the coach had tightened the scar tissue over her ribs. Jessie Forbes was a bit taller than she was and probably five years younger. Fit and strong and clear-eyed. Everything Vance no longer was. Oddly, she didn't resent the careful offer of assistance. On a day when she wasn't so weary, in so much pain, and wishing for nothing more but drink and a bed, she might have wondered why she wasn't bothered. As it was, she just nodded and turned in the direction Jessie had indicated. "Thanks again."

"Don't mention it."

Jessie went back to loading supplies, then checked her watch. She had almost an hour before she was due to collect Kate at the Beecher home. Just enough time for a little socializing of her own.

The saloon was nearly empty at five in the afternoon. Four men played cards at a back table, a bottle of whiskey in the center. A few cowboys stood drinking at the bar that ran along one side of the long, narrow room. An upright piano was pushed against the opposite wall, but the piano player was nowhere in sight. A staircase at the rear led up to a narrow balcony and a hallway beyond. The girls who populated the rooms down that hall wouldn't make an appearance until after ten that evening, when the cowboys and townsmen would be in the mood for company. One woman stood at the far end of the bar talking quietly to the bartender, and when she saw Jessie, she smiled and waved. Jessie tipped her hat and went to join her. "Hello, Mae."

"Why, hello, Montana," Mae said, using the nickname she had coined when Jessie, just eighteen, had first started coming into the saloon with her ranch hands after taking over the running of the Rising Star Ranch when her father died.

"How are you?" Jessie regarded with real pleasure the elegantly made-up blond in her signature off-the-shoulder emerald green dress, cut so low in the front as to flout propriety. Still, she carefully kept her gaze above the level of that creamy expanse of skin, looking into Mae's deep green eyes instead.

"The week after roundup?" Mae laughed sharply. "About ready to shoot half the men in this town. I can't wait till they spend their last dollar and ride on out of here for another year."

Jessie hid her grin and said seriously, "I surely hope it's none of my boys giving you any trouble."

Mae gave her an arch look, one carefully plucked brow rising. "And I suppose you think because they take orders from you out there on that ranch that they're different than ordinary men? When they've been out on the range for a few months with nothing but their own ornery selves for company, there's only two things they're looking for when they got money in their pocket. Liquor and women."

"If any one of them causes you or your girls any trou—"

"No," Mae said, resting her soft hand on Jessie's forearm. "The Rising Star boys are usually the best in the bunch. Still, I've had my hands full all this week keeping peace down here and making sure that my girls aren't in the middle when some of these hotheads start in on whose ranch raises the finest horses, who can shoot the farthest, who's the best card player…" She shook her head. "You name it, men will argue over it."

"I can't see as there's much to argue about," Jessie said. "Everyone knows the Rising Star has the best horses and the best hands."

Mae threw back her head, her shoulder-length gold ringlets, worn fashionably free that evening, dancing over milky shoulders. "I forget sometimes you're not all that much different than those men of yours." Her expression grew tender as she took in the handsome rancher's sky blue eyes, her sun-kissed hair caught carelessly at the back of her neck with a leather tie, her worn and trail-stained clothes. Everything about her was so much more appealing than any of the cowboys who frequented the bar or her bed. Her smoky voice grew deeper. "Just different in all the ways that count."

"Mae." Jessie laughed. "I'm about as ordinary as they come."

Mae forced lightness into her voice, reminding herself that things were different for Jessie now, and anything she might have once dreamed about her would never come to pass. Leaning close, she whispered conspiratorially, "I'd bet that's not what your young Miss Kate Beecher would say."

Blushing, Jessie hooked her thumbs in her front pockets and glanced around, grateful that no one was in earshot. "Uh...well, I—"

"Oh, Montana," Mae said, taking pity on her. "You are a wonder. Where is she? With her folks?"

Jessie nodded. "I had to come into town for supplies, and Kate stopped by for a visit with her mother."

"But not you?"

"I think it's going to be a spell before the Beechers are real comfortable with me."

"Or with Kate living with you."

"Yes."

"Well, never you mind. They'll come around," Mae said kindly, though she doubted that Martha Beecher would ever accept what Kate and Jessie shared—what Kate refused to give up or deny. As much as she'd once mistrusted Kate's motives, Mae had to give her credit for standing up for what she wanted, and for standing by Jessie. "How is Kate after her first week out on the ranch?"

"She's fine," Jessie said with relief. "She still gets a little tired if she overdoes it, which she usually does, but she's nearly back to her old self."

"I think we were lucky that the grippe didn't take more," Mae said angrily. "Seems like life out here is hard enough with the weather, and the outlaws, and the troubles between the army and Indians. We don't need to be dying in droves from the grippe and cholera, too."

Mae's tone was bitter, and Jessie wondered who she had lost in her life. As long as they had been friends, there was far more she didn't know about Mae than what little she did.

"Hate to go through anything like that again," Jessie agreed. "Looks like the doc is going to have some help, though."

"What do you mean?"

"A new doctor came in on the stage today. At least, I guess she's going to be working with the doc. She was headed in that direction."

"She?" Mae's eyes brightened with curiosity. "I never heard of a woman being a doctor."

"I saw something about it in the newspaper not that long ago. There are schools back East especially for women to be doctors."

"You don't say. And now we've got us one." Mae tapped an impatient finger on Jessie's arm. "Well. What's she like?"

"I don't know. I only talked to her for a minute." Jessie recalled her encounter with Vance Phelps. She'd seen that look of quiet desperation in men's eyes before and felt a pang of sympathy. "I have a feeling you'll be meeting her soon, though."

"Me? Why?"

"Isn't this where everyone comes for comfort of one kind or another?"

"Why, Montana," Mae whispered. "How'd you ever get to be so smart."

Jessie smiled wistfully. "It doesn't come from being smart, Mae. It comes from being lonely."

"But you're not anymore, are you?"

"No. I'm not." Jessie leaned forward and kissed Mae's cheek. "It's about time I go collect Kate."

"You tell her I said hello," Mae called as she watched Jessie walk away, her heart aching. She wanted to be happy that Jessie had found someone to love, but remained inestimably sad that she hadn't been the one to claim Jessie's heart.

## CHAPTER THREE

Vance knocked on the plain wooden door marked by a small sign that said Doctor's Office in unadorned hand printing. When no one answered, she peered through the rectangular pane of glass adjacent to the door and, in the murky interior light, could make out a desk, several chairs, and a bookcase. An unlit oil lamp stood on top of the bookcase. After she knocked again to no response, she tried the door handle and, as she expected, it opened. She entered, put her valise down just inside the door, and took a seat in the straight-backed wooden chair opposite the desk. She felt no particular sense of urgency since there was nowhere else she needed to be. She'd long since learned how to let time slip away, so that the passage of it was no longer a painful burden. Closing her eyes, her mind carefully blank, she settled in to wait.

❖

"Really, Kate," Martha Beecher said with an aggrieved expression. "Just because Jessie refuses to dress appropriately is no excuse for you to disregard your upbringing."

Kate Beecher took a deep breath, having known that she would invite such a conversation when she'd come to visit her mother wearing only her plain cotton walking dress, without her crinoline underneath. The wide-hooped understructure made her dresses far too cumbersome to move about easily on the ranch or to sit comfortably in the buckboard. She'd never understood why women had considered such an imposition to activity fashionable to begin with, and intended never to wear one again. Nevertheless, she was resolved to keep her temper in check when her mother criticized Jessie. She and her parents, especially her mother, were still on tenuous terms when it came to her new living arrangements and, more critically, her personal relationship with Jessie. "Jessie could hardly be expected to do the work she does dressed any differently, and," she said with a small pleased smile, "she looks wonderful just as she is."

"I'm well aware of Jessie's…differences," Martha said primly, "but I see no reason that *you* should suddenly forget yourself and the things you've been taught."

Laughing, Kate regarded her mother fondly. She knew how great the sacrifice had been for her mother to leave Boston society and to travel into a wild and unknown land for the sake of her husband's dreams. And for Kate's dreams, too. "Believe me, I haven't forgotten any of the important things that you've taught me."

"Sometimes I wonder."

"Oh! That will be Jessie!" Kate set her teacup aside and rose swiftly at the jangle of spurs on the wide wooden porch. Although it was only May and snow still covered the Rockies well down into the foothills, the afternoon was warm, and they'd left the front door ajar to take advantage of the breeze as they'd visited.

"Why don't you tell her she needn't wait," Martha said stiffly. "Then you could stay for supper and your father will take you…home… in the morning."

"Oh, no," Kate said on her way into the foyer. "I don't want to be away overnight." She opened the door wide and leaned up to give Jessie a quick kiss on the mouth. "Hello, sweetheart. Come inside. We were just finishing our tea."

"Hello, Kate." Jessie's heart swelled the way it always did when she first saw Kate after they'd been apart. Kate was every bit as breathtaking, with her lustrous wavy black hair and midnight eyes, as she had been the first morning Jessie had seen her. And even though every morning for the last week she'd awakened with Kate beside her in the four-poster bed that had been her parents', marveling at the wonder of their bodies curled together, she knew she'd never get used to having Kate in her life. It felt like a dream, and she imagined that it always would. Lowering her voice to a whisper, she said, "I've missed you."

"And I you," Kate murmured, resting her palm on Jessie's chest just above her heart.

Jessie drew her fingers over Kate's cheek, relieved to see the healthy flush of color where the angry hue of fever had been all too recently. Then she looked beyond Kate into the sitting room and caught a glimpse of the tea things set out on the buffet. A silver serving tray, plates with small sandwiches, and impossibly delicate, hand-painted china cups. The kinds of things that Kate's mother had been used to in Boston and no doubt missed out here on the frontier. To Jessie, they represented something uncomfortably foreign, and she would prefer roping a dozen wild mustangs at once to balancing one of those cups on her knee. "I don't want to interrupt. I'll just wait out here on the porch. It's a nice enough day and I'd enjoy—"

"You will do nothing of the sort," Kate chided, linking her arm through Jessie's and pulling her inside. "You'll have some tea and sandwiches."

"Good day, Mrs. Beecher." Jessie swiftly removed her hat as she followed Kate to the sofa. She'd been in the parlor many times in the last five months while Kate had recovered from the influenza that had nearly cost her life. She'd never been entirely comfortable, especially since Martha Beecher had seen to it that they were never alone. She'd treated Jessie as the suitor she'd been, although an unwelcome one, with distant politeness and thinly veiled censure. It had been the happiest day of Jessie's life when Kate had left the Beecher home to move in with her as her lover and partner at the Rising Star Ranch. If she had her way, she'd never set foot in the Beecher home again, but she had promised Kate's father that she would not come between them, and she kept her word. Plus, Kate loved her parents and Kate's happiness was all that mattered to Jessie. If Kate wanted her there, she'd suffer the discomfort of Martha Beecher's displeasure.

"Jessie," Martha Beecher said with infinite civility. "I trust you're well?"

"Yes, ma'am."

"And things at the ranch?"

Jessie's face lit up. "The Rising Star did very well at the auction recently, and I've acquired some excellent breeding stock." She stopped at the faint flicker of distaste that crossed Kate's mother's face, belatedly realizing that ladies of class were not interested in the actual workings of a horse ranch. "Everything's going along well. Appreciate you asking."

Kate's eyes sparkled with excitement as she rested her hand on Jessie's knee. Touching Jessie was so automatic she never considered not doing so. "Jessie has some wonderful plans for supplying horses not just to the stagecoach lines, but to cattlemen all over the territory who need horses to drive their herds east—"

"Really, Kate," Martha interrupted. "I should think such things would be of no interest to a young lady."

"Oh, no—that's one of the wonderful things about living out here. Life is constantly changing. The West is growing, and we're right here to see it." She looked at Jessie—her love—with tender pride. "Jessie knows the land and the people. And what we need."

Blushing, but warmed by Kate's gaze, Jessie resisted the urge to take her lover's hand. She'd never been ashamed of what they shared, but she saw no need to force Kate's mother to witness what she so obviously wanted to pretend was not between them. Jessie still couldn't understand why anyone would resent something so beautiful and so precious as the love they shared, but she appreciated Kate's parents' concern for her welfare and her future. She intended to show them that they had nothing to worry about. She would take care of Kate as well as any man.

"If you still want to stop in at the store, Kate," Jessie said gently, "we should go so as not to be driving home too late. It still gets cold after sundown, and I don't want you getting chilled."

"We've blankets in the wagon, and I'm not going to be damaged by a little brisk air," Kate said.

"Jessie's right," Martha said in a rare moment of agreement. "You mustn't risk getting sick again." She'd not told Kate, but Jessie knew that the doctor had said Kate's recent brush with death had left her vulnerable. She'd recovered, almost miraculously, but she might not fare as well from another illness falling close upon the first.

Kate glanced from her mother to Jessie with affectionate irritation. "I'm quite all right and quite capable of making my own decisions about when I come and go." Nevertheless, she squeezed Jessie's hand and rose to kiss her mother's cheek. "But I do want to do some shopping before we start back."

Jessie followed Kate and Martha to the door, not really listening as they made plans for some ladies' gathering or another. She was wondering how long she could put off riding out to check the line with her foreman Jed. There were scattered pockets of horses all through the foothills of her property, and she needed to check on the yearlings and foals. Plus, she wanted to cull the herds of the strongest brood mares to put under the new stallion she'd acquired. The only reason she hadn't set out immediately after the auction was that she didn't want to leave Kate alone at the ranch just yet. She snapped back to the moment as Martha Beecher spoke her name.

"Jessie," Martha said, "you will look after our Kate now, won't you?"

Despite Kate's exasperated sound of protest, Jessie nodded seriously. "You can be sure of it."

"You worry too much," Kate said as she walked to the buckboard with her hand in Jessie's. She lifted her arms to Jessie shoulders and allowed Jessie to lift her up to the seat. She could have climbed aboard herself, even in her dress, but she loved the feel of Jessie's arms around her and the effortless way she swung her up. She wished never to miss an opportunity for Jessie to touch her.

"I worry enough," Jessie said as she settled next to Kate and tucked the woolen blanket around her waist and legs, letting it drape onto the footboard.

Kate waved to her mother, who stood in the doorway, then slipped her hand onto Jessie's thigh as they pulled away from the front of the house. "Haven't I shown you these last few nights that I'm quite well again?"

Jessie drew a sharp breath as Kate's fingers danced over the inside of her leg. "Can't say as I'd mind you showing me again."

Laughing, Kate leaned her cheek against Jessie's shoulder. "Then take me home, sweetheart. We'll shop another day."

❖

The sound of slow, heavy footsteps brought Vance awake in the nearly black room.

"Dr. Melbourne," she said immediately as the door behind her opened, lest she startle whoever was entering and find herself taken for an intruder. She had no desire to be shot ever again. "I'm Vance Phelps."

Caleb Melbourne crossed the room to the oil lamp, lit it with a stick match from his vest pocket, and adjusted the wick until the room was softly illuminated, leaving only the corners in shadow. He turned, a large man with a face furrowed and scarred by weather and life's cruelties. His full head of unruly dark hair and a thick mustache that draped the corners of his mouth would have lent him a rough, handsome look had he not appeared so careworn. His trousers and jacket were rumpled, and at first glance he gave the appearance of a man whose burdens had gained the upper hand. His dark eyes, however, were sharp and inquisitive, despite the puffed and weary lids. "Jonathan's daughter."

"Yes, sir."

Caleb nodded, pulled out the chair behind the rough wooden desk, and sagged into the chair with a sigh. "The last time I saw your father, you and your brother were barely toddlers." He looked past Vance out the filmy glass and into the darkened street beyond. Shapeless forms clattered by and the shouts of men coming and going filtered through the rough boarded walls. "That was in Philadelphia just after we graduated."

The past was not something Vance cared to revisit. Plus she was embarrassed, knowing that her father had asked a favor that could hardly be refused. "I know it's been a very long time, and I appreciate your kindness—"

"His letter said that you wanted to work."

Did she? She couldn't remember anymore what it was she wanted, if she wanted anything at all. She had come because to stay would have meant facing her father's grief and worry day after day and having no way to assuage it. He had already suffered so much, she couldn't bring herself to add to it. And there were far too many reminders of what they had all lost even for *her* to block out. She thought of the vast unsettled countryside she had crossed in the last weeks, the crude frontier towns so different from the paved and gaslit streets of Philadelphia, and the glimpse of New Hope she had had on her short walk down the hard-packed, rutted street. There was nothing here to remind her of her old life, her old self, and what might have been. That disconnection from all she'd known, all she'd been, that at least was something she did want.

With a start, she realized that Dr. Melbourne still waited, watching her with intent regard.

"Yes," Vance said, holding his gaze and giving him the answer he required. "I want to work."

"We're the only doctors," he grimaced, "the only *real* doctors, in two hundred miles in every direction. There's plenty passing through selling miracle cures who don't know as much about medicine as the average housewife. There's some out there, untrained though they may be, who do know enough to be of use in the places where there's no one else. For them, I'm thankful."

"I've seen some gifted healers with never a day of formal training."

Caleb looked at her empty coat sleeve and then back to her face. "I imagine you have. It was a brave thing you did."

"Or foolish." Vance thought of Milton and missed him with the same sharp bright pain of those first moments knowing he was gone. "I don't know how to judge it anymore."

"You were in till the end?"

She nodded. "The last official battle, at any rate."

As if sensing her reluctance, and appreciating a person's right to keep their feelings private, Caleb asked no more, although there were worlds left unsaid in her tormented eyes. "A lot of the people we see to are out on the range. Can you ride?"

"Yes. And drive a buggy. And shoot."

"Good, you'll need to do all three. For the first couple of weeks I'll take you around with me until you get acquainted with the land and the folks."

"You haven't asked me about my skills."

"Didn't figure I had to. If you were Grant's regimental surgeon, I guess you know what you're about." He rubbed both hands over his face, then stood. "There is one task I'm going to give you straight off. That's looking after the girls down at the saloon."

"Prostitutes?"

He nodded. "They're a good bunch for the most part, and in better shape than most, too—physically and in every other way. There's a spitfire of a woman there who looks after them."

"Is she the madam?"

"Nothing quite that fancy out here, but she does what she can to see that the girls aren't mistreated. When you get settled, drop around there and ask for Mae."

"Does this Mae have a last name?"

Caleb looked surprised. "Now that you mention it, not that I ever heard."

Vance said nothing, thinking that there was probably more than one person in New Hope with secrets they didn't care to share. Perhaps this was the right place for her after all.

"You won't have any trouble finding her," Caleb said with a small smile. "She's the finest-looking thing west of the Mississippi."

"I'm sure I'll have no difficulty," Vance replied, although she suspected that his assessment was colored by the fact that there were very few women on the frontier compared to the number of men. "I'll take a room at the hotel if you should need me before morning."

"Get some rest. I expect you'll need it."

Vance stood and extended her hand across the desk. "Thank you."

"You might want to hold off on the thanks until you've had a chance to see what you've gotten into."

Whatever it was, Vance thought as she hefted her valise once more and walked out into the night, it would never be as bad as what she'd left behind.

## CHAPTER FOUR

"A doctor? Imagine that." The rotund bespectacled man behind the counter perused Vance with open curiosity. "I can't say as I've ever seen a woman doctor before." When Vance said nothing, he cleared his throat and went on hurriedly, "Need a room, you say."

"Yes."

"We've got weekly rates, but if you think you'll be here longer, you might try the boarding house on the far end of town."

"Thank you," Vance said wearily, finding any day beyond the next more than she cared to contemplate. It had become far easier not to consider the future. "A room here will be fine for now."

"The name's Silas, in case you'll be needing anything."

Vance started toward the stairs. "No, there's nothing I need."

"G'night, then," he called after her, craning his neck to follow her as she slowly made her way up the wide wooden staircase. "Imagine that."

The room Vance let herself into on the second floor was a clean but unadorned space with a small hooked rug next to a single bed. The thin, cotton-stuffed mattress was covered by a thinner plain blue woolen blanket of the kind she had slept under in the army. She remembered that she'd always been cold and had often wondered if she would ever be warm again. A single chest of drawers stood against the wall with a round mirror nailed above it. A washbasin, lamp, and pitcher were the only items on its scarred surface. She did not light the lamp.

She set her valise at the foot of the bed, hung her coat on the back of the single chair that stood against the opposite wall, and wandered to the single casement window. The saloon, unmarked by any sign, was visible on the opposite side of the street. If she angled her head, she could see Caleb's office. Moving back to the bed, she sat to kick off her boots and then stretched out on top of the covers. Splinters of moonlight shafted across the ceiling, making random patterns that she watched take shape and dissolve and reshape while she waited for sleep. It was an exercise that she had discovered would bring some temporary respite from her memories, if not slumber.

Sleep stole unsuspectingly through her consciousness, and she found herself once again at Appomattox Court House, sweating in the cold morning mist of fear and smoke. The rough wooden table was awash with blood. No matter how fast she worked, every time she looked up there were more wounded. Her arms were crimson to the elbows, and still they came, the ruined and the broken, crying her name. Milton stood beside her, repeating over and over, *no more time, no more time, no more time*. She ignored the panic in his voice, the terror in his eyes, and just kept cutting. Her chest ached. Her lungs burned. She reached for the amputation knife. Just one more. Just one more. Just one more. The ground heaved, fire erupted at her feet, and red-hot pain seared her flesh. She looked down and saw herself writhing on the table, a faceless man poised above her with a saw in his hand.

Vance jolted upright, screaming. Quickly, she wrapped her arm around her bent knees and pressed her face against the rough wool of her trousers. She stifled her sobs as she fought for breath, her shirt soaked with the sweat of night terrors. When the clutch of the nightmare began to recede, she turned her face to the window and rested her cheek against the top of her knee. It hadn't been this bad in a long time. For a second, as her own harsh breath filled the room to overflowing, she thought she heard the sound of the fife and drum. As her heart stopped thundering in her ears, she realized it was a piano.

She stood, her legs still a little shaky, and walked to the window. Across the street, the saloon and some of the rooms on the upper floors were ablaze. Every few seconds a figure would go in or out through the swinging doors. In a lighted second-floor window she saw a man and a woman locked in an embrace, her dress lifted up to her hips as his hands roamed beneath it. Vance didn't immediately look away, taken with the urgent sense of life that surrounded the couple, thinking of what Caleb had said about the girls who lived there. She wondered if the woman who bent beneath the weight of the cowboy's passion welcomed his touch or was merely an indifferent player in an oft-repeated drama.

She tried to imagine desire and couldn't. Her pocket watch read a few minutes past one. Turning away, she walked to the dresser and found, to her surprise, that the pitcher was full. She poured a few inches of tepid water into the tin basin and splashed her face before stripping off the sour shirt. Then she soaked the tail of her shirt and rubbed it over her chest and shoulders before tossing it aside and pulling another from her valise. She also retrieved her holster and Colt .45, the same weapon she had worn throughout the war, and strapped it on.

Silas looked up at the sound of footsteps on the stairs. "Couldn't sleep?"

Vance regarded him impassively. "No. I could."

She walked out, unaware that he stared after her with a mixture of curiosity and unease.

The saloon was still half full, mostly with men drinking at the bar or tables, a few apparently asleep with their heads on their folded arms, and the remainder playing cards. In the far corner a scantily clad woman sat in a man's lap with her head on his shoulder while he fondled her breasts. Vance walked to the bar.

"Help you?" asked a middle-aged man with full sideburns, a barrel chest, and dark eyes that had seen all there was to see.

"Whiskey."

The bartender poured a shot and then set the bottle down next to Vance's right hand. "I'm Frank."

She pushed several coins toward his side of the bar. "Thanks."

"If you want everybody in town to know who you are, you can tell me now and be done with it." Frank shrugged. "If you don't, it might take a little longer, but sooner or later the same thing will happen."

"If I stay here more than a week, word will get around anyhow." Vance tossed back the shot and poured another one. "And if I don't, it won't matter." She held out her hand. "Vance Phelps. One-time surgeon and, now, Dr. Melbourne's new assistant."

"From back East." He said it as if it were a statement, not a question.

"More or less." Vance sensed someone move up beside her and glanced sideways. A woman with deep green eyes, golden hair, and the purest skin she'd ever seen stood beside her in a deep indigo dress with a low-cut, tight bodice that cradled her breasts like a lover's hands. Sparkling blue stones set in gold swung lightly from her earlobes, brushing her neck with a mesmerizing caress. Despite the whiskey she'd just drunk, Vance's throat was dry and her mind blank of everything except the tantalizing scent of perfume and the pale perfection of the woman's face. Frank, the other men in the saloon, even the remnants of her dream, vanished.

"Frank talked your ear off yet?" Mae asked, her voice low and sultry.

"Not yet," Vance managed. She downed her whiskey, her nerves jangling. "You must be Mae."

"Now why would you say that?" Mae nodded when Frank held up a bottle of brandy questioningly. She took the glass from him, but did not drink as she studied Vance. There were deep shadows under her eyes, and deeper ones within. She'd seen her come in, a stranger in a well-cut suit who seemed not to care that a woman, even one whose dress and carriage indicated she gave no credence to the opinions of others, might draw unwanted attention in a place like this. Attention that Mae was not certain that a woman with one arm could turn aside.

"Caleb Melbourne said you were the finest-looking thing west of the Mississippi." Vance spoke quietly with neither sarcasm nor insinuation. "He was right."

Mae threw back her head and laughed. "It would appear that both the town's doctors are sweet-talkers, then."

Vance frantically searched for something to say just to hear this woman's full, vibrant voice a little longer. After the cold, dark embrace of her dreams, she found herself inexplicably craving the vitality and warmth that surrounded Mae. "Since I'm speechless, I beg to differ."

"Well," Mae said, sipping her brandy. "Why don't you start with your name."

"Something tells me you might already know that and more."

Mae smiled. "Smart, too. But I imagine a woman wanting to be a doctor would have to be."

"Or stubborn."

"Both, I'll wager." Mae watched Vance pour another shot, saw her hand tremble. "I can't say that I'm not curious. Since I know you're no fool, you have to know folks will want to know your story."

Vance tilted her chin toward the room and the men—drifters, gamblers, trail hands, and businessmen. All had one thing in common. They were all here in the middle of the night staving off loneliness or simply trying to fill the hours until the habit of their day began again. One thing was certain, they all had stories. "I'd have thought you'd have heard enough of those by now."

"I expect yours is different."

"Why?" Vance finished her whiskey, contemplated the bottle, and pushed her glass aside. While the temptation to slide inside the bottle was strong, Mae's presence was stronger.

"You're not a man." Mae watched a bitter smile flicker across Vance's face. Even in men's clothing, in a place no decent woman would be seen, drinking whiskey in the middle of a lonely night, no one would ever take her for a man. Her face was strong, with a tightness along her jaw that suggested she wouldn't yield easily to trouble when it came her way. But there was a fineness to her skin, as if it were silk, and a delicate beauty in the elegant curve of her brow and the length of her dark lashes. It was easy to see the woman in her, which made the thinly veiled anger and pain that rode just beneath the surface all the more compelling.

"Maybe not, but my story might be the same."

"Oh," Mae said, sipping her brandy and resting her fingers on the top of Vance's hand where it lay on the bartop. "Are you going to tell me someone stole your stake and cashed in on your claim while you were on your way into town to file the deed?"

The corner of Vance's mouth twitched. "Never got the gold fever."

"Some no-account cheated at cards and won your horse, your saddle, and your last dollar?"

Vance shook her head. "I know when I'm beat, and I know when to fold them."

"I wonder," Mae mused, idly tracing the length of Vance's fingers, one after the other, with a ruby red fingernail. "I'd be willing to bet you don't give up easily."

"Like I said," Vance said roughly. "Stubborn doesn't always mean smart."

"Or," Mae went on, knowing that whatever caused the anguish in Vance's voice was something Vance wasn't going to talk about now. Maybe never. "You're going to tell me a woman broke your heart and ran off with the lying, yellow-bellied preacher."

"Couldn't be that," Vance replied seriously, aware that Mae was watching her intently. "I make it a point to stay away from church."

Mae smiled. "If you're not worried about the preacher, you might want to attend the services come Sunday. The townsfolk are likely to take to you more if you do."

Vance sighed. "Some things never change no matter how far away you go."

"You been traveling a long time?" Mae asked gently.

"A little more than a year," Vance answered, surprising herself at the admission. "Well, not the whole time. Part of it I spent in a hospital in Richmond."

"How long?"

"Seven months." Vance reached into her watch pocket, tipped out her pocket watch and looked at the time. "The night's pretty well along and I've taken up enough of yours."

"You're not keeping me from anything I'd rather be doing."

"Dr. Melbourne asked me to see to the young ladies here."

"The young ladies." Mae laughed quietly. She heard no hint of censure in Vance's deep, rough-edged voice. Whatever anger lived inside her, it was for herself and not others. "The young ladies and I rarely rise before midafternoon."

"I was counting you among their number," Vance said with a trace of gallantry long unpracticed. "Surely you're no older than your charges."

"It seems you know quite a bit about me, as well, Dr. Phelps."

Vance inclined her head and smiled fleetingly. "No more than what you want anyone to know, I'm sure."

"Come by around six tomorrow and have supper with me. I'll tell you about the girls then."

Vance hesitated. She wasn't in the habit of socializing, even casually. She had nothing to say that others could hear or that she would want to recount. It was enough for her to live with her past without inflicting it upon others.

"You'll not be required to tell me your secrets."

"And what if I should want to?" Vance held her breath, wondering just what she hoped to hear. Despite the circumstances or appearances, Mae was clever and far from the kind of beaten-down, destitute woman who ordinarily turned to prostitution as the last form of survival. Vance had been in enough large cities and desolate frontier towns to know what became of women who had no men to provide for them, no family to support them, and no skills to make their own way. Perhaps it was precisely because Mae defied expectations that she was drawn to her.

Mae closed her fingers around Vance's wrist and leaned close enough that had Vance looked down, she would have been able to see the blush of rouge highlighting the deeper rose of her nipples. "I would be very pleased to listen."

"Then I shall be pleased to attend you tomorrow evening." Vance gently disengaged her wrist from Mae's warm grasp and stepped away. "Good night, Mae."

"Good night, Vance."

Frank leaned on the bar as Mae watched Vance leave. "I can't say as I've ever seen quite the likes of her before," he said, not unkindly.

"No," Mae said quietly, "neither have I."

# CHAPTER FIVE

Kate stretched and smiled contentedly beneath the cotton quilt, enjoying the feeling of awakening in her new home. Her home. Her home with Jessie. Although the bed beside her was empty, the warmth that lingered told her that Jessie had just gotten up. The sun was not yet high enough to brighten the room, and she sensed that it was just before dawn. She'd learned in just the few days she'd been there that Jessie always rose before the sun, as did the men in the bunkhouse that stood not far from the main house. The horses and other stock needed tending, and after a quick meal and coffee, the men often had to ride miles before they would reach whatever part of the ranch they would be working on that day. The hours of daylight were precious, and Jessie and her men worked from first light until last.

Although Jessie had insisted the first morning that Kate needed her rest and should not get up with her, Kate decided it was time for her to establish her presence in the daily life of the ranch. It was her life now, too. She rose and quickly dressed in the chill room, adding one of Jessie's shirts over her dress for extra warmth. She liked the feel of the soft cotton because it reminded her of resting her cheek against Jessie's shoulder when they embraced. Immediately, her body quickened to the memory of Jessie's warm, supple form against hers.

"Oh, Jessie," Kate murmured with a soft laugh. "I never could have imagined you."

She hurried downstairs and into the kitchen. The lamp glowed on the counter, and when she checked the coals in the cast-iron stove, she saw that Jessie had laid on wood. The bucket sitting next to the dry sink was filled with fresh water, too, but the coffeepot was still cold.

Humming quietly, Kate set about making coffee and gathering the ingredients to cook breakfast. She was just pulling biscuits from the oven when the kitchen door opened and a brisk breeze preceded her lover.

"Good morning." Kate set the baking tray on a cooling stone, dusted her hands on her apron, and met Jessie just inside the door. Jessie wore her work clothes—denim pants, cotton shirt, leather vest, and a sheepskin coat. Her blue eyes were bright, her face flushed from the chill and wind, and she looked gorgeous. Kate wrapped her arms around Jessie's shoulders and kissed her. "Coffee's on and the bacon's almost done."

Jessie held her tightly and rubbed her face against Kate's hair. She was so wonderfully warm, so beautiful. "I still can't believe you're here."

Kate stroked Jessie's neck and ran her fingers through her hair. "Where else would I be? I'm home."

"I love you."

"Mmm, I love you." Kate leaned back in Jessie's arms and regarded her playfully. "You took advantage of me last evening."

Feigning innocence, Jessie gave Kate one more squeeze, then let her go. She hung her Stetson on a peg inside the door, removed her coat, and draped it over the back of the wooden chair. Without looking directly at Kate, she said, "Can't think what you mean."

"Well," Kate said as she poured coffee into the large tin cups they used for everyday, "after we had a fine dinner, you laid on a fire in the bedroom and turned the lamp down so we could snuggle under the covers. Watch the fire a bit, you said."

Jessie laid out strips of bacon on two plates, added a biscuit to each, and carried them to the table. She sat down and gestured to the chair beside her. "This looks wonderful."

Kate sat and tapped her finger on the top of Jessie's hand. "Don't think I'm going to forget what I was saying."

"I can't think of any place I'd rather be than lying in our bed with you in my arms watching the flames dance in the fireplace," Jessie said quietly.

"You made it so I was so comfortable I'd fall asleep," Kate said, stroking Jessie's arm as she sipped her coffee.

"Now you're giving me credit for predicting the future," Jessie said with a laugh. She bit into the biscuit and made a small groan of approval. "They never taste like this when Sam makes them."

"Well, if I can't bake better than your trail cook, Hannah Schroeder will have my hide. She spent all of last summer teaching me how."

Jessie grinned. "Lucky for me."

"You let me sleep when you knew I wanted to do something altogether different last evening," Kate said accusingly, although she smiled tenderly.

"You needed to sleep, love," Jessie said quietly. If she had her way, Kate would not be up now cooking breakfast for her when it wasn't necessary. She was used to eating with the men at the bunkhouse or doing for herself. She didn't expect Kate to do it.

Kate narrowed her eyes. "You *did* plan it."

"Not planned, exactly. I just wanted you to be warm and comfortable in case you were tired." Jessie toyed with Kate's fingers. "Besides, in another month we'll not need the fire at night, and I didn't want to miss an opportunity to lie close with you underneath the covers."

"We don't need an excuse to lie together, cold or warm, day or night." Kate stood and walked round behind Jessie's chair. She draped her arms around her neck and leaned down, her mouth close to Jessie's ear. "I bet the bed is still warm from last night. The sun isn't that high yet."

Jessie leaned back, pillowing her head between Kate's breasts, and closed her eyes. She shivered as Kate's hands brushed down her chest and inside her vest. "There might be something sinful about laying abed when it's time to be working."

"As hard as you work, I'm sure an hour would be forgiven." Kate opened the top button on Jessie's shirt and stroked her chest. The skin there was warm, silky soft, and in her mind's eye she saw the tanned triangle between Jessie's breasts. She had always loved how unconcerned Jessie was about the things that her mother had taught Kate were of great importance, and yet had seemed to matter so little. Jessie didn't hide her skin from the sun, and in the summer, she tanned a beautiful gold. Kate loved to follow that sun-kissed path down Jessie's throat until it blended with the smooth cream of her breasts. She traced her fingers along that route now, dipping beneath Jessie's undershirt to cup a small, firm breast.

"Lord, Kate," Jessie whispered, arching beneath her touch. "I can't think when you do that."

"How long do we have before Jed starts to worry and comes looking for you?"

"He won't, not for a good while." Jessie struggled for breath. "Especially with him knowing that you're new to the ranch."

"Then come upstairs and give me my hour."

Jessie pushed up on rubbery legs, her coffee forgotten, and turned to take Kate in her arms. She kissed her forehead, her eyes, her mouth. Kate had twisted her hair into a loose coil at the back of her neck and tethered it there with a ribbon. Jessie loosed the tie and released the black gossamer to shower around Kate's shoulders. "The way I'm feeling right this minute, I don't think I'll last anywhere near an hour."

"We'll see about that," Kate said, opening the next button on Jessie's shirt. She kissed the valley between her breasts, then higher into the hollow at the base of her throat, then the underside of her jaw. When she reached her mouth, she brushed her lips lightly back and forth until Jessie opened for her. With short, quick, teasing strokes, she danced her tongue over the moist, warm inner recesses until Jessie's hands fisted in her hair and pulled her head away.

"Kate," Jessie grated. "You can't know what you're doing to me."

"I know," Kate panted. "I know and I love it."

"All these months I waited, missing you so much. Wanting you so much." Trembling, her eyes hot, Jessie tugged at the laces on Kate's bodice. "Every time I went to your house, I was afraid they'd turn me away."

"No." Kate framed Jessie's face, her own steady, tender gaze soothing the apprehension in Jessie's eyes. "Nothing will ever keep me from you again. I promise."

But Jessie knew that something could. She'd almost lost her. She'd knelt by her bedside as Kate had slipped away. The agonizing desolation of that moment was burned into her consciousness deeper than any brand, the memory a living nightmare that haunted her day and night. She pulled open Kate's dress and filled her hands with her, lifting her breasts free and lowering her mouth to taste the life that coursed through her. "Oh, Kate, Kate. I need you so."

Kate cradled Jessie's head to her breast and caressed her cheek. When she felt tears, her own heart nearly broke. She had no words to ease her lover's fears, no reassurances where none could truly be given. Her pledge could only be to live, day by day, loving her. "Jessie, darling. Take me upstairs so we can touch everywhere. I want you everywhere."

Jessie, taller and stronger, was lost in the grip of remembered loss and desperate desire. The weight of her passion as she drew a nipple into her mouth forced Kate back against the wall. Groaning, Jessie wanted, *craved*, more. She grasped the bottom of Kate's dress and pulled it up, wanting flesh against her flesh.

"Jessie," Kate murmured tenderly, catching Jessie's hand where it roamed restlessly over her thigh. "Jed. Jed might come."

The sound of Kate's voice, the touch of her hand, splintered the pain like glass on stone. Joy rode through her, and the relentless, choking dread eased. Jessie drew a long, sweet breath, then raised her head and gently gathered the front of Kate's dress together, covering her breasts. She kissed her softly on the mouth. "Forgive me."

"Oh, my darling. There's nothing to forgive." Kate laughed shakily. "I can only hope you always want me this way."

"More." Jessie grasped her hand and pulled her into the hall and toward the stairs. "More every day."

Hastily, they shed clothing and hurried back into bed, finding it still warm beneath the quilt as Kate had predicted. Kate opened her arms and pulled Jessie on top of her, wrapping her legs around Jessie's lean hips.

"Now," Kate urged, "now touch me."

Jessie laughed, the memory of those long winter months of uncertainty dissolving like snow in the sunshine. Kate was here, alive and loving her. This time when she sought the beat of Kate's heart with her mouth pressed to her breast, it was with elation, not pain. Nothing ever made her feel as whole as these moments alone with Kate when there was nothing between them but the love they felt for one another. When she smoothed her hand down Kate's body and found her wet and waiting for her, she wanted to weep for the beauty of it. She held Kate's passion in her palm, lost in Kate's murmurs of pleasure and soft pleas for more.

"Don't make me wait." Kate clutched Jessie's shoulders as her body shivered with need. "Take me as many times as you want, but don't make me wait. Please, Jessie. Please."

Jessie pushed up on one arm to watch Kate's face as she filled her. Kate's eyes were hazy black pools reflecting the twisting urgency in Jessie's belly. She shifted to press her center against Kate's thigh, clenching against her in time to the slow, deep thrusts of her hand.

"More," Kate gasped. With one hand she touched Jessie's face, brushing trembling fingers over her mouth. She forced her other hand, palm up, between Jessie's legs and laughed unsteadily when Jessie jerked and cried out in surprise. "I missed you, too. All these months."

Now they were joined—by their flesh, by their passion, by their promise. They held one another's eyes as they pushed deeper, body and soul, rising together and finally, releasing together.

"Kate, Kate," Jessie groaned, trying to move her weight from atop Kate's body and failing. "How can you make me feel so strong and me not able to move a muscle?"

"You'd better catch your breath," Kate warned, sliding her hands up and down Jessie's back. "I don't think my hour is up yet."

"Can't." Jessie groaned. "I have to ride this morning."

Kate laughed. "Then you'll be thinking of me."

Jessie raised her head. "I'm always thinking of you." She kissed her swiftly, then rolled over onto her back. "I can see now why the boys get a little *loco* when they've been out on the line for a few weeks." She turned her head and grinned at Kate. "I think I'd get a little *loco* after a couple days without you."

"You'll have to leave me sometimes, won't you?" Kate asked quietly, turning on her side and curving an arm around Jessie's middle.

"Now and again." Jessie had been trying to work out how she was going to do that, and she mused aloud, "When I do, you can stay with your parents."

Kate grew very still. "I can?"

"Yes. That way, I figure you'll be safe and comfortable."

"You do?"

"Uh-huh."

"While you're out on the range—where there's outlaws and wild animals and every other kind of danger, I can stay with my parents in town." Kate sat up, her eyes blazing. "Like some pampered city girl. Someone you keep here to warm your bed and then send packing while you go off to do the real work."

Jessie gaped. "I didn't say that."

Kate threw back the covers and jumped from the bed, reaching for her chemise. She pulled it angrily over her head and glared at her confused lover. "You didn't have to. It's obvious you have it all figured out."

"Not all of it," Jessie muttered, climbing from the bed in search of her pants. She couldn't defend herself without her pants on. "I just thought it would be best—"

"You thought. *You* thought." Kate watched Jessie pull on her pants and remembered the first time she'd seen her undressed, in the hotel room in New Hope the first afternoon they'd gone walking together. She'd never seen such a beautiful woman before, so confident and strong. She had fallen in love with her in that moment. Because she was confident and strong and Jessie. "Jessie Forbes."

Something about the way Kate said her name made Jessie stop with one arm thrust into her shirt. The tender look on Kate's face made the tension in her belly drain away. Softly, she said, "What?"

"Do you love me?"

"Lord, yes." Jessie shrugged into her shirt and started toward Kate, but stopped when Kate held up her hand. Heart thundering, Jessie said urgently, "Kate, how could you ask me that?"

"Then what am I to you?"

"What…I…" Jessie pressed her hand to her heart. "You're my life."

"And you are mine." Shaking her head, Kate put her arms around her. "This is my home. I'll not leave it for any reason."

Jessie held her tightly. "Then I guess we're going to need some more shooting lessons if you're going to stay here while I'm away."

"Now that's a much better idea." Kate rested her cheek against Jessie's shoulder. "And I need to learn to ride astride."

"I can see you've got some ideas of your own you didn't mention."

Kate laughed, thinking they'd survived their first fight and were no worse for it. "Maybe just a few."

# CHAPTER SIX

Talk to you, Jess?" Jed Harper asked as Jessie was about to bring one of the horses she intended to saddle-break out of the corral.

"Sure." Jessie leaned an arm over the top rail of the gate and regarded her foreman. He was a good head shorter than her, tanned and tough like good leather. She could guess his age, but not from looking at him. He had the ageless, weather-beaten face of a man who'd spent his life outdoors doing hard work. She'd known him as far back as she could remember. He'd been one of her father's closest friends, and after Tom Forbes's death, he'd been Jessie's strongest ally. She was pretty certain that a lot of the men had stayed on with her as boss, even though she was a woman and only eighteen, because Jed had talked them into it. His faith in her had helped her get through a time in her life when she'd lost everything that mattered except her land. "Something wrong?"

"Could be."

Jessie made sure that all the hands at the Rising Star knew that she was the boss, but she also let Jed handle the day-to-day affairs with the twenty or so men who worked for her. Some were long-timers and lived permanently in the bunkhouse when they weren't out in the line shacks or riding herd on the stock. Almost as many were chuck-riders, men who showed up in the winter when work out on the range was scarce, looking for a warm place to roost until the weather turned friendly again. Some stayed on, but most moved on. Men who had no permanent home and no desire for one. Regardless, she could count on Jed to get an honest day's work out of them, and she paid them what they were worth, which made her as popular as a boss could be. When Jed brought a problem to her, she knew to listen. "Trouble with the men?"

He shook his head. "No more than usual. Charlie Baker came down from the north quarter late last night. He's been up there looking for stragglers and taking count of the mares and foals for the last couple weeks."

"I know. Isn't Johnny Earley up there with him?" Throughout the year, the horses free-roamed, searching out the best shelter and richest grazing land. The size of the scattered portions of the herd could range from a few dozen to over a hundred animals. The herd covered a territory that took men weeks to ride, so shacks were built at various intervals along the borders of the ranch and in the high country where a couple of the men would stay for weeks at a time keeping track of the horses.

"Yeah. He stayed behind while Charlie come down to say we're missing some stock."

Jessie's mouth tightened into a grim line. There were any number of reasons horses went missing. Sometimes they died in falls, were killed by wild animals, were stolen for food by Indians who had been displaced from their hunting grounds, or were rustled by men who drove them south to sell to the army or ranches along the way. "Charlie say how?"

"Thought at first it might be bear," Jed replied. "There's been signs of some around, but he hasn't seen any. Hasn't seen any carcasses either."

"Could be they're dragging them off to a cave somewhere."

Jed nodded. "Pretty unusual not to see any bits left behind, though."

"How many?"

"Charlie's not sure. At first he said he thought it was just one or two straying off, maybe joining another herd. But then he started keeping count every day. Says it's one or two every couple of days."

"That's a lot of horses." Jessie knew there was only one thing to do. "I guess we're going to have to go take a look. Get word to the rest of the men out on the line."

"That'll take a good few days. Maybe longer." Jed glanced up at the house. "No need for you to come."

"If it wasn't Charlie," Jessie said, "or if it wasn't more than a horse or two, I wouldn't. But Charlie's a good man. If he says there's a problem, then there is." Jessie flicked off her hat and slapped it rhythmically against her thigh. "If there's trouble on my land, then I have to see to it."

"Kate's not been here more than a week. I don't imagine she's settled yet." Jed looked uncomfortable. "She probably shouldn't be here on her own just yet."

Jessie smiled. "You might not want to say that around her."

"Wouldn't consider it." The angle of Jed's mouth danced upward for a second. "I've seen her when she's mad, that time in town when you took that bullet in the shoulder. If she could've got her hands on them that done it, she would've made short work of them."

"I'll talk to her. She doesn't know how lonely it can get way out here, and driving back and forth into town alone isn't such a good idea either." Jessie huffed out a breath. "Not until she can shoot a little bit better than she can right now."

"There's a couple of the boys I would trust to keep an eye on things here, if she stays."

"That's good." Jessie settled her hat low on her brow. "But not just yet."

Jed stared past Jessie to the foothills that rose into the mountains on the far-distant border of the Rising Star. The mountains, timeless and indestructible, provided a kind of comfort as they loomed above them, an anchor in the wide, wild country around them. He'd ridden the line for weeks at a time out there, never seeing another soul. He'd never been lonely. He'd forgotten that for all Jessie was capable of doing as good as any man, she wasn't one. "You never said."

"Never said what?" Jessie asked quizzically.

"That you were lonely."

Jessie heard the bit of hurt in his voice and smiled. "It's one of those things you don't know you are until you aren't anymore." She glanced up toward the house and saw Kate come out the kitchen door. "And now I'm not."

❖

Kate carried the washbasin to the side of the porch and poured the rinse water over the rail onto the wildflowers that were just beginning to break through the hard-packed crust. May mornings in Montana were cold, and she hadn't intended more than a very brief trip outside. Then she saw Jessie across the yard with her back to one of the corral gates talking to Jed. There was something in the way Jessie stood that caught Kate's attention. The first time she'd seen Jessie, Jessie had been walking down the street in town, and Kate had taken her for one of the cowboys who seemed to be everywhere. It had only taken her a moment of watching to realize that Jessie was not a man, and from that instant on, she'd loved to look at her. She liked nothing better than to view Jessie through the lens of her camera, capturing her unique combination of beauty and strength forever. She could tell Jessie's moods by the way she walked, by the way she tilted her hat, by the way she hooked her thumbs over the wide belt of her holster. Jessie was the only person she knew whose body and spirit were so intimately one. Kate flushed hot, thinking about lying with Jessie, knowing that when Jessie touched her, it was from the heart.

"Kate?" Jessie stood at the bottom of the steps looking up, wondering at the faraway expression in her lover's eyes. "You'll freeze out here."

Kate smiled secretly. "Not when I have my thoughts to keep me warm."

Jessie took the stairs in two long strides and slid her arm around Kate's waist. "You can do your thinking just as well inside." She drew Kate along with her and into the kitchen and then checked to see that the stove had enough wood.

"Is there some trouble?" Kate asked.

Jessie carefully replaced the lid on the top of the cast-iron stove and turned. Kate stood by the counter, drying dishes and watching her expectantly. "What makes you think so?"

"I saw you with Jed. You had that look you get when there's something serious going on."

"No trouble," Jessie said, at least none that she was certain of. "One of the men was worried that the herd was scattering in the high country." That part was true enough. She didn't see the point in discussing what might be the cause. Not when it would be sure to worry Kate.

Kate put down the dish towel. "And?"

"I need to see about it."

"When do you need to go?"

"If Jed and I get started today, we'll be there by first light tomorrow."

"You'll ride all night?" Kate asked as nonchalantly as she could.

"We'll overnight somewhere on the way. Rest the horses. Besides, a night ride's too hard on them if you don't have to do it."

As capable as Kate knew her lover to be, she hated to think about her sleeping on the cold ground in wild country that Kate had never seen. She had to remind herself that Jessie had been doing this since she was a young girl. And she wouldn't be alone. Jed would be with her. "I'll help you get ready. Tell me what you'll need."

"Kate," Jessie said, clasping both her hands. "I didn't plan to be away so soon after you came."

"You couldn't have predicted this." Kate kissed Jessie softly. "I'll make up some food."

"I would consider it a great favor to me if you would stay in town until I come back."

"Jessie," Kate said, her eyes flashing dangerously. "Didn't we talk about this just this morning?"

"I know," Jessie said, releasing Kate's hands and sliding her arms around her. "And you said that we should talk about things, so that's what I'm doing. It's too soon, Kate. You're not used to being here yet."

"I know how to cook, so I won't starve. I know where the well is and how to drop a bucket into it. I know where the chickens roost, how to feed them, and how to collect the eggs." Kate sighed. "I don't know about milking the cows, though."

"It's easy. I'll teach you." Jessie grinned and rubbed her cheek against Kate's hair. "That was on my list of things to do this morning, but somehow, I got waylaid."

"I'm not complaining about that," Kate murmured, kissing Jessie's throat. "I'm sure one of the men will milk the cows for me."

"It will only be for a few days." Jessie tightened her hold. "I don't want to ride out of here worrying."

"Oh, how unfair for you to say that." Kate smoothed her hand back and forth over Jessie's chest. Jessie would never realize how she felt each time Jessie rode out somewhere, even when there was no danger. She would never forget that Jessie had been brought back one morning shot and close to death. It was a horror Kate never wanted to relive. Nor, she thought with a sigh, would she wish that kind of worry upon her lover. "My mother has been wanting me to have dinner there and spend the night. The day after tomorrow is her sewing circle, and

I'd enjoy seeing some of my friends." She freed herself from Jessie's arms and stepped back, keeping hold of one of her hands. "I'll stay here tonight and go into town before dark tomorrow. Then I'll stay the next day for the sewing circle and that night, too. I'll be home the same day you will."

Jessie knew from the tone of Kate's voice that no amount of arguing would change her mind. And, when she considered it, it seemed fair. It wasn't entirely what she wanted, which was to have Kate always protected, if not by her, by her parents. But she'd always known that Kate was her own woman. She loved her for her fire and her fierce independence. She wouldn't want her to be any different now. "I want one of the men to drive in with you."

Kate wanted to resist. Eventually she would need to be able to come and go on her own. She did not want to be a prisoner at the ranch, and even more importantly, she wanted to be a real partner to Jessie. But there would be time for that, and she could not add to the worry that clouded Jessie's eyes. She caressed Jessie's cheek and nodded. "Until I've proven to you just what a good shot I'll be. Now let me help you get ready to go."

"Thank you," Jessie whispered.

Kate smiled. "You never have to thank me for loving you."

❖

"You can put that on the dresser over there, Billy," Mae said to the wide-eyed boy who carried a cloth-covered tray of food. He colored hotly and tried desperately not to look around her bedroom, which was visible just beyond her sitting area. Mae smothered a smile and wondered how long it would be until he was sneaking in the back door at night to visit one of her girls down the hall. "Thank you."

"Don't mention it, ma'am," he said as he stared at the floor and backed toward the door. The sound of feminine laughter coming toward him down the hall made him break into a sweat. He sidled past the two young women who were on their way into the room. They were dressed in things that he'd certainly never seen his sisters or any other young ladies in town wearing. He wasn't even sure they were dresses.

Mae chuckled at the sound of his footsteps clattering hurriedly away. "It's hard to believe there's a man alive as innocent as that one."

"Won't last much longer," Sissy said bitterly. She'd been around long enough to know what young boys turned into. At twenty she was one of the veterans among the girls. She eyed the bottle of good whiskey next to the food. “Looks like you’re doing some fancy entertaining.”

Annie, a plump redhead, eyed Mae eagerly. She was fifteen and still young enough to believe that she would save her money, move away, and make a new start. “Oh, that smells so good. Who’s coming?” She lowered her voice, although there was no one who could have heard. “Is it Mr. Mason from the bank?”

“Lord, I wouldn’t put on a spread for him,” Mae said, feigning horror. “I’m just having a little get-to-know-you dinner with the new doctor in town.”

“Is he handsome?” Annie enthused.

Sissy snorted. “Like that matters once the lights are out. What matters is how much he’s got in his wallet.”

“Now don’t you two start in,” Mae scolded good-naturedly. “And the doctor is a *she*.” Mae tilted her head as if considering. “And quite handsome.”

“Oh, that sounds so exciting,” Annie said. “A woman. I never heard of such a thing.”

“And handsome, you say?” Sissy looked intrigued. “Don’t be keeping her all to yourself then. Let us have a look.”

“Since she’s going to be taking over for Doc Melbourne, you’ll get your chance to meet her,” Mae said sharply, noting the predatory gleam in Sissy’s eye. She wasn’t at all certain that she wanted Vance at the mercy of some of her charges. She knew that the other side of loneliness was need, and Vance Phelps looked to have a lot of both.

## CHAPTER SEVEN

Mae answered the knock on her door to find Vance standing in the hall, a battered leather satchel in her hand and an equally weathered wide-brimmed black hat under her arm. Mae recognized the hat as the kind worn by army men, and the dark blue trousers looked like army, too. Her shirt was gray flannel and her coat a darker gray. Her black boots showed no trace of dirt on the well-shined leather. Although not dressed in finery, she had taken more care preparing for her visit than most well-to-do gentlemen bothered with. They often arrived in a state of dishabille or near inebriation, two conditions in which they would never admit to visiting a lady. But then again, Mae and the others were not ladies.

"Hello, Vance," Mae said with pleasure as she swung open the door.

"Frank told me to come on up when I inquired as to your whereabouts," Vance said, resisting the urge to stare before deciding that Mae probably intended her appearance to be noticed. Otherwise, why wear something that flattered the figure so thoroughly while leaving only the most tantalizing of secrets to be discovered? Her deep burgundy dress, almost as fancy as a ball gown with its elaborate black stitching along the scooped neck and hem, was cinched at her narrow waist to accentuate her voluptuous curves. Black silk laces on the bodice seemed barely capable of containing her full breasts. Her shoes were the color of blood and matched the silk that brushed against her ankles. When Vance completed her appreciative survey she raised her eyes to find Mae regarding her with the faintest of satisfied smiles. "I hope you don't mind me arriving unannounced."

"No, I don't mind." Mae let the door close behind them and held out her hand. "May I take your coat?"

Vance hesitated, then shrugged her right arm out of her sleeve and slid the coat off her left shoulder with a practiced motion, catching it in her hand before it could fall. She held it out. "Thank you."

Vance's left sleeve was empty from the region of the elbow down. Mae watched as Vance deftly rolled the cuff up several times. Then Mae draped the coat over the back of a brocade chair, walked to the sideboard, and poured two neat shots of whiskey. She turned and held one out. "Drink?"

"Please." Vance welcomed the familiar burn as she took stock of her surroundings. The sitting room was well appointed, with a thick rug, several cushioned chairs and a matching settee, tea tables, and a fireplace. An archway led into the adjoining bedroom, and she could just make out a deep blue coverlet on the corner of a poster bed. "If all the rooms are like this, perhaps I should be staying here rather than the hotel."

Mae laughed. "You'd be likely to find yourself with an unwanted visitor in the middle of the night, and the townsfolk would no doubt take up a petition if they heard that the new doctor was sharing rooms with the girls at the saloon." She indicated the settee. "Sit down. I'll get us our food in a minute."

"I have a feeling," Vance said as she settled into the plush seat, stretched out her legs, and crossed her ankles, "that the townspeople don't need too much of an excuse to take up a petition."

"Met some of them already, have you?" Mae topped off their whiskey and sat next to Vance.

"Mmm-hmm. I paid some visits with Caleb today on his rounds. I can't tell you how many people were scandalized."

"I imagine you're used to that. Couldn't have been that much different where you came from."

"Philadelphia," Vance said, answering the unasked question. "And no, it wasn't, although the outrage tends to be more subtly expressed in that social setting."

"There's nothing quite like polite indignation, is there," Mae said with a trace of bitterness.

Vance set down her glass. "You sound like you've experienced it firsthand."

"My mother was a lady's maid in Baltimore. I was raised around the privileged." She waved her hand as if swatting away a troublesome insect. "I could play with their children, even take lessons with them, until we were of a certain age." Her smile was brittle. "When the young men—the sons of the wealthy—began to find me of interest, I was suddenly no longer welcome in the same circles."

"I'm sorry."

"No need to be. Let me get you some dinner." Mae rose abruptly and moved to the sideboard, where she uncovered the platter of cold chicken, bread, and cheese. She lifted the tray. "You must be hungry if you spent the day with…" To her surprise, she felt Vance at her side. "What is it?"

"Let me take that for you."

Struck by the intensity in Vance's gaze, Mae extended the tray. "Why, thank you."

Vance gripped the tray on one side and steadied the opposite edge against her chest and her left upper arm. As she carried it back to the sitting area and carefully set it on the low table between the chairs, she said, "I can load and fire a rifle as quickly as I could with two arms. I can also saddle my own horse and do most other things."

"You think I was serving you because you've got one arm?" Mae gave her a look between exasperation and affection. "I'm used to serving men, who rarely lift a fing—"

"Although I can pass for a man, and have, I'll not have a woman do for me."

"Habit is all I meant," Mae said gently. Seated once more, she rested her chin in the palm of her hand. "I don't imagine you allow anyone to do for you." Her gaze fell on Vance's empty sleeve. "How did it happen?"

"No one ever asks," Vance said curiously, almost to herself, wondering how they had so quickly moved to such sensitive topics. It seemed that when she was with Mae, she revealed far more than she intended. With a conscious attempt to redirect the conversation, she said lightly, "I doubt you'd find the details of any interest and—"

"You should let me judge that." Mae leaned forward and prepared two plates, then handed one to Vance. "I know you were in the army. Did anyone know you were a woman?"

"How did you know that?"

"Your trousers. They're army issue. I've seen enough army men to know." She nibbled at a bit of cheese. "And you do not look like the kind of woman who buys secondhand clothes. Or steals them."

Vance laughed. "There was a time or two, especially when the campaigns were long and far from home, when I was tempted to…expropriate a new pair. But you're right, these are mine, and yes, I served in the Union Army for three years."

"All that time, and no one knew."

"Some did. I wasn't the only woman. I know of at least one officer whose wife joined at the same time he did and served in his outfit." Although she wasn't hungry, Vance ate a little. "The services of every able-bodied person were needed, especially doctors. No one cared what was under my clothes." She smiled grimly. "Or what wasn't."

"What about your family? Surely, they were opposed."

"My father was against it."

Vance's face closed on some hard memory, and Mae knew instinctively she'd gone as far as she could that night to assuage her not-inconsiderable curiosity about the mysterious doctor. "The war didn't touch us that much—not like it did you back East. We knew about it and the soldiers have been straggling through town more and more since it's been over. So many of them—like they have no purpose anymore."

"I imagine you've been fighting your own wars out here."

Thinking of the arduous trek by foot and wagon when food and shelter were always scarce, the deaths from accidents and disease along the way, and the harsh and unforgiving land at the end of the journey, Mae nodded. "True enough. It does feel that way at times."

"How many girls work here?"

"Around about a dozen or so at any time. Some get lucky, find a man who doesn't care what they've been, and they move on. Some hope they still have a home somewhere back East to go to and they leave." Mae shrugged. "Most stay because they've nowhere else to go."

"And you…look out for them."

"You could say that. I do what I can to see that they don't get hurt." She sighed and gave Vance a weary smile. "We live outside the law, what little of it there is here. No one will take our side against a man, no matter what the offense."

"But you protect them somehow."

With a delicate, well-manicured hand, Mae drew up the hem of her skirt to just above her shapely knee, revealing a small revolver secured with a thin strap above the top of her stocking. "I know how to use this, and I have."

A grin spread across Vance's face. "Fear is a powerful weapon."

"That it is." Mae rose, poured brandy, and returned. She handed one glass to Vance. "What was it like doctoring today?"

Vance considered her strange travels with Caleb to several outlying ranches as well as to the homes of some townspeople. "Funny, the people on the ranches seemed far less disturbed by me. Of course, most of the people we visited in town were ladies." Vance flicked her empty sleeve. "Not only is this shocking, but the rest of me is apparently just as bad."

Mae snorted derisively. "You could be wearing the finest Paris fashions, but as long as you're doing the work of a man, you're going to cause talk. Are you good at it?"

"I don't know," Vance said quietly. "I was. Once." She met Mae's eyes and saw acceptance, before she had even confessed. "I haven't been able to do much of anything since I was shot."

"That's when you lost your arm."

"Yes." Vance cleared her throat, which had gone tight. "My skills are...perhaps somewhat lacking now."

"Your skills," Mae rejoined, both amused and adamant, "have got to be far better than most anyone else's in the territory. Doc Melbourne is about the only real doctor out here." She leaned forward, displaying an alluring amount of cleavage, and tapped a delicate finger on Vance's thigh. "So don't let anyone in town or otherwise make you feel like you shouldn't be doing what you know how to do."

Vance registered the subtle sway of Mae's breasts but it was the hand on her leg that shocked her, the touch so foreign she barely recognized it. The only people in memory who had touched her had been those changing her bandages. They had come once a day, bringing unspeakable pain through no fault of their own. She saw the endless rows of beds, standing open like graves, heard the plaintive cries of the dying, felt the pathos seep into her bones. She shivered and a trickle of cold sweat ran down her neck.

Mae moved closer still, dabbed the sweat from Vance's throat with a white lace handkerchief she withdrew from her bodice, and murmured, "You're not there now, wherever it is."

"It's inside me," Vance gasped, not even meaning to speak.

"Well then, we'll just have to see about getting it out." She sat back and spoke in a normal tone, knowing that the only way to chase away the terror was to get on with the living. "One of my girls is pregnant."

Vance blinked and narrowed her eyes. The room came into sharp focus. She knew that Mae had witnessed her lapse, but it didn't embarrass or humiliate her the way it usually did. Mae regarded her with no hint of pity or morbid interest. She drew a breath and felt the nightmare release her. "Pregnant?" At Mae's nod, she went on, "How old is the girl?"

"Fourteen or so. She doesn't rightly know. Her parents died from typhoid while traveling overland and the wagon master brought her this far and left her on her own." Mae shook her head. "I suppose he should be given credit for that. She would have brought a fair price in one of the mining camps."

"Christ." Vance stood and paced, stopping before crossing the invisible border into Mae's boudoir. "How far along?"

"I'm guessing seven months. She's only been here five. Someone got at her before she arrived." Mae stiffened, her smooth delicate features hardening. "There's others here as young as her, younger. But when I saw she was in that way, I kept the men away from her."

"How does she support herself?"

"I see that she's fed and has a room."

"You could wear yourself out trying to save them all, I imagine," Vance said softly from across the room.

"I imagine you would know," Mae murmured, her gaze traveling gently over Vance's pale face.

❖

"How anyone ever took her for a man, I'll never know," Annie said a touch breathlessly. "She has the most beautiful eyes, so kind."

"Put her in a uniform with a couple of layers of long johns underneath," Sissy said, "smudge a little dirt on her face to cover up that lily-white skin, and who's to say she wasn't what she claimed."

Mae listened to the idle chatter with half a mind. She stood huddled with a few others against the railing on the second floor, looking down through a cloud of cigar smoke into the saloon hall below. It was packed with men whose voices converged to create a blanket of sound that nearly drowned out all other conversation.

"People see what they expect to see," Mae murmured.

"She's a darn sight easier to look at than Doc Melbourne," Sissy acknowledged grudgingly. "I'd rather have her poking at me than him."

"Doc Melbourne's always been a gentleman," Annie replied primly.

"That's because you've got a soft spot for him," Sissy griped.

"So what if I do? I saw you giving Vance a smile or two."

Mae bristled inwardly at the gossip that ordinarily she wouldn't pay any mind to. Hearing the other women discuss Vance so casually made her irrationally annoyed, even though she understood their interest. Vance was not just a newcomer, which always garnered curiosity for a few days, she was a woman doing something these young girls had never even imagined possible. On top of that, she was intriguing—in her independence and her differentness. Of course they were going to talk about her. Even flirt with her a little bit. Seduction was their primary means of survival, and it came as naturally to them as it did to Mae. Vance, however, had seemed to be immune to even the most flagrant flirtations. Still, the way Sissy had flaunted her youthful attributes had rankled.

At Vance's request, Mae had accompanied her while she made her initial examinations of all the girls, questioning them gently about past pregnancies or female troubles they might have had, asking if they knew how to take care of themselves and prevent disease and impregnation. Vance had been thorough and gentle and kind. She had neither judged nor attempted to change what they were. She had merely given them her attention and her caring. It was a wonder they all didn't fall in love with her, whether they were of a mind to lie with a woman or not.

"And so what if I did give her a little look." Sissy's voice interrupted Mae's musings. "You think men are the only ones who enjoy our company? You could do worse than having the town doctor take a shine to you. It might keep the cowboys off you for a while."

Startled, Annie looked at Mae. "You mean sometimes women might come to a place like this?"

"It's not unheard of," Mae snapped, giving Sissy a withering glance. "But just because a woman wears pants doesn't mean she likes to sleep with her own kind. Don't go jumping to conclusions."

"I'm not about to jump on anything," Sissy said with a toss of her head and a satisfied smile. "But I won't be jumping *out* of the way either if she should take an urge to climb aboard."

"I wouldn't be counting on that," Mae said. Vance had given no indication she was interested in lying with anyone, man or woman, but Mae had a feeling that might be because that part of her was buried under the pain and misery she'd suffered. Looking at the hungry gleam in Sissy's eye and the enchanted one in Annie's, she had no doubt there would be willing partners if it was women she wanted for comfort. She didn't want to think about to whom Vance would turn when her feelings came back to life.

"There's work to be done if we want to earn our keep," Mae said. "Let's get to it."

✣

Vance stood in a pack of men at the far end of the bar, nursing a whiskey that she didn't really want. It was the only company she was used to, however, and after leaving Mae, she hadn't wanted to go back to her room at the hotel. The little bit of her past she'd shared with Mae during dinner had opened a tiny chink in the wall that she had built to keep the pain at bay, but oddly, it wasn't pain that had surfaced through the hole in her defenses. It was longing. A restless sense of yearning for something she couldn't name. Whatever it was, it pulled at her belly, dragged at her heart, and she hadn't wanted to lie alone in the dark with it.

She sipped at her whiskey and saw Mae come down the stairs with some of the girls. Although Mae was only half a dozen years older than the oldest among them, she looked like a woman in full bloom and not a girl. Vance watched Mae move through the crowd, bestowing a touch or a smile on some lucky man or other. Watching her produced an odd combination of pleasure and pain, neither of which Vance could explain. She turned her back to the room and drained her whiskey, then signaled for another.

## CHAPTER EIGHT

Mae dabbed scent behind each ear and restoppered the small, pale green glass bottle. Just as she set it down on her dressing table, a knock sounded at the door. At four in the afternoon it was likely to be one of the girls. Frank knew better than to let anyone else upstairs before dark. There were a few wealthy *gentlemen* who had private arrangements for her time, and she no longer needed to bed a saddle tramp to secure her next meal. She was not expecting one of her special customers; they would be far too cautious to venture to her room during daylight, no matter how dire their circumstances. Still clad in only a camisole beneath her dressing gown—a blue and red China silk robe that had been a present from one of her admirers who had traveled to San Francisco—she opened her door expecting to find Annie or one of the other younger girls. They often came by before the night's activities to share gossip they'd overheard in the saloon or complain about one of the other girls. Or to share their fantasies about a future they were unlikely to realize. She didn't disabuse them of that notion, because they had little enough in life without stripping them of hope.

"Kate!" Mae took Kate by the arm and pulled her inside. "You're the last person I expected." She glanced up and down the hall, saw no one else, and firmly closed the door. "Where's Jess?"

"She's out on the range with Jed for a few days. I'm visiting my parents."

"Lord. Are you never going to learn you can't be seen here?"

Kate laughed, loosening her cloak and removing it as she deposited a basket on a nearby table. "Are *you* never going to learn that I intend to visit my friends regardless of where they may live?" She turned, meaning to give Mae a welcoming hug, then stopped when she saw that Mae was not dressed. "Oh, I'm sorry. You weren't expecting visitors and here I am barging in."

"Don't be silly. You'd be about the only visitor I don't mind having this time of day." Mae gave Kate a quick squeeze, drawing back with her hands on Kate's forearms when she felt her stiffen. She cocked her head and studied the faint blush on Kate's cheeks. "Something wrong?"

"Oh no, of course not," Kate said too quickly. Mae was barely dressed, and what little she did wear did nothing to hide her shapely figure.

"Why, Kate Beecher." Mae laughed, reading the discomfort in Kate's expression. "Don't tell me that a woman like me could stir you up when you've got the likes of Jessie Forbes in your bed at night."

"Certainly not," Kate said primly. "I consider myself as married as any woman with a husband."

"Oh, and I suppose you think that means they never appreciate a man other than the one they're tied to?" Mae poured tea from the late supper tray that Billy had just brought her from the hotel.

Kate took the offered cup and settled into one corner of the settee. "I don't know how they feel. No one but Jessie has ever made me…all churned up inside."

"But you notice women differently now, don't you?" Mae slipped behind a dressing screen angled in the corner of her bedroom and exchanged her robe for a dress. When she sat next to Kate, her own teacup in hand, she said, "Because of what being with Jessie has brought to life in you."

"I do, sometimes. Appreciate them." Kate regarded Mae seriously. "Is that…natural, do you think?"

"Oh, honey, you're asking the wrong person." Mae rose and exchanged her tea for brandy. She looked to Kate. "Are you of a mind for a small drink?"

"No, I shouldn't." Kate smiled in fond exasperation at the thought of her mother's reaction. "My mother is coping as best she can with me leaving home and being with Jessie, but if I arrive smelling of spirits, I'm afraid it will be her undoing."

Chuckling, Mae sat down again. "Natural, you asked. Lord, when you've seen the things I've seen, you learn pretty quickly that people are a complicated bunch. I know for a fact there are men and women who prefer their own kind, in and out of bed." She sipped her brandy and eyed Kate. "You know that's my way, but I can sit here and think you've got eyes prettier than a starry night and not get stirred up."

"And I think you're...beautiful," Kate confessed, "but I don't feel—" She blushed again. "I don't believe anyone could make me feel the way Jessie does."

"Mmm. Why thank you, for the beautiful part. And lucky for Jess to have a woman who sees only her." She patted Kate's knee. "And lucky *you* for having her, because I know for a fact it's the same with her."

Kate glowed with pleasure, feeling only a little strange talking to Mae about Jessie, when she knew that Mae had wanted Jessie. But she didn't know anyone else like herself in whom to confide. Now that she and Jessie were together, she felt different inside. It was more than just loving Jessie and wanting to express that love with her body. She knew it wasn't an accident that she had fallen in love with Jessie. She had fallen in love with a woman because somehow, that was meant to be. That was why she'd never cared for the suitors who had pursued her in Boston or for Ken Turner here in New Hope, either—a perfectly nice man for whom she had no feelings whatsoever. "I just know that I'm not the same as my friends, even though they don't seem to think I'm all that different."

Mae sipped her brandy thoughtfully. "Do any of them ask you about being with Jess?"

"You mean...about lying with her?" Kate laughed. "Goodness, no. Even when they're talking about relations with men, it's all whispers and secrets."

"Well, most folks just look the other way rather than see things they don't understand or that upset them." She shrugged. "It's not always a bad thing, I suppose."

"Why do you think we like one person and not another...that way?"

"I don't know how that comes about," Mae said with some consideration. "I always have admired the women like Jess."

"Like Jessie?" Kate considered her lover and found it impossible to define all that she was. She was beautiful and strong and tender and stubborn and oh so wonderfully loving. Surely there was not another woman in the world like her.

"The strong-minded, stubborn type who like doing what most folks call men's work because it comes natural to them. And," she said with a saucy grin, "I do like a woman in pants."

"Well, there's not much of a chance for you to see *that*." Kate smiled. "But I love the way she looks in pants, too, and I can't imagine her in anything else."

"Can't imagine you'd get her into anything else."

"Besides, wearing them makes perfect sense. Trying to do anything out on the ranch in a skirt is just impossible." Kate finished her tea and took one of the crackers from a saucer next to the pot. "I'm going to do something about my clothes so I can ride easier and get around without tripping myself."

"A lot of women on the ranches wear split skirts. Or pants. Nobody thinks much of it." Mae poked Kate's shoulder playfully. "But if you start wearing them around town, there'll be talk."

"Oh, I wasn't planning on that. I can just imagine how quickly my mother would hear about it."

"Faster than lightning." Because she was enjoying the rare moment of female confidence in which she felt no need to hide anything, Mae added, "The new doctor in town dresses a lot like Jess. She's pretty much the opposite in every other way, though. Like night and day."

"She? I knew a woman in Boston who was studying to be a doctor—a student in one of my father's classes. No one believed she would really do it." Kate sat forward eagerly. "You've met her? This doctor?"

Mae nodded.

"What's she like?"

"Hard to say," Mae said quietly, thinking of the ghosts and secrets that shimmered in Vance's dark eyes. "She doesn't say much about herself." She stood abruptly, unable to contain the urge she had to ease Vance's pain, and began to pace. "She's good with the girls. She doctored them last night."

Kate watched Mae, never recalling seeing her so agitated. Mae was always so cool, always standing back and laughing just a little bit at others' foolishness, and her own. Now her voice trembled and her expression was distant, as if she were somewhere else. Carefully, Kate asked, "And she's like Jessie? Like us?"

Mae halted abruptly and regarded Kate intently. "Like us? Liking women, you mean?"

Kate nodded.

"She hasn't given any sign of it, but then again, most don't." Mae sat down with a sigh. "Even out here where some women go our own way and make our own lives, it doesn't pay to remind folks of it." She squeezed Kate's knee when she saw her look of concern. "But don't you worry. Everyone loves Jessie. She's been part of this town almost as long as the town has been here. The way I hear, her father built that ranch when New Hope wasn't much more than a few mining tents beside a dusty road."

"But now I'm with her," Kate said quietly. "I won't have anyone hurt her because of me."

"No one's going to hurt either one of you," Mae said vehemently. "First of all, Jess wouldn't allow it. Secondly, neither would we."

Kate touched Mae's hand. "You're absolutely right." She gave Mae a sly smile. "So finish telling me about the new doctor. What does she look like?"

"Mmm, like I said, a little like Jess. Tall, like she is, with the same kind of strong face and rangy build. But she's dark, where Jess's light, and she's been…hurt." Mae closed her eyes against a sudden surge of pain that settled around her heart. "She lost her arm in the war back East. She joined up to doctor the wounded and was shot right near the end."

"Oh, my. How brave. How…wonderful of her."

"Crazy of her, you mean," Mae said bitterly. "Going off to fight in some war that even the damn foolish men should've had more sense than to get into."

"You don't mean that," Kate said gently. "You're just upset because she was hurt."

"I can see it, in her eyes. What it did to her." Mae's eyes swam with tears. "It broke something in her, and she's bleeding still."

"Maybe she just needs more time to heal."

"You can't heal a wound when the bullet's still in there." Mae rubbed her fingertips over her closed lids. "I don't even know her. Can't think why it upsets me so much."

"She means something to you, I can tell."

"No. Not that way." Mae shook her head impatiently. "Sometimes I just get tired of the misery."

"Well, maybe she'll find something in New Hope to help her heal." Kate smiled inwardly. *Or someone.*

"Maybe so."

"I brought you something." Kate rose to fetch her basket and then sat down again. She searched inside and then handed a slim volume to Mae. "Here."

Mae held the book gently, tenderly rubbing her hand over the surface. "*A Tale of Two Cities* by Mr. Charles Dickens." She looked at Kate with shining eyes. "Oh, this is fine, Kate. But you shouldn't be lending your books."

"Jessie brought me some books when I was sick. She bought them on one of her trips into Miles City for supplies. I already had this copy and she gave me another, so this is yours to keep." Kate ducked her head. "I know Jessie lends you books, because I saw a thank-you note from you in one of them."

"Kate, now that you and Jessie are together—"

"You and Jessie are friends, and I know she cares for you." Kate held Mae's gaze steadily. "And I know you care for her."

"You know a lot for someone who a year ago had never been kissed," Mae said with a soft laugh.

"I've made up for that."

"You know Jess would be mortified if she knew we were talking about these things, don't you?"

"And that's why she's not here." Kate looked at the timepiece pinned to her dress. "I must go before it gets much darker. I hope you like the book."

Mae held it to her breast. "I love it. Thank you."

Kate stood and gathered her things. At the door, she gave Mae a long hug. "I want to meet this doctor of yours sometime. Maybe you can bring her by the ranch."

"It's not like that, Kate. Besides, I don't think the town's doctor is going to want to be seen out riding with me."

"It seems to me that a woman brave enough to fight for what she believes in wouldn't put much stock in the opinions of foolish people."

"You think highly of people, Kate. You're young still."

"What's her name?" Kate asked, ignoring Mae's dark mood.

"Vance. Vance Phelps."

"I like the way that sounds. Good night, Mae."

"Good night." Mae carefully closed the door. Vance Phelps. She liked the way it sounded, too.

❖

"Well," Clarissa Mason said as she lifted a biscuit from the tray Martha Beecher extended. "Rose and I came in on the stage late last week with the town's new doctor."

Kate looked up from her sewing, alert to the censure in Clarissa's voice.

"Really?" Martha said, trying to hide her eager curiosity.

"Oh yes," Rose interjected before her mother could continue. "She's quite intriguing. She wa—"

"Hardly intriguing," Clarissa said sharply. "Impertinent and inappropriate would be more the word for it. Dressed like a man, for heaven's sakes. And who's to say she's even a doctor."

"Dr. Melbourne apparently believes her to be," Kate said reasonably, although her temper put an edge to her tone that had her mother giving her a frown.

"Well whatever she is, she would do well to behave like a proper lady." Clarissa cast a scathing glance Kate's way. "Some excuses can be made for our own, I suppose. But not for outsiders."

Kate rose and set her sewing aside. "Excuse me. Would anyone else like more tea?"

A few of the women in the sewing circle murmured, but most stared from Clarissa to Kate with rapt attention. Kate hurried from the room before she said something she knew she would eventually regret. Creating a scene in her mother's parlor would do no one any good.

"You shouldn't pay any attention to that old biddy," Millie, the town marshal's new wife and one of Kate's closest friends, whispered.

Kate turned from the icebox with a pitcher of tea in her hand and fury in her eyes. "How dare she attack Jessie in front of me? If it weren't for my mother, I'd—I'd..." She slammed the tea down on the kitchen table. "That's just the problem. I know there's nothing I could say that would make any difference to her. And strangling her is probably out of the question."

Millie smiled and put her arm around Kate's shoulders. "The way to get back at her is to show her that her opinion doesn't matter. And to anyone with half a brain, it doesn't."

"I don't understand why my mother even cares what people like that think."

"It's hard to be alone, especially out here."

"She's not alone. She has my father and she has me."

"Yes, and now you've got Jessie and your father…well, he's a wonderful man." Millie smiled. "But he *is* a man. Being as you don't have one, you probably don't realize how little they understand us."

Kate laughed. "You're right."

"Does Jessie understand you?" Millie asked shyly. "Seeing's how her and you are together and all."

"Yes, I think so. At least as well as I understand her." Kate took down two glasses and poured tea. Millie was the only one of her friends—aside from Mae—who ever acknowledged what Jessie was to her. She gave her an affectionate glance and set down the pitcher. "Which means not always. But when she doesn't, she tries."

"Can't ask for much more."

"No. I wouldn't ask for anything more."

"I've seen the new doctor. Have you?"

Kate shook her head. "No, not yet. I understand she's…solitary."

"I've heard she frequents the saloon at night."

"Really? I dearly wish I could. The conversation would certainly be more to my liking."

"Well, I think she looks very mysterious, and I can't wait to actually meet her."

"Yes, I'm looking forward to that, too." Kate considered that she hadn't spent any time with her father at the newspaper office of late, and today seemed like the perfect opportunity.

# CHAPTER NINE

"I can set the type while you block out the advertisements," Kate said to her father as she joined him at the print table in the rear of the single room that served as the office and production area for the *New Hope Chronicle*.

"You'll get ink on your hands and it's the devil to get out," Martin Beecher said mildly. "And your mother will likely take me to task for it."

Kate smiled and gently shouldered her father aside. Ever since she'd been a little girl she'd accompanied him when he went to work, although in those days it had been to the college where he'd taught. Since coming to New Hope, and especially now that she no longer lived at home, she didn't have nearly as much opportunity, and she missed their quiet camaraderie. "Anything I can't get out, I'll take care to hide. Let me see the copy."

More because he enjoyed her company than because he needed the help, Martin conceded and handed her the list of transactions he'd received that afternoon from the land claims office.

"Goodness, this is quite a list," Kate remarked.

"More and more homesteaders are arriving every day. Before long, Montana will be well settled and ready for statehood."

"The town certainly seems to be growing." As she spoke, Kate swiftly and efficiently set the type, letter by letter, into the preset frame. "Jessie said there were dozens of wagon trains moving West through Fort Laramie when last she was there."

"We're going to need some kind of law out on the range soon," Martin commented absently as he adjusted the layout of the notices and ads. "The town marshals can't be expected to chase across the entire territory after outlaws and cattle rustlers, and the army's got more than enough to do protecting the railroads and wagon trains from marauders."

"Cattle rustlers." Kate said the words slowly, realizing with an uneasy jitter in her stomach that she had no idea just how big the Rising Star was. Between the long winter and the months spent recovering from her sickness, she'd never been able to make the journey to see it that Jessie had promised long ago. But she knew from listening to Jessie speak of her land that it spread over many days' worth of travel. And that a great deal of it was remote mountain terrain. "I wouldn't imagine that's a very big problem around here, is it? I mean, perhaps a cow or two now and then for food or a horse to—"

"Oh no," Martin said. "According to all the reports that we've been getting from across the territories, gangs of rustlers are stealing hundreds of head of livestock."

"But surely not out here, so far from the rail centers."

"Apparently they're driving them hundreds of miles to markets in Colorado. Even as far south as Texas." Martin slid the finished plate into the hand press. "I'm surprised you haven't heard about it before this. What with the Rising Star being one of the biggest outfits in this part of the territory."

Kate had a feeling that she knew why she hadn't heard of this trouble before, and hoped she was wrong. Tomorrow Jessie would be back. Tomorrow she would have her answer. Stacking the single sheets as they slid from the press, she said, "I'll help you take the early editions around."

"I'll only be taking them a few places, my dear. You'll be more comfortable waiting here."

"I'll be bored is what I'll be. Give me the ones for the Golden Nugget. It's just down the street."

"Oh no," Martin said with a laugh. "If your mother ever heard—"

"I'll take them in the back. No one will see me, and even if they do, there isn't a soul who would know Mother to tell her."

"Kate, really. I know that you have an acquaintance—"

"I've a *friend* there, and this won't be my first visit. I'll be quite all right." Kate kissed her father's cheek. "I know you like to talk to Silas at the hotel in the evenings. You can come for me when you're done."

"If you promise to take care, I'll walk you there and be back shortly."

"I won't go anywhere I'm not safe."

❖

"Evenin', Doc," Frank said and poured a shot of whiskey without being asked. He slid it across the counter to Vance. "Late day or early night?"

"Just got back into town. Been riding all day." Vance smiled wryly. It hadn't taken more than a few weeks for the town's bartender to learn her schedule. She should probably take that as a sign that the whiskey was still winning. Nevertheless, she tossed back the drink and poured another from the bottle Frank had put down nearby. "Things are a lot farther apart out here than I'm used to."

Frank laughed. "I imagine so, if you're used to city living."

"Not for some time, but even farm country in the East is more populated. It took me most of the day to check on the three families Caleb wanted me to see."

"You making those calls by yourself?" Frank asked cautiously.

Vance stiffened. "That's right."

"Ever shot anyone with that sidearm you're carrying?" Frank leaned across the bar and kept his voice low.

"Would you ask me that if I were a man?"

Frank appeared unperturbed. "Might. If I thought you were a tenderfoot fixing to get himself killed."

"I'm not either one of those things," Vance replied evenly. "And I'm a dead shot."

"That's good to know." Frank swiped at a spill on the bar with the cloth he kept tucked into his belt. "I'm kind of getting used to your conversation."

Vance had to smile because they rarely exchanged more than a few words throughout an entire evening. His concern surprised her, not that she hadn't expected men to doubt her ability to protect herself. But Frank *hadn't* automatically assumed she was incapable. He hadn't made assumptions, any more than Milton had. Her sergeant had accepted her, first at face value because she *was* the regimental surgeon, and after a time because no one could do the job better. They hadn't talked much either, reading one another almost effortlessly, whether playing cards or caring for the wounded in the midst of Armageddon. For nearly three years they'd been as close as lovers, sharing danger and hardship and triumph. On that last day, she hadn't listened to his cautions, hadn't been able to hear anything except the thunder of death all around her. And he had paid for her mistake. Not her. He had remained out of loyalty and duty and friendship, and she had failed him. She gripped the edge of the bar, swaying as the room receded and the stench of battle filled her consciousness.

"Why don't you buy a lady a drink, Doc," Mae said as she smoothly caught up the whiskey bottle in one hand and threaded her opposite arm through Vance's. She nodded to Frank, who stared at Vance's ashen face with alarm. "Bring some glasses, Frank."

"Right away," he said hurriedly.

"I'm okay," Vance whispered hoarsely.

"Don't doubt it. Now me, I could use a few minutes off my feet with a good drink and better company." With practiced moves, Mae guided them through the crowd to a table tucked underneath the second-floor balcony. The illumination from rows of oil lamps set into sconces along the walls barely penetrated the space. "Looks like I got both."

Frank set glasses in the center of the table and melted away into the shadows.

"I wouldn't be too sure about the company," Vance said as she sank heavily onto the wooden chair. When Mae poured whiskey into a glass and handed it to her, she shook her head. "No, thanks. I need to clear my head, not muddle it up anymore."

"You looked like something hit you hard back there," Mae said gently. She'd come downstairs earlier than usual, unaccountably restless. She told herself she was only going to look over the crowd and make sure there were no troublemakers in the bunch. But the instant she'd reached the landing, she'd gazed toward the far end of the room where Vance usually spent an hour or two in the evening, quietly drinking alone. She'd seen her at once and, even at a distance, she'd known something was wrong. Something even the whiskey couldn't cure. Vance's face was a study in torment. Every thought had fled except for one. She would not stand by and watch Vance suffer alone.

"I'm sorry," Vance said.

"For what?"

Vance was glad for the dark so that Mae wouldn't see her humiliation. Or her shame. "I regret that I caused you any concern."

Mae laughed. "I don't believe worrying over someone ever caused a body any harm." She leaned close and put her hand on Vance's arm. "Have you had any dinner?"

"I…not as of yet." Vance refused to add to her embarrassment by admitting that she'd forgotten to eat. In fact, other than coffee and a biscuit at breakfast, she'd had nothing all day. She could smell Mae's perfume, the same scent that had clung to her coat after her visit to Mae's rooms. When she'd dressed the next morning and caught the hint of her in the air, she'd been shaken by a ripple of longing so intense it had left her weak. She'd deliberately put the moment from her mind, but now, with Mae so near and the warmth of her touch searing her to the bone, she couldn't resist. "Please allow me to buy you dinner."

For an instant, Mae was stunned to silence. Surely one of them misunderstood. "Well, that's very kind of you. If I'd known, I would have made arrangements for us to dine in my rooms. Perhaps another night."

"The hotel is just across the street."

"Vance," Mae said gently. "I can't eat there with you."

Vance's voice hardened. "And why would that be?"

"There are certain things that are…understood. In many other places, women like me would be living in shacks on the outskirts of town with nothing but tin and paper over our heads." Mae swept a hand toward the balcony above them. "Here we've got clean rooms, decent food, and doctoring when we need it. As long as we don't ask for too much, that is."

"I see." Vance wanted to protest, but she knew Mae spoke the truth. Prostitution was a part of life from the capital city to the smallest mining encampment. Most of the time, it was a dreary and dangerous life. She'd seen women worn out by it before they were twenty-five. She'd also seen parlor houses in St. Louis and Denver that were as fine as any hotel. The women who ran them and lived in them dressed in finery and often were among the wealthiest women in the community, earning far more for their labors than common workmen. But those success stories were not the norm. Out here on the frontier, the sporting women were fortunate if they did not fall prey to disease or mistreatment. "I want you to know that whatever the rules—or the consequences—they make no matter to me. I would be honored by your company."

Mae looked away, undone by the sincerity in Vance's voice and her own deep longing for the impossible. Impossible for so many reasons. She met Vance's eyes, because to do less would be to discount the gift she had been offered. The price that Vance was willing to pay for her beliefs was starkly evident in the empty sleeve and the ghosts of guilt and self-recrimination that haunted her eyes. Mae thought she had never known a braver soul. "It is you who honor me. Under other circumstances, there's nothing I would like more than to dine with you."

"I would not do anything to endanger you or any of the girls."

"It was kind of you to offer. And to understand." Mae forced a lightness into her voice that she did not feel. "You should go on over and have that dinner while you're still thinking about it."

"No." Vance caught Mae's hand as she started to withdraw. "Not just yet. I'd rather sit here with you. How much time do we have?"

"It will be a little while before the girls come down. The men need to know that I'm here, that I'm watching. That I know who the girls are going off with."

"And what about you? Will you be…going off with someone?"

Mae studied Vance's face in the dim light. Her dark eyes glinted, sharp as a knife's edge. Mae dared not ask the question she so desperately wanted answered. *What does it make me in your eyes?* She shook her head. "From time to time. Not tonight, I don't expect."

"Then I'd be pleased with your company."

"Will you tell me something?"

"If I can," Vance said immediately.

"What happened tonight?" Mae asked, her penetrating gaze just as unrelenting.

"Why does it matter?"

Mae couldn't think of any answer except the truth. "Because whatever is tearing you up hurts me every time I see it."

"I have…spells."

"Is it a sickness?"

Vance laughed hollowly. "Of a sort. Something happens to me and I end up thinking about the war. That last morning. I can…" She shivered. "It's like I'm there."

"You mean, more than just remembering? Feeling it?"

"Yes. Yes, that's exactly it. It's not a memory. I feel it. I hear it. I see it. *All* of it." She closed her eyes. "God. So real."

"Does it happen a lot?" As Vance spoke, Mae watched the pain etch itself into the lines of her face, saw her body shudder as if from invisible blows. She wanted to put herself between Vance and whatever was hurting her, but she knew it was too far inside her for anyone to touch. There would be no relief, no end to the agony, until Vance alone unearthed the source.

"Not as much as it used to." Vance reached for the whiskey bottle, pleased to see that her hand was steady. She poured them each a drink. "I don't remember very much about the first few months. My arm was infected, and I was delirious most of the time. I'd had pneumonia and that flared up. I couldn't talk, couldn't identify myself." She emptied the shot in a single gulp and closed her fingers hard around the glass. "I spent quite a long time in a hospital in Richmond before anyone figured out who I was."

"That you were a doctor?"

Vance nodded. "That and that my father was one of Lincoln's appointees to the Medical Bureau that organized medical care in the Union Army."

"So he's a doctor, too."

"Yes." Vance sighed. "Eventually I was sent home, back to Philadelphia to be cared for. Once my arm healed and it seemed that I was getting well, the episodes began."

"And there's no medicine? No treatment?"

"Laudanum effectively stops it," Vance said bitterly. "That's a bit like trading one devil for another. I finally refused it, against my father's wishes."

"I've seen what that can do," Mae said softly. "It's a way to escape, sure enough. But it's a little bit like dying, too, isn't it?"

Completely without thinking, Vance lifted Mae's hand and rested her cheek against Mae's palm. "How is it you understand so much?"

Mae brushed her fingers through Vance's hair. "I want to understand you."

"Why?"

They were dangerously close to crossing a line that Mae could barely see any longer, but she knew it was there. She knew who she was, what she was. And she sensed, no, she *knew*, that Vance was vulnerable. For all her strength, for all her brave certainty, she was wounded, and Mae would not risk having her hurt more. She eased away, smiling. "There's three people in town it's good to know—the banker, the marshal, and the doctor. You're the best looking of the lot."

Vance laughed. "Then I count myself fortunate."

"I suppose you know it might help if you ate right and tried to sleep regular," Mae said carefully. "With the spells."

"You're quite correct. I have never been an easy patient."

Mae laughed. "Somehow, I find that easy to believe."

"Will you dine with me tomorrow?"

"A friendship with me will be frowned upon by every important person in this town, and most that aren't."

Vance made an impatient gesture. When she spoke, it was with the unconscious force she had used to command men. "Will you dine with me tomorrow? Here or at the hotel or any place of your choosing."

The only other woman who had ever looked at her and seen more than a whore in a fancy dress had been Jessie. But even Jessie had never looked at her with the kind of fire that burned in Vance Phelps's eyes.

"Yes. Yes, I will."

# CHAPTER TEN

I shall return in thirty minutes." Martin looked dubious as Kate took a stack of the freshly printed broadsheets from his arms and started toward the side door of the Golden Nugget. The jaunty sound of the piano was muted, but still audible—an uncomfortable reminder of the raucous activities within.

"I'll go directly upstairs, so you needn't worry," Kate replied, as if reading her father's mind. "One of my friends will bring the papers down and leave them at the bar. I'll just have a visit, and I'll watch at the window for you to return. I'll be fine."

"I'm not entirely certain—"

"When Jessie was here, recovering from her wounds, I came every day and almost every evening. It was perfectly safe."

"Those were extraordinary circumstances. You were helping to nurse her." Martin smiled fondly. "And I knew I would not be able to keep you away."

"No, you couldn't, and I'll always appreciate you understanding that." Kate remembered the terrible few days after Jessie had been shot. Even now, the thought that she might have lost her caused her stomach to clench painfully. She hated being separated from her, even for a few days, and every time Jessie left with Jed or one of the other men on these increasingly frequent trips up into the mountains, she worried. She pushed away the uneasiness that came from not knowing just where Jessie was or what she was doing. It was something she supposed she would have to get used to, now that they lived together. It had been easier, in some ways, when she lived in town and Jessie was at the ranch. Then, what Jessie did every day was less real to her, and the dangers far more abstract. Now, she was learning just how difficult life could be in the untamed land where she'd chosen to make her home. "I have friends here. You needn't worry."

"I expect I shall always worry, as is a father's duty." He touched her shoulder affectionately. "But I have always known you to be sensible, so I will yield to your judgment." He turned as if to leave, and then looked back. "Are you still happy with your decision to…go with Jessie?"

Remembering that she was speaking to her father, Kate chose her words carefully. The love he would surely understand. The passion, the sense of completeness—those were things too private to share. "I love her, and she loves me. I have the life I want." She couldn't hide her joy. "I'm so happy that you and Mother have allowed it. Thank you."

Martin snorted softly, thinking of Kate's threat to run away with Jessie if anyone tried to keep them apart. He had no doubt she'd meant it. "You left us no choice, but I'll admit that I can see she suits you." He shook his head. "I never thought that I would see the things I've seen out here—men killing other men for a pocketful of gold dust, women doing for themselves and surviving, nature claiming lives like some merciless servant of an avenging God. Happiness can be a rare thing. If she gives you that, and you her, it's a gift."

"She does." Kate kissed his cheek. "Now, off with you or we'll be so late that Mother will surely want to know where we were."

With that threat hanging in the air, Martin waited until Kate entered the building, then hurried away.

❖

Kate climbed the back stairs to the hallway on the second floor and went directly to Mae's rooms. She knew Mae's habits from the weeks she'd spent in these very same rooms helping to care for Jessie, so she was surprised when no one answered her knock. Still, she knew where Mae would be and set off to find her.

She nodded a greeting to several of the young women who had rooms along the corridor and fell in behind them as they started down the stairs to the saloon. Rapidly, she scanned the already crowded room. By the time she reached the first floor and had not found Mae, she decided to leave the newspapers with Frank and return the way she had come. She had almost reached the end of the bar at the back of the room, where far fewer men were congregated, when she was stopped by a hand on her arm.

"Might I be of service, madam?" a man inquired. His black hair was slicked back with pomade and his thick mustache extravagantly curled. He sported a dark suit with a black satin cravat, a brown velvet waistcoat, and an appraising glint in his eye.

"Thank you, but no," Kate said politely, allowing more than a hint of Boston to show through in her speech. "I'm just going to give these to Mr. Williams and I'll be leaving."

"Allow me to accompany you, then," he said, smoothly tucking her hand into the bend of his arm. "Phineas Drake." He bowed slightly. "At your service."

Kate inclined her head. "I'm very pleased to meet you, Mr. Drake. I appreciate your offer of assistance, but I can assure you it's not necessary."

When she attempted to extract her hand, he clasped her fingers and drew her even more tightly to his side. Although there was nothing truly unseemly about his actions, she was uncomfortable with the press of his body against hers. Even when she had kept reluctant company with Ken Turner, he had rarely done more than lift her hand to his lips. She was unused to anyone other than Jessie so close to her. Rather than allow him to see her discomfort, she decided the best course was to complete her mission as quickly as possible. "Let me put these on the bar, and then I shall be done."

"Perhaps then you would do me the honor of sitting with me for a while. You are by far the finest company I could hope for."

Kate managed to deposit the newspapers, slip her hand from his grip, and move away. She faced him, her expression cold. "I'm sorry. I really must be going."

Something in his face hardened and he took a quick step toward her.

"Why, Kate," Mae said with a small laugh, twining her arm around Kate's waist. "I'm so sorry I'm late." She batted her lashes at Phineas. "Don't tell me your card game is over so soon? You're not losing, I hope?"

Through narrowed eyes he observed them both, then gave a conciliatory smile. "No, not at all. I was merely stretching my legs when it was my good fortune to come upon this beauty." He lifted Kate's hand and brushed his lips over her knuckles, his eyes fixed on her breasts. "Perhaps, Mae my sweet, you will support my humble plea that this dear lady grace me with her company for a few moments."

"And let those cards get cold?" Subtly, Mae drew Kate away. "You'll have plenty of time for company when you've relieved some of those eager gentleman of the coins weighing down their pockets." In a voice too low for Drake to hear, Mae said, "Just keep walking and pretend you're telling me the most amusing story."

Kate put on a bright smile as she hurried off with Mae, feeling the gambler's eyes burning on her skin. "I'm so sorry. I hope I haven't created trouble for you."

"Nothing of the sort," Mae said grimly, although her smile did not falter. "I enjoyed getting in the way of his plans." She pulled Kate under the stairs. "What in heaven's name are you doing here?"

"I just came—"

A deep voice said quietly, "I would be pleased to disabuse that gentleman of any ideas he might have regarding you, should you ladies require it."

Kate turned from Mae and looked into the deepest, darkest eyes she'd ever seen. For one brief instant she saw sympathy, gentle empathy, and more than a little temper. She smiled, recognizing a bit of Jessie in the handsome stranger. It was that more than the discreetly pinned-up coat sleeve that told her this was the woman Mae had told of. Like Jessie, she wore her unconventional attire with natural ease, as if anything else would be foreign to her.

"We *ladies*," Mae said archly, although her tone was playful, "are quite capable of handling a snake on two legs if we have to."

"He seems to have quite an interest in you." From her place in the shadows, Vance had observed the man watching Mae and Kate with sharp attention as they'd hurriedly left him. His expression had been both avaricious and angry, and she knew a dangerous man when she saw one. "I'd take some care around him."

Mae ran her fingers up and down the lapel of Vance's coat. "I will." She left her hand linger on Vance's chest for an instant as she indicated Kate. "This is my friend Kate Beecher. Kate, this is our new doctor. Vance Phelps."

"I'm pleased to meet you, Miss Beecher," Vance said, tipping her head slightly.

"Oh, and I you. I'm sorry if I caused any concern." She looked at Mae. "Really, I just wanted to say hello. Jessie's away again and I was helping my father. I thought I'd drop off the newspapers and then find you upstairs."

"I came down early tonight." Mae sighed in exasperation. "I can see that we're going to have to do something about you if you keep insisting on visiting."

Kate smiled. "Well, since you're one of my closest friends, I'd say that was very likely."

"*And* since you don't seem inclined to stay above stairs, we'll just have to be sure you're not bothered." Mae frowned. "Do your parents know you're here?"

"Actually, my father does. He's going to come for me in another few minutes."

"Well, you're not staying down here until then. I'll take you upstairs, and you can wait there."

"That's not necessary," Kate said. "If I'd known you were already busy, I wouldn't have bothered you."

"Hush, Kate. Don't be silly. I just want you away from here before one of these other *gentlemen* decides he wants your company and isn't as easily dissuaded as our friend Mr. Drake."

"I'll be happy to show Miss Beecher home," Vance said. She smiled at Kate. "Or to accompany you anywhere you'd like to go."

"Oh, no," Kate said quickly, casting Mae a sidelong glance. "I didn't mean to interrupt your visit."

"That's quite all right. I was about to leave." Vance turned to Mae. "Until tomorrow evening?"

"Come around five."

"Will you be all right? With this Drake fellow here tonight?"

Mae laughed harshly. "I'll be fine. He's a coward who uses his fists on women who won't fight back. I will."

Vance leaned close. "Use your gun if it comes to that."

"If I shot every man who tried to get over on me or one of my girls, the streets would be thick with bodies." Nevertheless, Mae was touched by Vance's concern and equally worried that Vance still might take it upon herself to warn Drake off. The gambler was not a man to be crossed, especially when his pride was at stake. She had no doubt that Vance could use the revolver holstered to her thigh, but she did not want to see her in danger. Certainly not by way of protecting her. If Vance went after every man who might be a threat to her, she'd have no time left for anything else. And Mae did not want to cast Vance in the role of protector. She'd made her choices, and she would take whatever consequences came of them. She could see the worry in Vance's eyes, although her expression was calm. More than calm. Mae imagined that Vance had looked like this before a battle. Unafraid, resolute, perhaps even willing to die. That single thought frightened her more than any possible risk to herself. "Promise me you won't try teaching him a lesson."

"If I did, you can be sure he would not come back around you."

"No." Mae shook her head vigorously and spoke the one truth she knew Vance would accept, even if she did not care for her own safety. "It can't be that way. Because if the men start thinking we'll fight them on what they want and what they think is theirs by rights, none of us will be safe then."

Vance looked away, her jaw set. After a moment, she nodded sharply. "I understand."

Kate watched the exchange, and although she could not hear the words that passed between them, she could feel the waves of anger emanate from the doctor. Likewise, she could see the barely contained fear in Mae's face. That was one thing she had never seen before. Although she knew that Mae's life was hard, dangerous, perhaps unspeakably so, it was not something that Mae let others see. The fact that she did not, *could* not, hide it now made Kate afraid for the first time.

"Please don't let my foolish—"

"Oh honey," Mae said with a tight smile, "you didn't do anything. The fact that a woman walks into a room shouldn't give every man within sniffing distance the idea that she was put there for his pleasure. Not even here."

"What's right isn't always what matters," Kate said quietly.

"It should be," Vance said, her voice low. She took Mae's hand. "If you're sure you'll be all right, I'll walk with Miss Beecher to her destination."

For a fleeting second, Mae pressed her palm to Vance's cheek. "Go. And don't forget your dinner."

"Oh," Kate said quickly. "I'd be happy to fix something for you at home. My parents' home, that is."

"I wouldn't think to inconvenience you, but—"

"Please, it's the least I can do." Kate laughed. "Although, I must warn you, my mother is very keen to meet you. Undoubtedly, she will wear you out with questions."

Vance considered refusing, because the last thing she wanted was a social encounter where she would have to be polite and conversant. She'd been using work as an excuse to decline the frequent invitations to tea or supper from patients and new acquaintances ever since her arrival in town. However, this offer was so genuine and Mae's look of relief so apparent that she couldn't refuse. "That would be very kind of you. Thank you."

"Good," Mae said briskly. "Now, the two of you get out of here." She smiled at Vance. "You be careful, now."

Vance held Mae's gaze. "And you."

❖

When Kate found Martin deep in conversation at the hotel with Silas, she informed him that Dr. Phelps would escort her home. "There's no need for you to hurry your visit."

Martin looked from one to the other in surprised confusion but saw no reason to object. "Of course, my dear. You may tell your mother I'll be along shortly." He nodded to Vance. "Nice to see you, Doctor. Perhaps we can talk sometime about the challenges you face out here. It would make for an interesting article in our paper."

Vance smiled noncommittally. "I'm sure it would."

As they began their walk through town, the only lights that flickered were in windows lit by candles and oil lamps. Kate said, "We're originally from Boston. We've been here just over a year. It's very different, isn't it?"

"Yes," Vance said, her mind still on the encounter in the saloon. "It's a strange place where men feel the bounds of propriety no longer apply and women have both great independence and none at all."

"Mae is an amazing woman," Kate said. "She's one of the strongest, most capable people I've ever met."

"She is." Vance rubbed her hand over her face. "Forgive me. I didn't mean to impose my ill mood upon you."

Kate laughed shortly. "You've hardly done that. It makes me so angry that anyone would think less of her for any reason."

Vance gave her a curious look.

"Oh, I know what she does to earn her way. Should I be shocked? That a woman would use one of the few tools at her disposal to survive on her own?" She shook her head angrily. "I think it's incredibly brave."

"You are not a typical young woman from Boston, Miss Beecher," Vance said.

"No, Dr. Phelps. It appears that I'm not." Kate slowed as they approached the walk to her parents' home. "If I had never come to this place, I might still be closed-minded and unforgiving of things I did not understand."

"Somehow, I doubt that. It takes more than a change of environment to alter who we are and what we believe."

"You're right," Kate said thoughtfully. "It's more than just my coming here. It's that I came here and found myself." She smiled at Vance. "And I found the only thing that matters to me."

"Indeed. And what might that be?"

"Love, Dr. Phelps. I found my love." Kate slid her arm through Vance's. "Please. Come inside and meet my mother."

"It would be my pleasure."

## Chapter Eleven

"Mother, this is Dr. Vance Phelps."

Looking at the women seated in the parlor, their expressions at once wary and curious, Vance sighed inwardly. She knew these women—she'd grown up with them, or women so like them that the differences made no difference. When Kate led her into the parlor and she came upon Kate's mother and her guests, Vance was reminded of the many afternoons of her youth spent in a similar fashion, conversing about matters of no importance and gossiping discreetly about people who were no doubt doing the same about them. Mercifully, she had always had the excuse of her studies to justify taking her leave after a polite interval, and if that failed, Victor could be counted on to fabricate ingenious distractions to effect her escape. Thinking about Victor brought the anticipated surge of pain, so familiar she didn't even bother to try to suppress it. For months there had been nothing but pain, to the point where pain was more natural than anything else she felt. Now, it was merely the backdrop against which the events of her day unfolded.

"I'm very pleased to meet you, Mrs. Beecher," Vance said. She turned to the other two women and smiled graciously, as if she were once more in the great room of the brownstone mansion in the heart of Philadelphia where she'd been born and raised. "And Mrs. Mason and Rose. How very nice to see you again."

"Yes, how nice," Clarissa Mason said coolly.

"Oh, do sit and have some tea," Rose gushed, sliding closer to her mother on the sofa to make room.

Vance remained standing, waiting for the lady of the house to make known her desires.

Watching the exchange, Martha Beecher was at a loss as to how to react. There was absolutely no doubt that the woman before her was bred to high society. It was evident in every line of her face and every cultured inflection of her speech. Despite the outlandish—even shocking—attire, she stood as if she were at the head of a reception line at a formal affair, greeting the elite of society with just the slightest hint of amused superiority. Oh, Clarissa Mason had clearly underestimated her, but then, how could Clarissa be expected to recognize someone of the doctor's station? Clarissa might be a banker's wife, but a banker's wife in New Hope, Montana, was a far cry from the upper class of Eastern society. Clarissa had undoubtedly looked at the newcomer's admittedly outrageous appearance and no further. Martha stood to greet her guest.

"Please, do sit down, Dr. Phelps. I'm so happy to have this opportunity to meet you at last," Martha said with just a hint of polite reserve. "I so hope you bring news of the East, as we very seldom have the opportunity to hear of events out here before they are no longer of consequence."

Declining the offer of a seat, Vance feared that she would disappoint Kate's mother on more than one level. Any news that she might relay of politics and the social upheaval that followed the end of the war would undoubtedly dissatisfy, and she knew nothing of the latest fashions and styles. "I've been traveling for quite some time, and I'm afraid I have no recent news about any matters of importance."

"And," Kate interrupted laughingly, slipping her hand into the crook of Vance's elbow once more, "I have invited Dr. Phelps home for a late meal. I'm going to take her into the kitchen and fix her a plate. She's been working all day."

"Indeed," Clarissa Mason said archly. "You're…" She hesitated as if searching for a polite term. "You're actually tending to patients, then, not just assisting Dr. Melbourne."

"I'm doing both," Vance said quietly, her tone subtly cooler. "Some procedures, particularly surgeries, are easier to perform with competent assistance." She smiled thinly. "But I am used to treating substantial injuries independently. The war taught me that."

"Oh," Clarissa gasped, as if finding the subject repellent.

Rose, however, sat forward, her face alight with excitement. "Oh, do tell us what that was like!"

"Surely not, Rose," Clarissa chided. "Such things are not fit conversation for a young lady."

"Is it true, that no one knew you weren't a man?" Rose persisted.

"I really couldn't say," Vance said. She was tired from riding all day and her shoulder ached. She was agitated and worried about Mae, and the fragile veneer of sociability she'd been able to assume cracked and slipped away. "I'm a physician, and I was there to treat the wounded. When the ground is littered with the dead and the dying as far as the eye can see, social conventions fall quickly aside."

"Oh, how terribly awful," Rose cried, looking even more intrigued.

Vance glanced toward the door. "Forgive me. It's been a very long day and you must excuse me."

"Come," Kate said, drawing Vance toward the hallway and the kitchen beyond. "Let me fix you that meal, and then you can head home and get some rest."

Rose jumped to her feet. "Let me help."

Before either of their mothers could object, Kate and Rose spirited Vance away.

"It's really not necessary for you to fuss," Vance said as Kate took the remainder of dinner from the icebox and placed the tray in the center of the table.

"Oh," Rose said, preempting Kate's reply as she pulled a chair close to where Vance sat at the table, "it's hardly a bother when here *you* are doing such important and so very difficult work."

Vance caught the amused look on Kate's face and managed not to laugh. "Well, I do appreciate it. I very seldom have home-cooked food. Miss Beecher, can I help you?"

"Nothing to do," Kate said as she placed the bread and cold meats in front of Vance. "And please, call me Kate." Then, shyly, she asked, "What was it like, going to medical school?"

"It's Vance, then." Vance struggled to bring into focus an experience that felt to her now as if it had occurred in a different lifetime. To a different person altogether. She answered from a place of sad remembering. "I attended Women's Medical College, which was an amazing thing in itself. An entire medical school established and devoted to training women." With an absent smile, she shook her head. "Originally, I wanted to attend the school that my father had, that my…" She took a breath. "Well, at any rate, I ended up being very happy where I trained. It was exciting, demanding work."

"Oh, I can just imagine how wonderful it must've been to be able to study like that," Kate said, her face flushed with enthusiasm.

Rose shuddered. "Well, I can't imagine it. Working around the sick and the dying all the time." She glanced quickly at Vance and amended, "But I think it's highly admirable, of course. Highly."

"Yes," Vance said solemnly, wishing that she could remove her coat. The kitchen was overly warm. However, she had no desire to invoke more rabid curiosity from the eager young Miss Mason.

"I know you're tired," Kate said gently. "But someday, when you have a moment to spare, I'd love for you to tell me what your courses were like."

"It's a promise." Vance pushed the barely eaten food away. She had little appetite for dinner and far less for company. The bounds of normal conversation took her far too close to the borders of memories best left unvisited. There were places she simply did not want to go again. "This was very kind of you. Thank you." She stood. "Now, I must say good night. Please give my regards to the other ladies."

"I shall." Kate held open the back door. "Be careful."

Vance regarded her quizzically, then smiled faintly, wondering if Kate too was still thinking of the onerous Phineas Drake. "Thank you. Good night."

"Good night," Kate said softly, closing the door behind Vance as she stepped out into the night.

"Oh," Rose said after Vance was gone. "Isn't she the most fascinating and exciting individual!"

"Yes, she's very strong and brave," Kate agreed, but for far different reasons, she suspected, than Rose, who seemed desperate only for a glimpse of anything outside the everyday routine of New Hope. It wasn't what Vance had achieved that drew Kate to her. It was the terrible sorrow that clung to her like a heavy cloak. Kate understood now why Mae had spoken of wounds unhealed.

❖

Vance walked back to the hotel through the dark streets, relieved to have left the gathering that had seemed foreign to her. She hadn't realized how poorly she had fit that social niche until she had left it, first peripherally, when she began her studies, and finally, completely, when she'd left for the war. She'd never felt completely comfortable with the conventions and restrictions that her sex and social status had dictated for her as a child and young woman. While her mother had been alive, she had done all the usual things that a well-bred young lady should do, including attending the required social events with young men of her class. Then, her happiest times had been the summers spent at her family's country estate. Her mother had paid far less attention to her comings and goings then, and she could ride, hunt, and secretly gamble with her brother and his friends without incurring her mother's censure. The young men had welcomed her as one of them, because they had all grown up together. By the time she was a teenager, she knew she wanted to be a doctor. Had her mother not died when she was fifteen, she might have had more of a battle convincing her father of her desires, but with no one to strenuously object, she had had her way. However, it wasn't until she had dressed in Victor's clothes and accompanied him to the recruiting station that she'd truly realized what freedom felt like. She'd never felt as comfortable or more like herself in her life.

Vance slowed at the mouth of the alley beside the Golden Nugget, having returned without realizing it. Briefly, she considered going back inside for one last drink and one final glance at Mae. However, at this time of night, Mae would certainly be working, and Vance wasn't certain that was something she wanted to witness. She was staring at the side door, contemplating the long evening ahead, when it opened and a woman stepped out. Her heart gave a lurch as she imagined that Mae had somehow conjured her thoughts and had slipped out to meet her. She took one step forward, then stopped, realizing her error. Pleasure was rapidly eclipsed by disappointment, a cycle that left an ache not totally unwelcome. It had been a long time since the anticipation of anything had pleased her. As she was about to turn and continue on her way to the hotel, a voice called out to her from the shadows.

"Dr. Phelps, wait, please."

Once more, Vance halted. This time she recognized the young blond woman, a younger but somehow more hardened version of Mae, and strode down the narrow passageway to meet her. "Sissy, isn't it?"

"Yes," Sissy said. Although she wore a shawl over her shoulders, she made no effort to pull it closed over the extremely low-cut bodice of her dress. Rather, she straightened her shoulders, which lifted her breasts even closer to the top of the confining fabric. "Must be fate. Mae sent me to fetch you."

Vance's chest tightened, and this time the pain was very real. She forced a breath and ground out the words that threatened to choke her. "Is she hurt?"

Sissy frowned. "Mae? No. It's about Lettie."

*Lettie. Not Mae. Mae is all right.* Vance struggled to make the connection, carefully averting her eyes from the display of flesh that was obvious, even by moonlight. "Lettie. I'm afraid I don't…wait." Her voice took on an edge. "Isn't she the young lady who is pregnant?"

"Well," Sissy snorted, "I won't vouch for the *lady* part, but she is pregnant sure enough."

"What's the problem?" Vance asked, already hurrying down the passageway toward the door.

"She's bleeding some and Mae said to see if you could come."

"Of course. Take me to her."

❖

The room was far smaller and plainer than Mae's, although clean and well furnished with a bed, dresser, chair, and even a small bookcase tucked into one corner. Lettie, dark-haired, pale, and clearly frightened, lay beneath a thin patchwork quilt. Vance removed her coat and folded it over the back of a nearby chair. Her cuff, which she never buttoned, she pushed upward by sliding her arm across her chest as she approached the bed.

"Hello, Lettie, do you remember me?"

The young girl nodded. "You were here before with Mae. You're the doctor."

"That's right. Are you having any pain?"

Lettie shook her head.

"How about earlier? Did anything unusual happen?"

Again, a head shake.

"All right then, what about the bleeding? When did you notice that?"

Lettie cast an uncertain glance in Sissy's direction.

"Go ahead, girl, tell her," Sissy said with a touch of impatience.

"Round about three days," Lettie said quietly.

Vance looked at Sissy. "Would you please pour a basin of water for me." Then she smiled encouragingly at Lettie. "All right, then, I'm going to take a look at you and then we'll talk. Okay?"

"Yes," Lettie whispered.

Vance went to the sideboard and used a cake of soap and the water Sissy had poured to wash her hand. She was aware of Sissy watching her curiously, and when she reached for the towel and dried her hand with the towel pressed to her chest, she met Sissy's eyes. "You must tell them not to wait when there's a problem. I will always come. There is nothing for them to be afraid of."

Wordlessly, Sissy took the towel and finished drying Vance's hand. When Vance tried to pull away, she shook her head. "I can do it faster." As she carefully patted each finger, she said, "Girls who are sick, who can't work, are used to being put out on the street."

"Surely not here. Surely, Mae would not…"

"Mae can't be everywhere, all the time," Sissy said, regarding Vance with blazing eyes. "And even if she was, she don't own the roof over our heads."

"Who does?"

Sissy shrugged. "Don't know. Don't make any difference to me."

"Nevertheless," Vance said firmly, "if they're sick, I need to know. Tell them they'll get back to work faster if they let me see to them."

"You're not going to tell us to change our evil ways?" Sissy asked sarcastically.

"That's not for me to say. My job is to treat the sick."

"Ain't that what we are?"

"No," Vance said gently. "Now let me see to Lettie."

Vance was in the midst of palpating Lettie's distended abdomen when she felt a subtle shift in the air in the room, as in the sky before an electrical storm. Then she caught a whiff of wildflowers on hot summer afternoons, and she smiled. Without looking up, she said, "Good evening, Mae."

"Looks like we're keeping you busy," Mae said, coming up behind Vance and brushing her shoulder in greeting. "Sorry to trouble you."

"No trouble," Vance murmured, sliding her palm over the outline of the uterus, pressing gently to discern the position of the developing head. Then she sat back and carefully pulled up the covers and gave

Lettie's hand a reassuring pat. "I'm going to speak with Mae for a few minutes. Everything seems to be fine, but you're going to need to stay in bed for several more days until I examine you again."

"Oh, but—"

Vance shook her head. "No buts. It's important." She stood and followed Mae outside into the corridor. It was less than two hours since she'd last seen her, but she was aware of having missed her.

"Thank you for coming," Mae said.

"There's no need to thank me." Vance resisted the urge to capture a golden ringlet that had escaped from the mass of curls and now dangled enticingly onto Mae's breast. It fluttered with each breath, a taunting invitation as it danced over ivory skin.

Mae followed the direction of Vance's gaze, wondering how much of what she saw in Vance's eyes Vance was actually aware of. Despite the pleasant flutter in the stomach the thought gave her, it was something best pursued another day. There were more important things to attend to now.

"What's wrong with her?"

"Possibly nothing. She has had some bleeding, which is not completely unheard of at this stage in the pregnancy." Vance watched a well-dressed man in a business suit accompany the redheaded Annie down the hall and disappear into a room. "But it could be the first sign of something serious. She needs to be at complete bed rest for at least the next several days."

"I'll see to that." Mae traced a line with her nails up and down Vance's forearm, which was bare below her pushed-up cuff. She smiled to herself when she saw Vance visibly shudder. "Maybe you can look in on her tomorrow before dinner."

"I'll do that," Vance said hoarsely, stunned by the twist of excitement that slivered through her.

"Good," Mae said, smiling sweetly. "Now you go on home." She touched Vance's cheek fleetingly. "And you have sweet dreams."

Vance leaned against the wall watching Mae as she glided away, wondering if any pleasure would ever have the power to replace her nightmares.

# CHAPTER TWELVE

Are you feeling ill?" Martha Beecher asked, studying Kate with concern as they cleared dishes from the table. "You ate very little for breakfast, and now nothing for lunch."

"No, I feel wonderful," Kate replied with forced brightness. "I'm quite recovered by now."

"Of course you are," Martha said, although she wouldn't believe the truth of that until many more weeks had passed. "But that doesn't mean you don't need to take care of yourself. It's important that you eat and get plenty of rest—"

"I know." Kate poured water into the dish basin. "Really, you needn't worry."

"You forget I'm your mother." Martha crossed her arms, frowning. "I can tell when you're not yourself."

"I never forget that." Kate sighed and set the dishrag aside. "I had hoped that Jessie would be here by now. She said she'd come into town as soon as she brought the horses down from the high country."

Martha's expression darkened subtly. "Your father and I are always happy to have you here, so staying another night—"

"That's not the point. Jessie always keeps her promises to me," Kate said, her eyes flashing. "She said she would be here *today*. The only reason she wouldn't be is if something happened."

"I'm sure you're worrying for nothing," Martha said dismissively. "She's been off on these…roundups…frequently lately."

"I don't think you understand what life is really like beyond the borders of this little town." Kate's unease made her forget her usual patience, and her mother's offhand rejection of her anxiety over Jessie—

and more, her persistent criticism of their life together—angered her. "She could be hur—"

"I know some of the things that could happen out there," Martha snapped. "I traveled for weeks across this hellacious countryside in that ungodly wagon the same as you and your father, only I didn't find it to be the great adventure of my life." She glanced around the kitchen, grand by New Hope's standards but humble compared to what she had been used to. "I'm trying hard to make this place my home, only to find my daughter has deserted me for a life that…"

"For a life that makes me happy," Kate said gently. She went to her mother and took her hand, giving it a small shake. "And I haven't deserted you. I'm right here. I want you to come to the ranch and see for yourself what my home is like. It's beautiful."

Martha sighed and nodded. "All right. I will."

"And I want you to be happy for me."

"It's hard, Kate, being happy about something I cannot understand." Martha regarded Kate with tender confusion. "All my life, I have tried to be what was expected of me. Woman, wife, mother. I don't understand choosing a way of life that will only bring hardship."

Kate smiled. "Every life is hard, whether we choose our path or not. But in choosing a life with Jessie, I also know I'll have what matters most. Love."

Martha raised her hands, signaling defeat. "I love your father, but I would have married him even had I not."

"And *I* would not have married without love," Kate said gently. "And it never would have happened with Ken Turner or any other man." She laughed. "Father's dream brought me here, and my own brought me Jessie. I feel like the luckiest woman in the world."

"You're my daughter. You must forgive me for wanting acceptability and security for you."

"Acceptability will come." Kate shrugged. "And if it doesn't, what does it really matter when I go to sleep at night knowing that I have everything I could want?"

Martha shook her head. "Is that really how you feel?"

"Yes."

"The world seems to be changing very quickly." Martha sat heavily at the table. "Women do things out here I would never have imagined. Why, look at the new doctor. She seems not to care what anyone thinks of her, dressing in men's clothes and wearing her hair far shorter than is suitable, too."

Kate couldn't help but smile as she sat beside her mother. "I don't think Vance worries overly about the length of her hair. She's doing important work."

"Yes, and look what it cost her. Her arm," Martha said, aghast.

"That's horrible, I agree." Kate shuddered. "I really can't imagine being that brave."

"Bravery should be left to the men."

"Why? Why can't women fight for what we believe in? Why should we be any less noble in our convictions than the men?"

"Wherever do you get such ideas?" Martha sounded exasperated as well as reluctantly impressed.

Kate laughed. "From my parents, of course." She leaned forward and kissed her mother's cheek. "Both of them."

Pleased, but trying not to show it, Martha said sternly, "I can assure you, I had no part in any of these outlandish ideas of yours."

"You taught me what it was to be loved, and how to recognize it." Thinking of Jessie, Kate struggled to keep her worry at bay. It was late afternoon, and with each passing minute, her concern grew. Hoping to occupy her mind, she said, "I'm going to walk into town and visit Father. If Jessie should arrive before I return, will you send her down for me?"

Martha nodded. "And when your Jessie arrives, regardless of the time, I expect you both to stay for dinner."

Touched, Kate said, "Thank you. I'll be home soon."

"Be careful."

Kate recalled the previous evening and her brief encounter with Phineas Drake. Although she hadn't actually been frightened, she wasn't foolish enough to think that there was no danger to a woman alone. "You needn't worry. I plan to be."

❖

Kate set her teacup aside and swiveled on the settee to face Mae. Since she had found her father busy completing an editorial on the controversy surrounding the use of "barbed wire" on the open range, it had seemed a perfect opportunity to visit. "I want to be able to protect myself from the likes of Phineas Drake when I'm going about town unescorted."

"I'd say that's very smart." At 4 p.m., Mae was not yet dressed for the evening in her silk finery, but wore a smart, simple dark blue linen dress and matching shoes. The neckline, although scooped, was modest compared to her working attire. She sipped her tea, her expression contemplative. "You know, some would see a woman walking about alone as an invitation for trouble."

"I know that, but I can hardly let such ridiculous notions make me a prisoner. Jessie is often out on the range all day, and unless I want to remain at home alone, I'll have to be free to move about independently."

"Have you talked to Jessie about this?" Mae asked, one eyebrow quirked in anticipation of Kate's response. She smiled faintly when she was not disappointed.

Kate sat up straighter, a frown forming between her brilliant dark eyes. "I certainly hope you're not going to start sounding like my mother."

"Heavens, save me from that!"

"I'm not in the habit of asking Jessie's permission to come and go, nor would she—"

"Lord, I know that by now." Laughing, Mae set her tea aside. "But I expect she'll have something to say about you gallivanting around the countryside on your own." Her expression grew serious. "And truth be told, Kate, it *is* dangerous. Not just out on the range, but here in town, too."

"I know that, and I don't intend to do anything foolish. But if Vance and Jessie can—"

"Things are different for them—"

"Why?" Agitated, Kate paced to the window that overlooked the street, watching the people, mostly men, come and go. She spun back. "Because they wear pants and carry guns?"

"Well, yes. Mostly."

"Well, as much as I like the way they both look in them, I'm not planning on wearing pants *just* so I won't be bothered when I walk down the street." She grinned. "The gun, however, is another matter."

"Well, I won't say I've never seen a woman in a dress carrying a sidearm," Mae said, walking to her bureau. She opened the top drawer and withdrew a pearl-handled Derringer, the twin to the one she carried.

She held it out to Kate. "But this is much less likely to draw attention, and that's what you want."

Kate took it and examined it enthusiastically. It felt wonderful in her hand, smooth and substantial. It made her feel stronger, and even more importantly, it made her feel free. "Will you show me how to use it? I've only ever shot the Winchester."

"Come here," Mae said, returning to the settee. "First, let me show you how to load it."

Kate was an apt student and within a few moments had grasped the mechanics of how to load and fire the weapon. "Oh, I want to go outside right now and find something to shoot at."

"Well, we could most likely go downstairs to the saloon and find you a target or two."

Kate's reply was interrupted by a knock at the door.

"Hold on, let me see who wants something now," Mae said, rising with a sigh. Her expression of annoyance changed to one of pleasure when she opened the door and saw Vance. "Hello. You're early." She indicated her dress. "And I'm unprepared."

"You look lovely, as always," Vance said. She looked past Mae and smiled at Kate. "Good afternoon."

Hastily, Kate began gathering her things. "I should be leaving."

"No, I'm interrupting," Vance said, taking a step back. "I merely stopped to say that I was going to look in on Lettie."

"We've been keeping her in bed, just like you said," Mae informed her.

"Good. Well, I'll just see to her, then."

"Do you need any help?" Mae asked quietly.

"I can manage, thank you," Vance replied gently. "But Lettie might like it if you were there."

"Of course. I'll be right—"

Annie came out of a room across the hall and hurried to Mae's door. "Mae, Sophie says her best black shoes are missing, and I think someone's been going through our things."

"All right," Mae said, "I'll be there in a few minutes."

Kate touched Mae's shoulder. "I can go with Vance, Mae, if you want to see what that's all about."

"I'd better, before they start accusing one another of stealing each other's things. Probably some visitor decided to make a present of those shoes to his wife and stuffed them in his saddle bag."

Mae disappeared into Sophie's room as Vance and Kate went down the hall.

"I've been meaning to ask Caleb who the midwife is in town," Vance said. "Would you happen to know?"

Kate frowned. "As far as I know, there isn't one."

"Really?" Vance stopped outside Lettie's door. "With a population this size, I would imagine there are quite a few births. That must mean a great number of women are delivering without any trained assistants, since I'm sure Caleb can't see to all of them."

"I never thought of that," Kate murmured. "Back in Boston, such things really weren't discussed very much. They just seemed to… happen."

Vance laughed softly. "Yes, conception and the practical aspects of delivery do tend to remain a mystery in polite society. But I can assure you, very few women would attempt delivery without a midwife present."

"What is it, exactly, that the midwife does?"

Leaning a shoulder against the wall, Vance said, "Well, in the early stages, the midwife monitors the progression of the pregnancy, checking on the general health of the mother and things of that nature. Closer to delivery, she performs the routine examinations to judge the position of the child and determines whether everything is on schedule. Then of course, during the delivery, she aids the mother up to and through the time of birth."

"It sounds very important."

"Oh, it is. Most physicians never arrive for the delivery until almost the last minute. The midwives perform an invaluable service." Vance straightened. "Let's go see Lettie."

Once in the room, Kate watched closely as Vance questioned the young girl as to her health and carefully examined her abdomen. Occasionally, Kate would ask a question which Vance answered thoroughly and unhurriedly.

"Here," Vance said, reaching for Kate's hand. She drew it to Lettie's belly and covered Kate's fingers with hers. Pressing lightly on Kate's fingers she said, "Feel here. That's the head."

Kate held her breath, trying to see through her fingertips as Vance slowly moved her hand over Lettie's pregnant abdomen.

"And here, that's probably the baby's rump."

"Oh," Kate gasped, amazed. She jumped when she felt a thump under her fingers. Eyes wide, she stared at Vance. "She moved."

Vance grinned. "She, or he, did indeed. At this stage, which I judge to be a little over seven months, the baby's very active." Vance looked up at Lettie. "Isn't that true?"

Lettie nodded vigorously, unused to having anyone pay her quite so much attention. "Sometimes it keeps me awake at night."

"How can you tell how far along she is?" Kate didn't think she'd ever felt anything quite as miraculous and, at that moment, didn't think she'd ever met anyone, other than Jessie, quite as thrilling as Vance Phelps.

"There are number of things," Vance said, standing. "If you'd like, I'll go over them with you once we're finished here."

"Yes," Kate said instantly. "Yes. I'd like that very much."

Delicately, Vance covered Lettie with the sheet. "You're doing fine. Another day or two, and if there's no more bleeding, you can start moving around again. But no lifting. All right?"

"Yes. You'll come back again?" Lettie asked.

"I will, in two days' time." She turned, surprised to find Kate holding out her coat. She slid her arm into the sleeve and waited, a bit self-consciously, as Kate drew it up her shoulders and settled it into place. "Thank you."

"It is I who should thank you," Kate said as they walked to the door. "That was the most exciting, wonderful, amazing—" She broke off, laughing. "You must think me ridiculous."

"Not at all." Vance smiled herself. "I remember just how excited I was the first time I felt something like that. I—" She stopped abruptly at the sound of hurried footsteps ascending the stairs at the far end of the hall. Mae suddenly appeared, her skirts held up in both hands as she rushed toward them. Urgently, Vance said, "What is it?"

"The doc…" Mae pressed a hand to her chest, trying to catch her breath. It wasn't the running, but the panic, that had stolen the air from her lungs. "The Doc sent a message for you to come quick. Says he needs you straightaway."

"All right." Vance hesitated only a second. "You're fine?"

"Yes, yes. I'm coming with you. I've helped him with this kind of thing before."

"What kind of thing?" Kate said, hurrying along beside them, a terrible fear rising in her throat. When Mae didn't answer immediately, Kate grasped her arm to slow her headlong rush. "Mae, what kind of thing?"

"Someone's been shot." Mae took Kate's hand. "Someone from the Rising Star. That's all I know, honey."

*No. No no no. Not again. This can't be happening again.* With fierce determination, Kate ran.

## CHAPTER THIRTEEN

Kate cursed the dark, the uneven rut-strewn street, her shoes with the short square heels as she hurried toward Doc Melbourne's office. A light flickered in the window from the oil lamp, and a shadow passed back and forth within, splintering the shaft of light that escaped. Despite her horribly slow pace, she was well ahead of Mae and Vance when she reached the wooden porch in front of the building. Even as she pushed through the door she was calling Jessie's name.

Jessie turned at the sound of the door slamming open. Blood streaked the right side of her face. Her shirt was soaked with sweat, caked with dirt, and a large stain over her left side looked frighteningly like blood.

Kate flung herself into Jessie's arms. "Oh my darling…are you hurt?" Frantically, she patted Jessie's shoulders, her chest, her face. "You are. You're hurt. Oh…sit down. Where's the doctor? He must look at you."

"Kate," Jessie said gently, catching her hands, stilling her motion. "I'm all right. It's nothing. Just some scratches." Then she wrapped her arms around Kate and buried her face against Kate's neck. Her voice was muffled as she choked out, "It's Jed, Kate. Lord. He's been shot."

Vance strode through the door followed immediately by Mae. In her rush toward the closed inner door that led to the treatment room, she spared Kate and Jessie a brief glance. It took a second for her to register that the cowboy holding Kate, or being held by her, was a woman. She put her surprise away and looked at Mae. "Can you help?"

"Yes, of course. I've done it before."

"And so can I, if you need me," Kate said firmly.

"It wouldn't hurt." Vance disappeared through the inner door with Mae.

Tenderly, Kate disengaged from Jessie's embrace and stroked her cheek. "He'll be all right, darling. Sit now. I'll be out very soon."

Not knowing what else to do, Jessie slumped into a chair, her hands dangling uselessly between her legs. "Please, Kate." Her eyes were deep pools of misery. "Please don't let him die."

"Vance and Dr. Melbourne will take care of him." Heart aching, hating to leave her but wanting desperately to *do* something, Kate kissed Jessie swiftly, then hurried away. Not even thinking about what awaited her, she rushed into the next room, only to halt abruptly just inside the door. Shocked, she stared at the sight of Jed lying facedown on the table. He was shirtless and his back was awash with blood. Doc Melbourne leaned over him, pressing a square of white cloth between his shoulder blades.

"Why, Kate, what are you doing here?" Caleb Melbourne glanced quickly from Kate to Vance.

"I thought we could use the help," Vance said.

"Might be right," he said. "Kate, we won't have time for the smelling salts."

She took two steady steps forward. "I won't faint. Just tell me what to do."

"Get some more of these bandages from the case over there," he said with a tip of his head. Over his shoulder, he said to Vance, "He's got a bullet in his back and he's lost a lot of blood. We need to get it out, and we need to get it out fast. I'd say you'd be the best one to do that."

Vance didn't bother examining Jed but took Caleb at his word. She shrugged out of her coat and pulled her surgical kit from the closet where she had stored it upon her arrival in New Hope. She hefted it onto a nearby table and jerked open the flaps. It was not the same kit she had used that last morning at Appomattox, but a spare she had brought from home after hers was lost. For one brief second, the shining instruments looked completely foreign. She gripped a gleaming silver probe, and at the first touch of the cold steel against her fingers, everything came back to her. She felt the ground shake with the thunder of the cannons, smelled the cordite and blood in the air, shuddered beneath the weight of the dying.

Mae covered Vance's hand with hers. "Why don't you tell me which ones of these you need, and I'll lay them out while you see to Jed."

Vance stared at Mae's hand, stunned as the warmth cut through the chill that entombed her. Mae's voice was so soft, and yet it penetrated the barrage of sounds that bombarded her. Her voice barely a whisper, she said, "Thank you."

"Nothing to thank me for," Mae said briskly, relieved to see a bit of color return to Vance's face. When she'd reached into the leather satchel, she'd turned chalk white and her eyes had gone flat, as if her body was still there but her soul had disappeared. It was about the most terrifying thing Mae had ever seen. The only thing she could think to do was touch her and try to pull her back from whatever hell she'd slid into. "Which ones, Doc?"

"All of...the probes. And the forceps...those are the clamps... there." Vance cleared her throat, her voice stronger. "If you could open that canister...Yes, that one...and pour some of the carbolic over my hand. And my sleeve...could you roll it up, please."

Swiftly, Mae took care of Vance's shirt and then unscrewed the metal top from the pint-sized canister. At the first whiff, she drew back in disgust. "Lord. You want that on your skin?"

"It won't hurt me," Vance said, holding her hand over a nearby basin. "Go ahead and pour it."

"Whiskey will do just as good," Caleb remarked.

Vance nodded. "You might be right." She shook her hand free of the liquid and walked up to the table. "Let me see."

Gingerly, Caleb moved the poultice aside, and blood immediately welled up from the hole adjacent to Jed's shoulder blade. He slapped the compress back down, his expression grave. "The bleeding might stop if I hold this on here long enough, but the bullet will still be in there."

Vance and Caleb both knew that leaving the bullet in place would lead to infection and certain death. Unfortunately, at the rate the wound was bleeding, Jed was likely to bleed to death before they could get the bullet out.

"Have you given him anything?" Vance asked.

"I didn't have to. He doesn't know anything that's happening." Caleb tossed the crimson-soaked bandage aside and held out a bloodied hand to Kate. "Could you hand me another, my dear. Just keep one ready at all times."

"Here you are." Kate extended the cloth, careful not to look at Jed's face. She'd discovered very quickly that if she just concentrated on the injury and what needed to be done, she could keep her fear and horror at bay. If she thought that this helpless man on the table was Jed, the kindhearted and gentle man who had welcomed her to the Rising Star as if she had been family, she thought that she might break down in tears. She couldn't even contemplate the terrible loss it would be for Jessie if Jed died. She could not think of those things and be of any assistance. And she was determined that she would help save this man she cared for and who meant so much to her Jessie.

"Caleb," Vance said, carefully pressing her fingers over the thick muscles along Jed's spine. "If you will steady the probe once I locate the bullet, I'll follow it down with the forceps and extract it."

"You just get me in the right spot," Caleb grunted. "Kate, you be ready to swab the blood, because we're not going to be able to see a damn thing. Mae, you'll be handing us the instruments."

Both women murmured their assent. Mae watched as Vance selected a silver probe ten inches long and as thick around as her small finger. It narrowed into a blunt rounded tip at each end. Vance's hand was steady, her face calm but determined. Despite the terrible circumstances, Mae couldn't help but think how beautiful she was. Her eyes met Vance's and held. "Just tell me what you need."

"This may be too thick. Have the next size down ready."

"Yes." Mae searched it out as Vance leaned over Jed.

"Ready?" Vance said to Caleb.

"Let's get this done."

The instant Caleb removed the bandage, blood gushed forth. Unperturbed, Vance inserted the end of the probe into the bullet wound, balancing it delicately across her fingers and angling it with slight pressure from her thumb until it naturally found the angle of the bullet track. Then she guided it forward with a gentle massaging motion, avoiding trauma to the surrounding tissues. She was unaware of time passing or of the swift intake of breath beside her. The air grew very still, the sounds of battle receded, and there was only the rush of blood through Jed's body, the pump of his heart, the ebb and flow of his life that rested now in her hands. When the steel probe touched the ball of lead lodged in the paraspinous muscles, she said without looking up, "Caleb, hold this just as it is. Don't push forward or change the angle."

Without looking away from the wound, Vance waited until Caleb placed his fingers next to hers on the probe. She noted absently that his hand was shaking. She repositioned the instrument slightly. "Do you have it?"

"Yes," Caleb said, the tension making his voice thin and tight.

Vance let go of the probe and opened her hand. "Mae. The forceps. Kate, very gently swab the blood away from the bullet site, but don't move the probe."

The smooth handle fit perfectly in her palm. Without needing to look at it, Vance slid her thumb and fourth finger through the grips. Had she had her left hand, she would be holding the probe and, together, one hand would have guided the other, a delicate *danse à deux*. She was partially blind because she could not feel the bullet or the probe as she pushed the forceps into the wound. Nevertheless, the track the probe had followed was imprinted on her mind, and she guided the forceps effortlessly. When she judged she was an inch away from the end of the probe, she said, "Now pull it back slowly. Slowly."

As Caleb retracted the probe, Vance opened the jaws of the forceps and pressed deeper into the wound, finally closing the instrument at the point where she knew the bullet to be. With a slight twist to free the surrounding tissue, she extracted the forceps with the bullet held firmly in its jaws. "Kate, press down on the wound now."

It had taken her just over a minute to complete the entire maneuver.

"Never seen it done slicker," Caleb murmured.

Wordlessly, Vance turned away from the table and laid the forceps with the bullet still clamped tightly in the jaws onto the cloth Mae had spread out beneath her other instruments. "I imagine you know what needs to be done, Caleb."

"Yes," Caleb said grimly, swabbing the area around the wound with a whiskey-soaked cloth. "Now we wait."

Vance walked to the sideboard and dunked her bloodied hand into a basin of water. Without bothering to dry it, she crossed the room to a door that led out into the alley behind the building, opened it, and stepped out into the dark.

"Is there anything I can do to help you?" Kate asked quietly.

"Let's turn him over and get him covered. I suspect he'll be as comfortable here as anywhere else for the next few hours." Smiling faintly at the two women, Caleb went on, "This is the part that's so wearing, because we've done all we can really do. I've never seen anyone get a bullet out that was in that deep so fast and with so little damage to all the other structures. No one could have given him a better chance." He slid his arm under Jed. "You two take his arm there and turn him toward you when I lift."

Once Jed was on his back, Mae retrieved a blanket from a cabinet along the wall, and she and Kate spread it over him.

"Jessie's in the other room," Kate said. "She's hurt. Could you look at her now?"

"Of course. Go get her."

When Kate returned to the anteroom, Jessie bolted to her feet, her face pale.

"Kate?"

Putting a smile on her face, Kate hurried to her. "He's alive. The bullet's out."

"Oh Lord," Jessie sighed, closing her eyes. They'd ridden more than twenty-four hours straight without stopping for food or water. The stress and fear made her weak, and she swayed.

"Here now," Kate said quickly, wrapping her arm around Jessie's waist. "You need some looking after. Come in the other room and let Dr. Melbourne check you."

"The horses. I have to see to the horses. They need to be stabled and fed."

"And so do you," Kate said firmly. "Now don't argue. As soon as *you're* taken care of, I'll make sure your horses get to the livery."

"Charlie. Charlie Baker came down with us. He should be right outside somewhere. He can do it."

Kate briefly recalled passing a man in the dark, slumped in a chair just outside the door, on her wild rush inside. "I'll find him. Now come with me."

Too weary to think anymore, Jessie allowed Kate to lead her by the hand into the back room. When she saw Jed lying so quiet on the table, his eyes shut, his chest just barely moving, she bit her lip to stop the tears and looked quickly away.

"He's tough as one of those wild horses of yours, Montana," Mae said compassionately. "He wouldn't take kindly to you doubting him."

Jessie nodded.

"I don't think you need me any longer, do you, Doc," Mae said as Kate started to gently unbutton Jessie's shirt. There was something so private about the way Jessie kept her eyes fixed on Kate's face, as if Kate were all the strength she'd ever need, that Mae had to turn away.

"No, we'll be fine," Caleb said absently as he rummaged in the cabinet for more supplies. He did not notice as Mae followed the path Vance had taken a few moments before and disappeared through the back door.

Kate opened Jessie's wool shirt, saw the bloody tear in the thin cotton shirt she wore under it, and gasped. "Oh, Jessie."

"I'm okay," Jessie said swiftly, gathering her wits when she realized how frightening this must look to Kate. "It barely touched me."

"It touched you," Kate murmured, cupping Jessie's chin and brushing a thumb over her cheek. "That's all that matters."

"Just don't worry," Jessie said, trying not to grimace when Caleb wiped at the blood caked onto her side with a damp cloth.

"Don't be silly." Kate kept one hand on Jessie's shoulder as she watched the doctor work. She felt Jessie tremble. "I love you. I'm allowed to worry."

If Caleb Melbourne heard, or cared, he gave no sign of it. At length he straightened. "I'm going to tape a clean cloth over this. It should be changed three times a day and the area cleansed." He looked at Kate. "I'm quite sure you can take care of that."

"Yes," Kate said steadily.

"No riding for a couple of days."

"She won't," Kate answered before Jessie could protest.

Jessie motioned toward Jed. "How long will he need to stay here?"

"He shouldn't be moved very far for at least a week. We'll get him over to the hotel or Mae's place in a day or so."

"I need to go out to the ranch to see to things tomorrow," Jessie said. She swallowed. "The men are going to be pretty stirred up about this."

Caleb frowned. "You'd best see they don't go doing something crazy. I might have a good surgeon here, but that doesn't mean I'm in the market for more patients."

Jessie said nothing.

"Let's go home, Jessie," Kate said gently. She intended to find out exactly what had happened and what Jessie intended to do about it. But for now, all she wanted to do was hold her.

## CHAPTER FOURTEEN

It had started to rain, and it was so dark in the alley behind Doc Melbourne's that Mae could not see her way around the puddles.

"Lord, could this night get any worse," she muttered, lifting her dress. Her shoes were already a ruin. Her heart lurched when a form materialized from the shadows ahead of her, and she reached into the inner pocket of her dress for her Derringer. As the figure approached, she drew a breath and steadied her hand. She'd not be taken in an alley. What she did—and with whom—she did by conscious will.

"You shouldn't be out here," Vance said. "It's far too dark and inclement."

"Is there something wrong with your brain?" Mae snapped, her fear overriding her manners. Shaking now, she secured her gun and tucked it away. "I almost shot you."

Vance slid out of her coat and swept it around Mae's shoulders. "Well, at least I would have been close to treatment if you had. Where's your shawl?"

"I left my room in rather a hurry, if you'll recall." It was difficult for Mae to see Vance's face, as the moon had disappeared behind the storm clouds. Still, she could make out enough to know that Vance had been standing in the rain for a long time. Her hair was plastered to her forehead and neck, and the coat that Vance had covered her with was soaked through. Mae placed her palm against Vance's chest. "You're wet to the skin."

"As you will be, if you stand here much longer." Vance cupped Mae's elbow and guided her down the passageway toward the main street. "You should go straight home and get warm. Have some tea and a fire or—"

"And while I'm getting all comfortable, just what are you planning to do?" Abruptly, Mae halted, jerked her arm away, and faced Vance in the street. "Wander around until you catch your death?"

"I think that unlikely. I've lived outside in weather like this for far longer—"

"I'm sure you have. I'm sure you've seen things that no one else could understand even if you explained them," Mae said sharply, "but you don't have to now." She took Vance's hand and gripped her cold fingers. She didn't need to see her face to know that whatever had plagued her in the doc's office still had a hold on her. Her voice had a hollow ring to it, as if she had to force the words out from some deep place. "Come back with me and let me make us both some tea."

Vance hesitated, still trapped between worlds, part of her reeling from the images of battle, the other drawn to the strength and tenderness in Mae's touch. She sensed Mae shiver with cold, and that made her decision. "If you've whiskey for the tea, I could use some."

Mae wrapped her arm around Vance's waist. "Living where I do, that's one thing I never run out of. Come along, now. The street's turning into a river of mud."

Vance very rarely lamented the loss of her arm, because there were far greater things to mourn. But at that particular moment, she wished she had two just so she could lift Mae in her arms and carry her across the treacherous thoroughfare. She'd never had the desire to do anything of the sort before in her life, but she wanted it now like an ache in her bones. She contented herself with resting her hand in the center of Mae's back to guide her. "I'm sorry for the weather."

Mae laughed as they set out, splashing through the puddles they couldn't see and sliding in inches of deep mud. "Unless you called the rain, you've no need to be."

"A lady shouldn't have to—"

"I know you don't mean yourself, because I'll wager you've tramped through worse than this. And believe me," Mae gasped, hurrying the last few feet down the alley to the stairs, "so have I. I walked behind a wagon most all the way out here."

"Well, you shouldn't have to do anything of the kind now."

"Are you all right?" Mae asked quietly. "I know you were bad there for a little bit."

"I'm recovered, I believe. Thanks to you." Vance leaned against the building, one leg up on the first stair, the other on the ground. Mae stood close to her, one arm still resting on her hip, her body angled between Vance's legs. The eaves sheltered them from the worst of the rain, and the lights in the windows on the second floor provided enough illumination for Vance to see Mae's face. She brushed the wet tendrils of hair away from Mae's throat, allowing her fingers to linger on the sleek column of her neck. Mae's skin was cool but the blood beat hot just beneath her smooth skin. That unmistakable rush of life made her all too aware of the void in her own being, and she realized how easily she could feed off Mae's passion, taking, with nothing to offer in return. "You should go upstairs now and draw a bath. Get warm."

"I think I might," Mae said, trying to decipher the brooding look on Vance's face. Their bodies nearly touched, and the slow brush of Vance's fingers over her skin stirred heat in places that the far more demanding caresses she endured from others never awakened. She could return to the saloon, back to the noise and press of bodies and mindless coupling, or she could spin out this fragile thread that fluttered between them a little longer. "Join me."

Vance gasped, not at the unexpected invitation but at the image of intimacy that came instantly to her mind. Mae's pale skin shimmering with crystal droplets in the lamplight, her lids languid with heat. She dropped her hand away, but she could not step out of the reach of danger. Mae was so close to her that she could feel the outline of Mae's body curving into her own. "I…can't."

Emboldened by the storm that raged around them and by the terrible tension of what they had just done for Jed, Mae skimmed her mouth over Vance's lips. It was a fleeting kiss, but one that could not be called anything less. "Then come upstairs and have that drink."

When Mae turned and started up the stairs, a chill far colder than the night's enveloped Vance with such swiftness she shook under it. She looked up the stairs, and when Mae paused on the landing to glance down at her, she followed.

❖

"I don't want to leave him here alone," Jessie said, standing in the open doorway of the doctor's office and staring out into the rain. Doc Melbourne had sent them out, saying there was nothing anyone could do just now. Charlie had been waiting and, after getting word on Jed's condition, had gone off to deal with the horses. "I'll walk you to your parents' and then come back."

"You'll do nothing of the kind," Kate said, pulling her cloak around her shoulders. Jessie, she noted, seemed oblivious to the weather, but Kate feared it was more shock than toughness. The only time she'd ever seen Jessie so shaken was when *she'd* been sick with the grippe last winter, and she knew firsthand that Jessie was capable of running herself into the ground from worry. Kate intended to see that did not happen now. "Caleb said he wouldn't wake up until tomorrow at the earliest, but if you're set on staying, we'll *both* stay."

"We can't do that. Your parents don't know where you are. They'll be beside themselves." Jessie hunched her shoulders and stepped out, pulling the door partly closed to prevent the rain from pouring into the room. Her shirt was immediately soaked but she didn't mind. The biting cold seemed to get her blood going. In between being sick with worry, she'd mostly felt numb. When her father had died in a stampede, it had been over so fast that the pain had been a swift slice to her heart. This…watching Jed's life seep away, was killing her bit by bit. The only thing she'd ever experienced that had been worse was when Kate had been sick, and that had been as close to dying while still breathing she ever wanted to come. She swept her fingers over Kate's cheek. "Besides, you should get some rest."

Kate crossed her arms. "Oh, and you don't need any?" Now that the crisis was at least somewhat controlled, her fear was giving way to anger. Anger that it might have been Jessie on that table bleeding to death. Anger that somehow Jessie must have known this kind of danger was possible and hadn't told her. "When is the last time you've slept? Or eaten anything?"

"Kate—after the shootout, with Jed hurt so bad, I couldn't think of anything except getting him here." Jessie passed a weary hand over her face. "All I could think was that this was his only chance."

"I know, darling. I know." Kate couldn't argue with her. She sounded so tired, so fragile. It was so unlike her, and all Kate wanted to do was protect her.

"Maybe I was still too late."

"No. No, you weren't. Mae's right. He's very strong, and Vance did a miraculous job of getting the bullet out. You got him here in time. I know it."

"I'll feel better if I can keep an eye on him."

Kate smoothed both hands over Jessie's shoulders and down her arms until she clasped her fingers lightly. "Jed was like this when you were shot, too. He didn't want to move from this spot until we knew something." She drew Jessie's hands to her breast and pressed them over her heart. "But he went about taking care of things at the ranch because he knew you would want him to. He would want you to take care of yourself and the Rising Star."

Jessie tugged Kate close and leaned her forehead against Kate's. They stood in the shadows as the rain beat down around them, the night so black that the few lighted windows along Main Street looked like the disembodied eyes of wild animals lurking in the wilderness. Despite the eerie sense of isolation born of her fear and fatigue, Jessie had never felt so completely anchored to this earth as she did in this moment with Kate in her arms. "If you weren't here with me right now, I don't think I could make it until morning."

Kate kissed the base of her throat, then laid her cheek against Jessie's chest. "You could. But you don't have to. You won't ever have to."

With a sigh, Jessie wrapped her arm around Kate's shoulders. "Let's go somewhere and get out of this rain. I think I'll feel a whole lot better if I can hold you."

"I know that I will," Kate murmured.

"Lord," Jessie muttered as they left the shelter of the porch and ventured into the street. "I think you better go back inside, and I'll go see if I can find a buckboard to borrow. You can't walk all the way to your parents' house in this."

"Why don't we check the Nugget. There must be someone there we'll know who has a wagon. My father's probably at the newspaper office, but I expect he walked."

"You stay here, then, and I'll go to the saloon."

"It makes more sense for me to come with you, especially if we find someone to give us a ride."

Jessie hesitated for a moment, not wanting to subject Kate to the unsavory atmosphere in the saloon, but she could see the point of Kate's suggestion. "Okay, then." She took off her Stetson and put it on Kate's head. "Might help a little."

Laughing, Kate reached up and held the brim of the unfamiliar headwear. "Now you'll drown instead of me."

"I'm more used to it." Jessie put an arm around Kate and tilted her head down to keep the stinging water out of her eyes. As they set off in the direction of the saloon, she tried to angle her body so that the winds struck her first and not Kate. Raising her voice to be heard over the howling storm, she shouted, "Stay close when we get there."

Unconsciously, Kate gripped her bag more tightly and felt the weight of Mae's recent gift inside. She thought it best to show it to Jessie later, when she could explain how she had come to have it. Nevertheless, she liked knowing that she could protect them both, if necessary. "Don't worry. I'll be fine."

When they reached the board sidewalk on the opposite side of the street and ducked beneath the short roofs that protected the doorways, they could hear one another without shouting. Jessie wiped a wet sleeve across her face. "If this keeps up, there'll be flooding in the gulches up in the hills." She shook her head. "The foals can get trapped. I'll have to get men up there tomorrow."

"The men, not you," Kate said as they hurried along. "You're exhausted, and I'm not letting you go back out there again so soon."

Jessie clenched her jaws, remembering the sounds of gunshots coming from behind as she and her men had ridden toward one of the line camps. Ambushed on her own land. Bile rose in her throat and fury threatened to burn a hole in her gut. She'd be going back, and soon. *She* was the law on the Rising Star, and she intended to send a message that no one could threaten her men or her livestock. But she thought it best to bring that up in the morning, when Kate was more likely to see reason.

"I'm thinking I should stay at the hotel for a few days," Jessie said. "That way, I can ride out to the ranch to see to things and then come back to town in case…in case the Doc needs me for anything."

Kate grasped Jessie's arm and tugged her to a stop just outside the Golden Nugget. "If you want to stay at the hotel and not my mother's, I'll understand. But wherever you're sleeping tonight, so am I."

"Kate," Jessie murmured, drawing her close to the building so they were not visible to anyone passing by. She took Kate in her arms and kissed her, the churning fear that lingered in her stomach making her embrace rough as she gave herself over to the heat of Kate's mouth. She held her tightly, kissed her fiercely, drawing heart from Kate's supple strength. She drove deeper, drank hungrily, until she heard a faint moan. With a gasp, she pulled her mouth away. "I'm sorry for doing that here. I just—"

"No, don't," Kate whispered, struggling to capture the breath that had fled with the force of Jessie's need. "I need you, too." She leaned away, but kept her arms around Jessie's shoulders, where she had flung them to steady herself beneath Jessie's kiss. "I want to go home and explain to my mother what's happened, but then I think we'd better stay at the hotel. I'm going to want you to do that again."

"Good," Jessie said hoarsely, taking a step back and reluctantly letting Kate loose. "Because I'm going to."

## Chapter Fifteen

Just stay here," Jessie said, pointing to a dim corner near the bar, "and I'll search out a few people I know. Shouldn't take long to find us a ride."

"Yes, all right." Kate didn't mind waiting so much as she hated the idea of Jessie being able to move about freely, and free from worry, when she could not. She could hardly be upset with Jessie, though, when the unfairness was none of her doing. If she had to linger in the shadows, then she was determined to make the most of her time. She'd only been in the saloon a few times before, and then only during the afternoon—when there were very few people about—and for those few regrettable moments the evening before. Now it was crowded with cowboys, gamblers, and businessmen as well as Mae's girls. The atmosphere was rowdy and raucous and, she admitted, exciting. There was a definite sense of life being lived with no hint of caution, and that thrill was intoxicating all on its own. She saw Sissy slip underneath the staircase with a man in a well-cut suit. A railroad man, perhaps. Kate watched them absently to occupy her time, until she became aware that the fervent movements of both parties could only mean one thing. Then, when the man pushed his hand into the front of Sissy's dress and lifted her breast free, she stared only a second longer before averting her gaze. Such a thing was far too personal to be viewed by strangers, and she felt for Sissy that it should be happening under these circumstances at all.

"I see that I was grievously mistaken last evening," Phineas Drake said as he slid into a space beside Kate at the bar. "I erroneously mistook you for one of Mae's…friends." He caught her hand and lifted it as if to brush a kiss across her fingers. "My sincere apologies."

Carefully but firmly, Kate withdrew from his grasp. "You have nothing to apologize for, Mr. Drake. I *am* a friend of Mae's."

His expression darkened, and Kate caught a glimpse of his cold temper and flagrant disdain before his features smoothed into an unctuous smile. "I had hoped that you would do me the honor of your company, since you're in need of an escort. Seeing as you are a lady and there are some here who are, unfortunately, not gentlemen." He took her by the elbow in a light but commanding grip. "I have rooms just across the way. I'll have supper sent up. A fire will help dry your damp clothing."

"That's most kind, but I'm not here alone." When she tried to move away from him, he shifted subtly closer, his fingers tightening on her flesh. A shiver of alarm coursed down her spine and had her reaching into her bag for the comfort of her gun. She didn't seriously believe he would do anything to threaten her person in public, but the force of his repellent regard for her was nearly as frightening as a blow. "Please, don't trouble yourself as to my welfare."

"I'm afraid you don't appreciate the gravity of your circumstances—"

"I assure you, sir—"

Jessie appeared beside them, her eyes as dark as the thunderclouds that raged overhead. "Kate? Is something wrong?" She took a moment to see that there was no fear in Kate's eyes, because if there had been, she would not have hesitated to make the man whose hand still held Kate's arm pay for his arrogance. As it was, she pushed the flap of her coat behind her back so it would not impair her reach for her gun.

"No, there's no problem," Kate said calmly, having seen Jessie's movement out of the corner of her eye. Under ordinary circumstances, Jessie was levelheaded, but tonight, after the emotional and physical stress of the last few days, Kate did not trust her lover to contain her temper. "Did you find us a wagon?"

Jessie's eyes were still on Drake. "Your attentions are not welcome here."

Drake's expression was calculating, and he made no move to let go of Kate. His muddy brown eyes slowly scanned Jessie's face, then flicked downward to her holstered revolver and back up again. He shifted his hips so his own gun was visible. "I'm afraid we've never been properly introduced. At the moment, the lady and I are having a private—"

"No, we're done," Kate said firmly, wrenching her arm from his grasp. "I appreciate your concern, Mr. Drake, but I'm quite all right." She turned her back as much as the crowded space would allow and gripped Jessie's left hand to get her notice. She had to tug before Jessie looked away from Drake and met her eyes. "Let's go now."

"All right," Jessie said gently. She could hardly instigate a brawl with Kate so close, and as much as she wanted to strike out at Drake, or anyone who threatened what was hers, she knew she couldn't. Not tonight. "I've got a buckboard out back."

"Good." Kate didn't bother to say good night to Phineas Drake, but as she and Jessie made their way through the crowd toward the rear exit, she imagined she could feel his anger follow them. She didn't relax her hold on her bag until they were outside. Even the rain was a welcome comfort after the stifling heat and oppressive atmosphere inside.

Wordlessly, Jessie grasped her around the waist and helped her clamber up onto the board seat. Kate then took Jessie's hand to steady her as she scrambled up beside Kate. When Kate put her hand on Jessie's thigh, as she always did when they rode together, she felt the muscles tighten like ropes beneath her fingers. "It's all right, darling. Nothing happened."

"The bastard put his hands on you. I wanted to kill him."

"I'm very glad you didn't, because he is hardly worth having the sheriff come after you and put you in jail." It was pitch black behind the saloon, and Kate leaned close and kissed Jessie's cheek. "We're getting soaked again."

Jessie shifted on the seat to face Kate, the reins held loosely in her gloved right hand. "What exactly do you have in your bag, Kate?"

"You're very observant, Jessie Forbes," Kate said with a rueful laugh.

"Well, I know it's not gold, but it's got to be something pretty close, the way you've been holding on to that since we left Doc Melbourne's. And I saw you reach into it from clear across the room back there in the Nugget."

For a second, Kate considered trying to postpone the discussion, but she had no reason not to explain, and it was unfair to worry Jessie any further. She opened her bag and held it up so Jessie could see. "Mae gave it to me this afternoon."

Jessie reached in and extracted the Derringer. "Did she show you how to shoot it, too?"

"Not yet, but under the circumstances, I thought I was too close to miss."

"Lord, Kate," Jessie groaned. "You weren't really planning on shooting him, were you?"

"Weren't you?"

"Well, yes, but…" Jessie trailed off with a slow nod of her head. She carefully replaced the gun and handed back the bag. "First thing tomorrow, we'll have a lesson."

❖

Mae unlocked her door and held it for Vance. "You go on ahead. I'll just be a minute while I find someone to take care of the bath water." She handed Vance the soaked suit coat. "Hang this up to dry somewhere, too."

Inside the room, Vance shook out the dripping coat and draped it over the back of a chair. Then she knelt by the small hearth and stacked several logs. She found matches in the inside pocket of her vest that were miraculously still dry and started the fire. She turned at the sound of the door opening. A young man in pants several inches too short and a voluminous shirt that must have belonged to an older brother bustled in carrying two steaming pails of water. He did not look in her direction, and she suspected that he thought her one of Mae's customers. The thought made her smile bitterly as she considered that in many ways she *was* like some of the lonely, dispossessed people who found comfort in the arms of a tender woman. She turned her back to the room, ignoring the continued activity behind her, and watched the struggling flames flicker and finally catch. She would not come to Mae offering nothing but a broken spirit. It was enough that she allowed Mae to comfort her with her words and gentle touches. Those she imagined Mae gave willingly and often, because that's the kind of woman she was. As hard as Mae's life had been, her heart remained generous and kind.

"What are you thinking about so hard, Vance?" Mae had been watching Vance, who'd stood with her arm braced against the mantle, head down, staring into the fire, for more than a minute. The story that was written across Vance's stark features was easy to read, even if Mae couldn't discern each of the details. Loneliness was common enough out here—hell, anywhere—but the terrible sadness that radiated from Vance's still form made Mae's heart ache.

"You, actually," Vance said quietly. She faced Mae and rested her shoulder against the side of the fireplace.

"I was hoping that thinking of me might make you look a little happier," Mae said as she approached.

Vance braced herself for a touch, because the slightest contact from Mae tended to unbalance her. "I was thinking how extraordinary you are."

Blushing, Mae halted abruptly an arm's length from Vance. "I'm used to people…men…saying I'm beautiful, but I—"

"You *are* beautiful."

Mae waved a hand impatiently. "Stop that talk so I can finish my thought."

Vance grinned and settled with her back fully against the wall, her legs crossed at the ankles, her hand in her pocket. "Go ahead."

Now it wasn't Vance's words that drove every thought from her mind, but the sight of her all long and lean and her dark hair still dripping wet. Despite that, her face revealed just a touch of arrogance that Mae found quite appealing. "The water's going to get cold."

Vance said nothing, but it was suddenly very hard to breathe as Mae reached for the laces on her bodice. "Mae—"

"Don't talk," Mae whispered as she loosed the ties. The dress slid from her shoulders to reveal the thin lace chemise that barely covered her nipples. "Just watch."

"I can't, not without dying." The dress fell to the floor. She wore silk and little else below. Vance turned her head away. "The most I've ever done is kiss a woman. And then, I was young and I was…it was before."

The pain in Vance's voice was so raw Mae shuddered. She would never willingly do anything to put that sound there, so she slipped behind the dressing screen and quickly removed the rest of her clothes.

She pulled on her China blue robe, and when she emerged, found Vance struggling to put on the still wet coat. "Put that down," Mae said as she walked over to Vance. "Now hold still."

"No," Vance said sharply as Mae reached for the buttons on her vest. She grasped Mae's wrist to stop her. "Please. No."

Mae looked up into Vance's eyes. "I'm not going to hurt you. I'm going to put you into the tub, which is what I should've thought of doing to begin with. You're the one who went through hell in that room back there, not me. You're the one who stood out in the rain. You're the one who's shaking with cold."

"It's not all the cold," Vance whispered.

Tenderly, Mae touched Vance's face. "I know. I didn't realize you'd be scared. I'm sorry."

Vance closed her eyes, but kept hold of Mae's hand, preventing Mae from undressing her any further. "Maybe we can just…sit together by the fire."

"And waste all that hot water? At least one of us is getting a bath before we do anything else." Carefully, Mae shook off Vance's hand and finished unbuttoning her vest. Then she started on her shirt. "I think you should be first." When she finished opening all the shirt buttons she waited to remove the garment. "Open your eyes. I want you to see that there's nothing about you that bothers me."

"Why are you doing this?" Vance whispered.

"Because I like looking at you." Shorter by two inches—and without her shoes, even more—Mae raised up on her tiptoes and glanced another kiss over Vance's mouth. "Because I like touching you." She took Vance's face in both hands and kissed her with intent. Slowly, she moved her lips on Vance's, accustoming herself to the taste and texture of her. She played her tongue lightly just inside Vance's mouth, enjoying the slick smooth heat and the barest whisper of Vance's tongue meeting hers. When she drew away, she knew she'd only skimmed the surface of passions buried so deep it might take a lifetime to search them out. "Because you make things come alive inside of me that I thought had died and disappeared forever."

"What things?" Vance rasped. "Pity? I don't want you taking care of—"

Mae pressed her fingers to Vance's lips. "You'd best stop before you say something that's really going to get me riled. Maybe back East people pity someone like you, someone who paid the price for doing what she felt was right. Out here, we respect it." She moved her hand beneath Vance's chin, her fingers stroking her neck. "Now I'm going to take your shirt off and see what's been done to you. And if it makes me cry, it's not because I pity you. It's because I can't undo the hurt that you've suffered."

"You already *have*." Vance jerked her head away, grabbed Mae around the waist, and dragged Mae against her body. And then she took her mouth with all the fury of those long months of pain and loneliness. Yearning and need and desire tangled in the crush of lips and teeth and tongue. She could feel Mae's naked body beneath the silk, could feel the heat—the *life*—in her, and she desperately grasped for it like a drowning man clutched at rocks in a rushing river. "Oh, Mae," she moaned. "Mae."

Mae had to fight to gather enough breath to speak, but she knew, knew in her heart despite her terrible desire for Vance, that this was not the time. It was the time for *her,* but not for Vance. If she took Vance to her bed, it would be like letting a man who'd been lost in the desert for weeks drink himself to death at the first taste of water. They would have a few minutes, a few hours even, of unbearable pleasure in one another's arms, and in the morning, Vance would walk away and never come back. It had never mattered so much that that not happen. Trembling, heart on fire, Mae braced her hands against Vance's shoulders and pushed her gently away. "I want you in my bed. Do you hear me?"

Vance—chest heaving, eyes glazed—nodded mutely.

"I want you, but not when we're both so hungry we'll tear each other to pieces." She grasped handfuls of Vance's shirt when Vance tried to back away. "*Listen* to me. You're not alone. I feel what you feel. I need what you need." She took Vance's hand and eased it inside her robe, then pressed Vance's palm over her breast where her heart lurched wildly. "Feel what you've done."

Vance dropped her head with a groan as she cupped Mae's breast. She'd never touched another human being with passion, and now she could think of nothing else. "I need you. Please. I can't stop."

Laughing softly, Mae clasped Vance's wrist and moved her hand from her breast. "Now I know you're just playing on my sympathy."

Shakily, Vance laughed and her mind cleared a fraction. "I was hoping you'd find it in your heart to be charitable, considering how I've been…wounded and all."

"Oh, I might find a soft spot or two for you in my heart." Mae backed toward the other room where the tub awaited, pulling Vance along by her hand. "Now I want you in the tub with me."

Mae's robe had fallen open and her breasts were bare. They were full and firm and rose-kissed. Her body was hot and passionate. She was beautiful. But what gave Vance the courage to answer was the tender welcome in Mae's eyes.

"Yes," Vance said quietly. "I want that, too."

## CHAPTER SIXTEEN

Oh my goodness!" Martha Beecher stood in the middle of the kitchen with her hand pressed to her heart, her gaze darting from Kate to Jessie. "Whatever has happened! Kate—look at you, you're soaked. You're sure to get ill again behaving this way." She cast a quick but disapproving glance in Jessie's direction.

"We're quite all right, Mother," Kate said with the slightest hint of ire. After all she'd experienced that evening, such fuss over a little bit of rain felt ridiculous. "We just need to get into some dry clothes and everything will be fine."

"Go on into the parlor and stand by the fire," Martha instructed. "I'll make some tea."

As Kate and Jessie started from the room, Martha gasped and caught Jessie's arm. Anxiously, she asked, "Is that blood on your shirt? Are you hurt?"

"It's just a scratch. I'm fine, thank you," Jessie said quietly.

"What's happened?" This time, Martha spoke calmly, as if the true gravity of the situation had settled her nerves.

Jessie glanced quickly at Kate, who nodded. "Horse thieves shot at me and some of my men up in the hills yesterday. My friend Jed is at the doc's right now."

"Is it serious?"

"Yes, ma'am." Jessie's voice trembled and she reached for Kate's hand.

Kate moved quickly to Jessie's side and slipped an arm around her waist, hugging her close. "Tea would be good, Mother, if you could make some. We're both chilled."

Martha regarded the way Jessie leaned against Kate for support, heard the quiet steady strength in her daughter's voice, and saw, *truly* saw for the first time, the woman Kate had become. It was impossible to deny the powerful feelings between the two younger women, no matter how dearly she might have wished it otherwise. She remembered those terrible hours when she had thought she would lose Kate to illness. She recalled Jessie never moving from Kate's bedside and promising any sacrifice if Kate would only live. And after, when Kate was barely days from death's door, Kate's determination that nothing would keep her from being with Jessie, even if they had to leave the territory to be together. It was foolish to think that anything as petty as the small-mindedness of others would ever keep these two apart.

"Take Jessie upstairs to your room and get out of those wet things. I'll find some clothes of your father's that will fit Jessie well enough for now. You both need to get dry before you catch your death."

"Thank you," Kate whispered, hugging her mother tightly.

❖

The large tin tub stood behind the dressing screen in one corner of Mae's bedroom. Vance took comfort in the fact that the area was only dimly lit by a single oil lamp burning on the dresser on the far side of the bed, which took up the center of the room. She hoped that the scars on her chest and shoulder would blend with the shadows of the room and be less shocking, if no less unsightly. Even her father, a physician and a man used to seeing the worst of the human condition, had exclaimed at the state of the wounds the first time he'd seen her. To give him his due, however, she had only just arrived home from the hospital in Richmond and not everything had healed by that time.

"Whatever you're worrying about," Mae murmured, "it's probably a waste of good energy."

"Mae, you don't know—"

"You don't know where *I've* been, what I've seen," Mae whispered, slipping both hands beneath the edges of Vance's open shirt and pressing her palms to Vance's chest. "Stand still now and be quiet. Let me see you." When she felt Vance shiver violently, she added, "Put your hand inside my robe, on my waist. Hold me."

With a shuddering breath, Vance parted Mae's robe completely and curved her arm around Mae's waist.

"Ready?" Mae leaned into Vance's body and kissed her throat.

"Yes."

Mae skimmed her hands from Vance's chest to her shoulders and over her upper arms, pushing off her shirt. It fell to the floor next to the tub behind them. Vance's pale skin shimmered like silver in the lamplight. Her breasts were small and taut, her chest lean and tightly muscled like the rest of her body. A patch of scar tissue, the skin pebbled and rough, stretched from the outer edge of her left breast around her side. Carefully, Mae stroked the uneven surface.

"Is it painful?"

"No," Vance rasped, keeping her eyes on Mae's face. "Not when you do that. Sometimes…sometimes when I'm tired, or I've ridden for a long time, it gets sore."

"Does it help to touch it?"

Vance laughed unsteadily. "I don't know. It feels rather nice just at this moment."

Mae kissed the tip of Vance's chin. "You might not be thinking altogether clearly right now. We'll have to find out later."

"All right." Vance was having a hard time sorting out all the conflicting feelings that were warring inside her. Mae was so close that the heat of her body penetrated Vance's trousers, warming her thighs and pelvis. Mae's perfume, a bold scent sweetened by Mae's own distinctive flavor, assaulted her senses, making her dizzy with desire. Her belly was tight with longing, and she wanted to touch Mae everywhere. The brief wonder of Mae's breast in her hand was almost all she could think about. If she'd been whole, if she'd had two arms, she would never have stood so quietly, waiting. She would have touched Mae the way she hungered to, would have given free rein to the fire that was rapidly consuming her sanity. She remembered what Mae had said just moments before. *I feel what you feel. I need what you need.* She had to believe that, or her feelings of impotence would drive her mad.

"You're still shaking. Are you still scared?" Mae asked tenderly.

"No. I…oh!" Vance stumbled back a step as Mae moved her hand from Vance's chest to what remained of her left arm.

"Tell me if I hurt you." Mae spoke slowly, taking care to keep her voice level and firm. She'd seen far worse than the stump that ended just above where Vance's elbow should have been. She'd seen men trampled by horses, women torn apart by deliveries gone wrong, children dead from the pox. Vance's arm ended in a rounded lump of scar tissue that was far less horrible than she would have expected. Still, this was the woman she cared for, and no matter how well healed the wound appeared now, she knew that the damage extended far deeper than flesh, and she ached for that pain. She did the only thing she could think to do. She curled her fingers gently around Vance's arm and tenderly kissed the scar.

Vance gasped again. It was so unexpected, so unlike anything anyone had ever done, that she couldn't take it in. Her knees gave way and the next thing she knew, her cheek was pressed to Mae's bare stomach as sobs racked her body. Dimly, she was aware of Mae stroking her hair, her neck, her shoulders. Mae was saying something, crooning words that had no meaning but that caressed and soothed the raw weeping places in her soul. "Sorry," she choked out, "sorry."

Tears streaked Mae's cheeks unheeded. She had not imagined it possible that something as simple as a kiss could do this to one so strong, so brave. Brokenly, she whispered, "It's all right, sweetheart," although she doubted the truth of her own words. Sometimes there was nothing to do but to live with the pain.

"I wish…" Vance rubbed her cheek against Mae's skin. Desire warred brutally with need, and it was the need she feared more than loneliness. The desperate longing to be comforted, to be healed, that she'd kept chained for so long was dangerously close to escaping now. Unleashed, it would swallow her alive and destroy any hope of friendship with Mae. "I wish I had come to you whole."

Mae bit back her sharp protest, because she understood pride and independence. She understood too that Vance would allow nothing to grow between them until she was certain that the feelings rose from love, and not pity. "Looking at you pleases me to no end." She caressed Vance's tear-streaked face. "And you're about as brave a person as I've ever met."

Sighing, Vance closed her eyes. "I don't see what you see."

"I know." For an instant, Mae pressed Vance's face hard against her body, then gently pushed her away a few inches. "Vance, you're getting chilled. Let's both get in the tub so I can hold you."

After a moment, Vance got unsteadily to her feet and fumbled with the buttons on her trousers. "If we wait much longer, it will be cold."

Mae smiled. "I don't think we're going to notice."

"You're the only person other than the doctors and nurses and my father, who's a doctor, too, who has touched me there."

"I didn't mean to open old hurts." She brushed Vance's hand aside and finished unbuttoning her trousers for her.

Vance trailed her fingers through Mae's curls as she worked, then dipped her head and kissed Mae softly. "You didn't. Sometimes healing hurts."

Nodding silently, afraid that *she* might burst into tears now, Mae pushed Vance's clothing down and shed her own robe. She stepped into the tub, settled down with her back against one end, and held out her hand. "Come sit against me."

Carefully, Vance climbed in and eased down between Mae's legs so her back nestled against Mae's front. The water was still warm, and, despite her exhaustion, at the first contact with Mae's body, she came instantly awake. Mae's breasts pressed against her back, and when Mae angled her legs over Vance's beneath the water, the intimate contact caused her skin to flush with heat. Vance groaned and let her head fall back against Mae's shoulder. "I never want to move."

Mae nuzzled Vance's neck and wrapped both arms around her waist. "Then we won't."

Lazily, Vance turned her head and kissed Mae's neck. "The steam smells like you."

"It's the scent I use. I put some in the water."

"It does things to my insides."

"Nice things, I hope," Mae said a bit breathlessly. Everywhere their bodies touched, which was everywhere possible, her skin tingled. Her breasts were full and aching to be caressed. She was hot and pulsing below, desperately needing to be filled. Still, she only smoothed her hand up and down Vance's belly while pressing her cheek to Vance's throat. What there was between them was not to be hurried, but to be savored. This moment was about trust as much as passion.

"Wonderful things." Vance caught Mae's hand and drew it to her breast, stiffening when Mae's fingers glanced over her nipple. She groaned softly. "I've never been like this with anyone before. Man or woman."

"I wish I could say the same thing to you." Mae closed her eyes and kissed Vance's temple. "I'm sorry that I—"

"Don't." Vance kissed Mae's hand before shifting until she could look into Mae's face. "Nothing you have ever done or ever *might* do will matter more to me than what lies between us." She kissed Mae's lips, gently at first, then more demandingly. She kissed her first with reverence, then with desire. She kissed her, taking her time, exploring her mouth as she wished to explore all of her, body and soul. The hunger to possess her, to be possessed *by* her had not abated, but she discovered with each passing second that there was something beyond need. There was knowing. Above all, she wanted to know Mae, in her heart as well as her body. When she drew back from the kiss and settled once more into Mae's arms, her head resting on Mae's shoulder, she murmured, "I just wanted you to know why I might not be so…adept…at some things. If we do…"

"When." Mae laughed breathlessly and caressed Vance's chest, skimming her breasts just enough to appease her longing for her. "Lord, if you were any better, my heart might climb right out of my chest."

Vance smiled, a lazy, pleased smile. "My brother always had a way with the ladies. I never thought to experience such things for myself."

"But you knew you had…feelings…in that direction?"

"Yes. I didn't recognize exactly what they were at first, because as I'm sure you're aware, such matters are rarely discussed. But there was one girl in my medical school class. We were close, good friends." Vance sighed. "Our fondness led to the beginnings of something more intimate, but then the war came and…everything changed."

"Your brother? Where is he?"

Vance found Mae's hand and clasped her fingers. She closed her eyes and said, "Victor and I were twins. We did everything together from the time we were children. We went to different medical schools, but we often saw patients together. When the war came and Lincoln called for physicians, we enlisted together, too." She smiled. "It was Victor's idea for me to cut my hair and borrow his clothes so we could sign up for the same regiment. He knew I would find a way to go, and we always had more fun together than apart." She shivered although the water still held some heat. "We served in the same regiment for the first year and a half. There were very few formally trained surgeons, and before long we were both promoted to brigade surgeon. The Union forces fought on several fronts, and we ended up being separated. The mail, what there was of it, often took months to catch up to us when we were in the field. I hadn't heard anything from him for the last six months of the war."

Mae waited, saying nothing when Vance fell silent, but she recognized the hollow note in Vance's voice for what it was. Terrible loss. She tightened her arms in a futile attempt to shield Vance from a pain that had already struck her heart.

"I didn't know until I finally returned to Philadelphia upon my release from the hospital that Victor had been killed in the fall of Richmond just a few weeks before I was shot." Vance turned her face to Mae's neck. "I'll always wonder if I'd been with him if I could have saved him."

*Not whether he could have saved you.* Mae kissed Vance's forehead. "I'm sorry."

"Victor's death nearly destroyed my father. My…injury was more than he could cope with. Our relationship was never the same again, and when I wanted to leave Philadelphia, he contacted Caleb Melbourne on my behalf. I think he was glad when I left."

"Surely he didn't blame you for what happened."

"Not exactly. He didn't know either of us had enlisted, although he wouldn't have been able to stop us. We wrote to him once we arrived at our first post, and he tried to get me to come home." She sighed. "When I finally did come home, I was a reminder of everything he'd lost."

"I'm sorry about Victor, but I'm so very glad that you survived."

"Thank you," Vance whispered. She had once hoped to hear similar words from her father, but hearing them now, from the woman she was coming to treasure, meant even more.

"You're trembling." Gently Mae moved Vance forward, stood, and stepped from the tub. "Let me get a blanket."

By the time Vance climbed out, Mae had a blanket ready to wrap around her shoulders. "You'll get cold, too," Vance protested. She took one edge of the blanket and drew it around Mae so they were both covered. "I don't know how it is that I end up telling you things I never speak of with anyone else."

"Because," Mae said with a small smile, embracing Vance within the confines of their makeshift shelter, "I want to know."

Vance rested her cheek against Mae's hair. "I'm so glad."

"Come to bed," Mae said. When Vance tensed, she shook her head and kissed the hollow at the base of Vance's throat. "I want you to hold me. That's all."

Vance wanted more at the same time as she feared it, and because of that uncertainty, she was grateful that Mae did not demand greater intimacy. "Are you sure? What about the others?"

"Lord, Vance," Mae said with a laugh. "You don't think it matters to anyone who shares a bed here, do you? No one will take note, and even if they did, what of it? Unless you don't want anyone to—"

"No," Vance said fiercely, silencing Mae with a kiss. "I just don't want to cause trouble for you."

Mae felt the sudden threat of tears again, unable to recall when the last time had been that anyone had worried about her. "The only trouble for me would be if you left me now, seeing's how I have a terrible need to be with you."

Vance rested her forehead against Mae's. "And for tonight, just holding will be enough?"

"It will be just right."

When she settled in bed on her side and Mae came into the curve of her body, Vance discovered that Mae was correct. Nothing she'd ever known had felt so right. Mae's heart beat against her breast, Mae's thigh fit perfectly between her thighs, Mae's breath caressed her throat like a soothing balm. She wrapped her arm around Mae's shoulders and cupped the back of Mae's neck, caressing her gently. "I don't know that I'll sleep tonight," Vance said. "You feel too wonderful to miss a second of being with you."

"You don't have to worry," Mae murmured, melting into Vance as if they had been in one another's arms a thousand times before. "This won't be the last time."

With that assurance playing through her mind, Vance closed her eyes and slept. For the first time in a thousand nights, she did not dream of death.

# Chapter Seventeen

Jessie paced to the window and flicked the curtain aside, even though there was nothing to see outside in the dark. From the sounds of men shouting in the street below, she wasn't the only one wide awake. "Lord, Kate, I don't know how I'm going to sleep tonight. It would've been better if you'd stayed with your parents."

"No, it wouldn't," Kate said calmly as she leaned over and turned down the oil lamp before unbuttoning her dress and slipping it off over her head, leaving only her chemise and stockings. She sat on the edge of the bed to remove her undergarments. "I would lie awake worrying about you, and you would undoubtedly stay awake doing just what you're doing now, and neither one of us would have changed what's going to happen."

"Kate, I—" The protest died on Jessie's lips when she caught a glimpse of Kate slipping naked beneath the rough cotton sheets. Unsettled in an entirely new way than just seconds before, she leaned against the window casing, her arms crossed. "You could be safely tucked away at home right now instead of climbing into an uncomfortable bed in a noisy hotel."

"Jessie," Kate said quietly. "It's somewhere in the middle of the night. It's been a hard, frightening few days for you and I've missed you terribly. How you could think that I would let you sleep alone now escapes reason." She patted the bed beside her. "I know it's because you're worn out and scared for Jed that you could even question why I'm here. For now, just accept that I need you."

"You need me." Jessie said the words as if they had been spoken in a strange language. "Sometimes it scares me how much *I* need you." As she had the first afternoon that Kate had spent with her, Jessie crossed to the bed, unbuttoning her shirt as she walked. As she had that day as well, she unbuckled her gun belt and hung it on the bedpost.

"I love you," Kate said, watching Jessie unbutton her pants and step free, marveling just as she had a little over a year before at how beautiful and strong she appeared. She moved over to make room as Jessie removed her long johns and settled beside her. "And I need you terribly. It's all rolled up in what we share."

Jessie gathered Kate into her arms and buried her face in Kate's hair. She lay silently for several minutes as Kate stroked her back and her shoulders and her chest. She breathed in Kate's scent, listened to her heartbeat, concentrated on each small point where their bodies touched. As the essence of Kate filled her up inside, she sensed the bruised and bleeding places starting to heal. She wasn't aware of her tears until Kate's fingers brushed over her cheek.

"Tell me," Kate whispered.

"When they started shooting I couldn't really believe it. I knew what was happening, but I couldn't take it in. They were trying to kill me, on my own land."

Kate's heart was seized with a sudden chill. She knew firsthand the dangers that nature and accidents wrought upon the unsuspecting or unlucky. She had learned to accept that part of the life she had chosen. Now she added human treachery to the forces that threatened Jessie and their life together. Anger mixed with her fear and worry. "Will you be able to catch them?"

"I don't know. If they were only stealing a few to sell to the army or a passing wagon train, they could be a hundred miles away by now. If they're aiming to cut out a big part of the herd and drive them south to market, we'll run into them again."

"And if you do?"

Jessie answered instantly. "Then we'll hold them accountable for what they did to Jed."

"You mustn't go out there without more men."

"Don't worry, there won't be any shortage of hands willing to go."

"There's nothing I can say that will prevent you from going, is there?"

"Don't ask it of me, Kate. You know I will do anything I can to make you happy, but..."

Kate pressed her fingers to Jessie's mouth. "Shh. I'm not asking. I wouldn't. As much as I would like you to stay home where it's safe and let Jed and the men take care of these problems, I know that you can't. And I know that you might try if I asked you." She leaned close and kissed Jessie's forehead, then her eyes. "Which is why I won't."

"Thank you," Jessie whispered.

Kate doubted that Jessie would ever know what it cost her to say those words, but loving Jessie meant letting her *be* Jessie, so Kate kissed her softly and held her more tightly. "You're welcome."

Jessie raised up on her elbow so she could look into Kate's face. "Your mother was different with me tonight. Almost like...she was saying it was okay. About us."

"It *is* okay, darling," Kate murmured, fisting her hands in Jessie's hair. Jessie had long since removed the leather tie she usually used to hold it back, and it fanned out just above the spot where her collar touched the back of her neck. In the day, in the sunlight, it shone like the gold that the miners chased in the hills and rivers that surrounded them, but as it streamed between her fingers, it felt like the finest silk. Caught up in the vision of sunlight and heat that was her lover, Kate pushed Jessie onto her back and followed. She stretched out along Jessie's smooth, lean form, settling into her, body to body and heart to heart.

"Kate," Jessie murmured hoarsely. "I don't know if I can—"

"You don't need to." Kate kissed Jessie's mouth, her throat, her breast. "I will."

With a groan, Jessie closed her eyes and arched under Kate, willing to be commanded. Kate's were the only hands she trusted to guide her. Kate was the only person with whom she could be less than strong, less than sure. She trembled as Kate lavished attention on her breasts, her belly, her thighs. She cried out softly when Kate's mouth found her and again when she dissolved beneath the heat and relentless tenderness of Kate's caress. When Kate returned to her arms, Jessie pressed her face to Kate's throat. "When you love me, I'm not afraid anymore."

Kate framed Jessie's face, softly tracing Jessie's cheekbones and jaw before kissing her gently. "You are my home." She kissed Jessie's breast above her heart. "This is my life." She smiled and shook her head. "I guess stubborn is the other side of strong, and you've got plenty of both."

Jessie grinned and bumped her hips, rolling Kate over. She played her finger down the center of Kate's chest. "I'd say we're pretty even there. You were the one with the gun in her bag all set to do in that snake in the Nugget."

"That just shows I have good sense," Kate replied primly. She caught her breath unevenly as Jessie's fingers skimmed lower, dancing between her thighs. She clutched Jessie's arm as a quiver of excitement shot through her. "I miss lying with you at night when you're out on the trail."

"I'm careful, Kate," Jessie whispered, slowly working her way down Kate's body. She rested her cheek against Kate's stomach and looked up, studying Kate's face in the moonlight. "I'm always careful because I want to come back to you."

"Promise me you always will," Kate gasped.

"I will. Always." Jessie eased inside her with the joy of a lost voyager returning home. Slowly at first, then—as passion eclipsed wonder—with deeper, more demanding strokes, she carried Kate to the peak and over. When Kate's quiet moans of contentment stilled, Jessie slipped out to hold her again. "When I wake up in the morning and see you lying next to me, I don't think I could love you more. When I look across the yard and see you on the porch, carrying water or stacking wood or any of the other dozens of things you do, I don't think I could love you more. When I'm with you like this, when you've touched me in the places no one else sees, and you've let me touch you back, I don't think I could love you more." She kissed the tip of Kate's chin, then her lips. "Every day, I love you more."

Kate wrapped her arms around Jessie's shoulders and pulled her down tight against her. With her mouth against Jessie's ear, she whispered fiercely, "You are my heart. I love you so."

"As soon as Jed can travel safely, I want to bring him back to the Rising Star," Jessie said. "I want him to be looked after with his friends around him."

"Of course. I'm sure I can do whatever needs to be done."

Jessie shook her head. "I'm not asking you to do that. I can—"

"You can, and you will. But not alone." Kate gave Jessie a small shake. "Heavens, didn't we just have this conversation a few weeks ago?"

Jessie smiled and snuggled against Kate's shoulder. "Might be we need to have it a few more times."

"As many times as it takes," Kate said drowsily. "Go to sleep, darling."

"It will be morning soon. I'll try not to wake you."

Softly, Kate laughed. "You always say that, but I always know when you leave me."

Jessie smiled. "I'm glad."

"So am I."

❖

At the crack of gunfire, Vance shot upright. When another volley reverberated, closer this time, she threw herself over the wounded soldier beside her. "Stay down! Enemy fire."

The ground heaved with the force of cannonballs gouging its surface, and the torn earth rained down upon her, a deadly shower of mud and blood. She groaned as fire scorched her flesh, and she pressed the body beneath her down more forcefully.

"Vance, what is it?" Mae cried, awakened from a sound sleep by Vance's shouts. She pushed instinctively at the heavy weight pinning her to the bed, then relented when she realized she might hurt Vance unknowingly. Instead, she forced herself to lie still and stroked Vance's back. She cradled Vance's head against her breasts, shaken to find that Vance's hair was soaked with sweat and her body ice cold. "Oh, sweetheart, it's all right. It's outside. Some fool is shooting outside in the street."

"Shooting," Vance said urgently. "Someone is shooting."

"It's outside," Mae repeated. The room was growing light, so it had to be close to dawn. She caught Vance's chin in her hand and forced Vance to look at her. She waited until Vance's dark eyes cleared and focused on her face. "No one is shooting at us. We're safe. You're all right."

Vance frowned, struggling to orient herself before memories of the previous evening returned and she realized where she was. Then she became aware, all too acutely, just *exactly* where she was—lying naked on top of Mae's similarly naked body. With a start, she rolled away onto her back, her chest heaving with the remnants of her nightmare and an altogether different kind of excitement. She'd never experienced the touch of another's body all along the length of her own before, and Mae was lush and warm and arousing.

"You here with me now?" Mae asked as she reached for Vance's hand. Abruptly, pain stabbed at her heart when she realized she was lying on Vance's left side and there was no hand to find. She rolled closer and reached across Vance's stiff body until she could clasp her fingers. "Vance, honey?"

"You see why I shouldn't be lying with you," Vance said, forcing each word out through a throat tight with anger. "I could've hurt you."

"I was the one who almost hurt you," Mae pointed out in what she thought was a reasonable voice considering the swell of fear that coursed through her at Vance's words. It had been a long time since anyone had frightened her. Hurt her body, perhaps, but not her heart. She stroked Vance's face. "I'm not hurt."

Vance turned her head away. "You could've been. I do things sometimes in my sleep." She laughed unevenly. "I broke an antique lamp one night and had a hard time explaining that to my father in the morning."

"I'm not china, and I don't break easily."

"That's not the point, Mae." Vance withdrew her hand from Mae's grasp and pushed herself up on the bed. "*I'm* the one who's broken. I've got no business being here."

"What is it you think I need, Vance?" Mae said, heat in her voice now. She sat up, too, unmindful of the sheet falling away and leaving her body bare. "I haven't asked you to do anything for me. I've been taking care of myself for quite some time."

"And I'm not asking you to take care of me." Vance swung her legs over the side of the bed, waiting until she felt steadier before she stood.

"Lord," Mae sighed. "I'm not offering to. What I had in mind was sharing a little comfort and a little pleasure."

Vance said nothing, because she knew it would be far more than that for her. "I appreciate it." She stood and scanned the room, trying to recall where she'd left her pants. "I should get over to the office to check on Jed. I shouldn't have left Caleb alone there all night."

"It hasn't been but a few hours," Mae pointed out as she rose and pulled on her robe. "And you needed some rest."

"I'm sorry I disturbed yours." Vance pulled on her shirt and started working the buttons through the holes.

"You didn't." Mae pushed Vance's hand aside and buttoned her shirt. "I've seen what your spells look like now. Awake and asleep. Is this as bad as they get?"

"No." Vance looked past Mae to the gray light outside the window, feeling very much the same inside. Drained and desolate. "Sometimes they're worse."

The thought of being visited by such horrors made Mae's eyes dim with tears, but she quickly blinked them away, knowing that they would only hurt Vance's already bruised spirit. "Don't seem all that terrifying to me."

Vance smiled wearily. "I don't believe that I've ever met anyone like you."

Mae tilted her head back and met Vance's gaze. "I'll take that as a compliment since you seem to be short on those right now."

"I don't know why you would trouble yourself with me."

"I know you don't." Mae brushed a kiss across Vance's mouth. "That's probably why I do."

"I do need to see to Jed."

"And I need to be sure that everyone here is tucked safely away." Mae smoothed her hands over Vance's shirtfront. "I like the way you felt in my bed last night. I want you to come back."

"You're a beautiful woman." Vance played her fingers lightly over Mae's neck and underneath the edge of her robe to skim her collarbone. "A kind and tender woman."

"Vance—"

"Shh." Vance stepped away, letting her hand fall to her side. "I liked the way it felt to be in your bed last night. I'd like to come back, someday when I'm not empty inside. When there's something for me to give you."

"Maybe there already is," Mae whispered, "only you can't see it."

Vance nodded seriously as she collected her coat. "Maybe you're right. I hope you are."

"Don't stay away because you don't know how it will turn out," Mae called as Vance walked to the door. "Some things you only learn by doing."

"I'm not certain I'm as brave as you, Mae." Vance shook her head. "In fact, I'm quite certain that I'm not." She glanced over her shoulder as she reached for the doorknob. "I lost more than my arm."

"I don't know what it will take for those horrors to be undone, as much as they can be," Mae said, resisting the urge to go to her, to prevent her from leaving. "But I know you didn't lose the best part of you. You might have to trust me on that for a while."

Vance turned the knob but did not go out. "You make me wish for things I have learned to live without."

"Doing without and not wanting are different."

"Yes." Vance pushed open the door and stepped into the hall. "Good night, Mae."

Mae sat down on the edge of the bed as the door swung closed. She leaned her head against the bedpost and closed her eyes, remembering the way Vance had felt in her arms. *And what am I to do with the things you've made* me *want?*

## CHAPTER EIGHTEEN

Vance found Caleb asleep in the front room of the office with his feet up on the desk. She closed the door quietly behind her and started toward the dispensary area in the rear.

"He hasn't come around yet," Caleb said without opening his eyes.

"I'll stay with him now. You go on home."

Caleb eased his feet off the desk, his chair creaking in protest as he shifted his weight forward. Wearily, he rubbed at the stubble on his chin. "Must be about time to get up."

"It's going on six." Vance inclined her head toward the back room. "If you get a few more hours' sleep, you can spell me here later. Then I'll take care of the out calls."

"You spent most of yesterday on a horse, didn't you?"

Vance hesitated a second. The events of the day before seemed to be in the far-distant past. "I did, yes. But there's no reason I can't do it again."

"I wasn't entirely sure I needed help out here until you arrived," Caleb said as he stood and stretched. "Now I see that there's a lot of things that didn't get done because I didn't have time to do them before. There are a good many people who will be a lot better off because one of us will be able see to them more often. Since we're partners, we should share the work."

"I expect it will take a bit more time before I've earned that right," Vance said quietly.

"Out here, things are simpler than I expect you're used to. You're here, you're doing a good job, and I need you to keep doing it. That's all the time it takes for me to see how things should be."

With a shake of her head, Vance said, "I don't know that I would call your way of thinking *simple*. Practical, or perhaps honest."

Caleb shrugged. "The point is, life's too short to waste time thinking about how to live it. Best just to do it."

Vance thought of Mae's parting words and wondered if she really was afraid of living. She'd never thought of it before, never really considered her choices. The world was black and white and she knew her place in it. Now, with Victor gone, she was alone as she had never been before. She'd lost her home, her most intimate relationship, her sense of wholeness in less than a year. Along the way, she'd lost herself as well. She sighed. "I'd better see to him."

"I'll head on home for a while. See the missus and get something to eat." Caleb donned his hat and coat. "If something urgent comes up, send someone for me."

"I'll do that. Thank you."

He eyed her curiously. "For what?"

"For giving me this chance."

"Can't say as I've done anything except recognize a good deal when I see one. If it's something more than that for you, it's of your own making." He shrugged. "When you get down to it, everyone out here is working on another chance."

Vance smiled. "Then I guess I'm not so different."

"Nope," Caleb said as he opened the front door and breathed deeply of the crisp morning air. "Not much different where it counts. See you later, Vance."

"Good day, Caleb." When the door closed behind him, Vance opened the inner door and stepped into the dim back room. The air smelled of medicines and must and horses. The odor of death and decay that had been so pervasive in the hospital tents during the war was gone. As she approached the bed where Jed lay beneath a light cover, she saw his eyelids flicker. Quickly, she put her hand on his shoulder, anticipating his awakening.

"Jed," she said firmly, hoping to penetrate his drug- and pain-fogged mind. "You're at Doc Melbourne's. You've been shot, Jed, but you're still among the living."

Slowly, Jed opened his eyes, blinking rapidly. He clutched at the covers, as if they could shield him from further harm. He coughed and groaned quietly.

"I'm Dr. Phelps. You're at Doc Melbourne's now. We took the bullet out last night. You're doing very well."

"Where's Jess?"

Vance was caught off guard by the question and struggled to make sense of it. She hadn't paid any attention to the other cowboys who had been gathered near the office when she'd made her way in the night before. "I don't kno—" Jed pushed the covers back and struggled to sit. "Here now, don't try to get up."

The slightest pressure from Vance's hand on Jed's shoulder prevented him from rising. Frowning, he shifted in agitation beneath her restraining grip. "Is she hurt? Did they get her, too? I want to see her."

*Her.* Vance nodded in understanding, recalling Kate with the tall rangy blond the night before. Then she remembered where she'd first seen the unusual cowboy—the day she'd arrived on the stage they'd exchanged a few words in the street. So that was Jessie. *Kate's* Jessie, apparently, if the intimacy that was obvious between them meant anything. The night she'd escorted Kate home, Kate had said she'd found her love in New Hope. *Love for Jessie.* Vance was taken with a surge of wonder mixed with a bit of envy. This land was indeed filled with possibility.

"Jessie is fine," Vance said emphatically. "I expect she'll be along anytime. I'm going to give you something for your pain…and don't tell me you're not having any."

Jed closed his eyes. "I wasn't thinking I would."

"This won't take away all the discomfort," Vance said as she opened the bottle of laudanum. "Too much of this and you'll trade one misery for another."

"Don't want much of it."

"You needn't worry. I'll keep an eye on things." She rested the spoon against his lips and when he opened his mouth a fraction she tipped the liquid onto his tongue. She could remember the faintly bitter taste and the rapid spread of soothing heat through her bloodstream that softened her muscles, blunted her pain, and culminated in a blessed state of forgetfulness. On occasion she still succumbed to the need to escape, but a bottle of whiskey was all she would allow herself. The alcohol was far easier to leave behind the next day. "Go ahead and sleep."

When she was certain that Jed was resting comfortably, she returned to the front office, leaving the adjoining door ajar. She settled into Caleb's chair, propped her feet on the desk in the same scuffed spot where he obviously rested his with regularity, and closed her eyes. She did not expect to sleep; a light doze was all she usually was able to accomplish under any circumstances.

The thud of boot heels on wood brought her bolting to her feet, her hand on her revolver.

"Whoa," Jessie exclaimed, stopping abruptly. She recognized the doctor, but could tell from the wild fire in her eyes she'd been somewhere else just seconds before and wasn't quite altogether here even now. "I'm Jessie Forbes. That's my man back there. I've come to see him."

"I remember you." Vance took a deep breath and focused on the present. From the looks of the sunlight visible through the front windows, she'd been asleep for at least an hour, if not more. She couldn't remember dreaming, which was unusual. "He's probably asleep, but he was asking for you earlier."

Jessie's eyes lit up. "He was awake?"

"For a minute or so."

"So he's going to be all right?"

Vance walked to the dispensary door and closed it. "I don't know. The bullet came out cleanly but the wound is deep. He lost a fair amount of blood."

Jessie paled and forced her shoulders back, as if preparing for a fight. She studied the rail-thin, dark-haired doctor with the haunted eyes, trying to decide how much store to put in her opinion. She noticed her hand had relaxed and moved away from her sidearm. She'd come awake ready to fight, which meant she'd had to more than a time or two. Jessie respected that. The missing arm said a lot about her, too. Wounds like that killed most men. So she was strong as well as tough. Jessie judged that was as much as she needed to know. "What else?"

"In his favor," Vance went on, "he looks like a fighter."

Jessie smiled wryly. "I wouldn't want to take him on."

"That's good. He'll need to be tough." Vance settled a hip on the corner of the desk. "It'll be a few weeks before he's on his feet, if things go well. Another couple before he can ride."

"When can we move him to the ranch?"

"It might be better if he stayed in town. It would be easier for me or Doc Melbourne to check him, and he'll need some proper nursing."

"Mae would be willing to take care of him here," Jessie said. "She's done it before. She's done it for me. Still, I'd feel better if he was at the Rising Star."

"I didn't realize Mae did that kind of thing," Vance said quietly.

"There isn't much Mae can't do, and nothing she *wouldn't* do for a friend."

Vance heard the admiration and affection in Jessie's voice and felt a ripple of jealousy. Jessie Forbes gave every sign of being what Vance had once been—cocksure of herself, strong and fit, in charge of her life. She was also a handsome woman, clear eyed and well built. Vance could see her swinging Mae off her feet, Mae with her arms around those strong shoulders, laughing—

"Can I see him now?" Jessie asked.

"Yes," Vance said swiftly, forcing the painful images from her mind. "Of course."

❖

"Mae!" Kate called as she recognized her friend crossing the street toward the hotel. She hurried down the board sidewalk toward her.

"You're in town early," Mae said, lifting her skirts to climb the two stairs up to the raised walkway that ran along the front of the buildings.

"Jessie and I stayed at the hotel last night. Jessie has gone off to check on Jed. I was just on my way to the newspaper office to see if my father had come into work yet." Kate slipped her arm through Mae's. "What luck that I ran into you."

"I'm not usually up this early," Mae said wryly. "But since I am, I thought I'd get breakfast at the hotel."

"Oh, let's do. I couldn't keep Jessie still long enough to feed her. All she wanted was to see Jed. Then she was going to return the buckboard we borrowed last night and meet me back here."

"I imagine she'll be hungry once her worry is settled a bit." Mae paused as they neared the hotel. "You're really not fretting that there'll be gossip about us?"

Kate stopped and regarded Mae seriously. "Of course I'm not. You're my best friend."

"Lord, Kate," Mae said. "You're as stubborn as Jessie is. You just hide it better."

Laughing, Kate drew Mae inside. "It's a good thing I am, because between you and Jessie I've got my hands full."

They crossed the lobby, which was empty save for several worn sofas and chairs, to the dining room off to one side. To Kate's surprise, Rose Mason and her mother sat at one of the small tables having tea and biscuits. Rose's face lit up when she saw them, but Clarissa Mason's turned to stony disapproval.

"Kate!" Rose exclaimed, waving. "Come join us."

Kate saw Clarissa lean close to her daughter and whisper into her ear with some urgency, a disapproving admonishment Kate surmised. Suppressing a smile of satisfaction at the thought of Clarissa Mason's distress, Kate nevertheless shook her head. She had no desire to put Mae in a situation where she would be uncomfortable. "Thank you, but we wouldn't want to intrude."

"We were just about to leave," Clarissa Mason said brittlely.

"Oh, Mama," Rose objected. "You know Anna said she wouldn't be ready for our fitting for at least another hour." As Kate and Mae started toward a nearby table, Rose announced, "We're having dresses made with some of the material we brought back from Denver. They're going to be in the latest style."

"That sounds wonderful," Kate said with what she hoped was an appropriate degree of enthusiasm. She thought of her plans to adjust her own clothing to suit her new activities at the ranch and how appalled Rose would be at the outcome. How much her life had changed since coming to New Hope and finding Jessie. Finding herself. Although never as interested in fashion and social dealings as her girlfriends had been, she now found such concerns frivolous in the extreme.

"You go on ahead, Mama. I know you want to talk to Mrs. Frankel at the store. I'll have tea with Kate and…" Rose stared at Mae with added interest.

"I'm so sorry for my bad manners," Kate said, turning aside for a moment to ask for tea and biscuits from the boy who had come out from the kitchen to inquire. She smiled at Rose, who hurried to join them despite a disapproving cluck from her mother. "This is my friend Mae."

"Hello," Mae said.

"I'm so happy to meet you," Rose said as she settled at the table Kate and Mae had chosen.

"Likewise, I'm sure," Mae said, one elegant eyebrow raised.

Clarissa Mason paused by the table long enough to give her daughter a hard stare, then said coolly, "Don't be long. We have a great many things to do this morning before our appointment for tea at the Millers'."

"I'll be there shortly," Rose said. As soon as her mother disappeared, Rose leaned forward conspiratorially. "I heard that there was excitement last night at Doc Melbourne's." She glanced at Kate. "Is it true that someone from the Rising Star was shot?"

"Yes," Kate said quietly. "Our foreman, Jed."

"Did Vance take care of him?"

Mae didn't miss the eager emphasis Rose placed on Vance's name. She narrowed her eyes and studied her thoughtfully. Rose was very much like the young girls she had grown up with, the daughters of privileged families who rebelled against the restrictions imposed upon them by dabbling in what they perceived to be exotic or dangerous pursuits. Sometimes that took the form of romantic liaisons with men their parents would find unsuitable. She could imagine that Vance, being so very different from any of the women *or* men with whom Rose was familiar, would seem exciting and intriguing. Vance was surely handsome enough to turn any woman's eye, if only out of sheer appreciation for simple beauty. She wondered if the woman Vance had mentioned being attracted to in medical school had been anything like Rose, delicately lovely and undoubtedly eagerly passionate. She pushed the thought aside, because envisioning Vance with Rose or any other woman was more than she could tolerate under the best of circumstances. After a tempestuous night and very little sleep, she was likely to become dangerously ill-tempered.

"Yes, she did. She was wonderful," Kate enthused. "I've never seen anything like it."

"I really think we should have some kind of welcoming party

for her, don't you?" Rose said. "After all, she's a very important new member of our community. I think we should let her know how much we appreciate her."

Kate glanced quickly at Mae, whose expression suggested she was contemplating violence. "I'm sure Dr. Phelps would appreciate that. Right now, I imagine she'll be very busy taking care of Jed and all her other responsibilities."

"Will Jed be recuperating here in town?" Rose asked.

Kate shook her head. "No, Jessie will want him back at the ranch as soon as possible."

"You'll need help looking after him," Rose said. "I'm sure my mother would give me permission to help you. After all, it's the neighborly thing to—"

"That's very kind of you," Mae said flatly. "I've already offered to give Kate a hand, and I've had a great deal of experience with it."

"Oh." Rose looked crestfallen and then brightened after a few seconds. "Well, I'm sure you'll be needing extra food prepared and things like that. I'll be sure to bring some out."

"That would be very nice," Kate said, carefully not looking in Mae's direction. It wouldn't do to laugh.

"Well," Rose said, rising. "I should go before my mother gets upset." She smiled at Mae. "It was very nice to meet you."

Mae found it hard not to like her naïve friendliness and smiled despite the nagging image of Rose turning her considerable charms on Vance. "Same here."

Kate waited a beat until Rose was out of earshot, then said, "You don't really have to come all the way out to the ranch to help with Jed."

"I don't mind." Mae sipped the tea that had been delivered while Rose had been scheming to find a way to see Vance. "It's difficult work."

"I'm not afraid of that."

"I know, but I might be able to show you some things."

Kate nodded. "I'd appreciate that. And you know you're always welcome at the ranch, without needing a reason." Kate reached for a biscuit and grinned at Mae. "Rose is very curious about Vance."

"I noticed that."

"Vance is very striking."

"I noticed that, too."

"I thought perhaps you had." Kate grew suddenly serious. "I think she's quite marvelous."

"So do I," Mae said softly.

"Well, then it's a good thing you'll be coming out to the ranch to help with Jed."

"I wonder when Vance will let Jessie take him home."

Kate glanced across the room. "Why don't we ask her?"

Mae looked over her shoulder and saw Vance and Jessie approaching. It was the first time she'd seen them together. They were as different as night and day, Jessie golden and radiantly vigorous, Vance dark and broodingly potent. They were of a kind, and yet completely individual. They were painfully beautiful. "Oh my."

"Yes," Kate murmured. "I always thought that Jessie was just Jessie. But it's more than that, isn't it?"

"I think so," Mae said.

"It's something wonderful."

"Yes." Mae smiled up at Vance, who stood beside her chair. "Yes, it is."

# CHAPTER NINETEEN

Hello," Mae said, noticing in the bright light of day the smudges of weariness beneath Vance's eyes. She wondered if there would ever come a time when those shadows would lift.

"Good morning." Vance nodded to Kate as she took the chair next to Mae's. She registered absently the look of open affection that Kate gave to Jessie, but her attention was completely focused on Mae. When they'd parted some hours before, Mae had been disheveled from sleep. Beautiful in the way that women were when at their most natural. Now, she was dressed in a midnight blue dress that was considerably less revealing than what she wore in the evenings, but she was no less striking. Her hair was piled high and held with delicate combs; here and there a twisting strand of gold fell free. Her hands were unadorned save for a single emerald ring on her wedding finger. Her hands were delicate and small, and Vance was immediately assaulted with the memory of those fingers skimming her breasts. Without being aware of it, she clenched her fist on the table, her body vibrating with tension.

"How is Jed?" Kate asked, brushing her hand down Jessie's arm as her lover settled beside her.

"Doing as well as can be expected." Jessie tilted her chin toward Vance. "Thanks to the doctor, here." She glanced at the scrawny boy who approached the table with an inquiring look on his face. "Coffee. Vance?"

"Lots of it," Vance replied. "And the thanks are mostly due to the fact that Jed's stubborn and strong."

"Neither would do him much good," Mae pointed out gently, "if you hadn't gotten the bullet out as slick as you did."

"We got lucky there." When Mae smiled and briefly stroked the back of Vance's hand, a knot of tension coiled in the pit of Vance's stomach. She wanted to open her hand and lace her fingers through Mae's, just to feel more of her skin. She caught a whiff of spice and warm earth, and longed to press her face to Mae's neck. It was dangerous being anywhere near her, because all she wanted was to lose herself in the sensation of her. She straightened and moved her hand away. "Another twenty-four hours and you can take him back to the ranch."

"We're used to tending our wounded," Jessie said quietly.

"I imagine that you are. That's good." Vance looked across the table into Jessie's eyes. "I imagine you spend a goodly amount of time on the range. Jed's going to need fairly constant care for the first week or so. If I can, I'll come out a couple of times a day to look after his dressings."

"I can help with that," Kate said quickly.

"So can I," Mae added.

"I expect that's so," Vance said. "But I'll need to watch him closely for the first four or five days. Then, if he's coming along with no problems, you two can take over." She shifted and glanced at Mae. "It's quite some distance to the ranch, and you shouldn't be out riding alone. I'd be pleased to escort you if you intend to visit."

Mae's eyes widened in surprise. She was used to coming and going at all hours of the night and day with no one but herself to guard her well-being. That Vance should even concern herself sent a thrill through her. Still, it wasn't necessary. "You'll have better things to do than take me arou—"

"Vance is right," Jessie said firmly. "It's too far for you to go alone."

"Now listen here, both of you," Mae said in exasperation. While she was touched, it did not escape her notice that both Jessie and Vance came and went unescorted. "I don't need any more protection than what I already have. I can shoot as well as either one of you, I'll wager."

"I expect you can." Vance smiled. "But since I will be going that way, there's no reason you can't come along to protect *me.*"

Despite her indignation, Mae laughed. "Why the two of you seem to think that you're the only capable ones is beyond me."

Vance and Jessie exchanged a commiserating glance. Catching

sight of the stubborn set to Jessie's jaw, Kate bumped her shoulder. "Neither Mae nor I are careless. You're just going to have to trust us."

Jessie sighed in exasperation. "It's not about trust, it's about... it's about..." She looked across the table at Mae and Vance, then said quietly to Kate, "It's about loving you."

"I know it is." Kate's expression softened and she smoothed her palm over Jessie's thigh. "And I feel exactly the same way about you. Do you see how it goes both ways?"

"I suppose." Jessie cast one more hopeful look in Vance's direction, but got only a shake of her head in return. "Then I think you and I should take a ride outside town for some target practice."

Kate's face lit up. "Now?"

Jessie laughed. "I don't see why not."

"Mae, do you mind?" Kate asked.

"Lord, no. I think it's a great idea." She gave Jessie a knowing look. "And you ought to get her something with a little more power than what she's got in that bag right now."

"I intend to." Jessie stood and held out her hand. "Ready, Kate?"

Kate jumped up and clasped Jessie's hand briefly before gathering her things. "I'll come by later, Mae, since it looks like we'll be staying in town one more night."

"You do that. I want to hear all about your lesson." Mae watched Kate and Jessie hurry away with a fond expression. "Sometimes I forget that she's little more than a girl."

"Kate?" Vance asked.

"Yes," Mae said, returning her attention to Vance. "I don't think she's seen twenty yet."

"You can't be much ahead of her."

"You have a very smooth way with words, Vance. Let's say I'm closer to thirty than twenty."

Vance drank deeply from the bitter coffee the young boy had left and thought of all the other young boys she had watched die by the hundreds during the war. "Years don't matter nearly as much as how we spend them. Kate strikes me as being a very sensible woman."

"She is. They both are." Mae pushed her tea aside. "I can tell when you're thinking about the war. Your eyes get so sad."

"You mustn't worry for me," Vance said.

"But you know that I do, don't you."

"I know that it's in your nature to care for others." Vance looked away from the deep green of Mae's eyes, fearing she would surrender to their gentle beckoning. "Last night, you comforted me. That was kindness."

"Last night I held you. Does it matter why?" Mae whispered.

"I don't know."

"I want to be holding you again right now."

Vance shivered and the cup she held in her hand rattled against the tabletop. "I have work to do."

"I know. Will you come back tonight?"

"Even if I don't know why?"

"I don't care." Aware that they were in public, Mae rested a fingertip delicately against Vance's wrist. She would have liked to have taken her hand. "Late, after midnight."

Vance knew why Mae made the request. She would be busy during the evening and most of the night seeing that the girls were not abused by customers, or taking care of customers herself. Mae had never made a secret nor given an apology for what she did to make her way in the world. Vance did not expect her to, yet the thought of a man using her made her tremble with fury. She looked away, not wanting Mae to see her anger.

"Do you think it means something to me?" Mae asked quietly.

Vance snapped her head back and searched Mae's troubled gaze. "Do you think I judge you?"

"I don't know." Mae shook her head. "I can't change what—"

"I don't like to see your goodness wasted."

Mae felt a shock of surprise. She was used to disdain or distaste, but never concern. "Do you think that's what I give them? No. I give them a lie, and everyone knows it. But sometimes a lie is better than nothing."

Vance looked down at the table where Mae's hand lay close to hers. She imagined the softness and the heat in her touch, the tenderness and the care. She covered Mae's hand with hers, and when Mae would have pulled away, closed her fingers around Mae's.

"Vance, someone might see—"

"I do not want lies between us."

As her breath fled, Mae turned her hand over and felt Vance's fingers slip through hers. She clasped them gently. "There won't be."

"I'll come tonight if I can," Vance said. "I'm not sure I can give you anything. At least not enough." She lifted her eyes to Mae's. "That's the truth."

"Then that's enough."

❖

The tree branch danced and skittered across the ground as if possessed.

"Good shot," Jessie said with pride. She stood behind Kate, both hands lightly on Kate's hips, sighting over Kate's shoulder as Kate fired Jessie's revolver. "Now, try the stone off to the side there. The reddish one."

"It looks so small."

"Make it even smaller. Sight a spot no bigger than your thumb. That's your target." She pressed closer, steadying Kate against the front of her body. "Remember, squeeze all the way through the shot."

Kate imagined a white circle in the center of the dusty stone and allowed her awareness of everything else to slip away. She felt the curved metal of the trigger against her finger, and when they blended together as a whole, she closed her hand, increasing the pressure until the gun fired. A puff of dirt kicked up six inches from her target. "Damn."

Jessie laughed. "That would do the job if you can get that close."

Kate stepped away and handed the revolver, grip first, to Jessie. "Let me see you do it."

"Kate," Jessie protested. "I learned to shoot almost as soon as I learned to ride, and I learned to ride before I could walk."

"*Jessie*," Kate said threateningly.

"All right," Jessie said quickly in surrender. She reholstered her Colt .45 and moved several more feet away. Then, almost faster than Kate could follow, she drew and fired. The stone jumped straight up and she fired again, hitting it in the air and splitting it into pieces.

"I want to be able to do that," Kate said. "That was wonderful."

"It might be better if we practiced with the rifle. You can keep that beside you in the buckboard, and the range is better."

"Both," Kate said with determination.

Jessie gave Kate a long look. "What are you planning, Kate?"

Kate smiled and held out her hand. "Come sit beside me and I'll tell you."

After they climbed into the buckboard, Jessie put her arm around Kate's shoulders. "All right. Seems like a lot happened while I was away for a few days."

"You have no right to talk, Jessie Forbes. Not after what happened to you out there." To soften her words, Kate kissed Jessie quickly. "Vance said a town this size needs a midwife. I think she'd teach me."

"Midwife," Jessie said slowly. "I…why, Kate, I…"

Anxiously, Kate went on quickly. "I know I'd be away from the ranch some of the time, but I'm sure I can take care of everything at home and still—"

"I think it sounds wonderful," Jessie said firmly. "I think you would make a fine midwife." She turned on the seat and took both of Kate's hands, studying her seriously. "This is what you want? It would make you happy?"

"*You* make me happy," Kate said. "Wonderfully happy. But sometimes I feel like I want to *do* more. To do something that…" She sighed, frustrated, searching for words. "I want to have something of my own that matters."

Jessie nodded. "Like the ranch matters to me."

"Yes. Like that."

"Well," Jessie said, "then you have to be able to shoot. And ride astride. As soon as we get back to the ranch, we'll pick you out a horse."

"I was rather thinking of Rory."

Jessie laughed out loud. "Kate, Rory is a wild mustang. I can barely sit him."

"He likes me."

"He likes the sugar and apples you give him."

Kate grinned. "That too." She kissed Jessie again. "Sometimes bribery works."

Jessie put both arms around Kate and pulled her close. With her mouth on Kate's, she muttered, "So do kisses."

❖

Mae removed the key from the inside pocket of her dress and fit it to the lock in the door to her room. As she stepped inside, she was propelled forward by a sharp blow in the center of her back. She would have stumbled and fallen, but large hands grasped her arms and swung her around so forcefully that she banged against the wall, striking her head hard enough to cause her vision to blur.

"Been holding back on the profits, Mae?" a deep male voice grated. "Or have you just been too busy entertaining the new doctor to work the way you ought to?"

"I don't know what you're talking about," Mae said sharply, trying to twist out of the painful grasp. She turned her face away from the fetid odor of stale whiskey and tobacco. He was larger than her by half, and he leaned his weight against her, leaving no doubt as to the pleasure he got from handling her. "You've been getting your money just like always."

Michael Hanrahan came around once a week to collect the money she and the girls earned entertaining men. She had never been certain to whom he reported, but she was sure that he did not own the Golden Nugget. He was too often drunk and far too ignorant to run a successful business, and she doubted that Frank would work for the likes of him. Nevertheless, he had power by virtue of the fact that he represented whoever controlled them all from behind the scenes.

"I've got what you've come for in my dresser," Mae said calmly. "Let me go and I'll get it for you."

He put his hand beneath her dress and dragged his fingers up her thigh to clasp her roughly between the legs. "How do you know what I've come for?"

She stayed perfectly still and kept her eyes on his, refusing to allow him the pleasure of seeing her pain or her fear. She couldn't reach her Derringer, which was strapped just above her knee, and even if she could, she wouldn't shoot him. Killing him would only bring down the wrath of other men. Men who were most certainly more dangerous. "I imagine you've got somewhere to be with that money."

His gaze flickered away, and she knew that he was considering how much time he had before he needed to deliver what he'd come to collect. When he roughly covered her mouth with his and forced his tongue past her lips, she reacted instinctively. She bit him, and he pulled away swearing. She didn't have time to raise her arm and block the vicious backhand he swung at her face. When brutal pain exploded inside her head, she slumped to the floor.

## CHAPTER TWENTY

"Hey, Jed," Jessie said, gently resting a hand on her friend's shoulder. "How are you feeling?"

"Not bad," Jed said, his voice rough and raspy. He smiled weakly at Kate, who stood by Jessie's side.

"The doctor says you're doing very well," Kate said, leaning down to kiss his cheek. "Tomorrow, we're going to take you home."

"That sounds right fine." He coughed and grimaced. "Sorry to be so much trouble."

"Guess you must've fallen on your head when you pitched off that horse," Jessie said roughly, "seeing as how you're talking foolishness."

"I can't say as I'll mind going home."

Vance came in just in time to hear Jed's remark. "Something wrong with our hospitality?"

"No," he said, turning his head slowly as she approached. "But being here makes me feel like something mighty serious might be ailing me."

"Oh," Vance said musingly, "nothing that a little time won't take care of." She took off her coat and hung it on a pine clothes rack inside the door. "I'm going to need to take a look at that back of yours now."

"All right," Jed said.

As Vance opened a cabinet against the wall and withdrew a stack of clean bandages, she said, "It might be a bit painful. I'll give you some laudanum before we start."

"Can't say as I like that stuff overmuch. Makes my head feel like it's filled with wool."

"It can do that. You won't need as much this time." She placed the supplies on a stand by the bed and regarded Jessie and Kate. "This will take me a little while."

"I'd like to help," Kate said. "Then I'll know what needs to be done."

"All right. Jess?"

"I'll just wait over here out of the way." Jessie patted Jed's shoulder again before moving to the opposite side of the room. She leaned against the wall and watched Vance and Kate as they worked. Despite having only one arm, Vance was obviously strong and was able to move Jed onto his side with only a little assistance from Kate. When they pulled the blanket down, Jessie saw that the bandage over the center of Jed's back was dark with blood. She tensed, knowing he was a long way from being all right and that it could easily have been her lying there instead of him.

Vance said something to Kate that Jessie couldn't hear, and then both women went to a sideboard where they rinsed their hands in an enamel basin with something Vance poured from one of the containers she withdrew from a cabinet. Then Vance removed the poultice over Jed's wound, pointing something out to Kate, whose face was a study in rapt attention. Jessie wondered whether Kate would have become a doctor like Vance if she had remained in Boston. It struck her that when Kate had come West, she'd given up far more than Jessie had ever considered. When Kate looked over at her and smiled with excitement, Jessie smiled back, but she felt a trickle of apprehension race along her spine.

Her attention and the stirrings of worry were diverted by the thud of running feet in the outer room and the bang of the door crashing open. All three women staring in surprise as a young boy of perhaps eight careened into the room, sweating and out of breath. He gaped at Vance.

"Help you?" Vance asked.

"I'm supposed to find a doctor," he exclaimed, dancing from one foot to the other and waving his arms. His canvas trousers were a size too big, his boots worn almost flat at the heels, and his face and hands streaked with grime. He smelled like a barnyard.

"I'm Dr. Phelps," Vance said as she threaded the last bit of linen packing into the tract of the bullet wound. "What's the trouble?"

"My ma. My ma says the baby is coming soon and I'm to get

the doctor." He looked from one woman to the next, clearly confused. "Where is he?"

"Aren't you Emily Jones's son?" Kate said kindly. "Tommy, right?"

The boy nodded vigorously.

Kate said to Vance, "Emily is a few years older than me. She's got…five already, I think."

"Then this one will come along quickly," Vance remarked, straightening up. "Jessie, can you help Jed get comfortable?"

Jessie pushed quickly away from the wall. "Sure."

"I'll be with you in just a minute, son," Vance said, collecting the instruments and placing them in a tray on the sideboard. "Don't worry, now. I can take care of your mother."

"Can I come with you?" Kate said hurriedly. "I could help." At Vance's look of inquiry, she added firmly, "I want to learn to be a midwife."

Vance regarded her steadily for a long moment, then nodded briskly. "All right. Let me show you the equipment we need to have available."

While Kate and Vance collected instruments and supplies, Jessie helped Jed ease onto his back. Jed's eyes were clouded with pain. "You okay there?"

"I expect I'll live."

"I sure hope so." Jessie smiled grimly. "We've got a score to settle."

"You'd best be waiting for me for that."

"I will if I can." Jessie shrugged. "I expect that won't be up to me. If they've a mind to keep stealing my stock, I'll have to set them right."

"You need to take care, Jess," Jed said urgently. "They won't think nothing of shooting—"

"Jessie," Kate said, resting her hand in the center of Jessie's back, "I might be gone for a while. Will you be all right?"

"I want to check on things out at the ranch, anyhow. Why don't you have Vance bring you back there when you're done?" She grinned at Jed. "Then tomorrow, we'll come back into town and collect this one."

"Yes, all right. If you're sure?" Suddenly, Kate was nervous. She had no idea what to expect, never having witnessed a birth, or if she would even be of any use to Vance. And she hadn't given Jessie very much time to grow accustomed to the idea of her taking on this new responsibility. She searched Jessie's face uncertainly. "If you think I shouldn't—"

"I think you and the doctor should get going," Jessie said gently. "Sounds like you're needed somewhere pretty fast." She stroked a finger down Kate's cheek. "You be careful."

"I love you," Kate whispered so that only Jessie could hear.

Jessie felt the words settle around her heart, next to the worry that she tried to push aside.

❖

"Don't push yet, Emily. This baby's almost out." Vance cupped the infant's head in the palm of her hand and gently eased her fingers inside the birth canal beneath the shoulders. "All right now, bear down nice and easy."

Kate stood just behind Vance's shoulder, holding a warm blanket and barely breathing. Emily had been almost ready to deliver when they'd arrived. They had hurriedly boiled water to cleanse the instruments Vance had packed and heated blankets and towels in the oven. Emily's husband Robert had retreated to the barn, muttering something about cows the instant they'd arrived. Kate and Tommy had settled the other children, ranging in age from toddler to six or seven years old, into their respective cribs and the single large bed the oldest ones shared in the loft above the main room of the house. Emily and Robert's bedroom occupied part of the first floor along with the kitchen and common living space.

"Once the head is delivered," Vance murmured, "all we need is a shoulder, and the rest will follow smoothly. I'm guiding the right shoulder out by angling the left back and the right forward with my finger and thumb." Vance looked up into Kate's eager eyes. The room was sweltering because they'd built the fire up high in the fireplace, and Vance's hair glistened with sweat. "Once this little one starts coming, it won't take but a second. You need to be prepared to catch it."

"Yes," Kate whispered. "I understand."

"Here it comes. One more push, Emily," Vance told the laboring woman. An instant later the shoulder came into view, then an arm, and then, with a gush of fluid, the baby slid out along Vance's forearm and up against her chest, where she cradled it. "You did wonderfully, Mother. And you have a…daughter."

"Oh, at last," Emily sighed tiredly. "I love the boys, but I could use some help in the house."

"Here you go, Kate," Vance said, straightening and angling the baby toward Kate. "Wrap her up and put her up on the mother's belly. Then we'll take care of the cord."

Vance took a length of cotton twine from the items she and Kate had assembled on a chair beside her and held it out to Kate. "Tie this an inch from her belly, as tightly as you can, and then a second time several inches away."

Kate's hands trembled as she followed Vance's instructions. "There."

"Good. Now, take the scissors and cut the cord."

For an instant, Kate looked into Vance's face, seeking assurance. Vance's eyes were calm and encouraging. Steadier now, Kate removed a clean towel from around the scissors they had boiled earlier and snipped the cord.

"Go ahead and give her to Emily to nurse. The afterbirth will be coming soon." As Vance spoke, she massaged Emily's lower abdomen, feeling the uterus continue to contract weakly as it worked to expel the placenta. A trickle of blood flowed from the birth canal as the placenta separated from the wall of the uterus. The amount of blood flow was normal and the dark maroon color indicated that the uterus was already beginning to shrink. The tightening muscles were closing off the connections between Emily's body and the mass of arteries and veins that had nourished the fetus for nine months.

"Come here, Kate, and put your hand where mine is." Vance guided Kate's hand over the dome of the uterus which was still large enough to extend out of the pelvis. "Sometimes after a prolonged labor the muscles fatigue, and you have to help the contractions along by massaging the womb. Emily is doing fine without our help."

"It's the most amazing thing I've ever experienced." Kate had never felt so connected to the essence of life before. Moments earlier she had seen, and now she could feel, the breathtaking elegance of birth.

"Yes," Vance said softly. "It's a wonder."

"Thank you so much for letting me be here."

Vance smiled. "There'll be nights when you'll be so tired you won't thank me, but I promise you'll never grow weary of the moment when you hand the baby to the mother."

Kate laughed softly. "I know you're right."

An hour later when Vance steered the buggy into the yard in front of Kate's house, it was close to midnight. It was cool enough that they had pulled the blanket over their legs. The sky was cloud filled and totally black. Even the moon and stars were obscured. A lamp glowed in the front room, lighting their way. Vance set the traces onto the floor, jumped down, and hurried around to Kate's side. She held up her hand as Kate stepped onto the running board. "I'll see you in the morning when you come for Jed."

"All right," Kate said, taking Vance's hand. She squeezed it gently. "Thank you again for tonight."

Nodding, Vance took a step back. "It was my pleasure. It's been some time since I've had the opportunity to teach. If you'd like to continue—"

"Oh, yes. Please." Kate shivered and pulled her cloak more tightly around her shoulders. "Any time. Please."

"It's almost always in the middle of the night," Vance warned, laughing softly.

"That's all right. Do you want to come in for something hot to drink before you drive back to town? Or you could spend the night here."

"No, thank you. I'll just wait until you're inside." Vance climbed back up into the buggy. It would take an hour or more to return to town, and unless there was another call waiting for her at the office, she would still be able to see Mae.

"Be careful, then."

"Yes." Vance nodded absently. "Good night, Kate."

"Good night." Kate had not yet reached the front door when it opened and Jessie stepped out. Kate took her hand. "Have you been waiting up, darling?"

"Couldn't sleep," Jessie said as she watched Vance's buggy turn from the yard. "She could have stayed here."

"I asked," Kate said, slipping her arm around Jessie's waist. "Let me get warm. Then I have so much to tell you."

"I've a fire going in the library. I can make some tea."

Kate removed her bonnet and cloak as they walked down the hallway that formed the center of the house, ending at the kitchen in the rear. She shook out her hair with a sigh as she removed the pins that held it up. "No, I don't think I'll get to sleep as it is. I'm far too excited."

Jessie said nothing as she followed Kate into the library, but walked to a heavy wooden sideboard against the far wall and poured a short shot of whiskey. "Spirits?"

"Oh, I don't know. That might not make me sleepy, but it will certainly make me silly. And I mustn't forget anything about tonight." Kate stretched both hands out toward the fire and rubbed her palms together. "Oh, you can't imagine what it was like."

Jessie came to join her by the fire and sipped the whiskey as she took in Kate's pleasure. She listened intently as Kate explained all she had experienced, enjoying her excitement. "It seems like you learned an awful lot from seeing one baby being born."

"Vance is the most wonderful teacher." Kate gripped Jessie's arm. "It's amazing everything she's accomplished. Schooling, the war, traveling across the country. I can hardly imagine."

"Women out here don't get the chance for a life like hers."

Kate looked at Jessie curiously, hearing a note of melancholy in her voice that was totally unlike her. "What do you mean?"

"Being a doctor." Jessie hunched her shoulders and moodily watched the fire. "Having the respect of other people because of how much you know and what you can do."

"Jessie," Kate said gently, encircling Jessie's waist and resting her cheek against Jessie's shoulder. "That's exactly the way people regard you."

"What?" Jessie laughed. "Why, Kate, there's nothing special about me. I'm just a rancher like half the other folks around here."

"How many women own their own ranch, breed their own horses, are in charge of so many men?" Kate squeezed Jessie in playful annoyance. "Why, the first time I saw you I realized I'd never seen a woman like you before. Not just how beautiful you were." Kate turned Jessie's head toward her and kissed her lingeringly. "But how certain and sure you were."

"There's plenty of women out here making their way alone. I'm lucky, I guess, because I had the ranch left to me. I could just as well have had nothing after my father died."

"That may be, but you've kept it going and made it something even more over the years. That's what people respect." Kate tightened her hold and kissed Jessie's throat. "You're doing everything I had always hoped to do. Living the life you've chosen. I've always loved that about you."

Jessie stroked Kate's back and nuzzled her hair. "You could be a doctor like Vance. You're every bit as smart."

Kate leaned away and studied Jessie's face. "Is that what you think I want?"

"I can see how happy it makes you doing for others. Working with Vance." Jessie kissed Kate's forehead. "You should be able to do anything you want to do."

"And if I said I wanted to go back East to go to school?" Kate spoke quietly, her gaze locked with Jessie's.

Jessie took a deep breath and fought not to tremble. "If that's what you want."

"I've a mind to torture you, because sometimes you irritate me so," Kate said in exasperation. She curled her fingers around Jessie's belt and pressed hard against her body. "Jessie Forbes, I love you. I have no intention of doing anything that would take me away from you for more than a few hours at a time. I am certainly not going back East for any reason under the sun. What's gotten into you?"

Jessie held Kate tightly. "I just see how excited you are to be working with Vance, and how much you think of her."

"I *love* you." Kate kissed Jessie soundly, then started opening her belt buckle. "It's time that I remind you of that."

"Maybe," Jessie laughed shakily as Kate tugged her shirt free from her pants, "I should work on irritating you more often."

"I don't expect you're going to stop anytime soon," Kate said as she slipped her hands inside Jessie's shirt. "And I'm glad."

## CHAPTER TWENTY-ONE

By the time Vance had stopped at the office to ensure that Caleb did not need her to see to any new emergencies, returned her buggy at the livery, and stopped at her room to change her soiled clothing, it was well after one. After stripping off the offending garments, she washed up with the lukewarm water in the pitcher on her dresser. She rummaged through her valise for her cleanest shirt, fresh drawers, and her least rumpled trousers. Once she'd donned her holster, she headed across the street to the saloon.

The room was nearly empty. A cowboy slept with his head down and his hand around a bottle of whiskey at one end of the bar, a boy of twelve or so who looked half asleep swept dust around on the plank floor, and the piano player tapped out single notes with one finger as he stared into his beer. Frank had removed his apron and was wiping down the surface of the bar with methodical strokes. He looked up as Vance approached, his usual friendly smile absent.

"Evening, Frank," Vance said, sliding a coin across the bar. "Whiskey, please."

As he poured the drink, Vance looked over the room again and then up to the balcony where one or two of the girls could usually be seen watching the activities or, occasionally, servicing a customer. There was no one there now. Vance downed the drink quickly and signaled for another. This one she sipped slowly as she watched Frank, wondering at his silence.

"Busy night?" Vance finally asked.

"'Bout like always." Frank carefully folded his damp towel into a neat square and draped it over the edge of the bar. He regarded Vance impassively. "Mae said I was to tell you she was busy tonight. If I was to see you."

Vance flushed, partly from the embarrassment of having Frank know why she had come and partly from sharp disappointment. She wasn't ashamed of her relationship with Mae, but she didn't want Frank to think that she was just another customer. That she would use Mae that way. Mostly, she was hurt to think that Mae was unavailable to her because someone else had a claim on her time, and her tenderness, and her body. It was hard to know which she resented more, because they all were precious to her. She quickly finished her drink.

"Thanks. No need to tell her I was by." Vance waved her hand when Frank went to give her change. "Give it to one of the girls."

Vance was halfway to the door when Frank spoke.

"She ain't busy."

Turning, Vance studied his face. What she had initially taken for indifference she now recognized as a concerted effort to control hot temper. His eyes burned with anger. A sick dread roiled in the pit of her stomach as she hastened toward the stairs. "Where is she?"

"In her room, I imagine. Here!" Frank called.

Vance turned and caught the bottle of whiskey he tossed to her solidly in her right hand. She tucked it under her left arm to keep her hand free in case she needed her gun. "Thanks."

❖

Once upstairs, Vance checked the length of the hall before going to Mae's room. All the other doors were closed and the rooms quiet except for one, from which the sounds of labored coupling filtered through to her. Assured that no particular threat lurked to take her unawares, she tapped on Mae's door. When she got no response, she tried the knob and found it locked. She knocked louder.

"Mae. It's Vance."

She waited a full minute and contemplated kicking in the door. The only reason she hesitated was because she knew it would frighten Mae. Louder now, she called, "Mae!"

The door opened an inch. "Hush. You'll raise everyone."

Vance couldn't see Mae's face, but she felt a flood of relief just to hear her voice. "May I come in?"

"Not tonight, sweetheart. I'll send a note for you when it's a good time to come by."

As the door started to close, Vance braced her arm against it. "No. Not until I see you."

"Vance, please."

"I'll stand right here. I won't step into your room. Just let me see you."

"There's nothing to trouble yourself over. It's just…not tonight."

"I'm not leaving."

Mae heard the iron in Vance's voice and knew that she would not win this battle. With a sigh, she stepped back and pulled the door open. The room was in shadow. A single candle burned on the dresser. Backing up as Vance walked toward her, Mae pulled her robe tightly across her breasts. "I'm sorry about tonight. You've got a right to be angry, but I—"

"Quiet, now. It's all right," Vance said softly as she veered away from Mae, who obviously did not want her too close. She put the whiskey bottle on the dresser and fished in her vest pocket for a stick match. Finding one, she lifted the globe on the oil lamp and lit it. She turned back and went very still as she saw Mae clearly for the first time. The confusion and uncertainty in her belly turned to fury. Her rage made her voice even more gentle. "Who did this?"

The right side of Mae's face was a massive purple bruise, her eyelid swollen shut. The corner of her mouth was split from what had obviously been a vicious blow. The thought that anyone would lay hands on her made Vance nearly insane. She swept the room as if the perpetrator might still be there and unconsciously slid out her revolver. "Where is he?"

"Gone," Mae said wearily. It was harder for her to have Vance see her like this, a victim, than to have the entire town look down upon her for being a whore. At least that she could claim to have chosen of her own free will, but to have it be so apparent that she could not protect herself shamed her. She looked away. "Go on home, now, Vance. I've had worse, and this will heal."

"You think I would leave you now?" Her barely restrained wrath made Vance tremble. She jammed the gun back into her holster. "Even if I had no feelings for you, I would want to see to you."

Mae shuffled slowly to the bed and sat down on the edge. She felt sore all over from the pummeling, and her head throbbed mercilessly. "There's nothing you can do."

"Motherless scum," Vance spat. "I'll kill him for this." She locked the door and shrugged out of her coat. Then she picked up the oil lamp and carried it into Mae's boudoir. She moved slowly, deliberately, tamping down her rage so as not to upset Mae further. She put the lamp on the dresser where the light would allow her to see Mae's face clearly. "How many times did he hit you?"

"I don't know. I only remember the first time." Mae looked down at her hands, which she had folded in her lap. "I didn't see it coming."

"What happened?"

"He was waiting when I came back today."

"Who?" Vance asked, her tone lethally dark.

"It doesn't matter."

"It *does*."

Mae looked up. "Don't you realize that if you went after him, *I* would be the one to lose? He would kill you, and if he didn't, someone else would to revenge him." She caught Vance's hand and drew it to her uninjured cheek. She closed her eye and took comfort from the heat and strength of Vance's touch. "That would be worse than anything he's ever done or *could* do to me."

Vance knelt in front of Mae and brought Mae's hand to her lips. She kissed each finger, then turned her hand over and kissed her palm. "You can't ask me to stand by when someone does this to you."

"I do. I do ask it of you." Mae cupped Vance's chin and lifted her head until their eyes met. Vance's were as hard as ebony shards of glass. "Don't let them really hurt me by hurting you."

"Oh, God," Vance groaned, closing her eyes. She'd gone to war believing that her skill and dedication would help right a terrible wrong, only to learn that she could do little more than add torment to agony. Her reward for her sacrifice had been further loss and suffering. A raging fire burned inside her now to answer this injustice with violence. *Don't let them really hurt me by hurting you.*

Vance took a shuddering breath and leaned back on her heels. She opened her eyes and smiled faintly. "I want to have a look at you. I'll not add to your pain, I promise."

"I don't fear your touch," Mae said gently. "But I fear your temper in this, Vance."

"No, you needn't. I won't do anything that would hurt you. You have my word."

Mae laughed softly. "You're a smart and clever woman. My head doesn't hurt so much I've forgotten that. Promise me you won't go after him."

Vance's jaw tightened. "And you're a stubborn woman, Mae."

"Never denied it."

"I won't kill him with my own hands, which is what I want to do." Vance stood, her expression growing hard. "That's all I'll promise for now."

"I know when I'll get no more." Mae smiled as much as she was able. "Thank you."

"Lie down now and let me look at you." Vance reached for the covers and pulled them back as Mae slowly slipped beneath them. Once Mae was propped against the pillows, Vance sat carefully on the edge of the bed. "Tell me what happened."

Mae drew a breath and then, in a quiet, even tone, related the incident. As she spoke, Vance studied her face, keeping her own expression carefully blank. Mae had been hit hard enough to leave the imprint of knuckles on her cheekbone. Carefully, Vance palpated the thin rim of bone beneath the discolored and swollen eyelid, some of her tension easing when she felt no telltale grating that would have suggested fractures. She ran her fingers along the edge of Mae's jaw, searching for irregularities, and again, found none. With her thumb and index finger she delicately teased apart the eyelids that Mae could not open on her own. Blood streaked the white sclera, but the pupil was round and the cornea clear.

"Can you see me?" Vance asked tenderly.

"Yes, and you look mighty serious."

"I am." Vance leaned forward and kissed Mae's forehead. "How long were you unconscious?"

"I don't know for sure. Not long," Mae added hastily when she saw the muscles in Vance's jaw bunch. "It was still afternoon, so I don't think more than an hour."

"Any dizziness, ringing in your ears, weakness in your arms or legs?" Just asking the question was so painful it took Vance's breath away. When Mae answered in the negative, she was almost afraid to believe it. "You're sure?"

Mae stroked Vance's thigh. "Yes. I would tell you."

Vance lifted the tie on Mae's robe. "I need to examine the rest of you."

"He didn't get at the rest of me," Mae said tightly.

"How do you know what he did when you were unconscious?"

"I'd know."

"If you're uncomfortable with me seeing you, I can put up a screen so that you won't—"

"Lord, Vance," Mae said with a sigh. "It's not the way I want you to be looking at me, but I'm not delicate about it. I just don't want you to waste your ti—"

"I've got all night, and there's nothing I'd rather be doing than seeing to you."

"And you call me stubborn," Mae murmured, touched nevertheless. She helped Vance open her robe. "He handled me a bit rough, but that's the worst of it. If I hadn't bit him, he most likely wouldn't have hit me."

"You should've shot the son of a bitch's balls off," Vance seethed. "He left his goddamn fingerprints on your arms."

"If I could have and not brought more trouble down on me and the girls, I would have," Mae said forcefully.

"Who is this man?"

"I told you I wasn't going to give you his name, because some night when you've had an extra shot or two, you're likely to go after him."

"I promised you I wouldn't." Vance gently pressed Mae's abdomen. "Does this hurt?"

"No. And I believe you. That you mean it, at least." Mae covered Vance's hand. "But sometimes we don't keep our promises because of well-meant intentions."

"Does he own the Golden Nugget?"

Mae sighed again. "Lord, you won't give up. I'm sure he doesn't." She pressed her fingers to Vance's mouth. "And before you ask, I don't know who does."

"You must have some idea."

"I don't think there's but three or four people in this town with enough money or brains to back this kind of operation, but whoever it is is very careful to keep it a secret."

Vance nodded thoughtfully as she closed Mae's robe. Gently, she met Mae's eyes. "You're sure he didn't violate you."

"Yes," Mae replied, her voice suddenly thick with tears. She hadn't expected so much tenderness. Even as a child, when she had led a life that many would have found enviable, especially for the child of a servant, she had not known such care. "The way you treat me makes me feel…special."

"You are." Vance stood, released the leather tie that tethered her holster to her thigh, and unbuckled the belt. She set her holster on the bedstead and unbuttoned her trousers. Then she kicked off her boots and stepped out of her pants. She was aware of Mae watching her as she draped them over a chair. She kept her shirt and drawers on and walked to the side of the bed. "I'd like to stay the night."

"I…why?"

When Mae did not protest, Vance lifted the covers and settled beside her. She eased her right arm over Mae's shoulder, carefully settling Mae against her side. "Because I feel good when I hold you."

Mae wrapped her arm around Vance's waist and rested her uninjured cheek against Vance's chest. "I told Frank to tell you not to come up."

"He did."

"I'm glad you didn't listen."

Vance kissed Mae's forehead, then the corner of her mouth. She kissed her gently, taking care not to brush the tender areas as she skimmed her lips over Mae's. She stroked her throat with her fingertips, then dipped beneath her robe to caress her breasts lightly. When she heard Mae's breath hitch and felt her tremble she stopped. "I'm sorry. I didn't mean to—"

"You have the most wonderful touch." Mae held Vance's hand to her breast. "I love your hand there."

"Close your eyes," Vance whispered, softly caressing her again. She rested her cheek against Mae's hair and breathed in her scent. She continued to hold her, stroking her shoulders, her arms, her breasts, until she was asleep. She lay awake listening to Mae's quiet breathing, absorbing the soothing rhythm of her heartbeat into her own chest. The rage was too potent to let her sleep, but the love would let her rest.

## Chapter Twenty-two

When Mae awakened to the sensation of Vance beside her in bed, she stayed perfectly still so as not to disturb the wonder of the moment. Vance's body was hot and firm, and her fingers glided slowly up and down Mae's arm in a steady, mesmerizing rhythm. Mae could tell she was awake from the quiet tension that suffused her body. Ordinarily, what Mae wanted more than anything else was for the person in her bed to leave her in peace. Now, she discovered that the presence of this particular woman delivered it to her.

"Did you sleep at all last night?" Mae murmured as she fit her body more tightly to Vance's.

"Some," Vance lied. She'd taken far too much pleasure in gently caressing Mae as she'd slept to want to sleep herself. While the human body had always fascinated her in its miraculous construction and ingenious workings, she'd never before felt the kind of excitement that lying next to Mae had stirred in her. Mae's skin was so soft, the curve of her hips and breasts so graceful, the heat of her flesh so enticing that Vance had to struggle not to wake her with the urgency of her response. She wanted more. She wanted to never stop touching her.

"You deliver some kind of personal service," Mae joked lightly, stretching to carefully kiss the corner of Vance's mouth.

"Only to you." Vance turned on her side and studied Mae's face in the early morning light. The unblemished portions of her face were beautiful. Pale, delicate skin over fine bones. Her bruises were even uglier in daylight, however, and fury tangled with tenderness. Vance shivered and lightly skimmed her fingertips over Mae's jaw. "How do you feel?"

"If I don't count the aches and pains, I've never felt better in my life."

Vance laughed. "I think my question has to do with those aches and pains."

Mae stroked the hair from Vance's forehead and kissed her softly. "I've never opened my eyes next to anyone I've loved before. That's all I can feel right now."

Vance jerked and drew a swift breath. "Mae."

"Oh, I know women like me aren't supposed to have feelings like tha—"

"Don't, now." Vance stopped Mae's words with a kiss, mindful of her injuries even as she slicked her tongue hungrily inside the moist recesses of Mae's mouth. The dam she had not known she had erected to hold back her wants and needs was crumbling, and she was helpless to stem the rush of desire. She yanked her mouth away from Mae's, panting. "I'm aching for you." Shuddering, she closed her eyes. "So much."

"No need to stop," Mae whispered. She found Vance's hand and drew it inside her robe to her breast. When warm, strong fingers closed over her nipple, she whimpered.

"I'll hurt you," Vance groaned. "You don't know what I'm feeling." She rested her forehead against Mae's, her eyes tightly closed. "I never thought to want anything, any*one*, the way I want you. Even if you weren't injured, I'd be afraid."

Mae laughed quietly even as her body quickened. "Oh, sweetheart. You think your touching me with caring will hurt me, ever?"

"I think if I do what I'm wanting to do right now, it might."

"Well then, why don't you do what *I* want you to do?"

Vance opened her eyes, her head thick with arousal. Mae's breast lay heavy in her hand and her green eyes shimmered, inviting her to touch, to take. Still, she had enough reason left to know she couldn't. Not when the price of her pleasure would be Mae's pain. "I want to. I don't know how good I'll be at it, but I'll do my best. But not until you're well."

"Oh, I think you'll do just fine," Mae said. The slow play of Vance's fingers over her breasts was nearly enough to carry her over, but she resisted the heavy swirl of passion between her thighs because there was something else she wanted more. "But just this minute it isn't you touching me I want."

Vance tensed. "I…I've never. With anyone."

"Mmm. I remember." Mae opened the top button on Vance's shirt. Then she started on the second. "I've been thinking about that. How much I like being the first to touch you."

"I'm not…I wish…" Vance stilled Mae's hand. "I wish I were as beautiful as you. That I could be as pleasing to you as you are—"

"For a woman so smart," Mae said, tears brimming on her lashes, "you're just plain stupid about some things."

Vance grinned. "That's what I've been trying to tell you."

Mae parted Vance's shirt, exposing her small, perfectly formed breasts. "I can't but think of you and my knees go weak." She smoothed her hand across Vance's chest, tracing breast and nipple and scar tissue as if all were priceless gems. "I see that handsome face of yours and I get tight inside, needing you to touch me, wanting you to take me places no one else ever has." She looked into Vance's eyes, circling one red fingernail around Vance's nipple, then squeezing until Vance arched and groaned. "You're just exactly the kind of woman who pleases me."

"I can't think what with wanting you to keep touching me." Vance's voice was tight, strained, nearly as tense as her body, which trembled with barely contained excitement. "I have this terrible need for you somewhere inside me."

Mae moaned softly. "Oh, I know. I know because I feel it, too." She rested her cheek between Vance's breasts. "Hold me."

Vance circled Mae's shoulders and pulled her near, telling herself that this would be enough for now. Desperately hoping that her body would not betray her. She feared that Mae's embrace alone would be enough to ignite the powder keg of arousal that simmered so near to brimming over. She felt so close to slipping over the edge that the slightest brush of Mae's fingertips caused dangerous ripples of pleasure to dance along her thighs. She groaned and clenched her jaws tightly. Urgently, she whispered, "Stop touching me now. Just let me get my senses back."

"Oh no. I plan to touch you senseless." Mae slid her hand beneath the waistband of Vance's drawers. "I want you to be still and let me."

Had she her other arm, Vance would have pulled Mae's hand from between her thighs where it had come to rest. As it was, one armed, she was too slow, and before she could protest, exquisite pleasure burst beneath Mae's ceaselessly caressing fingers. Had she been able to think enough to consider stopping, she couldn't have. Her body claimed its reward even as Mae claimed her heart. Her release started as a sweet fist in the pit of her stomach, then raged along her spine and down her legs, and finally exploded, burning all thought from her mind. She cried out, and then cried, her face buried in Mae's hair.

"Here now. Your heart's hammering like to burst," Mae marveled, her face still cradled against Vance's chest.

"It's about to break," Vance said unevenly, "from holding so much happiness."

"You don't have to hold it, sweetheart. There's lots more coming." Mae was satisfied in a way she had never imagined. She had given true pleasure from the heart, two things she had never experienced before. She felt full, sated, as if Vance's release had been her own. She wanted Vance's touch as much as ever, but for the moment, she was content. "I just couldn't wait any longer for you."

"I think it unfair," Vance said, her voice rusty from holding back the well of emotion that threatened to undo her, "that you have me at such a disadvantage." She tangled her fingers in Mae's hair and tilted her head back before gently kissing her eyelids, her bruised cheek, her mouth. "In that circumstances prevent me from taking my pleasure in you or returning what you have bestowed upon me."

"I consider it downright clever," Mae teased. "I'm hoping it will be enough to get you back again."

Suddenly serious, Vance said, "You can't think that a few moments of pleasure are all I seek?"

Mae grew still. "I don't like to think too much beyond the moment. I've learned that hoping for something often leads to disappointment."

"And what is it that you hope for?" Vance stroked down the center of Mae's back to her hip, then over the curve of her body to her stomach. She opened her fingers as if to encompass all of her in the palm of her hand. "Beyond today?"

Silently, Mae shook her head, fearing that putting words to her dreams would cause them to shatter.

"There was a time," Vance said quietly, "that I knew the shape of my future. I knew where I would live, what I would do. Who I would be. I did not know who or even *if* I would love, but knowing the other things made that loneliness bearable." She kissed Mae. "Now I am not certain who I am or what my future will be. But I know who I love. And that matters more than all the rest."

"I'm not the woman you should love," Mae whispered. "But I don't have it in me to tell you not to."

"How can you judge who I should love? Can you feel the pain in my heart that eases only when you touch me? Can you know the despair that lifts only when you smile?" Vance closed her eyes and rubbed her cheek against Mae's hair. "Can you imagine the loneliness that fades only when you're near?"

"Some of that I know," Mae said. "Because you give me that, too."

"I know that I come to you less than I once was," Vance tilted Mae's face up to hers with a fingertip beneath her chin, "and for that, I'm sorry."

Mae's eyes narrowed. "I still have that nice warm feeling that comes from loving you this way. But I can lose it pretty fast if you keep up that kind of talk. You might have thought you were more before you lost your arm. Before you lost your brother. Or your home, or your way of life. Maybe you were. I have no way of knowing. But I know who you are now. I see your strength, and your goodness, and your gentleness. That missing arm hurts me, but there's nothing about you that makes me wish for more."

Vance smiled crookedly. "Then I count myself extremely lucky."

"That's better." Mae sighed. "I hate for you to go, but I imagine the town is waking up about now. You can't be seen coming and going from my room at all hours."

"I have every intention of coming and going from your room whenever I am welcome." Vance made no move to get up and her voice had taken on an edge. "Which I hope is often."

"Lord, Vance. No matter what we are to each other, in the eyes of the townspeople we've no business being together. Two women, they might overlook. The town doctor and a whore? Never."

"I don't care what the opinion of others may be." Vance stirred with uneasiness. "Unless the anger is directed at you."

"What happened yesterday had nothing to do with you," Mae said quickly.

"Have you ever considered just leaving here? Giving this up?"

Mae laughed bitterly. "And what would I do? Even if I could leave my past behind, I have nothing with which to make a future. If I had, I wouldn't be here now."

Carefully, Vance said, "I have resources. I could lend you—"

"No," Mae said quickly. "I won't take money from you. Not now, not ever. What happens between us—"

"Has nothing to do with money," Vance said angrily. "You insult me to suggest that. And yourself."

Mae sat up, pulling the sheet above her breasts. "What am I to think, then?"

"That I care for you and want to help you. Or is it only *I* who should accept help without question?" Vance pushed up on the bed and started to button her shirt. "Is it only I who needs caring for?"

"No. No," Mae said softly. She stifled the urge to help Vance button her shirt. For her it would have been an act of love. For Vance, one of pity, and she would not risk that. "Tell me, then, what you're thinking."

Vance took a long breath and reined in her temper. When Mae reached over and tentatively began buttoning the rest of her buttons, she tilted her head back against the wall and sighed. "I was thinking I could help you buy a house or start a business or—buy coach fare to somewhere else."

"Leave here?"

"If that's what you wanted."

Mae stood up and fastened her robe. "You are lucky I don't have my gun, because if I did, I would likely shoot you."

"I can see that I've taken a misstep."

"A whole passel of them." Mae went to the sideboard, rinsed her face, and took her time drying off while she gathered her thoughts. She needed some distance from Vance because up close to her, her thoughts tended to scatter. "There are girls here who are my responsibility. If I'm gone, someone else will take my place. Someone who may not care any more for them than how much they can make in a night. Someone who may not care what's done to them if the price is right. I'll not have that on my conscience."

"I understand."

"Do you? I'm not sure that you really do." She took a breath and said quietly, "If not me here taking charge of things, someone else. If not Sissy and the others doing what they do here, then some other girls will come to do it. It's a part of life out here that isn't going away."

Vance stood, shook out her trousers, and stepped into them. She left her shirt out and went to the sideboard to wash as well. When she leaned back, towel in hand, her hair still dripping, she said, "You don't want to stop doing what you do."

"I wouldn't mind if I never had another stranger touch me," Mae said harshly. "But I have my independence, and I'm not starving, and those girls might have a chance for something more than I had."

"All right."

Mae frowned. "All right what?"

"There are brothels in St. Louis run by women who live in fine houses, who ride through town, day or night, in elegant carriages, and who are welcome in the best of company."

"That's St. Louis. I know about those places, but people out here aren't as accepting."

Vance shrugged. "Things change."

"That's not something you should count on."

Vance tucked in her shirt and buttoned her trousers. "The only thing I'm counting on is you."

With a shake of her head, Mae picked up Vance's holster and swung it around her narrow hips. "Hold still, now."

"I did that once for you already today," Vance murmured, circling Mae's waist and pulling her tight against her body. The crush of Mae's breasts against her chest stoked the urge to touch her that had not diminished since they'd lain together. She bit lightly at Mae's earlobe before skimming the rim of her ear with her tongue. "And look what happened then."

Mae sagged in Vance's embrace, the thunder of desire stealing her strength. "I see now what happens when you're feeling more *yourself*."

Vance laughed. "What?"

Mae spread her palms on Vance's back, cleaving to her, knowing that her passion would fuel Vance's. When she heard Vance gasp and felt her body twitch, she stepped away, a satisfied smile on her face. "You get insufferably sure of yourself."

"Should I apologize?" Vance asked, her breath coming fast as her insides twisted with want.

"You come back one of these days—" Forcing herself to do the opposite of what her body screamed for her to do, Mae backed away. "And we'll see."

"I promise you," Vance said, her eyes smoldering as she slung her coat over her shoulder and started for the door, "I intend to just as soon as I can."

There were other things she planned to do as well—things that for the moment, she did not intend to share.

## Chapter Twenty-three

Vance found Caleb in the midst of changing Jed's bandage. She hung up her coat and went to help out.

"Morning," she said as she spooled out a thin strip of clean linen from a basin. She passed it to Caleb, who gently threaded it into the bullet tract to help facilitate drainage. She didn't expect an answer. His nod of greeting and distracted smile were enough. She leaned over to check Jed. "How are you feeling?"

"Better than I should be, I suppose, with the two of you poking at me the way you're doing."

Vance smiled. Jed's color was good and the wound itself showed no evidence of swelling or purulent drainage. If he went another day or so without signs of festering, he would have a very good chance of making a full recovery.

"Am I going home today?" Jed asked.

"I wouldn't want to be the one to stand in Jessie's way when she shows up here for you," Vance said dryly. She glanced to Caleb, who nodded. "Seems like you'll get plenty of care at home. And the food will probably be better."

Jed laughed carefully as Caleb reapplied his bandages. "That will surely be true if Miss Kate is cooking."

Caleb and Vance got Jed resettled and returned to the office. Caleb closed the door.

"I can't think of a single reason why that wound isn't a stinking mess right now," Caleb said, pacing to the window and staring aimlessly into the street. "Except for all that fussing you did with the instruments and that carbolic acid."

Vance joined him and said mildly, "Before the war, I spent six months in Europe with my father and brother visiting various medical clinics. I heard Dr. Lister speak about his theories concerning contamination as a cause for wound purulence. It seems to make sense."

"I don't know if it makes sense or not, but if it gets results, I don't much care." Caleb frowned. "So tell me what I should be doing. Never mind the why, I don't have time for it."

"Well," Vance said, suppressing a smile, "here's what I recommend."

They were deep in conversation when Jessie and Kate came through the door.

"How is Jed?" Jessie asked immediately, looking from Caleb to Vance.

"Better," Caleb said with satisfaction. He started toward the dispensary. "He's not going to be able to walk to the wagon. I'll help you get him on a litter." Over his shoulder, he added, "Vance, why don't you go over with Kate what she'll need to do about the bandages."

"Right." Vance smiled at Kate and reviewed with her the routine for twice-daily bandage changes. "The most important thing is to look out for signs that the wound is festering. Is all that clear?"

"Yes. I understand."

"You're getting quite a lot of practice with treatment these days."

"It's wonderful," Kate enthused. "Jessie and I talked about the midwifery last night. I want you to know that I'm serious about learning."

"I never thought otherwise." Vance hesitated. "I could teach you medicine, Kate. Most medicine is still learned in apprenticeship, not school. Or you could spend a few months back East at one of the colleges, and then apprentice with me."

"I've thought of it. Jessie and I even spoke of it." Kate smiled. "I think what you do is amazing and so important." She glanced toward the partially opened door where a murmur of voices could be heard. "If I'd never come here, if I'd never met Jessie, I might want to do something like that. But I'm happy already with my life. I want to be a midwife. You said yourself it's something the people here need."

"That's true."

"It's what I need, too."

Vance nodded, thinking about choices that were made because they were right and not merely expected. She thought about her own choices and knew that she would make the same ones again. She would go to war with Victor because she believed it was right. She might have come to New Hope because she'd given up choosing, but she planned to stay because it was what she wanted. What she needed. She thought of Mae, and smiled. Yes, just what she needed.

"Once Jed is settled, I'll take you out with me so you can get acquainted with your future patients. That way, they'll know that we're working together and that you'll be looking in on them from time to time," Vance said. "All right?"

Kate nodded vigorously. "Oh yes. That would be just perfect."

Jessie returned in time to hear Kate's pleased exclamation. She imagined Kate and Vance were talking about Kate's schooling again. When Kate turned to her with shining eyes, Jessie smiled. "I'm going to go get some things the doc says we'll need, and then we can go."

"I'll walk with you," Vance said quickly.

Surprised, Jessie nodded. "Come on along."

There was something in Vance's expression that told Kate she wanted to talk to Jessie alone. Kate squeezed Jessie's arm briefly. "You go ahead. I want to say hello to Jed and talk to Caleb for a minute."

"All right." Jessie nodded to Vance and they stepped outside and into the street. "Something on your mind?"

Vance skirted the edge of a quagmire in the center of the street that was left over from the most recent rain. "What do you know about the Golden Nugget?"

"Besides the obvious?" Jessie nodded to a passerby and waited until they were out of earshot. "Not much. It's been the Nugget pretty much as long as I can remember. I think there was a time it was called something else, but the purpose was the same."

"You know who owns it?" Vance saw no reason to be circumspect with Jessie. Kate and Jessie and Mae were friends. From the fond looks that passed between Jessie and Mae, she had wondered on occasion if perhaps they had once been more than friends. She found it did not bother her as much now to think of it. In fact, she was glad if Mae had been with someone who appreciated her, and she imagined that Jessie would have.

Jessie glanced sideways at Vance, then straight ahead. She'd yet to be able to read anything behind the doctor's set expression. "The only one I've ever seen giving orders in the place is Frank, but I don't actually know that he owns it."

"Let's say he doesn't. Who might?"

Jessie slowed as they neared the general store, settled her back against a post facing the street, and set her boot heel on the edge of the raised board walkway. Vance draped her arm over the hitching rail, leaned against it, and crossed her ankles. Anyone watching would have thought they were just two friends out for a leisurely stroll.

"It would take some money," Jessie said thoughtfully. "Thaddeus Schroeder—he owns the newspaper along with Kate's father—might have enough. He's been here almost as long as the town has. He's a family man, though, and seems decent. I can't quite see him behind the Nugget."

"Caleb would have the resources as well," Vance said, "but I think that unlikely, too."

"There's Wallace Fitzpatrick—he owns the lumber and supply yard, and Mason at the bank." Jessie shrugged. "There might be one or two more, but I'd just be guessing."

"What about the land title office? You think anything might be recorded there?"

"Deeds are usually printed in the newspaper, but I don't know how far back those records go." Jessie studied Vance. "Kate might be able to tell you that, but if there is some trouble brewing, I don't want her a part of it."

Vance tightened her jaw and said nothing. It had been a long time since she'd confided in anyone. Since Milton—and Victor. The silence grew, and she knew that Jessie would not question her. If she gave no explanation for her concerns, she would be making a statement as to the limits of the friendship forming between them. "Whoever owns the place has a hired man to oversee it." Her words came out hard on the wave of her fury. "He took after Mae yesterday. Left bruises on her face and her arms."

"Bastard," Jessie swore.

"Yes."

"And you want to go after him?"

Vance met Jessie's hard blue gaze. "Wouldn't you?"

Wordlessly, Jessie nodded.

"Mae got me to promise I wouldn't," Vance said wryly. "I'm still not sure how that came about."

"I'll wager she worked it around to her being hurt if you went off and got yourself killed."

Vance laughed softly. "Something like that."

"The problem is, they're right. And if something happened to Kate, I wouldn't last."

"You and Kate," Vance said carefully. "People here don't make a fuss?"

Jessie grimaced. "Well, Kate's parents did. But most folks keep to their own business and let others mind theirs."

"I didn't promise Mae I wouldn't go after whoever's behind things. He as much gave his permission for this bastard to do what he wanted with the women at the Nugget."

"I'll ask around."

"I don't want you to put yourself in any jeopardy," Vance said quickly. "Any information you might—"

"Mae means something to me, too," Jessie said, her voice tight. "I'll see what I can find out."

Vance nodded curtly. "Thanks."

❖

"I'll come by this evening to take you back to town," Vance said three days later when she turned the buggy into the lane to Kate and Jessie's ranch. "It will probably be close to suppertime when I've seen to these calls."

"You don't need to be driving me around, you know," Mae said. "Lord knows, you spend enough time traipsing over the countryside. Have you been to bed at all in the last few days?"

Vance squinted in the bright sunlight. Her eyes felt gritty and she *was* tired, but having Mae beside her on a beautiful early summer morning seemed to infuse her with an energy she hadn't felt since before the war. "It's been one of those weeks when everyone seems to feel poorly at the same time. I've had a chance to nap a time or two."

"I won't mind if you come to visit late at night, you know," Mae said.

"I'm not sure how much sleep I'd get, in that case."

Mae flushed despite the wide-brimmed, feathered hat that protected her face from the sun. The deep green was a shade darker than her eyes and matched her silk dress. "That might depend on just how tired you really were."

Grinning, Vance jumped down and came around to Mae's side of the buggy. "That's one thing I don't seem to feel when I'm around you." She circled Mae's waist as she stepped down to the running board and swung her off and around to the ground, taking advantage of their closeness to brush her lips over Mae's cheek. "You look beautiful."

"Have I managed to cover the bruises?" Mae asked quietly.

Vance's heart twisted with sympathy and anger. "Yes. You needn't feel embarrassed by something that was not your fault."

"It's pride, I suppose." Mae waved as Kate came to the door of the ranch house. "But I don't have much more than that."

"You have the strength to make hard choices," Vance said as they walked toward the house. She kept her hand on Mae's back, in the hollow just above her hips, enjoying the way Mae's body moved beneath her fingers. "And you take responsibility for those young girls, when no one else, not even their families, is willing to. That's honorable."

"Hush," Mae whispered. "Your brain's getting soft from lack of sleep."

Vance laughed as she and Mae climbed up to the porch.

"Hello," Kate called, pushing loose strands of hair back from her face. The kitchen was still warm from the baking she had done early that morning, and the breeze felt wonderful against her hot skin. She regarded Mae and Vance fondly, thinking that when Vance laughed, she looked far younger than Kate had suspected. "I've got coffee on, if you'd like some."

"I'm afraid I can't stay," Vance said. "Mrs. Emerson sent word that all five of her children are complaining of stomachaches. And that's just the first of a long list." She smiled at Kate. "And before you ask, no, I'm not making any stops today on our expectant mothers. Plan on coming around with me again the day after tomorrow."

"Yes," Kate replied eagerly. "I will."

Mae touched Vance's hand in a fleeting caress as Vance stepped away. "Be careful today."

"I will. I'll see you later." She touched the brim of her black felt hat. "Kate."

"Supper's at six and I'm making chicken and biscuits." Kate took

Mae's arm as she fixed Vance with a stern look. "And I expect you to be here to help eat it."

"Then I certainly shall," Vance said with a small bow.

Mae watched Vance walk down the porch, climb into the buggy, and drive away. "She looks tired," she murmured anxiously.

"She looks happy," Kate said softly. "I don't think I've ever seen her look that way before. It's nice."

"I suppose if she were made of straw she wouldn't have come through all she has," Mae said with a sigh. "Silly of me to worry."

"Come inside and have something to drink. Jed's asleep, so we don't need to hurry." As she led Mae through to the kitchen, she said gently, "And it's natural to worry about someone you love."

"Why, I never said—"

Laughing, Kate held out her hand. "Here, give me your things, then sit down and we'll have some tea. And you didn't need to say. You just have to look at her and it shows."

"I'll have to be more careful."

"Why?" Kate sat down across from Mae and regarded her seriously. "You can't think Vance would mind?"

"Maybe not, but I imagine there's a fair number of people who would."

Kate took Mae's hand. "I know you could stand up to whatever might be said, and I'm sure Vance can. And if the look on Vance's face this morning means anything, she needs you to keep looking at her just the way you do."

"Lord, Kate. Feelings sure do complicate things."

"They do. Especially when they're wonderful." She sat back and worried her lower lip with her teeth for a second. Then she said quietly, "Anyone who doesn't know you as well as I do wouldn't have noticed, but I can see that someone's hurt you. What happened?"

Mae flushed for the second time in just a few minutes, this time with embarrassment. "Nothing to trouble yourself about."

Kate's dark eyes snapped. "Our friendship is very important to me. I'll not have you minimize it by thinking I shouldn't care about what happens to you."

"I…" Mae took an unsteady breath and smiled wanly. "I'd almost forgotten how stubborn you are. I won't even try to convince you it's not something you need to know about."

"Good. That's showing sense." Kate smiled tenderly. "Tell me."

Mae relayed the essentials of the event while leaving out much of the horror. "He won't catch me not paying attention again. And the next time, I won't worry about who else might be coming along if something happens to him. I'll just put a few holes where he'll be sure to feel them."

"Good." Kate's expression was grim. "I think it's terrible that you should have to worry about someone like him hurting you or the girls."

Mae studied her curiously. "But you don't think it's terrible that we're whores?"

Kate looked surprised. "Terrible? Of course not."

"How is it that a young girl from Boston has such a different way of looking at things than most folks do?"

"I think," Kate said, "it's because *I'm* different. Loving Jessie and knowing that some people would say I shouldn't—that makes me look at what people call *right* a little more carefully."

"Vance doesn't seem to set a lot of store in what people say about her."

"Well, it seems that you're outnumbered, then."

Mae laughed. "Seems so."

"Does Vance know what happened?" Kate asked carefully.

"She knows, and it was all I could do to keep her from rushing off to settle scores."

"I imagine." Kate knew that Jessie would behave precisely the same. And if anyone raised a hand to Jessie, so would she.

"It's a rare thing, being cared for that way." Mae shook her head. "I thought I'd run out of that kind of luck."

Kate smiled. "I'd say all four of us are lucky."

## CHAPTER TWENTY-FOUR

Jessie pushed away from the table with a sigh. "Lord, Kate. I'm going to get spoiled eating your cooking. It will be a chore swallowing what passes for food out on the trail."

Kate gave her a sharp look. "Is that going to be sometime soon?"

"I expect before long I'll have to see where the herds have wandered off to after all this rain," Jessie said vaguely.

"I thought you were going to wait for Jed to recover so he could go with you."

"That will be some time yet, I imagine," Jessie said. "What do you think, Vance?"

Vance, seated across the wide oak table, nodded as she looked from Kate to Mae, who sat beside her. "He's doing very well, largely due to the fine care from you two these last few weeks. But he's still a ways away from riding."

Kate kept her gaze on Jessie. "Can it wait until then?"

"It depends on what the linemen have to say about the state of things. Charlie will be down from the high country in a day or two. I'll know better then." Jessie glanced at Vance. "I've got a good saddle horse out in the barn. With all the riding you're doing, you might want to have a look at him."

After a second's hesitation, Vance stood. "You're right. I've been meaning to talk to you about that. I can't keep using Caleb's or paying the liveryman every time I need a mount."

"Let's take a walk and I'll show him to you."

Mae watched the two of them leave the room, Vance in her white shirt and trousers and Jessie in dusty denim and a sun-bleached blue cotton pullover. "I'm not so sure why I ever thought they were different. Times like this, I can't tell them apart."

"Yes," Kate said thoughtfully. "What do you think they're up to?"

Laughing, Mae shook her head. "Something too dangerous for us, I'll wager."

"Of course." Kate smiled fondly. "I'll torture it out of her later."

"A wonderful idea."

❖

Kate snuggled up against Jessie, wrapping an arm and a leg around her body for comfort more than warmth. "Mmm, you smell like hay and sunshine."

Jessie laughed. "I think you just said I resemble a barnyard. You want me to get a wash before we go to sleep?"

"You smell," Kate said, kissing Jessie soundly for emphasis, "healthy and strong and I like it."

"Lucky for me," Jessie murmured, gently guiding Kate on top of her body. She kissed the tip of Kate's chin, then her mouth, sliding both hands into Kate's long dark hair. She sighed her appreciation as she nibbled at Kate's lower lip.

Kate kissed her for as long as she dared, basking in the warmth of Jessie's embrace and the tender, persistent demands of her hands and her mouth. She lifted her face away just short of the point where she would be helpless to stop, smiling at Jessie's groan of protest. Her face felt hot and her body shimmered to the call of Jessie's desire. "Did you and Vance settle on the price of a horse?"

"What?" Jessie asked, her voice and expression befuddled. She caught the ribbon at the neck of Kate's nightgown in her fingers and tugged it loose. When she went to slide her hand beneath the soft cotton, to Kate's softer breast, Kate laughed and twisted away. Jessie frowned. "Wha…what?"

"You remember. You and Vance and the trip to the barn." Jessie looked so adorable in the glow of the firelight, edgy and confused and wanting, that Kate was fast losing her curiosity about Jessie and Vance's conversation.

"Kate." Jessie blinked. Her vision had already gone blurry the way it did when loving Kate got her insides all jittery and jumpy. She half sat up, holding Kate to her with one strong arm wrapped around her shoulders as she delved beneath her nightgown and lifted Kate's breast into her palm. She rubbed her mouth over the swiftly tightening nipple. "I can't make sense of anything right now."

"Oh," Kate sighed, cleaving to her, body to body, and went back to kissing Jessie where she had left off. When Jessie groaned and rolled her over, pinning her to the bed, Kate had already forgotten everything except Jessie's touch. She wanted to close her eyes and drift on the warm cloud of pleasure that built as Jessie kissed and stroked her way from Kate's throat to her breasts and lower, but she watched Jessie love her as long as she could. When Jessie murmured her name and took her with her mouth, Kate let passion steal the last of her reason.

When Jessie murmured her name again a few minutes later, her cheek pillowed on Kate's stomach, Kate stroked her damp hair and face. Contentedly, she whispered, "You drive every thought from my head."

"You were wanting to know something earlier," Jessie said drowsily. Pleasing Kate always set her off, like putting a match to dry tinder. The very sound of Kate's pleasure fired her own. Her head was still reeling and her legs felt heavy as iron. She didn't think she could move just then if the house went up in flames.

"What?" Kate asked dreamily, sifting strands of golden hair between her fingers. "Oh. I was wondering what you and Vance had to say that required a trip to the barn after supper."

Laughing softly, Jessie gathered all her willpower and managed to move a foot up the bed. She lay on her side and faced Kate. The firelight made her black hair shine and her skin rosy. "You look beautiful right after we've been loving."

Kate smiled lazily. "I feel beautiful."

Jessie rested her cheek in the bend of her arm and reveled in Kate's happiness, trying to imagine what it would be like if somebody put bruises on Kate's face the way they had done to Mae. Her stomach tightened until it ached, and her mind shied away from the image, but she forced herself to consider Mae's pain and Vance's helpless rage. "I love you."

The fervor in her voice bordered on sorrow, and, alarmed, Kate stroked her face. "What is it, darling?"

"I couldn't stand it if anything happened to you."

"Nothing's going to happen to me." Kate pulled Jessie's head to her breast and held her fiercely. "What's wrong?"

"You saw Mae's face."

Kate closed her eyes. "Yes."

"Did she tell you about it?"

"Yes."

"It's ripping Vance up inside." With a sigh, Jessie sat up with her back against the smooth plank headboard and pulled Kate into her arms, tucking Kate's head beneath her chin. With her free hand she reached down and drew the covers over them both. The fire was waning, and a chill crept in from the edges of the room. "She asked me a few weeks back, right after it happened, if I knew who owned the Nugget."

Kate's hand tightened on Jessie's shoulder. "She wants to punish whoever hurt Mae."

"Of course."

"Jessie," Kate said urgently. "If you get mixed up in this, it could be dangerous."

Jessie tilted her head back and looked down into Kate's face. "It's wrong, Kate."

"Oh, I know. I know." Kate struggled with the anxiety that rushed up into her throat, making her breath come fast and shallow. She would never get over watching Jessie almost die. She remembered the blood that covered the wagon bed, the deathly pallor of Jessie's face, the stillness in her body as life had drained away. "I can't have you getting hurt. I can't."

"We're a pair," Jessie murmured, kissing Kate's forehead.

"You can't take on men like that with force, Jessie."

"We aren't planning something like that, Kate. We aren't planning anything at all." Jessie rubbed her hand in steady circles over Kate's back. "Vance just wants someone to talk to about it."

"Don't tell me that's all she wants."

Jessie shrugged. "She wants to know who's accountable."

"And what's your part?"

"I just asked a few questions to see if anyone knew whose place it was, but when you put it right to folks, no one does."

"And you think that will satisfy Vance?"

"Probably not." Jessie chuckled. "I think she's of a mind to watch the place at night, to see if she can find him."

"Oh, she'll be in trouble if Mae finds out," Kate said vehemently.

"You're not going to tell her, are you?"

"No, because *you're* going to talk some sense into Vance." Kate thumped Jessie's chest for emphasis. "It won't do Mae any good if Vance gets hurt."

"I know." Jessie shifted restlessly. "But damn, it doesn't seem fair."

"It isn't. For either of them. And I *do* think we should try to find out who's responsible."

"We?"

"You don't think I'm going to just stand by and watch, do you?" She sat up and held Jessie's gaze for emphasis.

"Here I thought I was doing the right thing telling you what was going on, when I should've kept quiet." Jessie pushed a hand through her hair in frustration.

Kate laughed quietly and caught Jessie's hand. She rubbed Jessie's knuckles against her cheek. "You did exactly the right thing. Trying to protect me by keeping things from me will only drive us apart."

"I'm trying to work my way around to believing that."

"I know you are." Kate settled back down into Jessie's arms. "And I know it isn't easy for you."

"I wouldn't want something like my stubbornness to come between us."

"No," Kate said gently. "It's not stubbornness. I love the way you love me, and I don't ever want you to change. Just sometimes, you have to let me help you, too."

"Don't you know that you're what gets me through every day?" Jessie asked incredulously. "Before you came along, I was starting to wonder what my life was really all about. Working, living, always doing, but at the end of the day, there was still something missing." She eased down into the bed with a sigh of contentment. "Now there isn't."

Kate turned on her side and drew Jessie against her back, settling the arm that Jessie clasped around her middle between her breasts. She understood now the difference between existing and living. This connection they shared, unique beyond all others, was the essence of her life. As she lay waiting for sleep to come, satisfied in body and heart, she thought of Mae and Vance and what she might do to help them find the safety of one another's arms.

❖

Vance brought the buggy to a halt behind the Golden Nugget but made no move to get down. Instead, she turned on the seat and put her arm around Mae's waist, drawing her close. It was well after dark, and in the shadows, no one would take them for anything other than a man and a woman stealing a few moments of passion. She kissed Mae, a slow lingering exploration that deepened and grew more desperate until Mae circled her shoulders and pulled Vance down nearly on top of her.

"Mae," Vance warned, reluctantly pulling away when awareness finally penetrated the desire clouding her senses. "I've precious little control where you're concerned as it is. You must help me maintain command of myself."

Mae laughed, stroking Vance's face with shaking fingers. "And all this time I've been trying to do just the opposite."

"Ever since the night we lay together," Vance said, straightening up but keeping her hold on Mae, "I can't think of much else."

"I thought I was long past hoping for anything but a few minutes of kindness in bed," Mae murmured, sliding her hand inside Vance's coat to rest on her stomach. "But lying next to you has made me want a lot more than that."

Vince groaned softly and kissed Mae's neck. Mae's skin was cool beneath her fevered lips, and her belly tightened under Mae's softly caressing fingers. "I never knew what to hope for. Now I do, and…sometimes when I'm out riding, and I'm so tired I fear I won't make it to the next place on my list, I think of you. Then I forget about everything except how much I want you, and it carries me through."

"Oh," Mae gasped. "Come upstairs with me now."

"I can't. I expect there'll be messages for me at the office. This stomach ailment that's going around has half the town in bed," Vance said in frustration. "I still have calls left over from today. I don't think I'll be done before morning."

"I want you to come to me no matter the time," Mae insisted.

"I suspect the sun will be up by then." Vance laughed. "And I will be no more presentable than a barnyard rooster at that point. I think I had better wait for the laundry to open so that I can collect my clean clothes."

Mae fondled the buttons on Vance's shirt. "You need *new* clothes, not clean ones. It's time to get you out of these borrowed clothes and into your own."

"I decided after a few months in the army that my days of standing on a seamstress's platform were over," Vance said carefully. "Dresses never did suit me, even before I needed to spend my day in the saddle or a buggy."

"Oh, you can't think that's what I was suggesting?" Mae brushed her fingers through Vance's short, thick, unruly hair. "Oh no. I'm taking you to the tailor tomorrow to be fitted for proper trousers and shirts."

"I…do you think he will?" Vance asked uncertainly.

"Of course he will. As long as you intend to pay him."

"I thought I would just get something from the general store when I had time."

"They don't have much in the way of ready-made clothes, and what they do have would never fit you properly." Mae kissed Vance lightly. "No, I'll enjoy dressing you."

A shiver of wholly unexpected anticipation raced down Vance's spine and she groaned softly, eliciting further laughter from Mae. "You please me in ways I never imagined."

"I must go in," Mae said regretfully. "It's getting late, and I'll be missed." She kissed Vance again, both hands clasped behind Vance's neck. Breathlessly, she brushed her mouth over Vance's ear. "And if I stay here, I will need your hand on me very soon."

"Please, have you no mercy?"

"Where you're concerned?" Mae stepped down onto the running board. "None at all."

Laughing, Vance jumped down to assist her, not because Mae needed her arm, but because it pleased her to offer it. She was astounded and grateful that Mae understood that. She walked Mae to the stairs, suddenly loath to let her go. She knew what awaited Mae inside, and the image of fresh bruises on Mae's face caused a cold sweat to break out on her forehead.

"If he comes around again and I'm not here—"

"Vance, I'll not have you worry—"

"If he touches you again, kill him." Vance shivered as the thunder of cannon and hundreds of marching men closed in around her. "Don't wait. Fire first."

Mae studied Vance in the hazy yellow light that flickered from the windows above them, watching long-ago ghosts dance over her stark, haunted face. She took her hand, pulled her against the building, out of sight of the street, and framed her face with both hands. "Vance. Don't go back."

"It's all right," Vance said hoarsely, fighting back the mists of memory. "I'm here." She put her hand on Mae's waist and rested her forehead against Mae's. "I have nothing to go back to and everything to stay for."

"I'll be careful. Promise me that you will be, too." Mae pressed her fingers to Vance's mouth, then stepped away and started up the stairs. When she was out of touching range, she turned. "I love you, so you be sure to be here in the morning."

Vance pressed her hand to her heart. "You have my word."

## CHAPTER TWENTY-FIVE

The sun was just coming up as Vance rode back into town. She was pleased to see that the laundry was already open, and she stopped to collect her clothes. Despite Mae's admonition that she come directly to her rooms, Vance wanted to wash off the sweat and lingering hints of sickness before going to her. The cold-water wash refreshed her, and just before seven, dressed in her best clean clothes, she tapped lightly on Mae's door. Far from feeling tired, she felt alive with expectation. When the door opened and Mae smiled up at her, the thrill of possibility shot through her. It had been so long since she had looked upon a day with anticipation.

"Thank you," Vance murmured.

Mae's eyes widened in surprise. "Whatever for?" She took Vance's hand and drew her inside, closing the door behind them.

"For reminding me what pleasure feels like." Before Mae could reply, Vance slid a finger beneath her chin, tilted Mae's head up, and kissed her. "You always look beautiful, but in the morning, you're exquisite."

"I'm not wearing even a touch of powder on my face, my robe was once lovely but is no longer new, and I haven't had a chance to put up my hair." Mae caressed Vance's cheek. "But when you look at me the way you do, I feel—"

"Cherished, I hope," Vance broke in. She turned her head and kissed Mae's palm. "Because you are."

"I don't believe I'm ready for this conversation before breakfast."

Vance laughed. “Then I shall take you to breakfast and we can resume thereafter.”

“We’re paying a visit to George Smith after breakfast, so anything else you might have planned will have to wait.”

“I had nothing planned, only hoped for.”

“Hush now,” Mae said softly. She still didn’t quite know how to take the attention that Vance lavished on her. She’d never been the object of anyone’s true affection. Even her mother, who had cared for her as well as possible, often gave the impression that it was more duty than love that motivated her. Mae didn’t blame her for that. Widowed young and with no money to tempt another husband nor skills to provide for herself and a child, she had gone into service and managed to provide a home for them both. Nevertheless, the drudgery and disappointment of her life had hardened her heart without her even knowing it. “I must get dressed, and while I do, you’re to sit here on the settee.”

Vance lifted her brow. “I’m not to be trusted, then?”

Mae smiled. “You might be, but I most certainly am not. I dreamed of you last night and woke up wanting you.”

With a sound close to a growl, Vance caught her swiftly around the waist. She pulled her near and kissed her, harder this time, without apology for her demands. “The tailor can wait.”

“He can,” Mae said breathlessly. “But I fear if we don’t go now, we won’t go at all.” She nipped at Vance’s lower lip. “And you do need new clothes.”

“Mae,” Vance said with a warning glint in her eyes. “I’ll not be patient much longer.”

“I don’t want you to be. Just for a few more hours.”

❖

Two hours were beginning to feel like a life sentence. The only thing that made the process bearable was watching the way Mae’s eyes moved over her body when George Smith wasn’t looking. Vance stood in the center of the small, cluttered room in her undershirt, drawers, and boots while the impeccably dressed, fastidious tailor measured and fussed and remeasured. He’d blinked once in surprise when Mae had explained why they’d come, then given a small bow and gestured with an open arm toward the curtained-off back room.

"Three shirts, two trousers, and a coat for everyday and business both," Mae repeated. "Cotton for the shirts and wool for the coat and trousers. None of that linsey-woolsey that stretches out of shape after one wearing."

Smith looked affronted. "I assure you, I use only the finest materials that come all the way from St. Louis."

"Well, don't plan on charging us for the entire train."

Vance grinned and said nothing. She had to admit, it was rather enjoyable having clothes made for her that would actually fit and in which she would be comfortable. She also discovered that having Mae direct the tailor as to precisely how *she* wanted the clothes to look was unexpectedly arousing. When Mae circled her, a contemplative expression on her face, and touched her here and there to demonstrate where she wanted the shirt to fall or the trousers to start, Vance had to stifle a moan. Even though Mae gave no indication that she was aware of Vance's growing discomfort, it seemed that as the morning wore on, Mae found more and more excuses to touch her.

"There," Smith proclaimed as if he had just completed a work of art. "That should be everything we need. I'll have these for you, Dr. Phelps, within a week."

"Thank you," Vance said with as much dignity as she could muster while dressed only in her underwear. She gratefully took the pants that Mae held out to her, removed her boots, and pulled them on. The shirt she slid over the remnant of her left arm and across her shoulders with ease of habit. When Mae stepped close to do up the buttons, Vance caught a flicker of heat in her lovely eyes. Knowing that Mae warmed to her that way only increased Vance's desire.

Once dressed and outside, Vance cupped Mae's elbow and led her quickly down the street.

"Have you forgotten an appointment?" Mae asked, reaching up to settle her hat more firmly upon her now neatly pinned tresses.

"Something like that," Vance muttered, intent on reaching the Golden Nugget as quickly as possible. Caleb would not expect her until evening at the earliest, knowing that she had been out all night working. Of course he would assume she was sleeping, although that was the furthest thing from her mind.

"You're going to look very handsome in those clothes," Mae said somewhat breathlessly as she concentrated on not catching the heels of her shoes in the hard-packed ruts of the street. She held her hem above the dust with one gloved hand.

"If you like them, that's all that matters to me," Vance said with one swift glance in Mae's direction. "You seemed to enjoy the fitting enough."

Mae smiled pleasantly. "I find that I like having you half-dressed and helpless."

"Mae, so help me," Vance warned, "I'll not temper my urges much longer."

They'd reached the stairs in the alley leading up to Mae's rooms, and Mae stopped abruptly to kiss Vance full on the mouth. "I certainly hope not."

Vance led the way up the stairs, Mae's hand clasped in hers. She waited while Mae unlocked the door, dizzy with the scent of spice and invitation that wafted from Mae's faintly flushed skin. Once inside the room, she removed her coat while Mae locked the door. When Mae turned to her with a hint of uncertainty in her eyes, Vance's urgency drained away to be replaced with a sense of expectation that she had no desire to hurry.

"Before I'm through," Vance said with absolute certainty, "I'm going to know every inch of you."

Mae's lips parted but no sound emerged. With shaking hands, she deposited her bag and shawl on the nearby sideboard and reached for her hat.

"Let me do that," Vance said. Gently, she removed the pins that held the hat and set everything aside. Then she took Mae's hand. "Let's finish this in the other room."

The shutters were closed in Mae's bedroom, and Vance lit the oil lamp that sat on the bureau, suffusing the room in a golden glow. She crossed to Mae, who stood by the bed, and kissed her softly. "With only one hand I may be a little slow at it, but I'd like to undress you myself."

"Take forever, if you need," Mae whispered. "There's nowhere in the world I want to be except here with you."

Vance wanted her then, immediately. Wanted to revel in the taste and sound of her. Wanted to lose herself in the sensation of hot flesh against hot flesh. She knew if she broke the chains of her own restraint, Mae would let her have anything she wanted, would let her feast until she was sated, as selfishly as she desired. And that was the one thing she did not want. She would not take, even that which was freely given. She would show this one woman, the only woman she had ever truly wanted, what it was to be treasured.

"I don't believe there *is* a world for me without you," Vance murmured, reaching around to open the tiny row of buttons that closed the back of Mae's dress. She laughed quietly. "Did you choose this particular dress just to test me?"

Mae circled her arms around Vance's narrow waist and rested her head against her shoulder. She was already half lost in the hungry timbre of Vance's voice, and she hadn't yet felt those delicate fingers upon her skin. She wondered if she would be able to stand the intensity of that moment without tears. "I wore it because no one else has ever seen me in it. No one else has ever seen me take it off."

Vance's chest filled with a terrible ache, with a need so great she feared she would choke on it. She buried her face in the curve of Mae's neck, her hand pressed tightly to Mae's back. "You honor me."

"How is it possible that you don't see me the way everyone else does?" Mae laced her fingers through the thick dark hair that brushed Vance's collar and pulled her head up so she could search her face. "Does it truly not matter what I am?"

"What matters, my dearest Mae, is who you are," Vance said, her voice steady and her eyes as gentle as the first breath of spring, "and how tenderly you have taken me into your heart, when I have such great need for you."

"No greater need than mine for you."

Vance smiled and brushed her lips over Mae's. "I think you still do not know me, or my needs." With swift, delicate precision, she opened Mae's dress. She bent to kiss her bare shoulder, then smoothed her palm over her collarbone and down her arm, pushing the dress away. She repeated the motion on the opposite side, until the garment pooled in folds of lush green around Mae's feet. Vance traced a fingertip along the lacy edge of the chemise that peeked above the black silk corset that cradled Mae's breasts. Then she kissed the path her finger had taken, lingering over the spot where Mae's heart beat frantically.

"Your mouth is so soft, so warm," Mae marveled, trembling beneath that terribly gentle onslaught. She braced her hands on Vance's shoulders for support as her legs grew steadily weaker, but she was determined to stand as long as Vance wanted to touch her. She had never wanted to give so much to a single person in all her life.

"I love the way you smell," Vance murmured, closing her eyes as she rubbed her cheek over the swell of Mae's breast, her fingers busy with the hooks that held the corset closed. As it fell away, releasing the full beauty of Mae's breasts, she gasped. "So beautiful."

Unable to contain the ache of pleasure that filled her, Mae grasped Vance's head and guided Vance's mouth to her taut nipple. "Please."

Vance drew her in, rolling her tongue over the small hard peak, closing her fingers convulsively around the soft weight in her hand.

Mae's head dropped back, and eyes closed, she moaned. The sensation was pain and pleasure, too exquisite to distinguish. "I need you so."

Panting, Vance straightened, drawing trembling fingers down the delicate column of Mae's throat. With infinite care she plucked the pins from Mae's hair, watching it tumble like a golden sunrise around Mae's pale shoulders. "I must have you soon. I fear that if I wait, something inside me will break and I will hurt you in my hunger for you."

"No," Mae soothed. "You will not hurt me with love." She spread her hands over Vance's chest, then stroked downward over her stomach. She tugged at the buttons on her trousers. "But let it be soon."

Looking down as Mae opened her clothing, Vance felt the beast inside her slip its restraints. She caught a handful of silken curls in her fist and tugged until Mae let go of her clothing and stared up in surprise. Then she covered Mae's mouth, catching her swollen lip between her teeth, tugging it between her own and sucking until Mae whimpered and dug her fingers into Vance's back. Vance pulled away and, with an arm curved around Mae's waist, half carried her toward the bed. "Help me undress. I can't manage now with one hand."

"You've been managing just perfectly," Mae said unsteadily even as she pushed the shirt from Vance's shoulders. She grasped her undershirt and lifted upward, baring the scars that made her want to weep and the beautiful body that took her breath away. She smoothed her palm over the arch of Vance's shoulder and down her left arm, tenderly touching the terrible wound. "Be careful of this when we're together—"

"You needn't worry." Vance edged her fingers beneath Mae's chemise and drew it gently over her breasts and off. "The only thing that I will know when we lie together is joy." She reached down and pushed the covers aside on the bed, then motioned for Mae to lie down. She leaned over and whispered, "Will you take off the rest for me now?"

With her eyes on Vance, Mae removed her remaining garments. "Now you."

Vance felt Mae's gaze warm her skin as she stripped, baring far more than her flesh. She came to Mae with every emotion exposed, nearly helpless in her need. She lowered herself gently over Mae's body, leaning on her right arm to keep her weight from being too much. Because she had no other hand to explore Mae's body, she used her mouth, slowly, thoroughly, kissing Mae's forehead, her eyelids, her lips, before moving down to her throat, the valley between her breasts, the dip at her navel, the arch of hipbone and delicate curve of her thigh. It was a journey of discovery and adoration, and she did not hurry.

Mae's hands on her face and shoulders guided her, fluttering urgently when her mouth found a particularly sensitive spot, stroking languidly as the pleasure ebbed and flowed. When she reached Mae's center, Vance pushed up to her knees, leaning back between Mae's parted thighs and lifting her gaze to Mae's face. She barely recognized her own voice when she rasped, "I want only to please you. I want to be inside you, but if you would rather I not—"

"You are the only one I've ever wanted there," Mae whispered brokenly, "if you desire."

Vance gently cupped Mae's sex and stretched out upon her again, her hand between their bodies. She kissed her tenderly as she slipped into her, then closed her eyes and went completely still. In the faintest of whispers, she said, "I feel your heart pulse all around me. Even the beat of a new life in the palm of my hand has never felt as wondrous."

Mae cupped one hand behind Vance's head, drawing Vance's face to her breasts as she lifted her hips to take Vance even deeper. She moved with a rhythm as natural as life, as pure as love, and held Vance to her heart as she offered her own. Dimly she sensed Vance following her lead, stroke for stroke, knowing instinctively that Vance would fear to take more than Mae might want to give.

"Vance," Mae breathed against Vance's ear. "Make me yours. Please."

With a cry, Vance shifted her hips and rested her weight on her left shoulder so she could free her arm. She drove faster, harder, calling Mae's passion to hers. "Come to me, dearest. Come to me now."

Had Mae been able to think, she might have worried about Vance, but she could do nothing but give way to the fierce pleasure that blossomed with every thrust. She pressed her face to Vance's breast and let the wild beating of her lover's heart take her home.

# CHAPTER TWENTY-SIX

Did I fall asleep?" Mae asked. She had no memory of having been asleep, only of being delightfully free of fear or worry. Her body felt warm, soft, loved. She rubbed her fingers lightly down the center of Vance's chest, then kissed the base of her throat. "You're quiet. Are you all right?"

Vance nodded, her cheek brushing the top of Mae's head. "Yes. Just thinking."

"I'm not sure that's such a good thing at a time like this," Mae said, laughing lightly. "I believe I'd prefer that your brain be too addled to be entertaining any heavy ideas."

"You needn't worry. My head *and* body are nicely addled." Vance kissed Mae and smiled. "I thought I knew what it was to be happy, until these moments with you. Now I understand that happiness is not merely the absence of sorrow, but the presence of joy."

The tears that Mae had been able to contain earlier escaped now. She closed her eyes and savored the comfort and security of Vance's embrace.

"Have I upset you?" Vance said worriedly, feeling the tears against her skin.

"No," Mae whispered. "You've made me very happy, and apparently, when that happens, I cry."

"Then it seems we are in similar circumstances." Vance sighed. Judging from the light sifting through the spaces between the shutters on Mae's window, it was close to dusk. "I need to find Caleb and make sure he doesn't need me."

Frowning, Mae sat up. “I know you haven’t been to bed for more than a day. You can’t think of working tonight.”

“I won’t unless it’s necessary, but,” Vance said hurriedly, “if it is, I’ll be fine. Believe me, this kind of work is nothing compared to weeks on end with no shelter, no food, and no hope.”

“Why did you stay?” Mae asked quietly.

“After a while, I wondered that myself,” Vance admitted. “But I’d made a promise to serve, and when I was able to think clearly, I knew that the cause was just. I didn’t leave because I was needed. And part of me needed to be there.”

“Whatever comes of us in the future,” Mae said seriously, “I want you to stay only because you need to be here. Not because of what you think my needs—”

Vance sat up, her eyes glittering sharply. “Have I loved you so poorly just now that you can’t feel my need for you?”

Mae took a shuddering breath. “I never thought to be loved the way you do.” She pressed her hand to Vance’s heart. “But sometimes feelings change—”

“Not mine. Not about you.” Vance circled Mae’s shoulders and pulled her roughly against her chest. She kissed her hard with a mixture of frustration and affection, and didn’t release her until she was breathless. “I can see that you do not trust my feelings as of yet. I’ll have to work harder to convince you.”

“If you work any harder,” Mae whispered, pressing trembling fingers to Vance’s mouth, “I don’t know that I’ll survive.”

“I’ll see that you do.” Vance smiled and was about to kiss her again when frantic knocking at Mae’s door interrupted her. She threw back the covers and leapt up, reaching for her holster, which she’d left on the floor with her clothes. Out of the corner of her eye, she saw Mae pull on a robe and start toward the door. “Wait for me.”

“Who is it?” Mae called without opening the door.

“It’s me. Sissy.”

Mae glanced back and saw that Vance had her pants on and was working her shirt over her shoulders. She pulled the door open several inches. “What’s the matter?”

“It’s Lettie. She says the baby’s coming.”

“Lord, it’s too soon.”

“Only by a few weeks,” Vance said as she stepped up beside Mae. “Let me take a look at her.”

Sissy stared from Mae to Vance, but made no remark about the fact that they had clearly shared a bed. "I'll take you."

After Mae hastily threw on her dress, she followed. Vance leaned over Lettie, murmuring in a calming voice as she palpated the girl's swollen abdomen. Lettie's pale face was beaded with sweat and her eyes were wild with fear. Mae went to the head of the bed and stroked her hair. "Don't worry, honey. Everything is going to be all right."

"It hurts and I'm so scared."

"I know you are. I know." Mae looked at Vance over Lettie's head and saw her nod sharply to confirm that the baby was indeed on its way. "You're going to have this baby tonight, honey, and it's going to be a beautiful baby. You'll be just fine."

"Don't go. Please don't go."

Mae shook her head. "No, of course I won't." To Vance, she said, "How much time?"

"Hard to tell. A few hours at least." She smiled at Lettie. "You're going to have some work to do, but I know that you'll do a fine job. There's nothing to be afraid of." She stepped close to Mae. "I need to get my bag. Have the girls boil some water, bring fresh towels. You know what to do. I'll be back shortly. Until then, just stay with her."

"You go on ahead. I'll be here."

Vance smiled. "That's good. I'm counting on that."

❖

When Kate arrived nearly three hours later, it was well after dark and Mae, Vance, and several of the girls were huddled on chairs around the bed. Mae held Lettie's hand.

"I got here as soon as I could. Thank you for sending word for me to come," she said to Vance as she removed her bonnet and cloak.

"You've arrived in plenty of time," Vance said. "She's doing a wonderful job, but we've got a ways to go yet." She stood and led Kate to the bed. "Lettie, I'm going to show Kate how to tell what the baby's doing. It won't hurt you."

Panting, Lettie nodded, her face strained, but her eyes calm and trusting. "Okay."

After both Vance and Kate washed and dried their hands, Vance lifted the sheet and nodded to Mae to hold it up. "Thanks." She took Kate's hand and placed it on Lettie's lower abdomen just above her pelvic bone. "You can feel the head here, as it descends into the pelvis and the birth canal."

Heart pounding, Kate pressed gently. The smooth, firm curve of the infant's skull was easy to appreciate. She raised shining eyes to Vance's. "Yes."

"Now, I'm going to show you how to judge the progression of labor by the amount the cervix is open." She lifted the sheet to block what she and Kate were doing. "Mae, would you hold this, please."

"I have it," Mae said, watching as Vance gently placed Kate's hand between Lettie's legs and instructed her on what to feel for as she examined her inside. Mae had seen Doc Melbourne deliver babies before, and she knew the basics. He'd always seemed to do a good job, but there was a tenderness about the way Vance did everything that was just…special.

When Kate hesitated after slipping her fingers into the birth canal, Vance murmured, "You'll not hurt her. The nerves are stretched by the baby's head coming down, and not very sensitive right now."

"I feel something pounding," Kate said anxiously.

"Those are the uterine arteries, which are very large at this point because they're supplying blood to the uterus as well as the baby."

For the first time, Kate realized that she recognized this rapid pulse that beat against her fingers. It was a powerful sign of life and she'd felt it before, under different but just as miraculous circumstances. Reverently, she nodded.

"Now you'll feel a thick ring and then the smooth crown of the baby's head. That's the cervix opening to allow the baby to exit the uterus. When that ring is open five inches, she'll be very close to giving birth."

"It feels like it's about halfway there," Kate said, keeping her voice low.

"Good," Vance said. "You're right."

Carefully, Kate withdrew her hand. "What do we do now?"

Vance smiled. "We wait."

Four hours later they were still waiting. Lettie slept fitfully on and off, while Mae or Sissy sponged her hot, sweaty face with cool water. Vance and Kate sat on opposite sides of the bed, watching and checking the time between the contractions.

Mae squeezed Vance's shoulder. "You should have something to eat. It's closing in on midnight."

Vance smiled up at Mae. "I'm all right. Thanks. You can take a break, though. We might be in for a long night."

"It's hard when they're so young," Mae said, glancing up to where Lettie lay with her eyes closed. "Hard anytime I guess, when you're alone."

Vance caught Mae's hand and clasped it gently. "She's not alone. She has you and the others. She has more family than most."

Mae moved her hand to the back of Vance's neck and caressed her softly for a few seconds. "I'd forgotten how much you understand."

"I know what you mean to them. To all of us." Vance stood and stretched, then said, "Let's see how she's doing." When she pulled back the covers once again, she frowned. A trickle of blood pooled between Lettie's thighs. "Kate."

Kate jumped up and followed Vance's gaze. She caught her lip between her teeth but made no sound, merely looked into Vance's face questioningly.

"Feel her abdomen and tell me if anything has changed."

With a trembling hand, Kate probed gently the way she had been shown. She moved quickly, but carefully. "I don't feel the head where it was before," she said in a low whisper.

Vance repeated the examination and nodded, her face expressionless now. She looked over her shoulder to Mae. "I need my instruments and the basin with carbolic nearby. Will you lay them out for me like you did when Jed was injured?"

"Yes," Mae said. "What's happening?"

"I'll tell you in just a moment." Once again, Vance sat on the edge of the bed and carefully inserted her hand into the birth canal. She closed her eyes to focus her attention completely on the details she could discern with her fingertips, then withdrew her hand and stood. "The baby's shifted position. It's breech. I can feel an arm at the very top of the birth canal."

Mae's face went white. She glanced quickly up at Lettie, who did not appear to be listening, or, if she was, did not understand what was happening. Mae did, however. She'd seen women die trying to deliver a baby that was coming feet first or with just a hand or shoulder without the head preceding it. She'd never seen the baby delivered alive. "Oh Lord."

"The instruments, Mae," Vance said gently.

Wordlessly, Mae complied as Vance motioned Kate to step away from the bed.

"The baby's head is no longer in the birth canal, and if we can't change that, the baby or the mother will die."

"What can we do?" Kate asked through a dry, tight throat. The wonder and excitement of birth had changed in a heartbeat to a terrifying tableau of fear and desperation. She understood that there would be times when it was up to her to change that balance, and she was determined that she would not fail mother or child for lack of knowledge or courage. She looked to Vance for the answers and was reassured by the steady certainty of her gaze.

"Most often, to save the mother, the child would be sacrificed." Vance glanced at the bed where a young girl lay, weak and exhausted from the long hours of labor, having entrusted her life to Vance. "I'm not going to let that happen if I can help it."

Vance walked to the side table where Mae had arranged her instruments. "Would you help me with my sleeve, please?"

"Tell me what else I can do," Mae said, swiftly rolling Vance's cuff higher.

"You can reassure her, because this is going to be painful." Vance met Mae's worried eyes. "Give her your strength, as you do me."

Mae nodded. "We all trust you."

Vance dipped her hand into the carbolic and shook the excess liquid free. Sometimes, especially in the last two years of the war, the trust of others had felt like a burden, but not now. She felt an inner steadiness that had been gone since she'd learned of Victor's death. For the first time in months, she felt whole.

Vance turned, and with a clear head and certain mind, said to Mae and Sissy, "Put some pillows under her hips so that the uterus tilts back into the abdomen."

When that was done, she eased her hand into the birth canal and pushed upward until she felt the tiny arm between her fingers. She pushed farther until she encountered the thorax lying wedged across the uterine opening. Pressing her fingers together to form a funnel, she moved them alongside the small body until she reached the hips. Her hand was nearly inside the uterus now. She felt a contraction and the muscles closed down around her wrist. She held still, waiting for it to pass. She blocked out Lettie's screams, knowing that the girl would not die from the pain, and mercifully, that she would not remember it if she lived through the delivery. She looked at Kate, who was following her every movement with intense concentration, her eyes huge but clear.

"I'm going to try to move the baby ninety degrees inside the uterus. That's called a version." She took a breath and smiled slightly. "That should align the head again so that this baby can get out."

Kate didn't need to ask what would happen if Vance failed. She knew how small the opening was inside and that the only way the child was coming out was head first. She didn't quite know what they would do if this maneuver failed, so she simply prayed that it would not.

"Mae, hold Lettie tightly," Vance said gently.

"We've got her," Mae said in a firm, steady voice. "You go on ahead now and do what needs to be done."

Focusing all her attention on her hand and the small body cradled against her palm, she pushed steadily inward and upward, rotating the hips away from the cervical opening and drawing the head down. At first, nothing happened. Then it was as if the baby coiled in on itself and kicked away, as if swimming. When Vance felt the movement, she slid her hand out and guided the head down into the upper portion of the birth canal. She closed her eyes for a brief second, then grinned. "Shouldn't be long now."

Within the hour, a lusty cry pierced the air and mingled with the joyous exclamations of the women crowded around the bed.

"Honey, it's a boy. A big, loud, and beautiful boy," Mae exclaimed.

"Let me see him," Lettie said, smiling weakly.

"Kate, go ahead and deliver the placenta," Vance said as she walked away from the bed. Her hair and shirt were soaked with sweat, and the nerves she had not felt earlier snaked around in her belly now, making her queasy. After rinsing her hand and arm, she leaned against the window frame facing the street and closed her eyes.

"Here," Mae said quietly, handing her a glass of whiskey. "You look like you could use this."

Vance turned and set her back against the wall. She took the glass and drained it gratefully. "Thanks."

"I've never seen anyone do that before," Mae said.

"It's not a common technique, and it doesn't usually work."

Vance glanced across the room at Lettie, who was holding her child and rapidly regaining her strength. "But she is young and strong, and they deserved a chance."

Mae put her hand to the center of Vance's chest. Everyone else in the room was focused on the mother and baby. She stepped close. "You seem to have a knack for doing that for everyone."

Vance covered Mae's hand with hers and looked into her eyes. "We'll be each other's chance."

"Yes." Mae kissed her softly. "We will."

## CHAPTER TWENTY-SEVEN

As the sun set, Jessie stood on the front porch of the ranch house with a cup of coffee, watching with a wry smile as Vance climbed down from the buggy. "You missed dinner."

"Is Kate angry?" Vance asked as she climbed the stairs.

"She would have been most times, except she's done nothing but talk about Lettie's baby being born for the last three days." Jessie smiled. "So I think you've probably got another week's grace before she'll light into you about not getting back here in time for the evening meal."

Vance grinned. "How about Mae?"

"She'll probably fuss over you in between the scolding." Jessie looked past Vance, choosing her words carefully. "She looks good. I take it there hasn't been any more trouble?"

"None that she's told me of." Vance unbuttoned her shirt collar and took a deep breath of the fragrant, warm night air. "I haven't seen anyone come around the Nugget, and if he's been there, he hasn't caused any trouble."

"I've never seen a mark on Mae before." Jessie hooked her thumb over her gun belt. In the corral across the way, a colt fell asleep with his head resting against his mother's flank. "If I had, I would have done something about it."

"You weren't in town that often, I imagine, and she wouldn't have wanted you to know."

Jessie smiled faintly. "For all her gentle ways, she's strong in places I'm not sure I've got in me."

"She is quite remarkable." Vance rolled her shoulders, trying to work out the stiffness of the day and the tension from the conversation. Every night when the sun went down and she wasn't in town where she could watch after Mae, the anger ate at her, burning in her gut. "But it's only a matter of time before something else happens. Men like him take what they want."

"Whatever needs to be done to make her safe, you've got my help."

"Whoever owns the Nugget has gone to a lot of trouble to keep his identity a secret, and men with secrets are vulnerable." Vance pushed away the surge of anger when she thought of Mae or any of the girls being abused. "I'll find him."

"You still planning to follow Hanrahan when he reports in?"

"Seems like the simplest way to go about it." Vance shrugged. "I'm sure he doesn't expect anyone to pay attention to his comings and goings. I'd hoped to be able to do something before now, but I've been out on calls almost every night. It seems that this is baby-birthing time."

"I know. Kate's been right there with you most of the time."

Vance searched for any hint of dissatisfaction in Jessie's voice, but found none. "It's demanding work."

"Kate's strong and smart."

Smiling, Vance nodded. "She is. I meant that it can be difficult when your…" She frowned and glanced at Jessie. "Well I don't quite know what word to use. How do you think of Kate, as she is to you?"

"I think of her as my heart," Jessie said quietly.

"Yes," Vance replied, feeling the rightness of that as she thought of Mae. "When your…beloved…makes a habit of leaving in the middle of the night for hours at a time, it can be disrupting."

"I'm gone a lot, seeing to the stock and the men out on the line, and Kate never complains." Jessie chuckled. "Well, not much. More like worries."

"I imagine you worry a bit about her, too."

"If she weren't with you most of the time, I'd fret a lot more. But we've managed to get in some good practice the last few weeks, and she's getting to be handy with a revolver and a rifle."

"Doing the work she's doing will endear her to everyone in the territory. People will watch out for her. She'll be fine," Vance said gently, hearing the concern beneath the pride.

"It's what she wants to do." Jessie studied Vance. She didn't often speak to anyone other than Kate about her feelings. She and Vance were alike, she knew that without being able to put all the words to her knowledge. It wasn't just the way they dressed or the way they loved. It was something about how they worked inside, what was important to them. And what they feared. It made it easier to say what was in her heart knowing that she wouldn't have to explain or defend her feelings. "I figure that's part of loving, not getting in the way of what she needs to do."

"I think you're right."

"It can be a hard thing to do sometimes, just the same."

Solemnly, Vance nodded. Harder than hard sometimes. The breeze carried the scent of new grass and rich earth as golden shadows slanted across the dusty yard. "Summer's about here. It's beautiful country."

"It is." Jessie felt the calm in the center of her being that came from being on her land, being satisfied in her work, and being loved better than she had ever dreamed. "I've never been all the way back East, but I've been to the big cities a time or two. Enough to know there is no place for me there."

"I had to leave to understand that," Vance said, recognizing the absence of the restless unease that had always been part of her consciousness, even when Victor had been alive and she had been happy. Or what she had taken to be happiness. "It seems that we've come from different directions to the same place."

"I reckon that says something about us." Jessie grinned at Vance. "Good thing we're not of a mind to fit in."

Vance glanced behind her at the sound of the door opening. Mae stood in a shaft of lamplight, her face partially in shadows, her hair a golden halo framing the pale oval of her face. She wore a dress that resembled the blue of the Union uniforms when the troops had been young and fresh, before months of deprivation and death had changed them all. It was deceptively simple in design, the bodice and waist subtly accentuating her curvaceous body. It wasn't what she had been wearing when Vance had last seen her that morning. It occurred to Vance that she still wore the dusty, rumpled clothes she'd been in all day, and she wished for a bath.

"You two," Mae said, "don't need to worry about fitting in, because you're just where you belong. Vance, there's a bit of supper left, and if you don't have some soon, Kate's likely to take after you with a knife."

"I just need to get washed up," Vance said, wishing she could kiss her, but wanting to be fresher before she did.

Mae solved her dilemma by crossing the porch, curling an arm around Vance's neck, and kissing her soundly on the mouth.

Jessie looked hastily away and sidled toward the door. "I'll just…ah…be going. Help Kate…do something."

"Jed's been fussing about getting back to work," Mae called after Jessie, her arms still around Vance's neck. "If you tell him to stay in bed, he might just mind."

"How is he doing?" Vance decided that if Mae didn't mind the way she smelled, she might as well enjoy herself, so she leaned back against the post rail and snugged Mae into the curve of her body.

"We couldn't get even the smallest bit of cloth into that hole in his back today," Mae said with satisfaction. "I think he's healed."

"You've both done an excellent job with him." Vance sighed with contentment and rested her chin lightly on Mae's shoulder. "I'm sorry I'm so late."

"You make it hard for me to fuss at you when I'm so glad to see you," Mae murmured. She kissed Vance's neck. "And when you feel so good."

"With any luck, there won't be any calls waiting for me and I can stay the night with you."

"I don't care if there're a dozen calls, you're going to bed tonight." Mae frowned. "You'll not do anyone any good if you run yourself into the ground."

Vance laughed. "I'm fine. I've been known to take a nap beneath a tree while waiting for a baby to be born."

Mae smiled. "I bet that's a sight. But I still want you in bed with me tonight. Come by around one."

"Mae," Vance said carefully. "You told me once that you don't need to entertain very often because there are only a few customers you still see. How did that come about?"

"I think it would be better if we didn't speak of these things," Mae said quietly, her cheek against Vance's shoulder. "If it doesn't touch us, it can't drive us apar—"

"Nothing is going to come between us, my dearest Mae," Vance said. "Certainly not this."

Mae sighed. "Is it important?"

"I think so, yes."

"After I'd been here a few months, a gentleman from town told me one evening that he'd made an arrangement so that I would be available to him whenever he wanted."

"And you agreed?"

Mae laughed. "It's not a question of agreeing or not. He was polite, didn't come around very often, and made it clear that he would be generous with his money. He also made it clear that I was not to speak of our arrangement. He always uses the back entrance."

Vance remained perfectly still while Mae explained the arrangements, allowing none of her growing jealousy to show. "So he's the only one?"

"On occasion there are others, friends of his. Not very often."

"Who is he?"

"Oh, Vance, if you have a face, a name, to think about, I'm afraid that it will work on you. I don't want you to look at me and see him touching me, when he's nothin—"

"I love you," Vance said firmly. "I love to look at you, I love to touch you. I love it when you touch me. Nothing will ever change that." Tenderly, Vance skimmed her fingers over Mae's face and down her neck. She cupped her chin and kissed her softly. "When I look at you, I see my greatest fortune. I see my deepest hopes. All my dreams rest in your eyes." She pressed her cheek to Mae's and held her tightly. Against her ear she murmured, "I don't want to spend a day of my life without you. Please let me help you be safe."

"You make it hard to say no," Mae whispered. "Promise me you won't do anything foolish."

"You have my word," Vance said immediately.

"Wallace Fitzpatrick."

"The lumberman?"

"Yes."

"And you think he owns the Nugget?"

Mae shook her head. "I don't think so. But I think one of the others does. One of his friends."

"Who are they?"

Vance wasn't surprised when Mae named two of the men whom

Jessie had suggested had the means to own the establishment. At least now she could concentrate her efforts on them. If she couldn't track Hanrahan, she could watch them. She kissed Mae again. "Thank you."

"I can't seem to say no to you." Mae shook her head. "I'm not sure yet if that's a good thing."

Vance laughed. "I should get inside before Kate comes searching for me. I can't have the two of you after me at once."

"You needn't worry," Mae said, linking her arm through Vance's. "If anyone's going to be taking after you, it will be me."

"Then I shall consider myself lucky."

"Mary Willows asked me to bring my camera with me the next time I visit," Kate said. She sat at the table finishing her tea while Vance ate the supper she had saved for her. "To photograph the baby."

Vance smiled. "I have a feeling that's going to be a very frequent request."

"You're going to need a bigger buggy," Jessie teased.

"I love taking family pictures, but there are so many beautiful things about our life out here. I was wondering," Kate said shyly, watching Vance carefully, "if you would sit for me."

"Me?" Vance colored and cast about for some excuse. "Why, I hardly think there's anything about me—"

"I think that's a fine idea," Mae said firmly. "I'd like one of her, Kate."

"Actually," Kate said, "I've seen sketches in newspapers done from photographs. I'd like to try that for my father's paper. You're a new doctor in the territory, and a woman, and that seems like something people would be interested in knowing about."

Vance groaned. "I can't think why, and even if they did, I—"

"You might as well just agree, Vance," Jessie said. "Because you're going to sooner or later."

Kate cast her lover a stern glance, but her laughing eyes betrayed her amusement.

"I suppose it's the least I can do after all the nights you've fed me." Vance smiled at Kate. "Just tell me when you—"

The clatter of hoofbeats and the sound of someone riding hard interrupted her, and everyone glanced toward the kitchen door. Vance rose quickly as both she and Jessie automatically gripped their revolvers, and then she stepped between Mae and the window. When Jessie edged open the door to look outside, Vance started toward her, saying to Mae, "Stay inside."

Mae turned to Kate. "Where's the rifle?"

"By the fireplace." Kate opened a drawer, withdrew a revolver, and cocked it. "It's probably nothing, but ever since Jed—"

"I know," Mae said grimly, opening the door, the rifle resting in the crook of her arm. She could see shapes in the yard but not much else. She lifted the rifle as a figure approached, then lowered it again when she recognized Jessie's distinctive form. "What is it?"

Jessie strode inside, followed a few seconds later by Vance. "Charlie's outside. He said there are strangers following one of the herds. He thinks they're getting ready to cut the young horses out." She glanced at Kate. "I have to go."

"I want to come."

Jessie shook her head. "You can't, Kate. We're going to be riding hard. Charlie thinks we can reach their location before dawn."

"I'll need a horse and saddlebags for my equipment," Vance said. "I'll also need extra ammunition. I don't carry much when I'm out on calls."

"I appreciate it," Jessie said to Vance, "but there's no need for you to come."

"With Jed still down, you're short a gun." Vance grinned. "And I'm a good one."

Jessie studied Vance's face, saw the steady sureness in her eyes. "Okay, then."

Kate turned to Mae as Jessie and Vance hurried back outside. "Isn't there something we can do?"

"If I could think of a reason that made sense for them not to go, I'd say so." Mae frowned and set the rifle on the table. "But they're doing what needs to be done, and though I hate to admit it, they're the ones to do it."

As much as Kate didn't like the idea of staying behind, she knew that Mae and Jessie were right. She just had to believe that Jessie would come home unharmed.

## CHAPTER TWENTY-EIGHT

Just before dawn, Vance pulled her horse even with Jessie's. She, Jessie, and the ranch hands had been climbing steadily into the foothills through the night, and the air was noticeably thinner and colder than on the ranch. The terrain was rocky and the scattering of junipers and sagebrush fairly sparse, so there wasn't much in the way of cover. The openness made Vance more than a little uneasy. She was used to fighting in the woods and fields of Pennsylvania and Virginia, where trees and thickets provided plentiful shields. The sound of horses' hooves clattering on rock split the air like gunshots, and each time she heard it, her stomach tightened painfully. She knew where she was, and she knew that Lee's army did not wait over the crest of the next ridge. Still, the anticipation of battle was as familiar as the beat of her own heart. "How much farther, do you think?"

"We're pretty close to the line shack where Charlie and Johnny were staying when they saw the strangers following the herd," Jessie said.

"It might be better to leave most of the men back a ways, because fifteen riders are going to make a racket going up that last slope," Vance said, nodding toward the rocky ridge in front of them. "It will also prevent us from being flanked to have your guns at our back."

Jessie nodded. "I would never have brought this many men if Jed and Kate hadn't ganged up on me and threatened to follow us." She shook her head. "A few good hands are all we really need."

"It's a lot like trying to move an army without anyone noticing," Vance said. "It's far more effective to send advance skirmishers to secure an area and then bring up the main body."

"I guess you've been in situations like this before," Jessie said, slowing Star to a walk. The sun would be up within minutes, and any advantage of surprise they might have would be lost.

"A few times. Usually I stayed with the battalion, but when heavy forward skirmishes were anticipated, I went with the men."

Jessie turned in the saddle and motioned for Charlie to join them. "Tell four or five of the boys to wait here. The rest should work their way down into the valley, staying below the ridge line, so they can cut off any escape if the bastards decide to run. You, Vance, and I will go on up ahead so we can get a look over the rim of the valley. You can show us where you last saw them, and if we're lucky, they'll still be there."

"The boys won't take lightly to being left behind," Charlie observed conversationally.

"Maybe not. But I don't want to spook this bunch before we get a fix on their position."

Charlie nodded. "Makes sense, I guess. I'll tell them."

As he rode back to the group, Vance and Jessie trotted ahead. Just before they reached the top of the trail that bordered the valley below, Jessie slowed again. "You might want to think about staying back, too. We'll be visible on this ridge now that the sun is up, and if it's the same bunch as before, they won't waste any time shooting at us."

"I didn't come all this way to miss the action." Vance shrugged and grimaced as pain shot through her left shoulder and chest. The gray morning air hung thick with mist, and her leather duster kept the moisture but not the cold from settling into the damaged tissues. "Is it your plan to kill these men?"

"Might have to." Jessie regarded her pensively. "Is that going to be a problem for you?"

Vance held Jessie's steady gaze. "It wouldn't be if I knew they were the men who ambushed you and Jed. Attempted murder and horse thievery are hanging offenses."

"But we don't know for sure," Jessie said, spurring Star up a small rise off to one side of the trail.

Vance guided her horse up beside her, and together, they surveyed the valley below. "I'm not suggesting a friendly parlay. But once we find them, we might want to wait a bit to see if they're actually stealing—"

The small puff of smoke appearing from a clump of rocks two hundred feet away, the sound of the shot, and Jessie's horse rearing seemed to happen all at once. Then Jessie was falling and Vance was diving after her, her saddlebag clutched in her hand. Vance tucked her chin and rolled over her right shoulder, tossing the bag in front of her and pulling her revolver as she came to a teeth-jarring halt in the loose stones next to Jessie. A boulder blocked her view of the spot from which the shot had come, which also meant they couldn't be seen. Even if the shooters climbed up to their location, it would take them a few minutes.

"Jessie," Vance said urgently, a sick feeling clamping down on her throat. There was blood spatter on the ground, and Jessie had not moved since she'd landed. "Where are you hit?"

"Leg," Jessie said through gritted teeth, slowly turning onto her back and pushing upright against the largest rock with her right leg. "Just winged my thigh, but I think Star might have been hit. Bastards. I'll kill every one of them if they hurt my horse."

"I saw her bolt away. If she's hurt, it's not bad. Now let me see your leg." Vance jerked open the flap on her saddlebag and pulled out a trail knife. She slit Jessie's chaps and denim pants in the area of the bloody tear on the outside of her left thigh. Jessie winced but made no complaint. "It looks like it's skimmed you, but didn't lodge in the muscle or bone." Carefully, Vance palpated Jessie's thigh, pressing along the length of her femur and eliciting no increased pain or movement. "It's not broken."

"Just bind it up so we can climb up there and get a shot at these rustlers," Jessie said. "And don't tear my pants up too much while you're doing that, because Kate is going to be mad enough as it is."

"Just make sure you don't get any more holes in your clothes, and Kate will probably only take a few swats at you," Vance said as she withdrew a length of cotton from her bag. She folded the end and applied it to the slowly oozing wound. "Here. Hold this end so I can wrap it around and stop the bleeding."

A minute later, Jessie tested her leg. "Doesn't feel much worse than when one of my stallions kicks me. I can walk on it."

"Keep your damn head down," Vance said, her relief giving way to anger at whoever had shot at them. She turned at a sound behind her and saw Charlie and another man, Johnny probably, crab-walking up the slope toward them, guns drawn, faces grim. She pointed to the ridge. "The shooter was probably a lookout, hoping to scare us off.

The rest are probably down the other side, waiting to see if we'll keep coming." She looked to Jessie, who nodded agreement, then pointed Charlie and Johnny toward the right. "You two see if you can get over to that outcropping…there, and Jessie and I will work our way around this one here. Then we should have them in a crossfire down below us."

The two men glanced at Jessie.

"It's a good plan, boys. Let's do it."

The few minutes it took to reach the ridge felt like an hour to Vance as they cautiously darted from one outcropping to the next, half expecting gunfire from some quarter. She breathed a sigh of relief when she and Jessie reached the top without further shots being fired. From where they crouched behind a cluster of barrel-sized rocks, they could just make out Charlie and Johnny in a similar position partway around the ridge overlooking the deep narrow valley below. Scanning the area, she could make out portions of the herd grazing on the short grass that bordered a tortuously winding river. It wasn't surprising that the rustlers had chosen this location. Fifty prime mustangs grazed in the valley below, mares watching over their still-wobbly-legged foals as they ambled innocently beneath a clear dawn sky. Vance had seen bucolic scenes like this before erupt into gunfire and death in the blink of an eye. While a small corner of her mind noted the beauty, all of her senses were focused on detecting any sign of the enemy. She sniffed the crisp, sharp air and smiled, inching closer to Jessie.

"Cigarette."

"Where?"

Vance squinted in the sunlight and caught a puff of white out of the corner of her eye, come and gone so quickly it might have been a mirage, but she knew it wasn't. "There. Halfway down and just to the right of that lone pine."

Without moving, Jessie stared and, after a few seconds, saw the telltale whiff of smoke. "That's one. How many more do you think?"

"Charlie said they'd seen four men yesterday, right?"

Jessie nodded.

"Then they're probably all still here."

"Damn fools if they think they can ride onto our land and ride out with our horses." Jessie shook her head, then glanced at Vance. "Killing a man doesn't come easy to me."

"I understand. It might not come to that."

"I guess we'll see," Jessie said, eyes narrowing as she watched a prong-horned antelope bolt from behind a clump of sagebrush and gracefully dance down the rocky slope. She pointed. "Over there."

Vance followed her direction in time to see sunlight glint on a gun barrel. Then the air exploded with gunfire, and she was shooting back into the clouds of dirt and rock chips being kicked up by the fusillade of bullets from Jessie and the hands. She had one clear shot when a man ran across an open space between two rock formations, but before she could fire he went down and did not move. From Jessie's grim expression, she knew it had been her bullet that stopped him.

"Two of them are running," Jessie shouted.

Vance peered around the rocks and saw two men well down the valley pulling whinnying, nervous horses from behind a stand of juniper. "Your men will pick them up farther down the valley."

"One more up here, then."

"Maybe. Maybe he already left." Vance had barely gotten the words out when she was knocked onto her back. It felt as if a giant fist had punched her in the shoulder, and she immediately felt the familiar fire in her chest and arm. "I guess not," she grunted, pressing her hand to her left shoulder. She blinked the smoke and sweat from her eyes and saw her left hand lying useless in her lap, the arm bones shattered, the crimson pool gathering on earth so drenched with blood it could hold no more. Milton sprawled beside her, his sightless eyes accusing her. The sound of a thousand marching men bore down upon her, and for just an instant, she welcomed death.

"Don't think about going anywhere," Jessie said sharply as she shielded Vance with her body. "Mae will have my hide and then some."

*Mae. Mae will be angry. Worse, Mae will be hurt.* Vance took a deep breath and moved her right hand slowly over her shoulder and down the upper portion of her amputated arm. "I don't think it got much of me."

"Let me just get a look."

"Hand me my gun," Vance said, biting back the pain. "Dropped it."

"Here." Jessie put the revolver in Vance's surprisingly steady hand, then signaled for Charlie and Johnny to fire into the valley to give them some cover. She knelt beside Vance, shoved the duster aside, and ripped open her shirt. "Got a bit of a hole just above your collarbone. It's bleeding some."

"Through and through, I think. I can still move the shoulder joint. Help me sit u—" Vance caught movement out of the corner of her eye, rolled onto her side, and fired at the man who was pointing a rifle at Jessie's back. He groaned, fell to his knees, and then dropped face first into the dirt. "At least it's wasn't my gun arm."

When the pain surged again, she closed her eyes and let the sound of battle slip away.

❖

Kate found Jessie on the back porch, staring into the dark yard with a half-empty glass of whiskey in her hand. Coming up behind her, Kate put her arms around Jessie's waist and rested her cheek between her shoulder blades. "You shouldn't be standing on that leg, darling."

"It's fine, Kate. I've had worse after an afternoon in the corral."

"That might be, but it's a fresh wound and I don't want it bleeding again." It had taken her the better part of the evening to convince herself that Jessie wasn't badly injured. When she'd watched the cowboys' return, one leading a riderless horse, she'd thought her heart would stop. Then she'd seen Jessie on Star with Vance slumped in front of her, and she'd been able to breathe again. Until she'd seen the blood soaking Vance's shirt and heard Mae's agonized cry. "It's after midnight. You need to come to bed."

Jessie drank the whiskey down in one swallow and set the glass on the railing. She covered Kate's arms with hers, welcoming the warmth against her back. The sky was inky black, cloudless. Stars glittered like chips of diamonds. She felt so cold inside. "It was a night like this last fall when I was waiting for you to come to me. We were going to leave all this and run away. Remember that?"

"How could I not?" Kate gently drew her arms from beneath Jessie's and turned her lover to face her. She pressed both hands to Jessie's chest and leaned against her, searching her face. "What troubles you so?"

"Two people died today. It was my decision to go up there." Jessie sighed. "I knew it was right when I left here last night. I don't know why it doesn't feel that way just now."

Kate smiled softly and stroked Jessie's cheek. "Because life means something to you, and even though you did the right thing, protecting what's ours, it hurts to take a life."

"They fired first."

"Yes," Kate said gently. "And you protected yourself. And Vance protected you." She laid her cheek on Jessie's chest. "It takes a strong will to live in this land. Most people couldn't. It breaks them—destroys their dreams or corrupts their hearts. You have a good heart. I trust it. I trust you."

Jessie tightened her hold and closed her eyes as tears trembled on her lashes. "I'd have no heart at all without you," she whispered, her voice rough and shaking. "If I hadn't found you, I don't know that I could have lived my life out here, or anywhere, without becoming one of those people dying from broken dreams. I need you, Kate." She shivered. "So much."

"I knew from the first moment I saw you that you would change my life." Kate kissed Jessie and smoothed her tears away. "I knew in that instant that this was where I belonged, in this land, with you. I promise you will always have my heart, as I have yours."

"You think Mae will ever forgive me?"

"She loves you. She will."

## CHAPTER TWENTY-NINE

Mae watched Vance sleep. She turned the lamp down so low the wick threatened to gutter and go out. There was very little moon, and although the sound of Vance's steady breathing was comforting, she feared the dark this night. She couldn't remember the last time there was something she'd wanted so badly the thought of losing it made her scream inside. When she'd seen Vance slumped against Jessie, her face ashen, her white shirt soaked with blood, she'd known what dying felt like. Carefully, she reached over and brushed damp, dark strands of sweat-soaked hair from Vance's forehead.

Vance's lids flickered and she muttered hoarsely, "Mae?"

"Right here, sweetheart."

"Might you have some water?" Vance tried unsuccessfully to sit up but found that her limbs were strangely sluggish. Her left arm, especially, was an agonized mass of muscle and bone. She reached over, discovered the empty place where she knew her hand should be, and groaned.

"Shh, love," Mae crooned. "It's going to be all right." She settled carefully onto the bed next to Vance and slipped her arm behind her, taking care to support her back away from the area of the bandaged shoulder. "I've got water here. Let me raise your head."

Vance drank thirstily. The tepid water tasted like ambrosia. Mae's voice sounded like beautiful music. "Arm's gone."

"Yes," Mae said, tears nearly forcing her throat closed around the word.

"Remember now." Vance opened her eyes and focused on Mae's worried face. "Appomattox."

"No justice, is there?" Mae deposited the glass on the bedside table and stroked Vance's cheek. "That happening to you the last battle of the war."

"I don't know." Vance grimaced. "Divine justice?"

"Can't see why a hero should be rewarded that way."

"I'm no hero."

"You are." Mae kissed her tenderly. "And you're going to be all right. Caleb was here."

"What did he say?"

"That you were lucky, which all of us already knew." Mae settled her free arm around Vance's waist, caressing her gently, reassuring herself that Vance was really awake and with her. "The bullet missed all the important things, apparently. He said you'd feel weak for a spell, but there's no more damage to your arm that he could see."

"Damn thing hurts like it did right after I was first shot. Hasn't felt like that for half a year." Vance grinned crookedly. "Better than getting the other arm shot up, though."

"It would've been a damn sight better if neither one of them got shot up," Mae said fiercely, but her eyes, soft with concern, belied her anger.

"Wasn't my intention." Vance put all her effort into raising her right arm and found Mae's hand where it rested on her chest. She squeezed, surprised at how weak her grip seemed. "Sorry if I worried you."

Mae laughed, a sound that bordered on a sob. "Scared me half to death. Don't do it again."

"It will be my solemn endeavor not to." Vance took a deep breath, feeling a little stronger with each moment. "How's Jessie? Her leg okay?"

"Kate and I had gotten you both cleaned up before Caleb got here. He says she needs to be careful riding for a few days, but no real harm done."

Vance closed her eyes. "That's good." Suddenly, she stiffened. "What time is it?"

"Why, I don't know exactly. Going on toward one, I imagine." When Vance tried once more to sit up, Mae said sharply, "Here now, stop that. You'll start something bleeding."

"Won't you be missed back in town? I don't want you bringing trouble on yourself because of me." Frustrated, she raked her hand through her hair. "Especially when I'm laid up and can't be there to look after—"

"I sent a note round to Frank with Caleb telling him that I was sick in bed out here at Kate's. That will buy me another day or so." Mae took Vance's face gently between her fingers and waited until Vance met her gaze. "You'll have to get used to me caring for you, just like you look after me."

"I'll not have anyone hurt you again," Vance whispered. "Especially because of me."

Mae smiled and kissed Vance. "I can see that the things I love about you are also the things that are going to vex me to tears."

Vance grinned. "Love me?"

"Oh yes," Mae whispered. "I love you just about beyond reason."

Suddenly serious, Vance brought Mae's hand to her lips and kissed her palm gently. "For just a minute out there today—yesterday—I thought I was back at Appomattox. It hurt so much. Milton, my friend, was dead because of me. I knew Lee's soldiers were coming, and if I didn't die before they reached me, they'd probably shoot me where I lay. I expected to die and I didn't really mind."

Mae's heart thundered painfully, but she kept silent, knowing it was time for this wound to be purged.

"I got confused for a minute out there," Vance said, remembering the sweat and the pain and the soul-deep weariness. "I was ready to let go of everything, just to stop the hurt."

"Sweetheart," Mae whispered brokenly, kissing her forehead and holding her as closely as she dared without causing her injured shoulder more pain.

"But then Jessie reminded me of the one thing that mattered." Vance lay her head on Mae's breast. "She reminded me of you, and I realized I had the best reason of all for living." Mae's heart pulsed strong and steady beneath her cheek, and Vance felt the promise of happiness in every beat. "I love you." She tilted her head back and smiled into Mae's eyes. "You're all the reason I'll ever need."

"I never thought to have love like this in my life, not even when I was young enough to still believe that love existed. Not like this. Not all the way through me, in every breath I take."

"You can believe it." Vance held Mae's hand to her own heart. "I promise."

❖

Jessie peeked in the open door of the upstairs bedroom. Vance was asleep. Mae sat beside the bed, watching Vance with an expression of such tenderness on her face that Jessie was embarrassed to intrude. As she started to turn away, a soft voice said, "She's worn out. You'll not wake her."

Jessie turned back and waited while Mae quietly rose and crossed the room to her. In a whisper, she asked, "How is she feeling?"

"She'll admit to it hurting, which I imagine means the pain's fearsome, but her mind is clear." Mae smiled. "And she's showing signs of her usual stubbornness, so I imagine she'll be fine before long."

"I'm sorry."

Mae stepped into the hall and drew Jessie away from the door. She kept the door ajar so that she could see into the room in case Vance wakened. With a hand on Jessie's arm, she regarded her quietly. "I'm sorry for blaming you the way I did earlier. It's not your fault that Vance got hurt."

Jessie shrugged, remembering the terror in Mae's eyes when she'd first seen Vance. When Jessie had gotten down from Star after easing Vance into the arms of several waiting men, Mae had flung herself at her, accusing her of letting Vance get killed over nothing more than a few horses. She'd thought for a second that Mae was going to slap her. Then Mae had just run out of steam and turned away, shaking. At that moment, Jessie had wished that Mae *had* struck her. "It was my fight, not hers."

"Vance is your friend. She was only doing for you what you would've done for her." Mae sighed. "When I first saw her and all that blood…I thought I might lose her. I just needed a target for my fear. You were handy." She patted Jessie's chest. "And strong enough to take it. I'm sorry for forgetting that tender heart of yours."

Smiling, Jessie caught Mae's hand and held it. "She saved my life today. She's more than a friend." She kissed Mae's forehead. "You both are."

"Montana," Mae said softly. "I have loved you, I think, since the first time I saw you walk into the Nugget, covered in trail dust and sunshine." She laughed when Jessie blushed. "Somehow I always knew it wasn't meant to be, and it wasn't until I saw you with Kate that I understood why." She looked back into the room at the pale woman, so fragile appearing now, asleep in the bed. "Your heart was meant for Kate. And mine was meant for her."

"You'll always have a place in mine," Jessie whispered.

"And that means the world to me." Mae regarded Jessie intently. "I want you to do something for me."

"Anything."

"I want you to see that Vance doesn't try to change the way things are for me. At the Nugget." Even in the half-light of the hallway, Mae could see the muscle jump in Jessie's jaw. "You know how things are. That's not going to change, and there's no sense her getting killed trying." She grasped Jessie's hand again and squeezed, hard. "It would kill me to lose her. Please."

"I can't make that promise," Jessie said, adding quickly, "but I can promise she won't be alone. I won't let anything happen to her. I swear."

"You get yourself mixed up in this and end up getting hurt, Kate will never forgive you or me."

Jessie shook her head. "Kate understands."

Mae closed her eyes. "Lord. There's no talking sense into any of you."

"Don't worry." Jessie kissed Mae's cheek. "Vance isn't going to do anything foolish, and if she has a mind to, I'll see that she doesn't."

"I'll hold you to that, Montana."

"You can."

❖

The next time Vance woke, Mae was gone and Jessie was standing at the foot of the bed. "What time is it?"

"Morning. Mae's asleep down the hall. Kate made her finally lie down."

"Good." Vance braced her hand on the mattress but found she couldn't push herself up. Grimacing, she said, "Can you help me here?"

"I'm not sure I'm supposed to," Jessie said, coming around the side of the bed and easing an arm behind Vance's back. "You do anything to start that bleeding again, Mae and Kate will skin me."

"Don't worry. I don't want the both of them after me." Vance leaned back against the headboard with a sigh. "Thanks. How's the leg?"

"It's nothing. It'll be stiff for a day or two, but that's all."

"And Star?"

Jessie smiled. "She's fine. Little scratch no bigger than mine." She shifted and sighed. "You got the worst of it."

Vance grinned. "Not as bad as the two fellows we put down. Both dead?"

"Yep. Charlie went back up with a wagon after we got you down. He took them into town."

"What about the other two?"

"Long gone, and I don't think they'll be back." Jessie leaned a shoulder against the bedpost, her expression pensive. "At least those two won't. But I think we haven't seen the end of rustlers. Too many people came out here thinking there was gold running in the streets, and most of them ended up with nothing. Horses and cattle are money on the hoof."

"No matter where or when, it seems that it comes down to fighting to protect what's yours."

Jessie shrugged. "I never thought otherwise." She met Vance's gaze. "I owe you for what you did up there."

"You don't owe me for anything. You insult me to suggest it."

Jessie grinned. "You Easterners are pretty easy to insult."

Vance's brows rose. "Now you add injury to insult."

"Just the same, I expect you'll let me return the favor if needed."

"If needed," Vance said seriously, "I will."

"That's good enough."

Vance shifted restlessly. "Do you think you could have one of your men drive me into town later today? I never was a good patient, and I don't want to be any trouble."

"Could be you want to be closer to the Nugget?"

"Could be."

"I'll take you in myself if you promise not to try taking these men on until you've got your feet back under you."

Vance sighed. "I can see that Mae's gotten to you."

Jessie grinned. "Could be. But it makes sense."

"I'll wait till I'm healed, but I intend to right this wrong."

"You'll get no argument from me." Jessie gently squeezed Vance's shoulder. "I'll talk to Frank. I trust him. Between the two of us, we'll keep an eye on things until you're better."

"Thank you."

"No need. We're friends, right?"

Vance held up her hand. When Jessie took it, she said quietly, "That we are."

## CHAPTER THIRTY

When Vance stepped up to the bar shortly after midnight, Frank broke off his conversation with a grizzled cowboy who looked as if he had just come in off the trail, judging by his dirt-caked clothes and apparent thirst as he downed three shots of liquor in quick succession. On his way to the end of the bar where Vance stood half in shadow, Frank picked up his best bottle of whiskey.

"Good to see you up and about, Doc."

"Thanks. Even better to be here," Vance said. "More than a week indoors, most of it in bed, feels like a year."

"Been pretty quiet around here. Can't say as you've missed a whole lot."

Vance met Frank's deceptively placid gaze as she sipped the bracing drink. "I appreciate you keeping an eye on the situation."

"I'd do more but," he shrugged, "can't really change what ain't my affair."

"It wouldn't do anyone any good if you lost your job." Vance finished the shot and shook her head when he gestured with the bottle for a refill. "You do what you can." She turned sideways to survey the room. "Has our friend been around this week?"

"He was in and out a few nights ago. Picked up what he came for, but didn't linger."

"Does he have a regular time for coming by?"

"Not that I've noticed." Frank stepped away to pour a drink for a nearby customer, then leaned his elbows on the bar and lowered his voice. "One thing I do know. The bank transfers cash to the reserve in

Bradford once a month, and he always comes by the night before the stagecoach takes the shipment. Tidying up accounts, I suppose."

"And when would the next run to Bradford be?"

"Day after tomorrow."

"So we can expect a visit tomorrow night."

Frank nodded.

"Thanks." Vance studied the bartender, thinking that she had always been comfortable with him. He cared about Mae, and that was what mattered most to her. "Besides tending bar, what else do you do here, Frank?"

Frank was silent for a moment, as if deciding how much to reveal. Then, apparently coming to a decision, he said, "I suppose I manage the place, when it comes down to it. I order the stock, tally up what's in the till and take it to the bank, see that the place is looked after. Cleaned up and all that."

"So how is it you don't know who owns the Nugget?" Vance knew she was putting him on the spot, but it was time to put all the cards on the table.

"I've been tending bar here for almost ten years. Before Hanrahan, there was another fella who did pretty much the same as him. He hired me and spelled out how things would run. One day, he was gone, and Mike was doing his job." Frank blew out a breath. "I didn't ask any questions."

"I understand. I probably wouldn't either. You have any particular liking for the way the place is run now?"

"I like that I can do things my own way and don't have to answer to nobody. I take my wages out at the end of the week, leave receipts in the bag for whatever I spend to replace the liquor or the broken tables and chairs if things get rowdy, go about my business."

"Sounds like a pretty good deal."

"It suits me."

Vance tapped her hand lightly on the bar. "Thanks for the information. I think I'll head on upstairs."

"Mike Hanrahan's a mean son of a bitch," Frank said conversationally.

Vance smiled thinly, her eyes glittering dangerously. "So am I, when provoked."

She walked away to the sound of Frank's quiet laughter.

❖

Vance stopped in front of Mae's door and listened. Although Mae had been by Vance's hotel room that afternoon and had said that she would be free that evening, Vance was never certain that would be the case when she came around. She didn't completely trust herself to come face-to-face with someone who had just left Mae's bed, and it would do Mae no good for her to vent her jealousy on a customer. When she heard nothing from within, she tapped quietly.

"Mae, it's Vance."

The door opened almost immediately. Smiling, Mae reached out, took Vance's hand, and drew her inside. "How are you feeling?"

"Good as new." Vance caught Mae around the waist and kissed her soundly. "Like I haven't seen you in a month of Sundays."

Laughing, Mae slapped her hand against Vance's chest and held her away. "You might be feeling pretty frisky right now, but I saw that shoulder this afternoon, and you're not ready for romping just yet."

Vance ignored the restraining hand and tugged Mae close again. She nuzzled Mae's neck. "We don't have to romp. How about we stroll?"

Mae tilted her head back and gave her throat to Vance's kisses. Truth was, she missed her touch more than she would've imagined, even though she'd seen her every day. She never would have believed she could hunger for something she hadn't known she'd wanted until a few short weeks before. Loving Vance had opened her heart and her body to the possibility of not just pleasure, but communion. Now there were critical places inside her that only Vance could fill. She threaded her fingers through Vance's hair and tugged her head up so she could kiss her mouth. After she did, thoroughly, she whispered, "I think a nice long walk would be just perfect."

Grinning, Vance released her so that she could undress her. "Turn around."

"I took pity on you," Mae said as she turned her back. "This dress has laces."

"Buttons, ties…makes no matter," Vance muttered, rapidly loosening the laces that closed the back of Mae's dress. As she opened the material, she kissed along the edge of her shoulder blades and down the center of her spine. "Nothing's going to slow me down, let alone stop me."

The dark, edgy tone caught at Mae's heart and places lower down, and she turned back to Vance, suddenly just as eager to have her naked. She pushed at Vance's coat. "Let me help you get this off that shoulder."

"I thought you were anxious to see me in these new clothes," Vance protested.

"Right now," Mae murmured, "I want to see you *out* of them."

Vance laughed and held up her arm for Mae to help her out of the new coat. Then Mae went to work on the buttons on her shirt and Vance's patience disappeared. She gave a growl and tugged Mae's dress off her shoulders, then scooped her hand inside her bodice. The sensation of warm, soft flesh in her hand drove all caution from her mind, and if Mae hadn't gently restrained her, she would have tried to pick her up and carry her to the bed.

"Careful," Mae said breathlessly. "You start that shoulder bleeding, and I'm not letting you into my bed."

"Lord, Mae, I want you so much," Vance gasped. "Never. Never knew it could be like this."

"You can have me, for however long you want, as often as you like." Mae covered Vance's hand and held it still. "There's no need to rush, as much as I love the way you want me."

Vance laughed shakily. "I feel like I've been away from you for weeks."

"Well come to bed, and let's get reacquainted." Mae took Vance's hand and led her across the room. She stopped by the side of the bed and finished undressing Vance, taking her time, running her hands over Vance's body as if learning it for the first time. By the time she was done, Vance was shaking.

"Mae," Vance said, her voice a hoarse whisper. "What you're doing to me. I don't know that I'll last much longer."

"Just a few more minutes." Smiling, Mae stepped away and removed her undergarments. The way Vance's eyes darkened and her face tensed as Mae slowly uncovered herself sent spirals of pleasure curling through her. Naked at last, she lay on the fresh smooth sheets and opened her arms. "Come here where you belong."

With a sigh that spoke of a rightness she had never dreamed of, Vance settled into Mae's embrace.

❖

"Do you know what Vance intends to do about Mae's situation?" Kate asked, running her fingers lazily down the center of Jessie's chest. They lay curled together just before sunrise. The rooster would crow at any second, the day would begin, and it would be hours before they saw one another long enough to do more than wave or exchange a passing word. These quiet interludes at the end of one day and the beginning of the next were precious, because those were the times when she had Jessie all to herself. They were the moments when there was nothing between them except love.

Jessie lay on her back, Kate's head pillowed on her shoulder and their legs entwined. Fingers of red and gold stretched into the room as the sun broke over the horizon. She couldn't imagine wanting for anything else when she had this every morning. She kissed Kate's temple. "Not exactly. I got the feeling that she's going to use her wits and not her gun, if she can."

"I know she wouldn't do anything to endanger Mae, but I'm worried about her." Kate lifted her head and kissed the point of Jessie's chin. "And I'm worried about you."

Jessie shook her head and turned on her side so they faced one another. She kissed Kate softly. "No need. Vance won't do anything to hurt Mae. I feel the same way about you."

Kate traced the curve of Jessie's collarbone where it dipped into the hollow at the base of her throat. She kissed the pulse that rippled there. "You're precious to me above all else. Be careful."

"Don't worry." Jessie curled an arm around Kate's waist and pulled her near until their bodies fit together seamlessly. "You're the most important thing in my life."

"If you kiss me, you're going to be late for your morning chores."

"That's what's nice about being the boss." Jessie grinned and kissed her.

❖

Kate was in the kitchen when she heard the rider come into the yard. She went to the door, drying her hands on a towel, and looked out.

Vance dismounted and threw her horse's reins over the porch rail. Kate opened the door to greet her as Vance crossed the porch.

"You're just in time for coffee. I've got bacon and grits, too."

"I was hoping my timing would be good," Vance said with a grin.

"How are you feeling?"

"Happier than I thought I would be about going back to work." Vance scanned the yard. "Jessie around?"

"I think she's down talking to the men. She should be back any second, because she always knows when the coffee's ready." Kate led Vance into the kitchen. "Sit down. I'll get you a plate."

"I appreciate it." Rather than sitting, Vance hesitated on the threshold. "Maybe I'll just walk down and find Jessie."

Kate pursed her lips. "I take it you're in need of another horse?"

Vance opened her mouth, then closed it with a chuckle. "My apologies. Somewhere in the last few years I've learned some bad habits. I wanted to ask Jessie if she could come into town this evening."

"Because you intend to do something about Mae?"

"Yes."

Kate nodded. "My parents have been wanting Jessie and me to come in for supper. Tonight should suit."

"I don't know that—"

"If you're going to suggest that I stay here and wait, you should rethink that," Kate said mildly as she poured coffee. "The two of you have had quite enough adventure lately."

"I don't want Mae to know."

"I can imagine that you don't." Kate smiled. "I can even understand why. Do you realize that's unfair?"

"Yes." Vance crossed the room and took Kate's hand. "This is something I have to do, because I love her. I don't want her to worry because of my needs."

"Worrying comes with the territory when you love someone." Kate gave Vance's hand a little shake, her expression one of fond exasperation. "Mae is one of the strongest women I've ever known. A little worrying won't hurt her, and you should stop underestimating her."

Vance frowned. "I don't."

Kate shook her head. "I'm not saying Mae doesn't need you, that she wouldn't be devastated if something happened to you. Of course she would. And that's why you must take care of yourself and not take foolish chances. But Mae doesn't need you to stand between her and hardship. She needs you to stand beside her."

"Does Jessie understand all this?" Vance asked, her expression mildly perplexed.

"She's learning."

"Learning what?" Jessie said as she came through the door and tossed her hat onto the counter. "Hello, Vance."

"Learning how to let me help with the hard parts," Kate said.

Jessie winced. "Oh. That." She glanced at Vance. "I guess it's too late to go to the barn?"

"Way too late," Vance said, sitting down as Jessie pulled out a chair and settled at the table. She waited until Kate sat as well. "So this is what I've been thinking."

## CHAPTER THIRTY-ONE

"I don't understand how you can be so calm about this," Mae fumed, pacing in front of the settee in her parlor.

"I never said that I was calm." Kate sat at one end and waited for Mae to settle down enough to listen.

"You act like you're calm. You're sipping tea and nibbling on biscuits as if those two damn fools weren't working out a way to get themselves shot up again."

"They've both promised that won't happen."

Mae stopped dead in her tracks and planted both hands on her hips. She glared at Kate. "And you believe that?"

"I trust them."

"I noticed that you didn't let Jessie come into town by herself, just the same."

"I trust her, but I didn't say I wasn't worried."

"Oh, I know. I'm just taking my jitters out on you." Mae glanced at the watch pinned to her bodice and wished there were some way she could get out of working that night. But she knew it wasn't possible. Friday night was a big night out for ranch hands, and the saloon would be busy. "I'm sorry. Pay me no mind."

"It's all right. Vance is just getting over one injury. You have a right to be nervy."

Mae sat down with a weary sigh. "I can't see how anything she's planning to do will make a difference." She met Kate's gaze. "If I wanted to walk away from all of this, I could. It might be hard, but others have done it."

"Has she asked you to?"

Mae looked surprised. “No. Never.”

“Then I don’t expect that’s what’s behind her intentions. I have always been under the impression your safety was what concerned her.”

“I explained to her about looking after the girls. She understood that.”

Kate nodded.

“I explained to her about not wanting to be beholden to anyone. That I make my own way.”

“I imagine that Vance would respect that.”

“She does,” Mae said quietly. “In fact, everything would be just fine if she hadn’t decided that Michael Hanrahan needs a lesson taught to him.”

Kate set her teacup aside. “I think we both know it’s more than that.”

“Lord, I *do* know.” Mae pushed impatiently at an errant curl that fluttered around the corner of her mouth. “I just wish I knew what else she plans to do.”

“If I knew, I’d tell you,” Kate said reassuringly. “All I know is she and Jessie talked about meeting in the saloon tonight at midnight. I think they’re hoping to follow Michael Hanrahan and get some information that they can use to negotiate with whoever owns this place.”

Mae laughed harshly. “Negotiate? Is that what Vance said?”

“Well, not exactly, but that’s what I assumed.”

“Oh, honey, back East folks might negotiate. Out here? The only thing that changes anything is money or bullets.”

“Perhaps I misinterpreted,” Kate said worriedly. “But I have a feeling that Jessie understood Vance perfectly.”

❖

Vance leaned her back against the bar and watched Mae work her way through the crowded room in her direction. Every few steps a cowboy or gambler in fancy clothes would stop her with an arm around her waist and whisper something in her ear. She’d laugh and deftly extract herself from his grasp and move on. She was an expert at avoiding wandering caresses without giving affront. It was a talent, like those sleight-of-hand magic shows. Her smile was so brilliant, her laugh so alluring, that the men never realized they had never once truly touched her.

"You look like you're studying on something very serious," Mae said as she stepped close to Vance's side. She'd been aware of Vance's eyes on her since the moment she'd stepped out onto the balcony and started down the stairs. She'd also known that Vance could see every hand that touched her on her journey. "Something wrong?"

"I wonder if any of them knows how much they've just missed?"

Mae's heart gave a little jump of surprise and wonder. "You don't look at the world like anyone else I know."

Vance smiled faintly. "I've been told that before." She traced a fingertip down the sleek curve of Mae's arm, exposed below the narrow shoulder of her maroon gown. "You're an amazingly beautiful woman. But your true beauty lies somewhere no one touches."

"Except you," Mae murmured.

"Except me." Vance watched Mae's full, moist lips curve with pleasure. "I want to kiss you."

"I'm glad, but I wouldn't recommend it." Mae angled her body to block the view of anyone in the room and slid a hand inside Vance's coat. She caressed her, fingers dancing over her stomach. "If they saw how it was really done, they'd figure out they're being cheated."

"Not cheated," Vance said, her voice rough with desire. "Not if they've put one finger on you."

"You keep talking like that, and I'm—" Mae broke off as an arm came around her waist and tugged her roughly backward, away from Vance. She knew who it was without needing to see his face. "Is that any way to say hello?"

Michael Hanrahan pulled Mae against him and held her there. He bent his head and rubbed his stubbled cheek over her neck. With his mouth against her ear and his hand roaming over the front of her body, he muttered, "You don't look like you're real busy."

"The night is young and I was just getting started." Mae kept her voice light and her expression unconcerned, because she could feel Vance's fury from three feet away. She pointedly did not look at her, because she was afraid that any connection between them now would break Vance's fragile restraint. Instead, she turned as much as she could in Hanrahan's grasp, putting her back to Vance. "There's a full house tonight. Let's take care of your business so I can take care of mine."

Hanrahan grabbed Mae's hand and pressed it down on the front of his pants. "How about we take care of that business."

Mae didn't try to pull away, but met his hot gaze coolly. "I don't remember that being part of the arrangement."

"Nobody has to know."

"But I might forget myself and mention it."

His expression hardened, and he pushed her away. "Let's go upstairs."

When Vance started after them, she was brought up sharply by an iron grip on her shoulder. She whirled around, her eyes aflame.

"You don't want to be getting in the middle of that," Frank said. "You might end up satisfied, but Mae will pay for it."

"Not if he's dead," Vance said through clenched teeth.

"If he's gonna be dead, it would be better if no one knew just how that came about." He busied himself wiping nonexistent spills from the bar. "Could be I might lend a hand there."

Vance blew out a long breath and reined in her temper. "Appreciate it. But I think I'll keep you for the heavy work."

He grinned. "Still, you might want company."

"That's been arranged."

"Has it now?" He nodded approval. "Well then, stop around for a drink when you're finished."

"I'll do that."

When Vance scanned the room and balcony, Mae was gone. She'd taken Hanrahan to her room to give him the money that she and the other women earned. If that's all that was happening up there, he would be coming down soon. Vance motioned for Frank to fill her glass, which he did. She picked it up with a steady hand and drank it down in one fast swallow, welcoming the sharp burn that settled in the pit of her stomach. Then she placed the glass on the bar and walked out.

Vance waited in the shadows beneath the stairs that led to the second floor and Mae's rooms. She didn't think about what was happening upstairs, because if she did, she'd go upstairs and finish things before they even started. And in the end, she would accomplish nothing. She wished for a cigarette, something she hadn't wanted since waiting in the dark for the last battle. She didn't need to look at her watch. She knew what time it was. The night felt empty, devoid of life. Nothing stirred. Even the horses tethered in front of the saloon stood silently, their heads down, their breath streaming soundlessly through flared nostrils beneath the moonless sky.

Almost fifteen minutes passed before the door above her opened and boot heels thudded on the wooden staircase. She slid her revolver from the holster but did not cock it until he reached the ground. Then she stepped up behind him, forced the muzzle to the back of his neck, and thumbed the hammer.

The sound cut through the stillness like cannon shot.

Hanrahan stiffened.

"Hello, Michael," Vance said quietly.

The man relaxed slightly as if he recognized a woman's voice. "You might want to put that away before someone gets hurt."

His tone suggested that Vance would be the one to suffer. She laughed and pushed it harder into his skin. The pain forced him to stumble forward a step, and she shoved him face first against the wall with her hip. She pinned him with her left shoulder, welcoming the pain as it seared through her brain and cleared her head. Then she dropped the gun from the back of his head and forced it between his legs. She angled the barrel up and forward until it met resistance.

"Do you like it here better?"

Her voice was soft and cold, a sliver of ice slipping into his heart. He shivered and gasped, but didn't move. "What do you want?"

"To teach you some manners."

"Wha—" He grunted as the gun barrel stabbed into his tender parts. "I don't know—ow—*Jesus*—"

Vance jammed him harder into the wall and whispered in his ear. "You don't know how to treat a lady. I think this"— she jerked the gun barrel into him again and smiled in satisfaction when he whimpered—"might be getting in the way of your social skills." She saw Mae's face, battered and bruised. Saw the marks on her arms and imagined the stinking weight of Hanrahan's body pinning her down. She took a breath, savoring the moment. "So I'm going to relieve you of it."

Hanrahan pleaded. "Jesus, no."

"This is for Mae," she whispered as she tightened her finger on the trigger.

Jessie stepped away from the building where she'd been standing in the dark for over an hour, waiting to back up Vance in case of trouble.

In a conversational tone she said, "He hardly seems worth wasting good lead on."

"Everything's fine here," Vance said without looking around. "You go on."

"How you doing, Hanrahan?" Jessie continued as if Vance hadn't spoken.

"She's crazy. Get her off me," he said desperately, the stench of fear permeating the air around him.

"It's a big country out here," Jessie said. "Lot of mining camps where a man could disappear to."

Vance said sharply, "Let it be."

"Now, if I were to see you around here after sunrise," Jessie remarked, "I wouldn't stop her from finishing it next time."

"I'll go. I swear, I'll go." He tried to turn his head but in a move so fast even Vance couldn't catch it, Jessie had her gun out and shoved underneath the edge of his jaw. She leaned close.

"And if she doesn't kill you, I will."

Jessie straightened. "Now, before you go there's a few things we need to know."

He couldn't answer their questions fast enough. As he scurried off, Vance holstered her Colt and leaned against the wall. She tilted her head back and closed her eyes.

"You okay?" Jessie asked.

"Mostly."

Jessie leaned back beside her. "No moon again. Dark as pitch out here."

"No one would have cared about him," Vance said.

"Nope. No one would've given it a second's thought, even if they had heard a shot."

"I suppose you're going to tell me you think I would've regretted killing him, and you saved me from the guilt?"

Jessie laughed. "Not by a long shot. Hell, I wanted to do it myself."

"So why'd you stop me?"

"He might not have been able to tell us what we wanted to know if he was bleeding all over the ground."

"Forgot about that."

Jessie turned her head, just able to make out Vance's features in the near-total darkness. “Besides, that’s not what’s going to fix Mae’s situation. And it might be even easier the next time.”

“There’s not going to be a next time.” Vance rubbed her aching shoulder. “I’m going to see that Mae has the one thing that really matters to her.”

“What’s that?”

“Her independence.”

Taking care not to hit the area of the injury, Jessie patted Vance’s back. “You’re almost right. But I expect you’ll figure that out in time.”

❖

When Mae let Vance into her room after closing, she put her arms around Vance’s neck and held her close. She kissed her gently. “Are you all right?”

“I am now.”

“Did you kill him?”

“No. But he’s gone, and he won’t bother you again.”

“Thank you.”

Vance took Mae’s hand and walked with her toward the bed. “I’m not done yet. I have one more visit to make in the morning, and then this will be over.”

“Tell me.”

“Tomorrow.” Vance pulled Mae down beside her on the bed and buried her face in the curve of Mae’s neck. “Right now, the only thing I want is you.”

Mae opened her dressing gown and drew Vance’s hand inside. “Then that’s what you shall have.”

## CHAPTER THIRTY-TWO

Charles Mason came out of his office with his hand extended and an ingratiating smile. "Dr. Phelps. Mrs. Wainwright tells me that you're in need of assistance."

"Thank you for seeing me so quickly," Vance said, shaking his hand. "It's a private business matter that I thought you would be best suited to handle."

"Of course. Of course. I'm always happy to work with a new client of the bank." He swept his arm toward his office. "Please. Do come in."

Vance followed him into his office and took the chair he indicated across from his desk. She reached into the inner pocket of her new frock coat, the more formal of the two that Mae had insisted she have made, and drew out a sheaf of papers. Together with the starched white shirt, waistcoat, and trousers, she was attired as well as any wealthy businessman would have been. She took her time arranging the documents, aware that Mason was regarding her avidly. With a smile, she passed the papers across the desk. "As you can see, although I've been in town quite some time, I haven't had an opportunity to transfer my funds from the bank in Philadelphia. I'd like you to see to that."

"I'm sure we can take care of that for..."

Mason's voice trailed off as he studied the account summaries. He straightened, his expression bordering on obsequious. "I'll handle this personally." He fiddled with his tie, glanced down at the paperwork one more time, then back at Vance. "I'm sure our community will benefit greatly from your presence, Dr. Phelps. If there's anything that I can do to help you get settled...anything at all—"

"That's very kind," Vance said neutrally. "Your wife and daughter have been most gracious in arranging a small gathering for me tomorrow at your home. I certainly appreciate their kindness."

"Merely a small gesture, one neighbor to another," he said.

Vance doubted that he had any idea that the soirée was planned. She didn't imagine that the social calendar of his wife and daughter was something he paid much attention to, but she nodded in agreement. Then, as if in afterthought, she said, "Actually, there is one more matter that you can assist me with."

"Certainly."

"I'd like to purchase some property."

"I'd be more than happy to act as your agent in that matter," Mason said quickly. "If you will just provide me with the details, I can facilitate—"

"Oh, I think it's something we can finalize right now."

"I'm sorry?"

"I want you to sell me the Golden Nugget." She reached into her coat and withdrew the final sheet of paper and passed it across the desk. "A simple transfer of the deed should be all that is required. Shall we say for the sum of one hundred dollars?"

"I'm afraid I don't understand," Mason said, his face and neck growing red above the collar of his shirt.

"Really? Michael Hanrahan informed me last evening that you were the owner of the Golden Nugget."

"He was mistaken," Mason said flatly. He shuffled papers together, stacked them on the corner of his desk, and rose. "Now, if there's nothing else, I'll initiate the transfer of those funds for you."

Vance crossed her legs and settled more comfortably into her chair. "If Mr. Hanrahan was lying, then he was protecting someone else at your expense. Who might that be?"

"I'm sure I have no idea."

"Well, I can probably clear up the misunderstanding easily enough." Vance stood. "I've always found that the wives of powerful men know far more than they ever let on." She laughed. "I know that was certainly true for my mother. My father was often quite dense about the motives of other men who sought to take advantage of his largesse and trusting nature, but my mother…my mother always knew and saw that he didn't entangle himself in difficult situations. I daresay your wife will know who harbors some ill will toward you."

"Certainly you wouldn't involve a lady in such unsavory business," Mason blustered, although there was a look of panic around his eyes.

Vance took a step closer to the desk and leaned forward, resting her hand in the center of his blotter. "Why should you think that I would value the sensibilities of your women any more than you value those of mine?"

"I'm sure I have no idea what you're talking about."

"Of course you do," Vance said, her unwavering gaze boring into his until he looked uneasily away. "You have a special arrangement with one of the women at the Nugget. You pay her for your pleasure and for that of your friends. You think if you come and go by the back stairs and have someone else do your dirty work that everyone will look the other way." She straightened. "Well, I won't. Sign the bill of sale or I will make my inquiries so public that within a week everyone will know of your personal association with the Nugget."

Sweat beaded on his forehead. After a moment, he nodded and picked up the bill of sale in a trembling hand. He began to read it over, then stopped with a surprised grunt and looked at Vance in astonishment. "This isn't your name on the bill of sale."

"No," Vance said as she sat down and began to write the draft for the purchase price. "It isn't."

❖

Mae leaned against Vance in the buggy as they headed toward the Rising Star. "You look mighty fine in those new clothes."

Vance chuckled. "You'd better like them, since they were all your doing."

"A lot has to do with the body that's in them." Mae stroked Vance's cheek. "*You* are what's fine."

"Are you trying to flatter me into telling you what I've been up to?"

"Yes, even though it happens to be the truth and you do look handsome as all get out." Mae laughed. "I just don't think it's fair for you to make me wait until we get all the way out to the ranch."

"Truth be told, I don't want to wait either," Vance confessed. "Reach into my inside coat pocket and take out that paper."

"I'll take pity on you and not touch anything else along the way." Nevertheless, Mae indulged herself with a brief caress, stroking Vance's chest as she drew out the paper. Smiling at Vance's quick intake of breath, she unfolded the document and began to read. Then she gasped. "I…is this…how did you…oh my."

Vance grinned. "You are now one of the most influential business owners in New Hope." She slowed the rig so she could savor Mae's look of astonishment and pleasure. "You'll never have to worry about what anyone might do to you or your girls again."

"My Lord, Vance. I *own* it?"

"You do."

"But how?"

Vance told her, enjoying Mae's satisfied snort as she described Mason's discomfort. "And before you say it's too much for you to accept, I did it as much for my peace of mind as your safety."

Mae's eyes brimmed with tears but she nodded. "Thank you."

"My pleasure."

"I won't say no, because I want this, but…I plan to pay you back. Every dollar."

Vance smiled. "I thought you would."

Mae moved closer. "Would you really have told Clarissa Mason about her husband's philandering?"

"No, but I wouldn't have made it a secret either while I *investigated* who really did own it. Mason must have known she'd find out sooner or later if he forced me to search him out."

"Well." Mae's mind was going in a hundred different directions and she couldn't seem to take it all in. "What about Frank? The place won't run without Frank."

"I don't imagine he'll mind who pays his wages. In fact, I think he'll like it a whole lot better knowing that it's you." Vance halted the buggy at the entrance to the lane to the Rising Star. She dropped the reins over her knee and took Mae's hand. "You can turn the place into a respectable establishment. The girls will be protected, because you'll make the rules. And if not Frank, you can get someone else to enforce them."

"Are you going to ask me not to take care of customers?"

"That's not my place."

"Of course it is." Mae kissed Vance, a slow, tender kiss. "Unless you've been foolin' about loving me."

"Oh no," Vance murmured, her voice husky and low. She lifted

Mae's hand and kissed her fingers, then her mouth. "I love you with all my heart."

"There'll never be another in my bed." Mae held Vance's hand to her breast. "Or my heart."

"Nor shall there be in mine. You have my solemn promise," Vance whispered.

Mae curved an arm around Vance's waist and settled her head on her shoulder. "Then hurry up now. I can't wait to tell Kate and Jessie."

Laughing, Vance guided the buggy down the lane, holding Mae's promise in her heart, knowing she had come home at last.

# About the Author

Radclyffe is the author of over twenty lesbian romances, the Erotic Interlude series (*Change of Pace*, *Stolen Moments*, and *Lessons in Love* ed. with Stacia Seaman) and selections in multiple anthologies including *Call of the Dark* and *The Perfect Valentine* (Bella Books), *Best Lesbian Erotica 2006* and *After Midnight* (Cleis), *First-Timers* and *Ultimate Undies: Erotic Stories About Lingerie and Underwear* (Alyson), and *Naughty Spanking Stories 2* (Pretty Things Press). She is the recipient of the 2003 and 2004 Alice B. Readers' award, a 2005 Golden Crown Literary Society Award winner in both the romance category (*Fated Love*) and the mystery/intrigue/action category (*Justice in the Shadows*) and 2006 GCLS finalist for romance (*Distant Shores, Silent Thunder*) and mystery (*Justice Served*), and a 2006 Lammy finalist in the romance (*Distant Shores, Silent Thunder*), mystery (Justice Served), and erotica categories (*Erotic Interludes 2: Stolen Moments* ed. with Stacia Seaman). Her other 2006 novels include *Turn Back Time* and *Storms of Change*.

She is also the president of Bold Strokes Books, a publishing company offering acclaimed lesbian-themed general and genre fiction. She lives in New York state with her partner, Lee.

Look for information about these works at www.boldstrokesbooks.com.

## Books Available From Bold Strokes Books

**Whitewater Rendezvous** by Kim Baldwin. Two women on a wilderness kayak adventure—Chaz Herrick, a laid-back outdoorswoman, and Megan Maxwell, a workaholic news executive—discover that true love may be nothing at all like they imagined. (1-933110-38-4)

**Erotic Interludes 3: Lessons in Love** ed. by Radclyffe and Stacia Seaman. Sign on for a class in love…the best lesbian erotica writers take us to "school." (1-933110-39-2)

**Punk Like Me** by JD Glass. Twenty-one-year-old Nina writes lyrics and plays guitar in the rock band Adam's Rib, and she doesn't always play by the rules. And oh yeah—she has a way with the girls. (1-933110-40-6)

**Coffee Sonata** by Gun Brooke. Four women whose lives unexpectedly intersect in a small town by the sea share one thing in common—they all have secrets. (1-933110-41-4)

**The Clinic: Tristaine Book One** by Cate Culpepper. Brenna, a prison medic, finds herself deeply conflicted by her growing feelings for her patient Jesstin, a wild and rebellious warrior reputed to be descended from ancient Amazons. (1-933110-42-2)

**Forever Found** by JLee Meyer. Can time, tragedy, and shattered trust destroy a love that seemed destined? When chance reunites two childhood friends separated by tragedy, the past resurfaces to determine the shape of their future. (1-933110-37-6)

**Sword of the Guardian** by Merry Shannon. Princess Shasta's bold new bodyguard has a secret that could change both of their lives. *He* is actually a *she*. A passionate romance filled with courtly intrigue, chivalry, and devotion. (1-933110-36-8)

**Wild Abandon** by Ronica Black. From their first tumultuous meeting, Dr. Chandler Brogan and Officer Sarah Monroe are drawn together by their common obsessions—sex, speed, and danger. (1-933110-35-X)

**Turn Back Time** by Radclyffe. Pearce Rifkin and Wynter Thompson have nothing in common but a shared passion for surgery. They clash at every opportunity, especially when matters of the heart are suddenly at stake. (1-933110-34-1)

**Chance** by Grace Lennox. At twenty-six, Chance Delaney decides her life isn't working so she swaps it for a different one. What follows is the sexy, funny, touching story of two women who, in finding themselves, also find one another. (1-933110-31-7)

**The Exile and the Sorcerer** by Jane Fletcher. First in the Lyremouth Chronicles. Tevi, wounded and adrift, arrives in the courtyard of a shy young sorcerer. Together they face monsters, magic, and the challenge of loving despite their differences. (1-933110-32-5)

**A Matter of Trust** by Radclyffe. JT Sloan is a cybersleuth who doesn't like attachments. Michael Lassiter is leaving her husband, and she needs Sloan's expertise to safeguard her company. It should just be business—but it turns into much more. (1-933110-33-3)

**Sweet Creek** by Lee Lynch. A celebration of the enduring nature of love, friendship, and community in the quirky, heart-warming lesbian community of Waterfall Falls. (1-933110-29-5)

**The Devil Inside** by Ali Vali. Derby Cain Casey, head of a New Orleans crime organization, runs the family business with guts and grit, and no one crosses her. No one, that is, until Emma Verde claims her heart and turns her world upside down. (1-933110-30-9)

**Grave Silence** by Rose Beecham. Detective Jude Devine's investigation of a series of ritual murders is complicated by her torrid affair with the golden girl of Southwestern forensic pathology, Dr. Mercy Westmoreland. (1-933110-25-2)

**Honor Reclaimed** by Radclyffe. In the aftermath of 9/11, Secret Service Agent Cameron Roberts and Blair Powell close ranks with a trusted few to find the would-be assassins who nearly claimed Blair's life. (1-933110-18-X)

**Honor Bound** by Radclyffe. Secret Service Agent Cameron Roberts and Blair Powell face political intrigue, a clandestine threat to Blair's safety, and the seemingly irreconcilable personal differences that force them ever farther apart. (1-933110-20-1)

**Protector of the Realm: Supreme Constellations Book One** by Gun Brooke. A space adventure filled with suspense and a daring intergalactic romance featuring Commodore Rae Jacelon and the stunning, but decidedly lethal, Kellen O'Dal. (1-933110-26-0)

**Innocent Hearts** by Radclyffe. In a wild and unforgiving land, two women learn about love, passion, and the wonders of the heart. (1-933110-21-X)

**The Temple at Landfall** by Jane Fletcher. An imprinter, one of Celaeno's most revered servants of the Goddess, is also a prisoner to the faith—until a Ranger frees her by claiming her heart. The Celaeno series. (1-933110-27-9)

**Force of Nature** by Kim Baldwin. From tornados to forest fires, the forces of nature conspire to bring Gable McCoy and Erin Richards close to danger, and closer to each other. (1-933110-23-6)

**In Too Deep** by Ronica Black. Undercover homicide cop Erin McKenzie tracks a femme fatale who just might be a real killer…with love and danger hot on her heels. (1-933110-17-1)

**Stolen Moments: Erotic Interludes 2** by Stacia Seaman and Radclyffe, eds. Love on the run, in the office, in the shadows…Fast, furious, and almost too hot to handle. (1-933110-16-3)

**Course of Action** by Gun Brooke. Actress Carolyn Black desperately wants the starring role in an upcoming film produced by Annelie Peterson. Just how far will she go for the dream part of a lifetime? (1-933110-22-8)

**Rangers at Roadsend** by Jane Fletcher. Sergeant Chip Coppelli has learned to spot trouble coming, and that is exactly what she sees in her new recruit, Katryn Nagata. The Celaeno series. (1-933110-28-7)

**Justice Served** by Radclyffe. Lieutenant Rebecca Frye and her lover, Dr. Catherine Rawlings, embark on a deadly game of hide-and-seek with an underworld kingpin who traffics in human souls. (1-933110-15-5)

**Distant Shores, Silent Thunder** by Radclyffe. Dr. Tory King—along with the women who love her—is forced to examine the boundaries of love, friendship, and the ties that transcend time. (1-933110-08-2)

**Hunter's Pursuit** by Kim Baldwin. A raging blizzard, a mountain hideaway, and a killer-for-hire set a scene for disaster—or desire—when Katarzyna Demetrious rescues a beautiful stranger. (1-933110-09-0)

**The Walls of Westernfort** by Jane Fletcher. All Temple Guard Natasha Ionadis wants is to serve the Goddess—until she falls in love with one of the rebels she is sworn to destroy. The Celaeno series. (1-933110-24-4)

**Change Of Pace:** ***Erotic Interludes*** by Radclyffe. Twenty-five hot-wired encounters guaranteed to spark more than just your imagination. Erotica as you've always dreamed of it. (1-933110-07-4)

**Honor Guards** by Radclyffe. In a wild flight for their lives, the president's daughter and those who are sworn to protect her wage a desperate struggle for survival. (1-933110-01-5)

**Fated Love** by Radclyffe. Amidst the chaos and drama of a busy emergency room, two women must contend not only with the fragile nature of life, but also with the irresistible forces of fate. (1-933110-05-8)

**Justice in the Shadows** by Radclyffe. In a shadow world of secrets and lies, Detective Sergeant Rebecca Frye and her lover, Dr. Catherine Rawlings, join forces in the elusive search for justice. (1-933110-03-1)

**shadowland** by Radclyffe. In a world on the far edge of desire, two women are drawn together by power, passion, and dark pleasures. An erotic romance. (1-933110-11-2)

**Love's Masquerade** by Radclyffe. Plunged into the indistinguishable realms of fiction, fantasy, and hidden desires, Auden Frost is forced to question all she believes about the nature of love. (1-933110-14-7)

**Love & Honor** by Radclyffe. The president's daughter and her lover are faced with difficult choices as they battle a tangled web of Washington intrigue for...love and honor. (1-933110-10-4)

**Beyond the Breakwater** by Radclyffe. One Provincetown summer, three women learn the true meaning of love, friendship, and family. (1-933110-06-6)

**Tomorrow's Promise** by Radclyffe. One timeless summer, two very different women discover the power of passion to heal and the promise of hope that only love can bestow. (1-933110-12-0)

**Love's Tender Warriors** by Radclyffe. Two women who have accepted loneliness as a way of life learn that love is worth fighting for and a battle they cannot afford to lose. (1-933110-02-3)

**Love's Melody Lost** by Radclyffe. A secretive artist with a haunted past and a young woman escaping a life that has proved to be a lie find their destinies entwined. (1-933110-00-7)

**Safe Harbor** by Radclyffe. A mysterious newcomer, a reclusive doctor, and a troubled gay teenager learn about love, friendship, and trust during one tumultuous summer in Provincetown. (1-933110-13-9)

**Above All, Honor** by Radclyffe. Secret Service Agent Cameron Roberts fights her desire for the one woman she can't have—Blair Powell, the daughter of the president of the United States. (1-933110-04-X)